The
CHOICE

Also by Dan M. Appel:
A Bridge Across Time

To order, call 1-800-765-6955.

Visit us at www.AutumnHousePublishing.com
for information on other Autumn House® products.

The CHOICE

DAN M. APPEL

Autumn
House® Publishing
www.autumnhousepublishing.com
A Division of **REVIEW AND HERALD® PUBLISHING**
Since 1861

Published by Autumn House® Publishing, a division of Review and Herald® Publishing, Hagerstown, MD 21741-1119

This book was
Edited by Penny Estes Wheeler
Designed by Trent Truman
Cover illustration: Leather background: © istockphoto.com/rdegrie; Wings: © istockphoto.com
/77Dzign; Fence: © 123rf.com/Michael Ransburg; Grass: © 123rf.com/M.G. Mooij
Typeset: Bembo 11/13

PRINTED IN U.S.A.
12 11 10 09 08   5 4 3 2 1

Library of Congress Cataloging-in-Publication Data
Appel, Dan M., 1948-   .
    Brenda's husband had been dead almost a year, then he came back : the choice / Dan M. Appel.
        p. cm.
    Previous title: The choice
    Includes bibliographical references and index.
    1. Future life--Christianity. 2. Spiritualism. 3. Occultism. I. Title.

    BT903.A67 2007
    236'.2—dc22

                                    2007039071

ISBN 978-0-8127-0463-1

I DEDICATE THIS BOOK...

To my three best friends
My wife, Charla, and my two sons, Dan, Jr., and David

Being their husband and father is a privilege that
I surely do not deserve and for which I gratefully praise God
every day. They suffered through interminable rough drafts
and some phenomenally weird and disturbing happenings
while this book was being written. Their encouragement,
love, and patience are limitless!

And to
My parents and my sister

Who believed in me
in spite of knowing me my whole life.

ACKNOWLEDGMENTS

I would like to thank six extraordinary people for their help with this book.

Thelma Winter, teacher extraordinaire, English maven, and friend who inspired in me a love of good writing and the English language and whose attempts to teach me grammar and good sentence structure in high school were only partly successful and will be forever appreciated.

Jan Haluska, Ph.D., a friend of amazing integrity and unbounded grace whose ability to cut through all of the accretions obscuring the ideas of virtually any thinker and to discover and dialogue with the meat of what they teach and believe has astounded and inspired me ever since the first day I met him. Jan's kindness when I call (after not having contacted him for several years) to ask that he read through another book manuscript to find the flaws is undeserved and appreciated beyond words.

Penny Estes Wheeler, and her cohorts at Autumn House, for the opportunity to publish this book, and for their encouragement and wisdom as they guided this manuscript to print.

Christine Martello, Mary Lou Barber, and *Shirley Frangione,* whose life experiences sensitized me to the realities I have written about in this book. Thank you for your willingness to share your stories with me.

"Finally, be strong in the Lord and in the strength of his might. Put on the whole armor of God, that you may be able to stand *against the wiles of the devil*. For we are not contending against flesh and blood, but *against the principalities, against the powers, against the world rulers of this present darkness, against the spiritual hosts of wickedness in the heavenly places*. Therefore take the whole armor of God, that you may be able to withstand in the evil day, and haveing done all, to stand."

Ephesians 6:10-13

PREFACE

As you read this book, you need to be aware of my point of view.

The arrival of postmodernism on the intellectual and cultural scene has sensitized many to the existence of a spiritual—a supernatural—dimension that transcends the physical world we know and live in. That awareness coalesces, and at times harmonizes, the thinking and experience of a very broad range of individuals and movements, even as they, often strenuously, disagree about the details and implications of what they believe. People in groups ranging from the various "earth" and native religions and Wicca to Hinduism in all of its many forms; spiritists and occultists; Christians, Jews, and followers of the prophet Muhammad; those who believe in aliens and otherworldly life forms and inhabitants of the cosmos; and even a growing cadre of very pragmatic scientists and skeptics are becoming sensitized to the existence of good and evil forces, powers, or beings with supernatural power that are identified with good or evil and that are doing their best to influence human affairs.

Where there is the proverbial smoke there must be some fire, which brings us to a dilemma that we all must resolve in our own minds and hearts. Either we catch such dim and ill-defined glimpses of these supernatural forces and powers that every point of view contains just a little fragment of the whole truth, or we accept that only one picture is the correct one. That means the rest are a distortion of the truth and a threat to what is the truth and its adherents.

Only you can decide. What is important is that it behooves any thinking person to consider carefully the evidence with an open mind before accepting any explanation of the identity, personality, and power of any supernatural beings or powers and the philosophical system that supports and advocates for them.

After carefully considering the options, I have chosen to accept the Bible's explanation of the conflict between good and evil. I believe in a real God who created us and who intervenes in human time and space. He, in my understanding, is the source of all good. I also believe in a real devil, the one the Bible calls Satan, who is at war with God over the inhabitants and real estate of the universe and who is doing all that he can to distort the picture of who God really is in the minds and hearts of created beings. He is the author of evil. Whether that picture is right or wrong is up to you to decide. What is important is that you consider the issues, not just react emotionally.

So as you consider whether to read this book, I don't ask that you blindly accept my point of reference, my line of reasoning, or my conclusions. I would encourage you to consider them carefully and then to decide what is truth.

In writing this work of fiction, I have freely adapted the stories of a number of real people I have known. I have included nothing that could not happen, and much that has occurred to people I personally know and have talked with and respect. In some cases I have used so much literary license in constructing dialogue and sequences of events that only a skeleton of the actual occurrence remains. In other areas the stories are so close to actual events that those who participated in them will recognize themselves—even though I have changed names and places to protect their privacy.

Now, a word of caution. Some misguided and naive individuals reading similar accounts in the past have decided to make it their mission in life to confront demonic powers in person—a decision that they and others have lived to regret. No thinking person would willingly confront the devil or one of his demonic agents in person! I have written this story to inform and encourage thought and dialogue—not to serve as some kind of primer on how to confront evil. While personal, direct confrontation between loyal followers of God and the devil can and does occur, it is something any intelligent person would avoid unless there is no other choice, and then only after much prayer.

Whether or not you decide to accept the worldview espoused in this book, it is a good story that I hope will enrich your life. So grab a cup of something hot to drink, find a comfortable chair and a good light, and enjoy!

Cast of Major Characters

Abadon   a demonic entity charged with managing a specific territory in the kingdom of darkness

Brenda Barnes   widowed member of Cherry Pit Community Church

Cindy Marshall   former model and athlete—heavily involved in occult activities

Francis Baldwin   former pastor; now owner of Pine Burl Nursery, located on Cherry Pit Road

Gus and Millie Crossworthy   father and mother of Nadine

Johnny Barnes   deceased husband of Brenda Barnes

Juanita Parris   powerful church leader in Cherry Pit Community Church

Nadine Crossworthy   only child of Gus and Millie Crossworthy; witch; niece of Peggy

Peggy   aunt of Nadine Crossworthy, who introduces her to witchcraft

Stan Adkins   pastor of Cherry Pit Community Church

Steve Heinrich   young aeronautical engineer who befriends Cindy Marshall when they both work at Kroger's.

Chapter 1

Stan Adkins looked around the room, shook his head, and couldn't stifle an ironic smile. The scene was almost macabre, as though written by Alfred Hitchcock or Stephen King—a young pastor sitting alone in the shadows cast by a flickering fire in the study of a deserted Tennessee church; thunder rolling as lightning strobes across the churchyard; and a branch of a wild cherry tree, like one of Edgar Allan Poe's ravens, tap, tap, tapping against the window.

It had been a very strange evening, and Stan was having a hard time making sense of it. Making it worse, right outside the window, just past that cherry tree, was the cemetery where he had buried a number of people. Actually, Claude Ott had dug the graves and filled them in after the services, but it was Stan who had recited the words of the commitment that consigned their bodies to the ground. Sometimes, after saying the familiar "Ashes to ashes, dust to dust," he'd quietly add to himself, "If the worms don't get you you're bound to rust." Not irreverently, mind you, and not loud enough for anyone to hear, but just to help him keep his perspective.

Now with every gust of wind and rain that wailed and moaned through the trees, it sounded as if the denizens of the churchyard wanted into the warmth and security of Cherry Pit Community Church and away from the thunder and flashes of light bright enough to wake even the dead. Stan was glad that years ago Perry Parker had installed gas logs in the fireplace of the church study. Hurrying out to the back shed for more wood on a night like this would have been . . . well, let's just say that the fire would probably have gone out.

Not that Stan was afraid of ghosts. After all, he had always believed that when you died, you died. They lowered your body in a wood or metal box into the ground, and you were supposed to stay there. That's what he'd always thought. Your spirit or soul or whatever it was went to heaven or hell, or purgatory if you were a Catholic and there was some confusion over where you should go. After that, no one was sure what happened to you.

He guessed you burned or you billowed (isn't that what you do when you sit on a cloud?), depending on whether you went up or down, until Jesus came back and you were resurrected to face the judgment. Then you were sent to heaven or hell for eternity to continue to billow or burn. It didn't make a whole lot of sense when you thought about it, which Stan up to this point had preferred not to do. But one thing he had always known or believed or assumed was that once you were gone, you were gone. Until tonight at prayer meeting, that is.

Brenda Barnes had come to the midweek service at Cherry Pit Community Church with that special glow one has when they've fallen in love. They all saw it and assumed that Brenda's mourning was finally over. A year is a long time to grieve, and now it looked as if some lucky man had finally broken through the wall of sadness around her heart. It was time. In fact, it was long past time, and when she stood during the time for testimonies everyone eagerly waited to hear her speak.

Brenda had never looked lovelier, not even all those years back when she was crowned homecoming queen. The smile on her face made them all want to laugh. The color in her cheeks resembled someone who'd just come in from a long walk—a healthy flush that made her seem like a new bride. She looked around at the people who had nurtured her through so much pain. Her giggle brought to mind the tinkling of a thousand silver bells as she said, "I have the most wonderful news to tell you all. Johnny's back!"

Johnny Fletcher Barnes had died nearly a year before.

Cherry Pit Community Church hadn't been built large enough to contain the crowd that came to say their last goodbyes to Johnny Barnes. People who'd never been seen in a church were there, even Terry Hart, who'd always said the roof would fall in if he ever darkened the door. They'd had to open the windows to let the stragglers hear as best they could, and the police had been forced to close Cherry Pit Road to traffic because of the cars parked for more than a mile on the side of the road. Old Marge Peterson said it was the biggest funeral in the history of the town—even larger than Judge Bollinger's after the mine workers lynched him in 1911 during the strike.

"Johnny didn't go easy!" Gene Muncey had sobbed after the service as the guys drank beer and cried at the Sports Barn Bar and Grill.

It hadn't taken long. Johnny's stomach had been hurting for about a month. At first they'd thought it was indigestion, then maybe an ulcer. The guys even diagnosed it as an allergy to Brenda's cooking. But when his docs finally did a CT scan and saw the tentacles wrapping themselves around Johnny's liver and pancreas, they knew.

It had been the middle of the season. The softball team was counting on him to come in and save games the way he always had. His family was counting on picnics in the park, camping trips to the Indian wilderness area, and old movies in front of the fire at home. His boys were counting on him to teach them his secret pitch and to be there at graduations. They needed to have those man-to-man talks that dads and boys have when a girl leaves you for a Dennis Atkins or a Mike Esposito. Brenda was counting on being held and loved, and on Johnny's being there when she needed to smile, or the washer needed fixing, or the popcorn bowl needed retrieving from the top shelf in the pantry.

The doctors sadly told them there was no hope, but oh, how they still had hoped. All the experts said that cancer of the pancreas was incurable—that the doc just signed your death certificate when the diagnosis was certain. But they didn't know Johnny Fletcher Barnes. He'd always been a fighter. That's why the softball team had loved him the way they did. He'd never say die, and his pitching had saved more games then they were able to remember.

First they tried surgery. "A 10 percent chance of lengthening your life," the doctor told him. Then chemo. When that didn't work they tried wheat grass juice, New Age diets, and a doctor in Mexico who claimed a 90 percent cure rate. Next someone told them about a man in Montana who ground up a mixture of herbs that Johnny said was the worst-tasting garbage he'd had in his mouth since he was 5 and tried to eat his grandpa's chewing tobacco.

By then everyone realized that the cancer eating away at his pancreas and liver and then his kidneys and intestines was unstoppable. It grabbed its victims like a pit bull and shook them and ate them alive. The pain was like no other pain on earth.

Johnny had been in a morphine-induced coma for about a week when he suddenly awakened, struggled to sit up, and looked at Brenda wild-eyed with terror. He was still at home, where he wanted to die and where she had promised that he could. She took him in her arms and rocked him as he faced death. Brenda saw it in Johnny's eyes and felt it in the terrible trembling of his fragile body as she held him tight. He looked deeply in her eyes, searching her soul for her love, and gasped, "I'll see you, kitten." Then straining against the terrible pain, he died. And she had sat quietly rocking him and crying, until the hospice nurse came and together they bathed him and closed his eyes for the last time.

It was July when they found out what was causing his bellyache, and in February he was gone. February 14, to be exact. They engraved it on his tombstone next to a large heart that said "Loved" and "Resting in Jesus." It was ironic that, on the day of love, all of the love had gone out of Brenda's life.

And now Brenda had just announced, "Johnny's back!"

The silence thundered in the room. Time stopped. Deacon Warren's head jerked up and startled little Cassie Stenrud, who jumped and dropped her doll. Popping out of her arms, the doll hit the floor and tumbled down three rows to look up at Jennie Downer, who sat bolt upright, neck stiff, eyes darting wildly back and forth. Sylvia Bergstrom at the organ almost fell off the bench. Harold Downey coughed twice and looked over at his wife to see whether he'd really heard what he thought he'd heard. Sally Davis stopped chewing gum for probably the first time in her life. And Stan Adkins, whom nothing ever bothered, reached over for the corner of the Communion table to steady himself.

"Johnny's back?" he finally stuttered. "What do you mean, Brenda?"

"He's back, that's what I mean!"

"How . . . ? How . . . ?" Stan could think of nothing else to say. "How . . . ?" he tried again with no more success.

"He just came back," Brenda told them, her face shining like the sun. "One night I heard his key in the lock. I was in bed. It was almost 11:30. Johnny had this thing on his key ring. It was a memento of the first slow-pitch game he ever won. Carry Norton of the Rangers swung so hard that when he missed, the bat came out of his hands and flew foul into the parking lot. Bill Stadelmeyer, the team sponsor, had parked his Mercedes right next to the fence on the left field side. Carry's bat hit the hood and took off the ornament. Johnny found it after the game and added it to his key ring. He said it was his good-luck charm. It was so big he couldn't put his keys in his pocket anymore, so he bought one of those dumb things you hang on your belt that stretches out on a chain so you can use your keys.

"I hated the thing," Brenda said with a laugh. "Every night when he came home it made a weird noise as he pulled it out to unlock the door. And then that Mercedes hood ornament rattled against the sash as he turned his keys. We had to repaint the door several times because of the scratches. We buried the awful thing with him, along with his keys, and I felt so guilty, feeling so good about that whole ring going in the ground with him.

"Anyway, I was lying in bed one night, thinking about Johnny, when I heard his keys." She looked from the pastor to the congregation, willing them to believe her. "You couldn't mistake it. *Zing, rattle rattle*, then *clunk* as the deadbolt turned back.

"I was so scared I couldn't move. I could hardly breathe. Then I heard nothing for a minute or so until I heard the water in the sink.

"Johnny's throat was always dry when he came home from work. And he had this thing about drinking 12 glasses of water every day. So first thing when he came home, he always had a big glass of water. When he was done he'd rinse the glass, turn it over, and set it on the drainer to dry. It was like this routine he had. Every night the same thing. First the rattle of the keys at the door, then the clunk of the dead-bolt, next the water.

"That night I lay in bed for more than an hour, waiting and listen-ing. Finally I couldn't stand it any longer. I reached under the bed and got Johnny's favorite bat, put on my robe, and crept down the stairs. It was dark, and the house was so quiet I could hear the dog snoring in the kids' room.

"I looked through the whole house. There was nothing. Finally I turned on the lights and searched everywhere. It wasn't until I was reach-ing for the switch in the kitchen to turn out the lights and go to bed that I noticed the glass, turned upside down, dripping in the drainer."

Stan's hand slipped off of the Communion table, and he almost fell over.

Dead serious, Brenda continued. "I was so scared I wet my pants. I hadn't done that since I was in second grade. I couldn't move. I couldn't think. I couldn't breathe. I don't know how long I stood there, staring at that glass. It was long enough that I began to get cold from the wet that had run down my leg. When—scared to death—I finally turned to run, I slipped and fell on the kitchen floor. When I finally got my feet under me, I ran as I'd never run before. It startled Mox so badly that he woke up and started to bark. I could hear the boys muttering for him to shut up as I sprinted up the stairs.

"Steve heard me coming and stuck his head out their bedroom door. 'You OK, Mom?' he mumbled. 'You look like you've seen a ghost.'

"'I'm all right,' I said. 'I'm just in a hurry to get back to bed.' He looked down at my robe with a funny look on his face, shrugged, and shut his door.

"I locked my bedroom door, put a chair against it, crawled into bed, and spent the rest of the night crying. I didn't even change my gown, I was so frightened.

"A few nights later it happened again, then again, and again, until it became part of our routine. At first I was terrified. I'd creep down the stairs, bat in my hand, and check the house. It was always empty, but the glass was always there. After a while I didn't bother checking the house. I just went in and checked the kitchen for the glass and went back to bed.

"Once at breakfast, Johnny junior looked at me with a funny expres-sion and asked, 'Mom, why do you go downstairs every night in the mid-dle of the night?' I just laughed and told him I was thirsty.

"One night as I was sitting at the kitchen table, looking at that drip-ping glass and thinking about Johnny, I got to thinking about how he loved snickerdoodles. I used to make them for him fairly often, and almost every night after he drank his water he'd check the cookie jar to see if the boys had left him any or if I'd made some fresh. If he found cookies he'd pour himself a big glass of milk and take a plate of them in to watch the last of Johnny Carson. Well, I still make them for the kids, so one night I checked the cookie jar and saw that there were three left." She paused, took a deep breath, and let out a long sigh.

"On an impulse I took out the cookies, put them on a saucer, and poured a glass of milk. It made me feel close to Johnny for a minute, and I sat there in the kitchen and cried as I remembered him. Then I went to bed.

"When I came downstairs the next morning, Steve stuck his head around the corner. 'You forgot to put away the evidence,' he told me, laughing."

"'What do you mean?' I asked."

"Pulling me around the corner, he pointed at the empty glass and the crumbs on the saucer. 'Uh-huh, cookies and milk after the kiddies have gone to bed. You're going to start putting on pounds, Mom.'"

"I couldn't wait!" she continued, stumbling over the words in her eagerness to share the story. "As soon as the boys left for school, I started baking cookies. I know it sounds crazy, but I baked 10 dozen snicker-doodles. I couldn't stop. And that night when the boys went to bed I sneaked downstairs and poured a big glass of milk and set out three cookies. At 5:30 the next morning I ran downstairs and checked. Sure enough, they were gone.

"It was about two weeks later that I decided on a plan. After I put the cookies and milk out on the table, I went back upstairs and told the boys good night. When I was sure they were asleep, I put on my sweats, crept back downstairs, and lay down on the couch in the family room."

She looked from Stan to Sylvia to Howard, her face aglow. "I guess I should have been scared, but instead I felt excited—you know, the way you'd feel staying up late on Christmas Eve to see if you could catch Santa.

"I don't know how long I lay there in the dark, but I finally drifted off to sleep. I didn't wake up until Steve came down and startled rattling pans in the kitchen. Sticking his head in the family room, he saw me and grinned. 'At the cookies again, I see,' he said. 'Mom, I think you're an addict.'

"It wasn't until I started to get up that it hit me. The afghan! Sometimes when Johnny had to work late, I'd stay up to wait for him. But often I'd fall asleep on the couch. When he'd come in, he'd hate to wake me, so he'd cover me with the afghan my sister had crocheted for me. He'd tuck it under my chin and go on to bed. I'd wake up in the morning to find him sitting in his recliner with a cup of coffee, just grinning at me.

"When I reached up to pull back the afghan, I knew. Listen, everyone, I *knew*. Johnny had been there and had tucked me in."

Brenda looked around at the congregation. They sat in stunned silence. "I know that I'm taking an awful long time, but I need to tell you the rest of the story," she said.

Her friends and neighbors looked from each other to her. No one had the nerve to say a word.

"Do you remember your first date?" Brenda asked with a giggle. "How nervous and excited you were. How you wanted to look and even smell your best. Well, that day I took a nap so I'd be rested. And that night, after the boys went to bed, I showered and put on my best perfume. I hadn't worn Ysatis since Johnny died. He'd bought it for me for our anniversary, and I'd kept it in the refrigerator. It was our favorite. Anyway, I splashed a little of it on, then got out his favorite negligee. It was white, and sheer, and he used to say it made me look like an angel. Then I just went downstairs to wait.

"It was 11:45 when Johnny came home. I heard his key in the lock this time. He put his coat in the closet, just as he always did, then walked into the kitchen. The lights were out, but I could see him as clearly as if they were on. He went to the sink, filled his glass with water, drank it just as he'd done for years, and turned it upside down in the drainer to dry. Then he got another glass from the cupboard, went to the refrigerator, and poured himself some milk. I realized I was holding my breath as I watched.

"Finally he reached up, took the lid off the cookie jar, and fished out a handful of snickerdoodles." Then her words were little more than a sigh. "Johnny turned to me, and he smiled. It was a smile of love, and 'I miss you,' and 'I want you' all wrapped in one.

"I couldn't stand it any longer. I had to be close to him and touch him, to smell his aftershave and feel his arms around me. And you know, it was as if he could read my thoughts. He just stood there smiling at me as though he could eat me up. All these months I'd been dying for that smile. I'd even dreamed about it. Now Johnny was home.

"As I walked toward him I felt as nervous and excited as I did on our honeymoon. His eyes had that same twinkle of anticipation. Then I was in his arms and he was holding me and we were kissing—long, hungry, passionate . . . well, you know." And she actually blushed.

"It was almost dawn when he left me. After our love, we lay on the couch for the rest of the night just holding each other. Then he said he had to go. But he comes every night now. Sometimes I meet him in the kitchen, and we share cookies and milk, but other times"—a thousand stars shone in her eyes—"I just wait for him to come up to bed."

She looked at Pastor Stan, willing him to believe her.

"He always comes."

While she'd told her story Brenda had been on her feet. Now she sank down on the wooden pew and waited.

Feet shuffled. Someone coughed. Sylvia, nervous and frightened, set her foot on a bass pedal of her organ. Everyone jumped, yet stared straight ahead—afraid to look at their neighbors.

Stan finally found his voice. "Brenda, do the boys know about this?"

Standing again, she went on. "Oh, yes. We were grilling steaks for supper a couple of weeks ago when Steve asked me if I was seeing someone.

" 'You know that I've gone out once or twice,' I told him.

" 'That's not what I mean, Mom,' he said.

" 'Why do you ask?' I said. I think I was both scared and excited to hear what he'd say.

" 'Well, you're different,' he told me. 'You're smiling and singing while you work around the house, and you've started wearing that perfume Dad gave you. And several times lately Johnny and I've heard you talking to someone in your bedroom late at night. It even sounded like, uh . . .' His voice kind of trailed off.

" 'Steve!'

" 'Mom, I'm in high school. I know about these things,' he told me, his face flushing so red I wanted to laugh.

" 'Steven Blain Barnes, what goes on in my bedroom is my business!' I took after him with a spatula. We were both giggling as he ran out the door and into the yard, me right behind him. We ran around the lawn until I finally cornered him and gave him a playful whack across his backside.

" 'Well, Mom?' Steve said. He wasn't going to let me off the hook. 'You didn't answer my question. Are you seeing somebody? And if you are, why haven't we met him?' "

" 'You have!' I told him."

For the second time that night Stan Adkins' hand slipped off of the Communion table, and he almost fell. Looking out over the congregation, he could tell that they were all in about the same condition. In fact, for a minute he felt that he'd somehow stepped into a Norman Rockwell painting. All over the room people sat, transfixed, their mouths hanging open, their eyes forward in amazed stares as Brenda went on with her story.

"So I called Johnny junior to come on out, and I told them both,"

Brenda continued. "It hasn't been easy for them to adjust to the idea. Actually, Steve moved out and he's living with a friend right now, and Johnny sleeps every night with his bedroom door locked. But they'll come around—I know they will. They need their dad."

Ahem, Stan cleared his throat. "Brenda, we really appreciate your sharing this with us. Uh, . . . maybe . . . uh . . . it's late. Maybe we'd better close."

The members of Cherry Pit Community Church filed out of church in a daze. Now their pastor sat alone in his study, the church being assaulted by a wild rainstorm, trying to sort it all out. He had always believed that when you died, you died, and that was the end of it. It was all very neat and orderly. Nothing that had ever been human was ever heard from again after it died, despite what you might see in a horror movie, and he liked it that way. Now he wasn't so sure.

Brenda Barnes wasn't crazy, that he knew. And she wasn't given to strange fantasies. In fact, she was one of the most practical and down-to-earth people around. Sure, her grief seemed to be deeper than most, wilder somehow—but after all, Johnny had died young. Stan knew that people sometimes hallucinated under stress. But this sounded too real. He wanted to dismiss it. He wanted to think Brenda was nuts. But he could do neither.

Something else was happening, and he couldn't figure it out.

Because Stan was a stickler for organization, every sermon he had ever preached was neatly filed in one of two cabinets that stood in the corner. One shelf of his study contained notebooks neatly labeled with the titles of various Bible subjects. Through the years he had made a habit of systematically studying what the Scriptures taught on a whole range of topics. He took careful notes as he studied, recording what he'd learned and placing the pages in the binders. Now he went to the corner closet and took out a new notebook. Tearing off the plastic wrap, he savored the smell of the fresh vinyl. It always signaled the beginning of a new adventure in God's Word. Filling the binder with notebook paper, he neatly lettered a label with the words "What Happens When You Die," and taped it to the spine. Then, opening to the first page, he wrote "Initial Thoughts and Questions" and began making a list.

1. What exactly does the Bible say happens to you when you die?

2. What is the history of the Christian church's beliefs about the condition of people in death?

3. Does the Bible say anything about the dead contacting people on earth?

4. How about ghosts? Who and what are they? Ditto channeling.

What or whom are people contacting when they channel the spirits?

5. Lots of interest today in the occult. How does that connect with what the Bible teaches?

6. It makes sense that if people go to heaven or hell when they die, they would try to contact us if they could and if they really cared about us. Does the Bible say anything about this?

7. How about the after-life experiences that people talk about?

Stan paused, frowning and chewing the end of the ballpoint pen. Now he'd come to the heart of the matter, but he couldn't figure out how to phrase it. Rain still splattered against the windows. At last he took the pen out of his mouth and wrote:

8. Are the dead alive? (That's a contradiction of terms, isn't it?) And if the dead aren't alive, who on earth is making love with Brenda Barnes?

He placed the pen on his desk and closed the notebook. It had been a long, long day. Carefully placing the notebook on the corner of the desk, he crossed to the fireplace and turned off the gas.

Only as he was pulling on his coat did he realize that the wind had picked up. Instead of gusts and swirls, it now howled through the branches of the old cherry tree. Reaching for his hat, Stan switched off the light and opened the door.

Chapter 2

Francis Baldwin was proud of Pine Burl Nursery.

When the divorce was final and he had said his last goodbyes to the congregation and cleaned out his library at the church, he had wondered what he was going to do.

When you start dreaming of entering the ministry at the age of 5, when you preach your first sermon at 16, when all of your training—college and seminary—is in theology, what else is there to do?

The church—both local and corporate—had been kind, so he had had some time to adjust. After Ann had marched into the pulpit one Sunday morning and called him a fanatic and announced her intention to leave him and get a divorce, they could have terminated him with no pay at all. But they loved Francis. He'd been their pastor for more than 20 years, and he was like a member of the family. Between the severance package they offered him and his accumulated sick and vacation time, he had had almost a year and a half to sort out his life.

It hadn't been easy. When you've been married for 31 years and you lose your profession and your wife in one fell swoop, it's hard. No, more than hard. It takes your whole world and scrambles it until you wonder if the pieces will ever come together. You end up living in new places. Things and people you always counted on being there are suddenly gone. It is like a death in the family, only the person is still alive. You meet your former spouse in the grocery store or at the mall, and the knife in your stomach does another turn. And when you're in a profession that traditionally has expected its practitioner to be married, suddenly you're looking for a job—at the time when most men are settling into the best part of their ministry.

What do you work at when you leave the ministry? Most of the guys Francis knew who left the pastorate either became marriage counselors (if they'd been caught in an affair!) or insurance salesmen—neither of which appealed much to him. A few became hospital chaplains, but he found that prospect depressing. So he just drove around town, looking at people and businesses and wondering.

Suddenly relationships with lifelong friends became strained. For some, where once he'd been a welcome guest at dinner, he suddenly became a threat. It was awkward to share friends with his former wife. People who'd been his social intimates suddenly didn't know what to say or do. They were still cordial, but in a kind of arm's-length sort of way that made him want to, well, throw up and run away. He felt like an aspen leaf blowing around, not connected to anyone or anything. It was just easier to stay to himself. After a while he stopped contacting most of the people he'd once been close to.

One day he drove out to Cherry Pit Road to walk and think. It was a gorgeous fall morning, one of those days that make you glad to be alive and wish you could live forever.

As he walked, musing about the history of this strangely named road and thinking about his own future, he almost missed the sign. It was one of those small, neatly lettered placards that read "For Sale, Inquire Within," but made you wonder if the seller really wanted you to. On cardboard, it was tacked to the gatepost where you would have missed it if you hadn't been walking.

Stopping, he looked at the little nursery tucked back from the road in a small cove surrounded by a grove of wild cherry and hickory trees. *Don't I wish!* he thought as he looked back at the card, then up at the weathered cedar sign announcing the existence of Pine Burl Nursery. He thought all of the times he'd secretly dreamed of someday (maybe when he retired) owning a little lawn and garden center. Maybe this was his chance. This place wasn't much when it came to buildings, but it was obvious that someone here loved plants, and it was for sale. Shrugging, he turned into the lane.

Charla Jorgenson was Pine Burl Nursery. She started it, raising bedding plants for her neighbors on her back porch, and over the years it had grown into one of those places that have a little of everything. The office wasn't much to look at—how do you take time to paint a building when there are plants to care for? The fence needed repair. Potholes pocked the driveway, and her house hadn't had a good cleaning for years. But the shade houses and greenhouses and the 10 acres of nursery stock were the nicest Francis had ever seen. It was obvious that this woman loved plants.

And it was obvious to Charla Jorgenson that Francis Baldwin loved plants too. She watched him as he walked down the drive, and she just knew. She saw it on his face as he looked at the birches in the yard and when he stopped to caress a planter filled with petunias. She could see it in the way he smelled a rose he passed, and the way he smiled when he looked at the nursery stock.

She'd been waiting a long time for a Francis Baldwin; more than two years, to be exact, and had lost three different suites in the retirement center while she waited. After all, you can't just turn your children over to anyone.

Two weeks later Francis Baldwin was owner, proprietor, and the only employee of Pine Burl Nursery: one small house, one office badly in need of paint and repair, 10 acres of land filled with nursery stock, three shade houses, two greenhouses, and a cat named Arthur.

Now, looking out over the valley spreading before him like a huge rolling orange, green, and umber quilt on an unmade bed, Francis took off his sweater and tied it by the arms around his neck. He had never seen a prettier fall day in his life. The rain had washed the world, and the sun of an early morning made it feel like June.

When he was in the pastorate he had never allowed himself the luxury of an occasional walk. Now he was doing it every day and was feeling great. The walk to the end of Cherry Pit Road and back was an easy four and a half miles that left you exhilarated.

As he walked, he reflected on the origins of this strangely named road. Way back before the original Scottish settlers came to this part of south-central Tennessee nestled between the Cumberland Plateau and what would eventually become the Georgia border, wild black cherry trees had been sprinkled in among the hickory and pines. The Cherokees used the juice for dye, and the fruit was a staple of the bear and wild turkeys. Every time there was a fire, cherry sprouts sprang up in the clearings. In the fire of 1784 the whole hill had burned after a thunderstorm. Soon it was covered with wild cherry saplings. And when the first settlers cleared a road along the crest of the hill, it was soon lined with cherry trees.

Every fall, when the fruit ripened, dropped to the ground, and began to rot, the road was covered with cherry pits. They were everywhere. As you walked in the crisp, cold mornings of autumn they crunched under your feet, and the juice dyed the bottoms of your shoes a dark-reddish blue. After a while, when you walked into town and the folks saw your shoes, they'd say, "Hey, you've been up on Cherry Pit Road." The name stuck. And, when they built the little white church at the fork where Deacon Whithurst donated land during the fund-raising drive, the church came naturally by its name. In fact, they really had had no choice. Maddie Schaak, who said that this road, which wound along the hill above the Schaak farm, was the prettiest in the whole United States, had specified it in her will: *And to my beloved church family, $1,000 for the new church, if it's called Cherry Pit Community Church.*

That had been in 1844. The church burned in 1907 and was replaced by a much larger structure, but the name remained. Francis chuckled about the reactions it had to generate at church conventions when they called the roll.

Today, as he approached the church, it struck him how beautiful it really was. Currier and Ives would have painted it if they had ever made it this far south. Twin doors, four tall columns, tasteful stained-glass topped by clear, semicircular windows with beveled glass panes, and the prettiest cemetery he had ever seen. Claude Ott, the caretaker, had been in a few times for supplies, and it was obvious that the church and its grounds were his baby. There was hardly a twig out of place. Even now Claude was busy loading limbs and leaves that had blown down in last night's storm into an old pickup parked at the back of the cemetery.

"Pretty isn't it?"

Francis jumped and turned to see a young man in jeans and flannel shirt leaning against a tree that stood across the road from the church. "Sometimes," the stranger said with a grin, "I come out here and look at it just to get my perspective. Say, you're new around here, aren't you? My name's Stan Adkins, and I'm the pastor of this church."

Reaching out his hand, he said, "I was here late last night, so I'm taking my time getting started this morning. One of the advantages of a country pastorate is that you can come to your office to study in blue jeans. Ever been inside?"

Francis laughed. "No, I can't say as I have. I bought Pine Burl Nursery a little more than a month ago, and I'm still getting settled."

"Ah, you're the one who gave Claude the idea to use some dish soap with that liquid fertilizer he uses. He came back here telling me that the new guy down at Pine Burl knew what he was talking about. That, in case you don't know, is about as much of a compliment as you're ever going to get from Claude. Say, would you like a cup of coffee? I turned on the percolator just before I came out, so it should be about ready. You can tell when you see Claude edging over toward the door. He can smell coffee brewing clear across the valley."

Stan laughed an easy laugh and led the way toward the church. "My secretary doesn't come in until after 11:00 a.m. on Thursdays. She attends a Bible study fellowship. That leaves me free to be a little more relaxed. Come on in."

Chapter 3

Colonel Fred Marshall realized early on that his eight kids were all very gifted when it came to track and field. And he spared no time or expense to get them the best training that was available. It had paid off in ways that were beyond his highest expectations.

Fred's greatest joy in life was to load his kids into the family van, travel to an open meet where they weren't known, and then enter the whole bunch in the competition. The walls of the Marshall den, the mantel in the living room, and about 12 boxes in the attic all filled with trophies and ribbons were testimony to the fact that every one of his children was Olympic material if they chose to be.

They didn't. As they grew, they chose to be an engineer, a teacher, an attorney, a mechanic, a homemaker and mother, a pilot, a baker, and a model and nightclub singer.

It bothered Fred sometimes that his kids hadn't gone for the gold, but thinking of them, he was very proud. They were doing what they wanted, and that's what counted. That didn't mean that he wasn't concerned about them at times. Especially Cindy.

Cindy, his and Estelle's youngest daughter—the model/nightclub singer—had given Fred a lot of sleepless nights. It didn't seem like the place for his baby. But Cindy was one of the most independent women you would ever meet. So he'd held his tongue and hoped that she'd be safe. It wasn't that he didn't trust her. After 28 years in the military, he just knew the risks. In that environment there were too many guys on the prowl with one thing on their minds, and too many washed-up alcoholic bar singers who hadn't been able to resist the bottle. It just didn't seem to be worth the risk, and he wished his daughter had chosen a different profession. But she was as stubborn and hardheaded as she was beautiful, so he had expressed his concerns, then let her make the decision.

He had some other worries about Cindy that were even more pressing. He couldn't put his finger on the specifics. There was just a tugging uneasiness that something was going wrong. Fred Marshall wasn't a religious man, and he'd seen a great deal through the years, so there wasn't much that spooked him. But Cindy and Karen, her sister, were involved in something that made Fred Marshall very uncomfortable.

It had all started one night at supper when Karen had laughingly offered to read him his horoscope. Fred had about as much use for horoscopes as he did for television evangelists, so he had declined. But Cindy was interested, so they left the table and went into the living room to pore over an article Karen had brought with her.

At first it was a joke. They'd laugh as they read what the stars had to say about their present and future. Cindy and Karen had always been the closest of the sisters, and it all just seemed like harmless fun. Karen's husband didn't put much stock in it either, so he and Fred would roll their eyes and joke about it while the girls huddled over the latest predictions in the paper or one of the supermarket tabloids.

After a while, though, it began to get serious. Both girls began to invest in a fair number of books on the subject. Cindy purchased a program for her computer that was supposed to be able to chart the stars and their effects on our lives. Karen took most of her inheritance from a great-aunt and attended a seminar titled Charting Your Life by the Stars. It was led by no less than a Hollywood actress and her astrologer.

After a while it was as if they were possessed by the subject. Karen became almost missionary-like in her zeal. You couldn't escape from her without getting charted. As much as Fred loved his grandkids he began to dread the times Karen and her family came for supper. Family days, when all of them got together, became an ordeal.

Tony quit coming. There was no way, he said, that he was going to get involved. Donna came, but avoided Karen and Cindy any way she could. Ron, who still lived at home, retreated to his bedroom and turned on the stereo. The rest of the family endured the situation, but it was only because they had always been close and weren't going to let anything get in the way of their relationships.

Fred couldn't put his finger on what was happening, but he knew something wasn't right.

During the cold war he'd experienced the same vague uneasiness. He had known that something was wrong in his staff, but it wasn't something you could pin down. Call it a sixth sense. Call it whatever you want. He had just known. It had taken him two years to catch Starla Webster. She was a pro. Her East German handlers had trained their American recruit well. But when he caught the spy red-handed, in the middle of a pass, his hunch had been vindicated and the feeling had gone away. He knew that feeling. It was an alarm that never betrayed him when danger was near. Now it was sounding again, louder and more insistent than he'd ever heard and felt before.

Fred was worried about Cindy. He couldn't tell you what was wrong, but he knew she was in danger. And he knew—he felt it in his gut—that the enemy she faced was out to do everything it could to destroy her.

I wonder what Grandma T would say if she knew what I was doing now.

Cindy put down the latest copy of *New Age Magazine* and leaned back in her chair. It had been so very long since that day she and her grandmother had sat on the back porch of her old house on Hastings Street, gently swaying in the porch swing as they looked out at the park.

Setting down her lemonade, Grandma Terwilligar had gotten very serious for a moment. She was a Christian, and one of the happiest people Cindy knew. That was why the two weeks they spent together every year were the highlight of Cindy's summer. Grandma T was always smiling, so when she got serious Cindy knew that it was very important.

"Cindy," she had said, "there's something I need to talk to you about. I know that your mom and dad aren't very religious and that you don't go to church much. But you need to listen to Grandma now. Cindy, it's very important for you to get to know God. It will be hard for you because your family isn't interested, but you've got to read your Bible and pray every day. God has something very special planned for you. But you'll never experience it if you don't know Him."

Cindy had watched a couple dogs running circles around a woman leisurely walking with two leashes in her hand. Her mind wandered for a moment, but then, out of love and respect for her grandmother, she had turned her attention back to listen.

"Cindy, not only is there a real God who created you, and who loves you so much He sent Jesus to live and die for you—there is also a real devil who hates God and everything He has created. The Bible says that the devil rules this world and that we are his slaves unless we choose to be otherwise." She'd bent forward, her face serious and intent. "Honey, the devil wants to destroy you, and sometimes he can be very cruel. He has invented all kinds of ways to enslave us, but God is stronger, Cindy. God is stronger! If Satan ever tries to hurt you, remember that you can call on Jesus' name and He will save you. Will you promise to remember this?"

Cindy had nodded solemnly and said yes, but she had no idea what her grandmother was talking about.

Grandma T had died that year. Among her things was a letter, written to Cindy. After telling her how much she loved her, she reminded her of the conversation they'd had that day on the porch. And then she added, "Cindy, God showed me in prayer one day that He had some very special things in store for you. He also told me that His adversary, Satan, would do all that he could to keep you for himself. Whatever you do, don't ever have anything to do with him. You will know what I mean when you get old enough to understand. But Cindy, dear, please be careful! Heaven would be terribly lonely for Grandma without you. Love, Grandma T."

Chapter 4

Nadine Crossworthy had been born into one of the most prestigious homes in the town. Her father, Augustus Felix Crossworthy III, was president of its oldest financial institution—First. Federated Bank and Mortgage. Founded by her great-grandfather, Caesar Crossworthy, it was the only building of substance to escape the ravages of Sherman's march to the sea.

Tradition had it that when the Union general William T. Sherman and his aides rode into town, Caesar was there, on the front steps of the bank, to meet them. Flashing the secret Masonic sign for distress, he pointed silently to the compass and rule chiseled into the lintel above the door. While the rest of the town burned, it's said that the general sat impassively on his horse in front of the bank, never uttering a word, never taking his eyes off Caesar Crossworthy. It was rumored that the two of them never blinked the whole time it took for the Union soldiers to raze the town. When they were done, it was said that Sherman coughed once, reined his horse, and quietly rode away.

August Crossworthy, from the moment of his birth, had been destined to take over the bank. His father, August II, had died when he was 35 and little Gus was 5, so the mantle had passed to him. He wore it with pride and more than a little arrogance from the moment he was old enough to realize that it belonged to him. There were those who had questioned whether he had what it took to take his grandfather's place in the chair—some called it a throne—at the head of the boardroom. But from the moment he walked through the door, summoned home in the middle of his junior year at Emory University when his grandfather died, there was no doubt who was in charge.

There were two things that August III had always dreamed of. One ws to become president of the bank; the other was to father a little girl. When Millie Crossworthy became pregnant, he had prayed that God would give him a daughter. The moment she entered the world she became the delight of his life. She was the only thing that could coax him away from the bank.

Townspeople said that August Crossworthy was married to that bank. In fact, more than one person had chuckled and wondered how in the world he'd ever found the time to father a child since his hours were so long. But when Nadine was born, things changed. There was always time for his little girl.

As she grew, Gus saw to it that Nadine never lacked anything she ever wanted. The parties, and later the balls, held at the Crossworthy mansion were legendary in Gentry County. As a debutante, she made the rest of the girls and their coming out look plain. It was said that August Crossworthy would do anything for Nadine—even let her marry Tom Lawson.

Tom was every girl's dream and every father's nightmare. Captain of the football team, good-looking, built like a young Atlas, he bragged of bedding every good-looking woman in town, and some that weren't. When he appeared one evening at the massive Crossworthy front door, Gus's first reaction was to throw him off the porch—until he saw his daughter's face. Instead, he grimaced, bowed slightly, and invited him in. When Nadine gushed that Tom was taking her to a movie, the grim look returned for just a second. Then with a smile he had said that it sounded like fun and had promptly invited himself and Millie along. Calling Noc Johnson, the chauffeur, on the intercom, he ordered the car and, before anyone could protest, arranged the evening. Leaving Tom's convertible sitting on the curved drive that circled under the front portico, they went out to eat and then caught the movie.

Every date the two had that year went that way. After a while it became a determined game that both Tom and Gus played to the best of their considerable abilities. War was never officially declared, but Tom's interest and Nadine's willingness to get away alone were more than matched by Gus's determination that his daughter's virginity would survive this relationship intact. And it did for a while. But passion can afford to be patient.

That fall when Nadine left for Emory to begin her freshman year, there was a tearful goodbye out on the porch swing overlooking the valley. Gus did his best to look appropriately sad when Nadine told him of their decision to date around for a while. Then that evening he called a few friends whose sons were also attending his alma mater, to make sure Nadine had plenty of dates to keep her mind off Tom.

One night the following May, Bill Segna called Gus. President of the Atlanta Trust, an old-line bank whose headquarters on Peachtree Street was one of the city's landmarks, Bill's son was one of those Gus had hoped would pursue his daughter when she got to college.

"Gus, I think there's something you need to be aware of," he said after they'd exchanged some small talk about a couple of mutual funds they were both invested in. "I know it's a long drive, but I—well, maybe it would be a good idea if you dropped down to see Nadine."

Gus felt himself go weak all over. "What are you saying, Bill?" he demanded.

"I haven't wanted to alarm you—I know how you feel about your daughter—but there are some serious problems down here. Last fall Nadine began dating a young turk named Tom Lawson. Good-looking kid, but a bit of a hellion, I'm told."

Bill's words hit him like a punch in the belly. He feared he was going to throw up.

"Anyway, as I've been able to piece the story together, they got pretty physical; then the guy dumped her. From what Rocky, my son, told me it's had some, ah, serious effects."

Now Gus was pacing, his breath rapid, his footsteps slapping the polished Florentine terra-cotta in his den.

Bill's relentless voice droned on. "From the way things look she may need professional intervention of some kind, Gus. I'm sorry to call you, but I thought you'd want to know as soon as possible."

"What kind of effects, Bill?" He was close to shouting now.

"I think that you'd better come down and see for yourself, Gus. I'm no expert on these things, but if it was my daughter I think that I'd want to know as soon as possible. Well, listen, I've got to go. Louise has tickets for the opening night of symphony season, and I need to get ready. If there's anything I can do, let me know."

In less than an hour Gus and Millie were on their way to Atlanta.

Chapter 5

It all began innocuously enough. Cindy walked the two blocks from her apartment to the Jade Palace to pick up the Chinese food she had ordered. Jimmy Wong smiled as he brought her food, the take-out containers wrapped in newspaper inside a box. *It's a pity that such a beautiful woman is eating by herself,* he thought as he rang up her order. Oh well, he knew she didn't lack for male companionship, so it was probably OK.

The walk back to her apartment was a joy. Whoever had begun the custom of planting dogwood trees in town had bequeathed to their descendants a wonderful gift, she pondered. No place on earth was prettier in the spring.

Balancing the box containing her meal on one knee, she keyed the combination for the electric lock, opened the door, and stopped.

Curious people are often observant people. They notice things sooner because they are watching. They're interested, and take notice of things out of the ordinary. So the candle burning on the dining room table of Cindy's apartment caught her attention immediately. First of all, the candle had never been lit. She had replaced it that morning. Second, she knew she hadn't lit it. Slowly setting the box with her dinner on the floor, she opened the front door wide and shifted a leg of the coat rack against it to make sure it didn't close. Then she carefully and cautiously began a search of the apartment.

When she finished, she closed the front door and sat down at the table and studied the candle. Whoever had lit it was no longer there, she was sure of that. She'd even looked into the crawl space under her part of the building, and, standing on tiptoe on a chair, she had lifted up the hatch opening into the attic and checked there. Whoever they were, they had taken their matches with them or used a lighter of their own, because there was none on the table or in the trash. It was odd to say the least, and made her feel just a little insecure. Someone had entered her apartment and left without leaving a trace of evidence of how they had gotten there.

Blowing out the candle, she set the table and ate her dinner.

When she finished, she picked up the phone and called the manager's office. "Shelly, this is Cindy Marshall. Did maintenance do anything in my apartment today?"

"No, Cindy, I've been here all afternoon, and I haven't asked any of them to do anything at your place. Besides, Clarence is off for the day. Why?"

"Oh, nothing, really. I just wondered if anyone had been in my apartment. Say, how's the ceramics class going?"

"Fine. We spent all afternoon learning how to apply translucent washes. You should join us sometime."

Cindy laughed. "Thanks, Shelly, but ceramics just aren't my thing. Listen, I've got to go. I'll catch you later, OK?"

Cindy Marshall was about as independent a woman as you're ever likely to meet. Nothing much scared her, and if it did, she wasn't about to let it show. She'd spent too long working the nightclub circuit to be frightened easily. But that night, for the first time in at least seven years, she locked the second deadbolt—the one that could be opened only from the inside. Then she put the dowel rods her father had cut for her into the tracks of all of the sliding-glass windows.

It had been a long day, and for the first time in months she didn't have to work late. After a leisurely shower and the luxury of a half hour's soak in the Jacuzzi, she went straight to bed.

Francis Baldwin couldn't help feeling just a little twinge of loneliness as he walked through the door to Stan Adkins' office. There was something about the aroma of good coffee combined with the sight of the rows of books in a pastor's study that reminded him of his own office. As much as he was enjoying getting settled in at Pine Burl Nursery, he missed the pastorate. He missed the sacred agony of a new sermon every week. He missed the time to read and reflect and meditate. Yes, and he missed the uninterrupted time for prayer that his ministry had afforded.

"So how do you like your poison, black or with cream?" Stan asked.

"Cream, and no sugar, thanks." Francis let his eyes travel the room with open admiration. "Say, you've got a fine library, Stan. It makes me want to get some of my own books unpacked."

"Thanks. I'm afraid that they're all pretty narrowly focused, but if you'd ever like to borrow one I'm always open to lending what I have.

"So how are things going down at the nursery? Claude tells me that you're really sprucing things up around there!"

"Well, I'm trying," Francis told him. "Charla Jorgenson had one of the nicest collections of plants I've ever seen. But I'm afraid that organization and marketing were not her forte. I've gotten things looking pretty good cosmetically. And the bedding plants are selling well. But there's still a long way to go, I'm afraid, before things are the way I'd like them to be. This fall I plan to renovate the house and redo the office." He laughed. "Then maybe I'll feel that the place is really mine."

"Have you always been in the nursery business?" Stan asked, leaning back in his chair and placing his feet on the edge of a file drawer sticking out of his desk.

"No, it's new for me, although it's something I've always dreamed of doing. I had an office job before, so it's nice to get outdoors and work in nature. I'm really enjoying it, and it keeps me busy." The breeze blowing in through the alcove window rustled the curtains, and the smell of the honeysuckle growing on a trellis outside filled the room. For a minute or so the two of them sat in silence, savoring the glories of spring. "I guess it was time for a change, and I'm glad that God gave me the chance to do something I really enjoy. How about you? How long have you been pastoring?"

"Oh, about seven years now," Stan answered. "I came to Cherry Pit Community immediately after I left the seminary. We're not the largest church in town, but I wouldn't trade it for any other. The people have been great to me and my family, and we've had solid growth. I hope to retire here. Say, I don't know whether you're an active member of a local church, but we'd love to have you come and visit our services."

"Thanks," Francis smiled. "I think that I'd like that. I haven't found a church home since moving here, and I miss it. I'll drop by one Sunday really soon. Well, listen, I'd better get going, or I won't be there in time to open." He stood up and drank the last swallow from his cup. "Thanks for the great coffee. Oh, and I'll take you up on the offer of a book sometime."

Stan Adkins sat watching Francis walk down the road toward Pine Burl Nursery. Something told him that he should look forward to the opportunity of getting to know Francis better.

Chapter 6

Cindy, are you awake? I figured you probably had a gig tonight. But you sound as if I woke you up."

"Who is this?" Cindy struggled to crawl up out of the well of sleep that enveloped her like a huge quilt. "Karen, is that you? What are you doing, calling me this time of night?" Looking over at the clock, she groaned. "Karen, it's 4:00 in the morning. Are you drunk or something? What's going on?"

"I'm sorry, Cindy. I thought you'd be working tonight, so I stayed up to call you. You didn't sing tonight, huh?"

"No, Doc Sorenson called and said that he wanted to audition some new acts for this fall, and gave me the night off. I was kinda enjoying a good night's sleep for a change."

"Sorry. I wish I'd known."

"It's OK. What's so important that it kept my big sister up until this ungodly hour of the night?"

"Hey, older, but not bigger," Karen laughed, "unless you've lost some more weight lately."

"No, I still weigh what I did. It's not fair, though, that you're three inches shorter than I am. I'd have to be skin and bones to weigh what you do. So what's goin' on?" She pulled herself upright and leaned against the headboard. "I think I'm finally awake enough to carry on an intelligent conversation."

At that Karen fell silent. Cindy, listening to the slight crackle in the phone line and thinking she heard Karen's breathing, finally asked, "Karen, what's wrong?"

Her voice, when she found it again, seemed small. "I've been doing some reading, and I'm really worried."

"What about, Karen?"

"Do you remember Mary Haason, who attended Grandma T's church?"

"Yeah."

"Well, I ran into her at the A&P yesterday. I always liked her, even if she and Gam did bug us about going to church. Anyway, we got to talking, and I told her about some of the stuff we've been reading and the seminars we've been going to. I even invited her to the New Age fair at the college next week."

"And . . . ?"

"Well, Mary just listened, and when I wound down she said that she had a little brochure on the subject that she thought I might enjoy. I told her I was open to reading anything, so she went over to her car and got it for me."

"You called at 4:00 a.m. to tell me that Miss Mary gave you a brochure to read!"

"Well, *yes*."

"OK, what did it say?"

"Cindy, I'm really scared!"

Suddenly cold, Cindy reached down for the comforter that lay at the foot of the bed, hugging it to her body. "What are you talking about, Karen?"

"It started off with all that's happened since Alice Bailey, Benjamin

Creme, and the others decided to target the United States with an outreach of Hindu thought, and Marilyn Ferguson wrote the *Aquarian Conspiracy*. It talked about the explosion of interest in transcendental meditation, astrology, channeling, and all the other New Age stuff that, you know, has been going on and that we're pretty involved in. It even outlined the work of the Vishwa Hindu Parishad. I didn't even know, until I read this pamphlet, that it is one of the largest missionary organizations in the world. I was impressed and a little proud, actually. We've really made an impact! The author obviously knew what was happening and how it was affecting our Western society. It was neat to be a part of something so powerful and pervasive. It was like the old Judeo-Christian culture was finally on the run, and we were the ones chasing them in the white hats."

"But that sounds great!" Cindy interrupted. "I'd like a copy if I can get one."

"I already have one for you, but what I've shared with you isn't all."

"What is this?" Cindy asked. "Do I have to drag the details out of you a sentence at time? You woke me out of the best sleep I've had in three months. Now out with it!"

"Well, I told you that this talked about all the things we've been learning; then it asked a question. Actually, it started out saying that many people have a lot of confidence in the Bible and its views but that few have ever really studied what it says about things like this."

"This?"

"Don't be so dense. All this really neat stuff we do, the TM and channeling and so on. Anyway, I'm reading this paper, and at first I didn't agree, because I know a lot of people in the movement who talk a lot about Jesus and even consider Him one of the highest spiritual guides there is. We've both heard seminar speakers quote the Bible in their lectures along with the other great writings of the ages. We're even supposed to meet Jesus in person, next year, at Findhorn. So I didn't buy it.

"But then the author said that the Bible has a lot to say about the paranormal and asked if I'd personally ever seriously considered what it teaches on the subject. After that, he spent the next four pages showing verse by verse the things the Bible says."

"Well, what?" Cindy demanded crossly. "I thought the Bible was in favor of what we're doing. Didn't Jesus come to teach us how to be saved by reaching higher God consciousness? I'll bet Mary Jean Barger, at Silva, would love to get hold of this for her next seminar." She let go of her grip on the comforter. This was familiar territory, and she was at ease again. But Karen hadn't finished.

"Not so fast, little sister," Karen said. "This stuff is pretty scary—if you believe it. For instance, Deuteronomy 18:10-12 says—I'm reading it now—'Let no one be found among you . . . who practices divination or sorcery, interprets omens, engages in witchcraft, or casts spells, or who is a medium or spiritist or who consults the dead. Anyone who does these things is detestable to the Lord' [NIV]."

"So?"

"Cindy!" Karen's voice was shrill. "Divination is fortunetelling, and when J. Z. Knight channels Ramtha, she's consulting the *dead!*"

"In Leviticus 20 it says that God will be against anyone who consults a medium or a spiritist and that they should be put to death."

"How about Saul in the Bible?" Cindy asked defensively. "Remember the lecture up at Rainbow's End Ranch in Montana? Nomi Peterson told the story of Saul going to visit the woman who channeled Samuel's spirit. If God was against it then, it sure didn't sound like it! Saul was the first king of Israel. God had Samuel anoint him with sacred oil. What does your pamphlet say about that?"

She took a breath, then went on without letting Karen get a word in. "When Nomi channeled Samuel and he spoke to us," Cindy said, "it surely didn't sound to me that God was opposed to it. Remember that Samuel told us how he had been sent to comfort and strengthen Saul, and how the Endoran woman was God's medium to speak with him once he'd died. It was neat, Karen, and you or anyone else can't deny it!"

"Neither Nomi nor the spirit told us the rest of the story, Cindy."

What do you mean?

The Bible says that Saul had run all of the mediums out of Israel, and implies it was because of God's specific instructions. When he had so frustrated God by his disobedience that God wouldn't talk with him any longer, Saul turned to witchcraft, and then he lost his kingdom and was killed in the process."

"Where does it say that?"

"The story is in 1 Samuel 28-30. I looked it up for myself. But that's not all. There's about 10 other texts in the Bible that say about the same thing. Then there's the texts that say that the dead don't know anything—so obviously they can't be channeled."

"And you believe all this?" Cindy demanded.

"Remember what Grandma T told us, Cindy? I'm scared. If these aren't the spirits of the cosmic masters, then who are they? I don't want anything more to do with this. In fact, I burned most of my stuff tonight, and I've gone to my last seminar. I'm finished!"

By now Karen was sobbing. "This paper also says that astrology is from the devil, Cindy. That he uses it as a substitute for God. It says that the devil gets people sucked into astrology and tarot and then destroys their lives. That's why I called you. You've got to get out of this before it's too late."

"Karen, be quiet! Listen to yourself—"

"No! You listen," she sobbed. "I got you interested in all of this, and now it may destroy you. Cindy, please, please promise me that you'll read this if I give it to you. You've got to get out, Cindy. You've got to get out!"

"Karen, you're hysterical! Get hold of yourself. I don't know what you've been reading, but this is ridiculous. It was wrong of Mary to give you this silly stuff and get you all riled up. You know all of the people we've seen helped with astrology, and the seminars have been fantastic. This is a bunch of bunk. Our weekends at Silva have been the best thing that's happened to either one of us. So calm down. Is Gary there? Maybe I should come over. I know Mary Jean will come with me if I ask her. She can help you sort this out."

"No! Cindy, I'm not hysterical, and I'm not crazy. But I read all this and suddenly—I don't know how to describe it—it was so *clear*. If you believe the Bible, you've got to see it too. And I don't ever want to see Mary Barger ever again. We're in over our heads, and we don't even know it. We're like birds that have been hypnotized by a snake and think everything's OK even when we're about to be eaten."

"Karen!"

"I'm serious. I know you think that I've gone off the deep end, but I feel better than I've felt in years. For the first time in a long time I feel free. Gary's here, and I've told him everything. I thought I was free before, Cindy, but I was in chains. At first they were built of beautiful things like flowers and incense and the light of far-off stars, but they were still chains. And Cindy, I've felt them tightening around me like the coils of a snake. Tonight they're gone, they're gone. I'm free! You can be too. Please, for my sake, if nothing else, take a look at this!"

"OK, Karen, I'll gladly read anything you've got, you know that, but I doubt it's going to change my mind. Listen, it's 5:00 a.m. Why don't you let me buy you breakfast this morning? I'm off at the grocery store, and I've got an easy gig at the club tonight. I could pick you up around 10:00."

"That sounds good. We can talk some more. OK, I'll see you at 10:00."

Hanging up the phone, Cindy turned off the light, rolled onto her side, and pulled the comforter up around her shoulders. It was suddenly cold, and she shivered as she thought of all her sister had said. What if it were true? What if the astrology and the channeling and the meditation were all a trap? What if the self-hypnosis and the self-help weren't from the cosmic god-force? What if there were some sinister satanic plot to snare her and her sister and the millions of others who flocked to the seminars and the sessions and the fairs and read the books and the journals. What if . . . ?

For the first time in more than 10 years the words in Grandma T's letter, safely now in the box of keepsakes in the bottom of her dresser, came back to her. She could almost hear Grandma's voice even if she didn't remember her exact words: *Cindy, there's a devil who rules this world. He's ruthless, and sometimes he can be very cruel. He has invented all kinds of ways to enslave us. God has shown me that Satan wants you and that he will do all that can be done to keep you for himself. Please don't have anything to do with him. Please be careful, Cindy!*

Tossing and turning, she tried to go back to sleep. Why had Karen called? Why, especially at 4:00 in the morning, when she had been sleeping so delicious a sleep? Why had Mary Haason given her that paper, and why, like an idiot, had Karen read it? And why, if she had, had she chosen 4:00 in the morning to tell her sister about it?

Finally she gave up trying to sleep. Everything in life had been going so well, until this. What had her mother always given her when she couldn't sleep? Warm milk, that was it. Well, why not? It couldn't be any worse than counting stupid sheep.

Groping for her robe, she put it on and padded over to the bedroom door, opened it, and stopped in her tracks.

The kitchen glowed in the warm light of a single lighted candle burning on the dining room table.

Chapter 7

Hello, Daddy. What brings you to the great city of Atlanta?" Gus Crossworthy stood in the doorway of Nadine's condo silhouetted against a dogwood tree covered with a blizzard of flowers and glowing in the May sunshine, a look of confusion and disbelief on his face.

"Did you come to see what a witch looks like?" Nadine asked with a high, strained laugh. "Oh, I forgot. Bill Segna didn't tell you, did he? He just said that I had problems and needed my daddy. Well, come in, and I'll tell you all about it. Don't mind the goats. They're my friends. Mom may want to take off her straw hat. Mephisto—he's the one with the big horns—loves straw. That's why the paper in the dining room's in such bad shape. They should know better than to put straw paper on the walls of a house anyway."

In his shock Gus had forgotten all about Millie. Glancing to his right, he caught the look of horror and disbelief on her face. Taking her by the arm, they tentatively stepped through the doorway. He had never, in 67 years of life, seen or smelled anything like what he was seeing and smelling now. First there was the garbage, sacks and sacks of it stacked in every available corner, its stench mingling with the sickly, sweet smell of cheap Indian incense and goat manure. Then there were the goats themselves. Five of them, from what he could see—one standing on the dining room table, two lying on what once had been a very expensive couch, one peeking out from the kitchen door, and the biggest, meanest-looking billy he'd ever seen standing right in front of him, studying him, munching a mouthful of hay.

And finally, there was his daughter, the pride of Gentry County. Her hair was long and matted in what he'd once heard called dreadlocks. An old tattered dress and nothing more covered a body that couldn't have been washed in weeks. A large open boil on one leg oozed puss that ran down her leg, staining what were supposed to be shoes, or moccasins, but what in reality were gunny sacks tied around her feet with pieces of orange bailing twine.

"Come on in, Daddy, Mama. Mephisto won't bother you. He just looks mean. I'm sorry about the mess, but I've—well, it's a long story."

In a daze Gus shoved two protesting goats off the couch and gingerly sat down. "How, how are you, Nadine?" he asked. "And, and what's going on here?"

"Nothing much, Daddy. I guess I just haven't had the time to clean up lately, that's all."

"What's this about a witch? And how about Tom Lawson?"

"That's right, Bill told you about Tom, didn't he? Well, I guess I might as well start there."

"Before you start, honey, can Dad and I take you out to lunch?" Millie asked, glancing fearfully at a kitchen piled high with garbage and goat droppings. "You weren't expecting us, so it's not fair to ask you to fix us a meal."

"It's OK, Mom. I was expecting you. I don't feel like going out, so why don't we talk for a while? Then you two can go to your hotel. I made reservations at Peachtree Plaza."

"How'd you know?" Gus started to ask, then his banker's instincts took over and he said nothing. "So, Nady, tell us what's happening."

Nadine curled up on a love seat facing them, then sat for more than a minute staring out the window. "I guess I should start at the beginning.

Daddy, you and Mama did everything you could for me. I really appreciate it. But I've chosen to live my life in different ways.

"I guess it all started just after I turned 14. Remember, I started reading a lot of fantasy books, science fiction, and metaphysical stuff. You and Mom didn't approve, but neither did you want to stop me, which I appreciate very much. At first it was kind of spooky, what with all of the spells, crystals, dungeons, and dragons attacking shining princes, and trolls and Pegasus and spirits from other worlds and our netherworld. I used to lie awake at night reading, so scared I couldn't go to sleep, but fascinated by what I was discovering. After a while I began secretly to wonder if it could all be real. So I began to experiment. And why not? It was really exciting. I wanted it to be real because it was all so neat. I wanted to be a princess with a real prince fighting evil beings to save me. I wanted to defeat the wicked witches and terrorize the trolls. I dreamed of piloting space capsules into other dimensions and fighting the evil lords of other planets single-handed.

Not long after that Aunt Peg moved to town. Remember? I know how you feel about her, Mama, but she was great to me. She took an interest in me and eventually invited me to her house for her club. Daddy, I know you and Mom thought it was a garden club or something, but my eccentric old aunt was involved in something much more exciting than flowers and recipes, and her friends really took an interest in me. Every time you and Mom left town, I got to stay with my favorite aunt. And remember your Friday date nights?"

Gus nodded.

"You went out, and I stayed overnight with Aunt Peg. There was no school the next day, so you weren't worried if I stayed up late. I know that you believed that anything we would be doing would carry your seal of approval."

"Daddy, you were so naive when it came to your big sister," Nadine said gently. "You couldn't imagine her doing anything wrong, so you never bothered to ask much about what we did when we were together. It was just 'Did you have a good time with Peggy?' while you read your paper over coffee on Saturday morning. Don't feel bad, because it was perfectly OK with me. Once I discovered that they were involved in the same things I was, I really began to feel at home with them, and I wouldn't have told you anyway. Eventually I discovered that they were what you'd call a coven. You would say that they were witches."

"Witchcraft? Aunt Peg? Come on, Nadine. She was eccentric, but I don't really think that your aunt Peg was a witch."

"I always knew your sister was a witch," Millie muttered.

Gus shot her a glance that communicated paragraphs.

Nadine shifted on the couch, idly brushing goat pellets from a cushion. "Daddy, you asked me to tell you the story. Now, are you going to let me?"

"Go on."

"At first there were just hints, then stories. Some of the women lent me books that contained a lot more details than the novels I was reading. After a while they would let me watch while they cast their spells, even though I wasn't allowed to hear the incantations or see what they put in their potions.

"One day when Aunt Peg picked me up for a meeting, I could tell that she was excited about something. She hummed a little tuneless song as we drove, and she looked just like the Cheshire cat in *Alice in Wonderland*. When I asked her why she was so cheerful, she just smiled mysteriously and said that I'd know soon enough. When we got to her house for the meeting, I saw that all the ladies were dressed for a party. And it was. We had a wonderful time. Aunt Peg's cook had grilled salmon steaks. We had baby peas and new potatoes, and for dessert the best cheesecake I've ever eaten in my life. When we were done, we all went into the drawing room and had coffee."

"Then Aunt Peg came over and sat next to me and said that they had something special to tell me. All the ladies gathered around with excited looks on their faces. You'd have thought that I had gotten engaged or something. Looking very serious, Aunt Peg said, 'Nadine, as you know, we are a part of something very special. It is a sisterhood as old as humanity, and it stretches around the world. We have been called to share the truth about someone who is very special to us. He is very powerful. In fact, he rules the world, and we are his servants. Some call him Satan. Christians call him the devil or the adversary. But we know him as the Lord of our world.'

"You should have seen Aunt Peg, Daddy. She was just glowing. She went on to say that recently 'our Lord' had appeared to all of them to say that they were to bring another into their sisterhood and to prepare her for a special work. I know this doesn't mean much to you, Daddy and Mama, but Peg was told that when she died, that person was to take her place as the sisterhood's leader. Nadine's face lit up as if she had just been elected homecoming queen.

"And I'm the one he chose. I'm the one!"

"I'll kill Peg when I get my hands on her," Gus growled, grinding his teeth.

"You can't, Daddy," Nadine said with a sweet smile. "You know she's already dead."

"Go on with your story," Gus said slowly, his voice low and intense. "I want to hear it all."

"Well, I won't bore you with the details. They're secret anyway. But

I was in training for the three years before Aunt Peggy died. You remember that she died the spring of my senior year. When she was gone, and the time came for me to go to college, the sisters asked if there was anything special I wanted for a going-away present. I laughed and said, 'Yes. Tom Lawson for my college roommate.' You know that he was going to Australia for his first year, something about an unexpected, all-expense-paid scholarship in rugby if he went, I believe." She winked at her father. "Know anything about that, Daddy? Anyway, two days later, Tom called. 'You'll never guess what happened, Nad,' he said. 'I just got a full football scholarship to Emory, and I hadn't even applied.'

"We decided not to tell you and Mom about it, and Tom registered here in Atlanta. Daddy, we'd waited for years for some time alone. I know you won't want to hear this, but our first night together in this condo was heaven on earth. For days we didn't even go to class. These six rooms became our world, our love, our nourishment."

Nadine's eyes were closed, her face lifted. *She's reliving it*, Millie thought. *I can't handle this.*

"Tom had promised me for years that when I finally became his, it would be forever," Nadine continued. "We even started planning our wedding, lying together with the air-conditioner on, in front of a fire in the fireplace. Then one morning several weeks later I woke up and he was gone. No note. Nothing. At first I was frantic. I called the police. I drove around campus. I called everyone I knew who might have seen Tom. No one would tell me anything. Later I found out that he was shacked up with one of the cheerleaders in a little apartment just off campus. When I confronted him, he just shrugged his shoulders and said that that was life and that it was time I grew up." Tears filled her eyes, and she angrily brushed them away. "Then do you know what he did?" she demanded. She didn't wait for an answer. "He laughed and walked away."

"Oh, Nadine," Millie cried, reaching over to pat her daughter's knee. "I am so sorry!"

"Don't be, Mom. It's OK. Everything Dad said all those years was true. And the next day Tom was killed in a car accident. It was a freak crash, they said. He was doing only 40 when he suddenly veered off the road and into the Chattahoochee River on the north side of town. But," she looked her dad straight in the eye, "I know better. That morning I received a hand-delivered card from my 'sisters' expressing their pain for me and promising it would not go unpunished."

Gus gasped. "You're saying that these witches—?"

Nadine shrugged. "I've probably said too much. Let's just say that fate dealt Tom what he had coming to him. Shortly after that I discovered I was pregnant. My friends helped me with an abortion, and I . . . ." Nadine bit her lip, trying to control the tears that were struggling to start down her cheeks. "I committed myself to go on living. It's been hard. I don't seem to care about anything anymore. And it's been hard to sleep. I hear voices and see things . . ." Her voice trailed off into silence.

Gus and Millie looked at each other. Nadine seemed spent from the effort of telling her story. In the kitchen one of the goats slurped water from a bucket. When it lifted its head, water streamed off its beard onto the floor.

"So now you know." Nadine's words brought her parents back from their private thoughts. "I'm what you'd call a witch. My goats are my friends and my fellow ministers. They told me that you were coming and that you'd try to have me institutionalized. Daddy, I don't know how to say this, but whatever you do, don't try to put me away somewhere. I know that you don't understand what you see here, and that you probably never will. But I'm not crazy, at least no more so than most of the people in Atlanta. I've just chosen a different life. I'll be moving back to our hometown, and I'd like to see you both from time to time, but I'll be living in my own place. Aunt Peg left me her house in a trust. It was a secret until the time was right. Now I need to move back and begin my ministry. I hope that you both will understand."

She pushed herself up from the couch. Her eyes were coals in her pale, drawn face. "Well, it sounds like the cab I called earlier is right on time," she said. "I've got an appointment." She let her hand brush her father's shoulder. "I love you both."

Then Nadine crossed the living room and opened the front door.

Chapter 8

So what did your friends at church have to say?"

"About what?" Brenda asked sleepily, snuggling down a little deeper into Johnny's arms.

"About us. You know, what you had to say in prayer meeting last night."

"How'd you know?" Brenda asked. "I wasn't going to tell you for a while."

"Oh, we know these things," Johnny laughed. "You didn't answer my question. What was their reaction?"

She snuggled in a little closer. "Just what you'd expect. It was like I was consorting with a ghost or something," she said with a laugh. "Pastor Adkins nearly fainted, and the rest of them were in shock—except for a couple of them, that is. Juanita Parris stopped me afterward and whispered that it was wonderful I had you back. She said that she'd been hearing from Luke for years since he died. And Ben Gladden called me later and confided that he holds little Patty every night and rocks her to sleep after an angel lays her in his arms."

"Ah, little Patty," Johnny said. "Isn't she a cutie?"

"I don't know," Brenda replied. "I've only seen pictures."

"Well, take it from me, she's a little doll."

"What's it like, Johnny?"

"What's what like?"

"What's it like over there, wherever there is?"

"You mean heaven? What's heaven like?"

"Yeah, is it like in the movies? Have you ever met Jacob Marley?"

"As in Scrooge and Marley?" he asked.

"Yes!" Brenda sat up.

"No, I haven't met Marley, or his ghost," Johnny chuckled, pulling her back down beside him. "He was only a figment of Charles Dickens' imagination, Brenda, or as Scrooge himself said, 'probably an undigested bit of beef.' No, I haven't met Marley, or Scrooge, either, for that matter. But I have met a lot of other people you'd probably find interesting."

She sat up again. "Who?"

"Ty Cobb, for one."

"You're kidding! The baseball player?"

"No, the football player. Who do you think?"

"Johnny!"

"Just kidding."

"How about the Babe?"

"Babe Ruth? No, I'm afraid he went somewhere else. But I did meet Honus Wagner and Shoeless Joe Jackson. You know the movie *Field of Dreams*? It's almost like that, in some ways. A lot of people getting to do things they really enjoyed here on earth."

"Who else?"

"Well, let's see, I saw David, the king from the Bible, the other day. And Peter the apostle has a villa right up the road from me. Mahatma Gandhi sits under a tree with some of his disciples at the park down by the river in the center of town. And—he grinned—Martin Luther King is free at last. There are a bunch of important spiritual leaders from down through history who teach there. It's not nearly as restricted as we imagined it here on earth."

"Oh, and I almost forgot." Johnny leaned forward and gently tapped her nose. "Your mom says hello. She says that she really misses being able to be with you, but that she's been keeping track of you and praying for you. She was really excited when she discovered I was seeing you down here. She wants you to know that you're still her favorite daughter."

"You know I'm her only one," Brenda giggled. "She was always saying that. It was our little joke with each other." She sat quietly a moment, missing her mom, wishing her sons could have gotten to know their grandma. Then she thought of something else.

"Johnny, have you met Him?"

"Who's him?"

"You know. Jesus."

"Jesus?"

"Yes, Jesus! Isn't He the one we always dreamed of seeing when we got to heaven?"

"Yeah, I've seen Him."

"Well?"

"Well, what?"

"Well what? What is He like?"

"He's awesome, Brenda. Absolutely awesome. You're going to enjoy meeting Him one of these days. Very intelligent and perceptive. He's someone you won't want to miss." Johnny stood up, suddenly in a hurry. "Hey, it's almost daylight. I'd like to tell you more, but I'd better get going. Give the boys my love."

Quickly pulling on his pants and buttoning his shirt, Johnny smiled down on Brenda. "Listen, B, there may be some people who don't understand what's happening with us. Just ignore them, OK? And don't listen to their gossip. They're just a bunch of busybodies who've got nothing better to talk about. I'll see you tomorrow night."

"Johnny?"

"Yeah."

"Tell Mama hi for me."

"Will do, babe."

Chapter 9

It was another late night for Stan Adkins. It followed a long afternoon. First, Stan got his sermon to the stage where he knew where he was going, and had a basic outline down on paper. He'd even thought of a couple of good illustrations. Next, he caught up on his correspondence. Finally, he developed the agenda for the upcoming church board meeting and made sure that Madge had it typed correctly. Stopping on his way home to see a couple who'd visited church last Sunday, he then ate supper with his family, mowed and edged the front lawn, and took Shelly to her ballet lesson. Finally, when the kids were in bed and Barb was busy with the curtains she was making for the front room, he put on a sweater and walked the mile and a quarter down to the church.

Now, a cup of fresh coffee in his hand, he was deep in thought. There had to be something he was missing.

In the real world of the average pastorate there are some things you don't spend much time thinking about or studying. They are givens that you've always known and that don't bear much consideration in light of the millions of other things jostling for your attention. It's not that they aren't important—it's just that you don't have any reason to spend time focusing on them. These things are sort of like breathing, or your heart beating, or the sun coming up in the morning. Often they are caught from the faith of your parents or the ones who discipled you into a relationship with God. They are so basic that you never bother studying them for yourself, and in the process you can get yourself into real trouble.

But when a crisis arises and you have to face it head-on, sometimes you aren't as well prepared as you thought you would be. And sometimes what your parents have assumed and taught you, or your seminary professors told you many years before, isn't the case when you take the time to study it out for yourself. It can shake your foundations when you begin to discover that some of your basic assumptions might be wrong. Even worse, it can be pretty embarrassing to begin to question something you've preached and taught for years. But Stan had long ago decided that the most important thing to him was his spiritual integrity. In that, he was a kind of maverick. What counted in life was not what his church taught, as important as that was to him, or what his parents or mentors had told him, as much as he honored them. What was most important was what God told him in His Word. The Bible, and the Bible alone, had long been his creed. He told the Lord a long time ago that he would go anywhere He told him to go, and would believe anything that could be proved from the Bible, no matter who believed and taught anything else. Now that commitment was being tested in ways he had never imagined could happen.

Brenda had really shaken him the other night, for reasons that took him a while to sort out. Finally he realized it was because of a contradiction in one of the very basic issues of life.

Every fall Stan took advantage of the Halloween season to preach a sermon on the occult and the inroads it was making in Western civilization. He believed in witches and ghosts and goblins and spells and spirits and all of the other macabre manifestations of spiritism. But he also believed that they were manifestations of what Paul, in Ephesians 6:12, 13, described as "the powers of this dark world" (NIV). They were the ones whom John, in Revelation 12:7-10, pictured as the angelic followers of Satan who accompanied him to earth when he rebelled and was thrown out of heaven. In other words, he believed that the Bible taught that ghosts and spirits, for example, were demons manifesting themselves in various forms to deceive human beings. Everything he read in the Bible on the subject only solidified that explanation.

So when Brenda Barnes stood up in prayer meeting and began to share what was happening in her life, Stan reacted with something close to horror. The reason? He realized that for the first time in his ministry he was facing those forces of darkness head-on. He wasn't scared. He had no doubt that Satan was a defeated foe, but hearing Brenda's story was a shock, and the unknown couldn't help making him nervous and uneasy. And it scared him to death for Brenda! This wasn't theoretical for her. As far as she was concerned, the most important person in her world was again sleeping with her every night. It was real, and for her ever to deny it would, he knew, take a miracle.

But facing the issue of the identity of Brenda's midnight visitor opened up another whole set of problems for Stan, other than the obvious one of what one did in a situation like this. Somehow his predicament reminded him of a Three Stooges movie he remembered seeing when he was a kid. Larry, Moe, and Curly were installing lawn sprinklers, and the piping sprang a leak. When they ran to stop the leak, two more leaks popped up. When they got their hands covering those, five more erupted.

The question Stan Adkins wrestled with that night was this: If my own spirit is a living entity that goes to heaven when I die, why couldn't it contact people still alive on earth? In fact, if they—the spirits of our friends and family—really loved us, why wouldn't they contact us?

And if that was true, why was he horrified by "Johnny's" return?

If that were true, what should he do with what he'd believed the Bible taught about ghosts and such?

Searching for answers, he went to his Bible. The answers he found weren't what he expected. Pulling out his concordance, he looked up every text he could find that talked about the condition of humans in death. With two exceptions they unanimously declared that the dead didn't know anything, do anything, or feel anything after they died.

Of the two exceptions, Stan read that when Saul consulted a medium to channel the "spirit" of Samuel, he was condemned for it and died. Not exactly a ringing endorsement of the practice or the reality of whom the spirit claimed to be.

The other was the story of the rich man and Lazarus, found in Luke 16. Initially that story seemed to infer that the dead were in heaven and that they were conscious and interested in what was going on here on earth. It even sounded as if they could communicate with us if they were given permission. But looking it up in a couple of Bible commentaries, he discovered that while it was a good story, it was an allegory told to make a point about our generosity while we're alive. Allegories, he knew, rarely make literal sense, and the more he looked at this one the more he knew that anyone who took it literally and based a theology of life after death on it was in trouble.

The founders of Cherry Pit Community had been what is known in the south as hard-shell Baptists. They were deeply committed to the Bible and the Bible alone as their source of understanding of God's will. They believed in what was then called "soul sleep." Soul sleep was what some called their belief that when you died you simply slept until the resurrection. He'd run across it one day while leafing through the old leather-bound volumes carefully preserved in a display case in the church's lobby. Stan remembered shaking his head in disbelief that anyone could believe such a strange thing. It was so foreign to his thinking that he'd had to laugh. Now he wasn't so sure.

As he stared at the list of texts in the notebook on his desk, he couldn't escape the fact that the Bible *does* teach that the dead are "asleep," that they know nothing, and that they won't know anything until the resurrection at the end of the world.

"But how about one's spirit?" he wondered aloud. But when he looked up "spirit," it appeared to be nothing more than just what the Greek word for it implied—breath, or air. It was life, but not entity; it was breath, it was existence. It was not something that had a life of its own.

Whew, Stan thought. *If that's the case, then Brenda has real problems, and so do we.* Any way he went on this, he knew he was going to get bloody, hopefully in the figurative sense. Something like this could splinter a church and spell the end of a pastor's ministry. No matter what you did, it was like playing with a skunk. You were sure to end up smelling bad.

He knew he had several choices. He could simply ignore what was happening and pretend it would all go away. He knew plenty of guys who would do just that. But was that what pastors were for? He could also deal with it. If the eternal life of his parishioners and his integrity as a person and a leader were worth anything, then he'd have to face this thing head-on, no matter the cost. The truth was the truth. He might end up pastoring in Nome, Alaska, when the dust settled, but at least he'd know that he'd done the right thing.

Kneeling on the rug in front of the fire, he prayed, "Lord, the battle isn't in the distance anymore. It's not something I'm seeing on the evening news. It's right here in our own little town. It's affecting my congregation, the people whose souls you have made me the shepherd of. Yet I somehow sense that this whole thing is bigger than just my local church. The forces of evil are apparently choosing this place to make a stand.

"I'd just like to recommit myself and my family to You, tonight. And, once again, I give our church back to You. You're going to have to deal with all of this. I'm willing to be used any way You want to use me. I just pray for the protection it is my right to claim because of Jesus' death on Calvary. And I'd like to ask for Your wisdom. You know how easily I can run ahead or lag behind You. I also ask You to raise up other Christians to stand by me in this. I know that at times it's going to feel that I'm all alone, and I need support. Please give me people who will pray us through this. I pray this in Jesus' name—"

The phone rang. He said a quick "Amen."

Getting up from his knees, Stan crossed the study and picked up the receiver.

"Stan, are you OK?" It was his wife, Barbara.

"Yes, why?"

"Carlene Jaginski just called and said that she woke up with the distinct feeling that she should be praying for you—urgently. She had the impression you were facing some danger, and she wanted you to know that whatever it was, she'd be on her knees supporting you. She also called Eldene Richards and Dave Donaldson, her prayer partners. They said they're going to be praying for you until this passes."

She paused. Clasping her words to his heart, Stan didn't reply.

"Stan, what's going on?" Barbara demanded. "Does this have anything to do with what Brenda shared in prayer meeting?"

"I don't know what's going on, Barb," he said, smiling even in his distress. "I haven't gotten it all sorted out yet myself. But I am convinced that I am going to need all of the prayers I can get for the next few weeks. I'll tell you all about it when I get home."

"Stan, I don't like the idea of your being in that spooky old church all by yourself late at night. It's not safe. Something could happen to you. You need to bring your books up here to the house so that you don't have to go down there at night."

"I'm OK, Barb. God will take care of me. I will be careful, though, I promise. And I'll be home soon."

Hanging up the phone, Stan turned off the gas flame in the fireplace and turned out the lights. Stopping for a few minutes, he listened in the darkness to the sounds of the old church. It could be a spooky place if you let it be. But it was also a very special place. God's people had done battle with the forces of darkness here for more than 100 years. This was hallowed ground, and he knew that God loved it even more than he did. There might be another battle shaping up in the war that had been going on since the creation of the world, but Stan knew he was on the winning side.

Smiling, he opened the door, and stopped in his tracks.

Chapter 10

It had been a long time since Gus Crossworthy had been to church. In fact, aside from funerals and the occasional Easter or Christmas service that the president of the town's oldest bank was obligated to attend, he never went. Not that he didn't believe in God, mind you. Gus just believed that God could take care of His business while he took care of the bank. As long as God didn't interfere in the bank, Gus tried not to interfere in God's business. His membership, and the occasional offerings he mailed to the office of the church down the street from the bank's office, were to him like taxes or a license fee. If you were a pillar in the community, you were expected to belong to First Church. It was a social obligation that didn't entail active participation, so Gus had paid his dues and ignored the church most of his life. He didn't even know what they believed, and if it weren't for his membership in the Rotary Club he would have had no idea who the pastor was. So he felt a little strange, and not a little sheepish, as he dialed Darrel Widmer's office number.

"Darrel," Gus said heartily when the church secretary had connected him with the pastor, "how are you this morning?"

"Fine; what's up?"

"It's been a while since I've been out to Aspen Meadows, so I picked up a tee time for later this morning. Any chance that you're up to 18 holes? We haven't played together since the hospital tournament three years ago. I figured it was time we both got some R & R."

"Let me check my schedule. Thursday mornings are usually pretty flexible for me, so I should be able to work it out. Yep, I'm free. When's your tee time?"

"We tee off at 11:00," Gus answered. "I'm going to hit a bucket of balls ahead of time, so I'll meet you on the first tee when they call us. We can eat lunch in the clubhouse on the turn. It's on me today."

"Great," Darrel said as he wrote in his appointment book. "See you at 11:00, then."

That's providential, Darrel thought as he hung up the phone. *Last night the board decided to build a new educational wing, and first thing this morning the bank president calls wanting to play golf. With any luck at all, they might have that wing done in time to be chosen to host the next state conference on the church and environmental unity. It's about time the city boys got out into the hinterland and discovered that small-town pastors and their churches aren't all a bunch of hicks.*

For a guy who plays golf only three or four times a year, Gus sure can hit the ball, Darrel realized a couple of hours later as he watched the bank president's tee shot land in the middle of the fairway about 240 yards out. Somehow it wasn't fair that you could practice until you had blisters on your hands and struggle to break 90, and some of these old guys could walk out on the course occasionally and play scratch golf. Dropping his driver into the bag on the back of the cart, he shook his head. Maybe in some afterlife, somewhere, he'd be a decent golfer.

"So how are things at the church?" Gus asked a few minutes later, swerving to miss a rut in the cart path. "Didn't I hear a rumor that you're planning to do some building?"

"Yes," Darrel answered. "We bought Dennis Rutan's old place about 10 years ago in anticipation of adding a new educational wing to the church. With the money we got from Alice Carty's trust the other day, we have enough to start. So we're planning to break ground as soon as we get the plans finalized.

"Say, can you always drop it on from 160 yards out?" Darrel shook his head appreciatively as he watched Gus's second shot roll to within about a club length of the hole. "I sure am glad we're not betting on this game.

You make it look as if you've got a practice range in your basement."

"Ah, I'm just lucky today," Gus smiled. "I play so seldom that I guess I get to take advantage of beginner's luck every time out.

"So how are you financing this new building?" he asked a few minutes later as they replaced the pin and headed for the cart.

"Well, it looks as though we have 20 percent on hand. There are two trusts that we expect will eventually mature and give us about another 20 percent. We're currently planning to borrow the rest. With interest rates being as low as they are, we're hoping to apply for a construction loan within three weeks, as soon as the architect completes some things on the plans. When the structure's up, we expect to explore the possibility of selling some short-term bonds to some of the members and will be coming to the bank to finance the rest."

Darrel turned to look at the driver of the cart. "How are things with you, Gus? Didn't I hear that Nadine's at Emory? I imagine she took Tom Lawson's death pretty hard. I was surprised that she wasn't at the funeral. Weren't they pretty close at one time?"

"That's one of the things I want to talk to you about over lunch," Gus answered. "Until then, why don't we make this a little interesting? Say, a dollar a hole, and I'll spot you six strokes."

"You're on."

Later, after they had finished the first nine and had ordered lunch, Darrel put on his pastoral voice. "Gus, I sense that something's really bothering you. What's going on?"

"Well," Gus said with a frown, setting down his glass and wiping his mouth with his napkin, "tell me what you know about witchcraft."

"Witchcraft!" Darrel choked. "What are you talking about?"

"Just what I said. Tell me what you know about witchcraft. Is it real? Does it work? If it does, who or what's behind it? Your wife palled around with my sister, didn't she? So you should know something about it."

"Well, I, uh, don't know what to say, I—"

"Don't give me that, Darrel." Gus almost spit out the words. "We both know better. What are you, afraid that somebody's going to hear that the wife of the pastor of the prestigious First Church is involved in witchcraft? That should make for some interesting gossip around the bar. 'Hey, did you hear that Darrel's wife sacrifices chickens on the Communion table?'"

"Listen, Gus, I don't have to—"

Gus leaned forward. His voice was low and urgent. "You listen to me, Darrel. I don't know how much you know about your wife's business, but I know she's involved with some of the other women in town in something that they claim is a coven of witches. My sister Peggy was one of the leaders, and they've gotten my daughter involved. I don't know what's going on, but I want some answers, and I want them now, or your new building plans can rot in hell as far as I'm concerned. And if I don't get some straight answers, when I'm done with you there won't be a bank in Georgia that will lend you enough money to build the front steps. I'm trying to be civil about this, but I want to know what's happened to my daughter, and I want to know where all of this is coming from. Do you understand me?"

"OK," Darrel said slowly. Sweat beaded his forehead. "Where do you want to start? But I'll warn you, Gus—you spread what I tell you around town, and you're toast. Do you understand *me*? Every time you think about opening your mouth, think about Tom Lawson. Now"—he paused to wipe a napkin across his forehead—"what do you want to know?"

"Well, for starters, is my daughter what she claims to be? Is she a witch, or has she gone off the deep end after what happened with Tom?"

"You want straight answers, I'll give 'em to you, Gus. She's a witch. Don't look so surprised. There's more than a million of them, at last count, in the United States. That's about one in every 200 people you meet on the street, and it's growing all the time. Most of them don't look like Nadine, and most don't keep goats for roommates. I'd say that's probably the result of the shock of what happened with Tom. But you'd be amazed, Gus, the people in this town who are involved in what used to be called the occult. Your daughter was inducted into that coven several years ago, and, as I understand it, has risen to a place of some prominence. It seems that they're planning on making some sort of stand here, and she has been selected to lead them. Now, what else?"

Gus sat slumped in his chair, trying to comprehend what he was hearing. "I thought witchcraft was a superstition uneducated people in undeveloped countries believed in. You know—witch doctors and such. I know there were witches in colonial America, but I always figured it was fancy sleight of hand, designed to frighten unsophisticated people into some kind of submission." He let out a long, deep sigh. "You're talking about educated people, here, Darrel. People who should know better."

"Watch any TV lately, Gus? Gone to a movie? Wandered down the aisles of your local book or video store?" His short laugh was more of a snort. "Read a newspaper or listened to a talk show in the past few years? Witchcraft and its cousins in the New Age movement are taking over the world, and it's been going on for a long time. Remember all of the Disney flicks we watched as kids? Remember the TV programs such as *Bewitched*, *Topper*, and *My Mother the Car* that we all laughed at? Oh, and there was that sort of romance the women swooned over, *The Ghost and Mrs. Muir*.

Well, they were just preparing the way in all of our awareness for what's happening today.

"Christianity, as our forebears knew it, is dead, or close to it. It was all a myth anyway." Another laugh. "Don't look so shocked. The Bible, we discovered a long time ago, Gus, is *the* myth. Oh, it's a great collection of the ideas of some pretty good but unsophisticated people, but the Word of God? No way! The Bible is just stories, Gus, the same as the rest of the fairy tales you read to your kids. The real reality is the unseen world that's all around us. It's in the power of our thoughts. It's in our thinking. It's in our stewardship of Mother Earth. It's in the power of the forces and beings that surround us. It's in the words of the masters from other times and other worlds who are ushering in a whole new age of existence on Planet Earth. We are inaugurating the next step in the progression of this planet."

Gus shuddered, sinking his head in his hands, but if Darrel noticed, he didn't even take a breath. "Remember in the sixties when we sang about ushering in the Age of Aquarius? Well, Gus, it's happening, and your daughter's a part of it. She's going to have a very significant role, from what I hear. But how about you, Gus? You going to let her do it by herself, or are you going to support her?"

"But how are you mixed up in all of this?" Gus asked. He sounded defeated. "I thought church and this kind of stuff didn't go together."

"Oh, there have always been some of us in the church involved in this. Some of the greatest leaders in spiritualism in the nineteenth century were churchgoers. Contact with the dead and their associated powers is natural if they're actually still alive, isn't it? If the spirits of the dead are conscious, then there's no reason we shouldn't contact them and they shouldn't contact us. We've been doing it for years. It just so happens that our way of doing it hasn't been seen as respectable by most in the religious community. Now, thanks largely to the cooperation of the media, a lot more is becoming accepted. Shamanism, witchcraft, Santeria, satanism, holistic health, and pantheism are all branches of a movement that's going to take this planet back to its true roots. Combine it with channeling, fortunetelling, astrology, and TM, and you've got a juggernaut that's rolling all over our nation. Look around, Gus. It's everywhere.

"If you think that Christianity is the dominant culture in the Western world anymore, you're living in la-la land. The war's already largely won; pretty soon it's just going to be a mopping-up operation to wipe out the last remnants of traditional Christianity." Darrel spoke with such authority that Gus had to gather his courage before replying.

"You're telling me that this whole thing is part of some huge media conspiracy to take us back to the Dark Ages?" Gus countered after a moment. "Come on, Darrel, give me a break."

"No, I'm not saying that at all. There are many in America who feel as I suspect you do right now. But it's who controls the media that calls the shots." He laughed. "That's what counts. It doesn't take a rocket scientist to tell you that for now, at least in that arena, we're in the driver's seat."

"I guess I still don't understand," Gus said. "You're telling me that everything I've ever heard about this stuff is not true and that you—whoever you are—are taking control of the world? You're saying that all the stuff we joke about at Halloween is reality, and that one day soon we're all going to be dancing around maypoles and sitting in séances or meditating or casting spells? I'm sorry, Darrel; I guess I just don't buy it."

"Why not, Gus? You've never taken the other reality seriously. Other than an occasional visit at Easter you've never attended church, and I'll bet you never pray, unless it's over a putt you're afraid you'll miss. I'll wager you haven't cracked your Bible in years, if you've even got one. You don't believe in a supernatural God any more than I do. Your god is yourself. The only difference between us is that I'm being honest about it.

"People are hungry to know that there's power outside of themselves, Gus. They want to believe in a supernatural world. How long has it been since the God I'd imagine you'd say you believe in has done anything for you? Where are the miracles? How long has it been since you've talked to Him? Or better yet, how long has it been since He's talked to you? Seen any angels lately? Heard any voices? No, the real reality is in what is happening all around you today. And you watch, Gus, when it comes to a showdown between Christianity and the real powers, you'll discover what reality really is. Your neat little world is bankrupt, and if you live long enough, you will be too—if you stick with it."

Gus felt as though he might throw up.

"Darrel, do all church people feel as you do?" he asked weakly.

"More and more of them, all the time," Darrel said with a smile. "Better get on board, Gus."

"Listen," Gus growled as he pulled out his credit card and placed it in the tray that held the bill. "I think you and your broom jockeys can all go to hell. You're the sorriest excuse for a pastor I've ever heard of. I come to you for help with my daughter, who's involved in who knows what kind of black satanic business, and all I get is the good news that black is now white and white is now black. You disgust me!"

"And you're a jerk, Gus," Darrel tossed back, "an old jerk who is stuck in a past that makes Mother Goose look real. You're going to get eaten alive by this. And your sweet little daughter's going to be right in the forefront of it all. Listen, if you're so all-fired committed to the past, why don't you go out to Cherry Pit Community Church? I can imagine they'd appreciate someone like you. That'd sound great, wouldn't it?" he chuckled. "Gus Crossworthy, bank president and deacon in Cherry Pit Community Church."

Maybe I will, Gus thought angrily. *If they don't believe what this guy believes, maybe I will.*

"Oh, and Gus," Darrel said as he tossed a tip on the table, "don't bother with the loan. We don't have to worry about the money."

Chapter 11

Kudzu has to be a result of sin, Francis Baldwin told himself as he hacked at the vines that kept creeping over the fence from a neighbor's tree. So were neighbors who didn't keep the lousy stuff in check! Why on earth the Marines had imported the stuff in the first place was beyond him. It did grow fast, but no self-respecting horse he'd ever been around would have touched the stuff. "Horsefeed! More like the vine from the black lagoon, if you ask me," he mumbled as he wiped the sweat from his forehead with a big blue handkerchief. The stuff grew more than a foot a day, and there was no killing it. It had taken over whole forests in the South, a foot at a time, wrapping its tendrils from tree to tree until each and every one was covered with a blanket of green vines and were dead. The only way to stay ahead of kudzu was to be out there every other day whacking off the vines as they snaked their way over the fence. Oh, well, he needed the exercise, and he guessed he was lucky it wasn't poison ivy or something else even worse.

"Who says the East isn't taking over the West?"

Francis spun around to see Stan Adkins grinning at him.

"Isn't that the truth! When those Marine horse soldiers imported the stuff from Korea, they didn't know it would someday rule the South, I'll bet, or it never would have gotten across the border. Had a guy in here the other day who said it was just another Yankee trick to destroy Dixie, and I'm about to believe him. This stuff's nasty! Say, how are you doing?"

"Fine," Stan said, grinning. "I didn't mean to startle you. That's twice, isn't it?"

"I'll get even," Francis answered, laughing. "You'll never know when the phantom will strike. So, how's life treating you?"

"OK, I guess. I've been doing a lot of studying lately, and my brain's been getting fried. I decided I needed a change of scenery and thought I'd take a walk down old Cherry Pit. Beautiful this time of the year, isn't it!"

"It surely is! I've missed my walks the past couple of weeks. I've been so busy. But every time I drive it, I marvel. I took a couple of art classes in college and really enjoyed the landscape part, so this fall, when things slow down, I think I'm going to try to paint the view out over the valley from up by the church. I haven't touched a brush since school, but I figured, why not? Say, would you like some juice? I just made some fresh."

"That sounds great. While we're walking, let me ask you about something. I've got two arborvitaes in my front yard that act as if they're dying. When you look close, there are little red mites all over them. Any idea what I should use to get rid of them?"

"Well, mites are common this time of year with certain ornamental conifers. I've got some stuff up front that should have your shrubs back in shape in no time.

"How are things at the church?" Francis asked a few minutes later as he poured them both a tall glass of fresh lemonade.

"All right, I guess. We're growing steadily, and the people seem happy." He paused, taking a long sip and weighing what to say next. "Well, to be honest with you, church hasn't been so great. I've come across a problem I've never thought about before, and it's giving me fits. Everything I study on the subject comes out different from what I was always taught. It's got me tied up in knots trying to sort it all out."

"Tell me about it."

"Well, I've always believed that when people died, they died. But as I think back, I see that I always realized there were also some real inconsistencies in that view. I remember my grandmother's funeral. The pastor read all of these texts that talked about her going into the grave and sleeping until Jesus comes, and Jesus' second coming, when she'd be resurrected and be taken to heaven with Him. Then in the same breath he preached about her being in heaven and looking down on us in love, and enjoying the things God had created for her there. I remember, at the time, leaning over and asking my mother how Grandma could be both places at once. She just shushed me and told me we'd talk about it later. When I asked her about it the next day, she said that I was too young to be thinking about things like that, and that was that. It never came up again.

"I used to think about it, though. One time Pastor Rasmussen preached a wonderful sermon about the Second Coming, and about the resurrection and our loved ones coming out of the ground and joining with us to go on a fantastic white cloud of angels to heaven together. I was thrilled. But I was also curious about something. If the dead were already in heaven, why have a resurrection? They could just meet those of us who were alive at the gates. If God needed to give them bodies, as my Sunday school teacher said the next week when I asked about it in class, couldn't God do it just as easily in heaven? It didn't make sense to make someone who was up there come all the way back down here to climb into a body in a cold grave so that they could go back to heaven."

Stan tipped his glass and finished it. Francis picked up the pitcher and filled it again. Stan hardly noticed. "I've imagined Jesus' friend Lazarus when he died. I could almost see him leaving his body and floating up to heaven, and being met at the gate and taken to a beautiful mansion. You know, an angel opens the door, and it's everything Lazarus has always dreamed of. In back is a giant olive tree, which Lazarus loves, and four huge mango trees loaded with fruit. The house, the decor, everything, is perfect for him. He's excited, and he settles in for eternity.

"Then I've pictured him about three days later, when Jesus is walking to the cemetery in Bethany. All of the mourners are wailing behind Him, and He . . . has them roll away the stone at Lazarus' tomb. OK, Francis, now picture this. Lazarus is sitting out under that olive tree, the juice of a fresh mango dribbling down his throat, his eyes closed in ecstasy, when out through the universe booms the sound of Jesus' voice, 'Lazarus, come forth!'

"One minute the poor man is in seventh heaven, eating mangoes and enjoying the sunshine. The next he's back in his aching body, wrapped in graveclothes, struggling to breathe, while he hops or even crawls out the door of the tomb. It doesn't make sense.

"Something else has been bothering me. I got to thinking about my grandmother. In order for heaven to be such a happy place for her, she couldn't have had much contact with Planet Earth once she got to heaven. You see, about a year after she died my dad left our family for another woman. It was terrible. We were dirt-poor, living in a little cove up in Sevier County, Tennessee. Many days we had nothing to eat but poke salad and some cornmeal mush. Sometimes during winters it was just the cornmeal. Eventually my mom remarried, and after a while we discovered that my stepdad was molesting my sisters. When, believe it or not, Mom wouldn't leave him I went to live with my uncle Hiram, who worked me like one of his mules. Now, if my grandmother could look down from heaven on all that and be happy, something is dreadfully wrong. It just didn't make sense to me then and"—his voice dropped—"to tell you the truth, it still doesn't."

"So what happened?"

"Well, after a while I forgot about those theological questions. You know, when everyone in your world believes something, and you hear it from the pulpit and even from people you respect, after a while you start believing it yourself. You never question it or really study it; you just accept it. It's much easier to go with the flow, I guess. It was for me, until about a month ago."

"What happened a month ago?" Francis asked.

"Well, one of my members stood up in church and . . ." His voice trailed into silence, both hands clasped around the glass. "Say, man, I apologize. I don't know why I'm telling you all of this."

"It's OK," Francis answered. "It sounds as if you're right where I've been a couple of times in my life."

"Really?"

"Yeah, it's a long story, but I've had to come face to face with finding that the Bible says one thing and my church another. It can be devastating, I know. So, what happened at church?"

"To make a long story short, recently during sharing time at Wednesday night prayer meeting one of the women stood up and said that her dead husband had come back and was sleeping with her."

Francis exhaled slowly. "Whew."

"Apparently it had been going on for some weeks, and she's so thrilled to have him back that she had to tell us."

"What'd you do?" Francis laughed incredulously.

"I almost fainted, that's what I did!"

"And the congregation?"

"Most of them were in as much shock as I was. What's made it tough is that I've now had to go back and face all those things I thought about as a kid. You know, where do the dead really go? What condition are they in? If they're still alive, why don't they contact us?"

"What have you found out?"

"Well," Stan said, "I'll tell you.

"I've discovered that nowhere in the Bible does it even remotely imply that the dead do anything but go down into the grave and stay there until Jesus comes," Stan said. "Remember Lazarus? Jesus said that he was asleep, and equated it with death. Ecclesiastes says that the dead don't do anything or know anything. The books of Job and Psalms say that they have no knowledge of anything on heaven or earth, and that they can't think or praise God. David was called a man after God's own heart, yet Acts says that he is still in his grave waiting for the resurrection. Apparently the Bible teaches that when people die they sleep in the grave until Jesus comes. No thoughts, no actions, no nothing." Stan shook his head as if he couldn't believe it himself.

"How about the spirit and the soul?" Francis asked. "I understand that the spirit and soul go to heaven."

"Not according to the Bible," Stan replied. "I have looked at all these texts upside down, inside out, and sideways. I can't make them say anything else! Genesis says that a soul is nothing more than the combination of spirit and flesh, breath and body. In fact, there's almost a formula. You take a body, you add what's called the breath of life, and you have a soul.[1] It's the same word translated in other places as 'living creature.'[2] And it's used in several places for any living animal.[3]

"And the spirit—it's breath, nothing more. Same word as what's used for wind. The way the Bible uses it, the breath of life shows that you're alive. Animals and man both have it.[4]

Of course, we do the same thing even today. When we happen on an accident victim, we say that the person's either breathing or not. When God created Adam, He put life within him, and the whole creation knew he was alive when he started breathing."

"Then where'd the idea that people can be divided up come from?" Francis asked him.

"The Greeks," Stan replied. "In the first three or four centuries after Christ a lot of pagan ideas crept into the church. One was the Greek idea that there was a spirit, an essence that was separate and made up the life of human beings. Spirit was supposed to be good, and the body—it was bad. It was an idea that originated with Zoroaster in Persia but was popularized and best articulated by Plato and then Augustine."

"Hmmph," Francis grunted. "So what are you going to do about all of this, Stan?"

"That's my dilemma. I told the Lord a long time ago that I would follow Him where He led and do whatever He said. So far it's been pretty easy, but now I don't know."

"Following God can cost you everything," Francis said quietly. "Your church, your family, maybe someday even your life."

Stan stood up and crossed to the kitchen window. "I know. I know. But what do you have if you don't have your integrity? Besides, this stuff is flooding our whole society. If somebody doesn't speak up, there's going to be no stopping it. Look around you, Francis. It's everywhere. It's crept in so slowly that we've all accepted it—even in the church. And I've got my kids' eternity to think about—if they should get caught up in this. And the church members God has entrusted me with. I don't think I have a choice. I just need to know that it's God's timing and God's way. That's all."

He turned back to his friend. "Listen, I've taken up too much of your time," he said. "I'd better get back to the church."

"Stan," Francis said, reaching out to touch his arm. "I don't know how to say this. Sometimes you come to the place in your life where everything hangs in the balance. It can be pretty scary. I know. But you never go wrong, no matter what the cost, if you go with what God teaches in His Word. I just want you to know that I'll be praying for you, and if there's anything I can do to be supportive, I want to be there."

"Thanks, Francis. I'll count on that." He had his hand on the doorknob now. "I have to go, and you have a customer. See you one of these Sundays?"

"I'll be there this week."

---

[1] Genesis 2:7.
[2] *Nephesh chayyah.*
[3] Genesis 1:21; Genesis 2:19.
[4] Genesis 7:21, 22.

Chapter 12

Cindy set another box on the table and carefully unpacked its contents. This was her third fair, and she was becoming well known. She'd even considered giving up the grocery story job she worked between gigs, and depend on New Age fairs for a living.

Glancing down the aisle, she was amazed at the assortment of people who came to these things. In the next booth was a palm reader with bleached-white hair, wearing a black dress, and sporting more jewelry than Cindy had ever seen on one person. Down the way, the followers of Maharishi Mahesh Yogi chanted a mantra. As usual, the Lucis Trust book display was huge. A couple aisles over was a booth selling videos featuring Shirley MacLaine, and there were hundreds of other astrologers, tarot card readers, psychic healers, and witches. There was a polyglot of Hindus, Buddhists, animists, various New Age organizations, and self-actualization groups from around the world, all crammed into one large gym. There was even a quiet corner reserved for self-hypnosis and channeling.

The mystical was big business in America today, no doubt about it. Every year Dungeons and Dragons and the other fantasy games designed to introduce people to the fascinating world of the occult accounted for multiplied millions spent. She even figured they'd surpassed Ouija boards as the number one psychic game in the world. It was funny. People who called themselves Christians and who claimed to be against everything in-volved with the occult bought these things for their kids like the proverbial hotcakes. Between TV and movies, most rock music, and all of the adventure games on computers and in video arcades, Cindy pondered, they'd done more to involve kids in the occult than everything the rest of them had done put together. Oh well, it was a strange world.

Stopping to savor the potpourri of sounds and smells drifting across the large room, Cindy thought about what her sister had said when she called. Astrology *had* become her life. It was a cause she could believe in. People respected her. It made sense. She had made friends who took a real interest in her, who considered her opinion important. And it was a good source of revenue. What she earned working checkout at the grocery store was nothing compared to what she made selling astrology books and charts to the tens of thousands of people who paid admission to discover the latest at the New Age fairs. That didn't include everything sold on the Internet.

Yet for the first time a nagging uneasiness wouldn't leave her alone. Cindy had felt it, and dismissed it, as she packed the materials for the fair. But when she arrived and walked through the doorway, instead of the warm, golden glow she usually felt, there seemed to hang over the room an ethereal darkness that no bright colors and lights could overcome. She decided that it was just her low blood sugar and went to one of the food booths and bought a meal of black beans, rice, and tabouli. The food helped, but the feeling came back again. It was like a small, quiet voice in the back of her mind—questioning, probing, cutting through all of the hype and the philosophy, even the things she had experienced, and warning her to be careful. Shaking off her feelings, she smoothed the black velvet cloth that covered her table and slowly arranged a large stack of star charts on its dark, smooth surface. There. She was ready. She even had time to wander around a little bit.

As she stopped to read the neatly lettered sign on front of a third-aisle booth Cindy began to sense the uneasiness a deer must feel just before a cougar leaps. She felt enveloped by a frantic, panicky desire to run. Glancing up, she looked into the eyes of one of the strangest creatures she had ever seen. It wasn't the dreadlocks or the way she was dressed. It wasn't even the goats that stood on either side of the woman. It was the look in her eyes, much like those of a falcon who'd waited hours for a mouse to emerge from its burrow. The eyes penetrated to her very soul and seemed to hold her captive—so rooted to the spot she couldn't even think of moving.

"May I help you?"

The voice was so incongruous that Cindy suddenly wanted to laugh. This creature had a beautiful, cultured voice. It was the same reaction she would have had if one of the baboons at the Atlanta zoo had suddenly turned and, in a very refined accent, asked the same question. It was crazy!

Stifling her smile, she answered, "No, I'm just browsing until things open up."

"My name is Nadine Crossworthy," the apparition said. Then she introduced Cindy to the other women in the booth, Wilma Filsinger, Sharon Creizon, and Carol Widmer. The three of them were nicely dressed. In fact, their clothes had the understated expensive look you'd see on women at a garden club. What they were doing with this creature didn't make any sense.

"Is this your first fair?" Nadine asked.

"No," Cindy replied. "But it's the first I've done in this town."

"Same here. We drove in from Georgia last night," Sharon said.

"Oh, yeah, so did I."

"Then we have something in common." The goat woman again.

"Maybe." Cindy smiled at the thought.

"So, what are you showing, Cindy?"

"Oh, astrology mostly. How about you? Your sign says that you're a coven."

"Yes, we are. Ever explored witchcraft?"

"No, I can't say that I have." There was that uncomfortable feeling again. This time the feeling was that of a net being slowly but surely tightened around her. "Listen, I'd love to talk more, but I've got to get ready for opening," she said, quickly turning away. "Maybe we can talk more later."

It wasn't until she was at the far end of the aisle that it dawned on her. *How'd she know my name? That's odd!* Turning, she looked square into those eyes. Even 100 yards away they stared into hers, unblinking.

"Cindy?" Her father's questioning voice came through the phone.

It was three days later, and Cindy had just finished emptying her car of the fair items and putting her personal things away.

"Daddy, how are you?"

"Fine, honey. I just had to call and see how my baby was doing."

"Oh, I'm fine, Dad. I just got back from my trip to North Carolina. How's Mom?"

"Great! We were just thinking that you might enjoy a good home-cooked meal. Why don't you come over for supper?"

"I'd love to Daddy, but I'm exhausted."

"Your mama made peach pie."

"You're trying to bribe me, Dad. I really can't, but I'd sure love a rain check."

"How about tomorrow night?"

There was a long pause.

"Dad, is there something else?"

"I don't know, Cindy. I, uh, are you OK?"

"Sure Dad. Why?"

"Well, sweetheart, you know that I'm not a very religious person, but I've been having some really strange feelings the past couple of months. It's like you're in some kind of terrible danger. You'd tell me if you were in trouble, wouldn't you?"

"You know I would."

"No, I don't," Fred retorted. "I know that you're so independent you wouldn't tell me if you were surrounded by lions and tigers." He laughed. "I just want you to know that I love you. If you need me, I'm there. Oh, and Cindy, I'm praying for you."

"Praying, Dad?"

"Yeah, I'm praying that you'll be safe. See you tomorrow night?"

"Good night, Daddy."

"Good night, baby."

Later Cindy stopped by the table and blew out the candle. By now it had ceased to amaze her. It was always lit whenever she came in, and it never seemed to burn down. *It's as if someone's trying to tell me that they're here,* she thought. *Sort of like the motel ads the announcer closes with: 'We'll leave the light on for you!' I wonder who 'we' is.*

Closing the door to the bedroom, she wondered at the strange feelings she'd experienced at the fair. Then she locked the door. Pulling back the duvet, she crawled in and snuggled it and the blankets around her. There might be troubles in the rest of the world, but this place was safe. It always had been. Stretching and yawning, she savored the cool freshness of the sheets. *Be it ever so humble, there's no place like home—and your own bed,* she thought as she started to drift off.

At first she thought it was a dream. Then she jerked awake. The footsteps had stopped in front of the door to her apartment; she was sure of it. Now, as she listened, she heard them enter. Sliding out of the covers, she quietly pulled the chair out from the dressing table and jammed it under the doorknob. Crawling back under the covers, she sat back against the headboard, wrapped the feather quilt around her, pulled her knees up next to her chin, and listened.

She couldn't figure it out. These weren't the searching steps of a burglar. They weren't the intense creaking of someone bent on doing her harm. And they weren't the aimless steps of someone who was lost or demented. It took her a while until she realized that they were the footsteps of someone padding around in his own living room. The sounds were of someone who was comfortable and at ease and felt they belonged there. Then suddenly the steps were gone.

Creeping to the door, she listened intently for a while, then quietly levered the back of the chair out from under the knob. *Boy, I'm glad I put some WD-40 on those hinges before I left for Carolina,* she thought as she pulled the door open. Stepping quietly out into the living room, she looked around. Windows were closed and latched. The deadbolt on the front door was locked, the safety chain in place. And the candle on the table burned brightly. *Maybe I imagined it,* she comforted herself. *Or maybe the building's settling. No, buildings don't settle a step at a time. It has to be something more.* But what, or who, and how? It was as if whoever was there had walked right through her door and made themselves at home. Shivering a little, Cindy blew out the candle and headed back to bed.

Chapter 13

"Something bothering you, Brenda?"

Brenda sat with her back against the headboard of the bed, her head on her arms, which were wrapped around her knees. She stared out the window.

"No," she answered pensively. "Just thinking, that's all."

"The moon's pretty tonight, isn't it?" Johnny said, scooting up in the bed so that he was sitting beside her. "Remember our honeymoon, and the moon on Lake Lanier? You were as pretty in the moonlight as you are now."

"Ah, c'mon, Johnny, I've gained 20 pounds, have at least 100 white hairs, and to top it all off, I've had two kids."

"You're beautiful to me, Brenda!"

"Just goes to show you that beauty is in the eye of the beholder, doesn't it?"

"So what's bothering you?" he asked, putting his arm around her. "You've been sitting here for the past two hours staring out that window at the moon. Something's eating at you."

"Oh, nothin'. At least not anything anyone can do anything about."

"Oh?"

"Johnny, it's not fair!"

"What?"

"It's wonderful having you here every night and all, but how about the other times? They're the ones that really count—the PTA meetings, the baseball games, shopping for groceries, going camping, all the things other families do together. Making love and sleeping together is wonderful, but real love is built on other things.

"We built our relationship on going to your games together and laughing at old movies and walking in the park and swimming in Lake Allatoona and watching our boys grow and all of the other things that make sleeping together important and exciting. Sex is great, Johnny. In fact, you know, it's never been better. But how about all of the other things that couples share? We don't have a real relationship. We can't."

"Brenda, I . . ."

"Don't interrupt me, Johnny!"

"OK."

"Why can't you be here all of the time, like everyone else's husband? Why can't you be here when the screen door needs fixing or the boys are fighting or I can't get that old rototiller running to till the flower beds. I have a husband, I guess, but I don't. I want to be with you all of the time. I can't wait for you to come and hold me. Yet at the same time I'm starting to dread it.

"It's even worse now that Steve's moved out, and Johnny junior will hardly talk to me. They act as if I'm a candidate for the guys in the white coats. Johnny, I just can't take it. I've got you, but not my kids or a normal life, and now that I've told the church, most of my friends avoid me as if they think I've got Dracula living in my basement." She sniffed. "I'm sorry, Johnny; that wasn't fair.

"Anyway, I feel as if I'm being torn in two, and I don't know how much more I can stand. Johnny, if you can come at night, is there any reason they wouldn't let you come all the time? I mean, you're down here anyway. Think of all the energy they could save teleporting you down here or whatever it is that they do. If they're as concerned about our happiness as you say they are, wouldn't it be easier just to leave you here? We could be a family again. Steve and Johnny would adjust to the idea; and I know that if you started coming to church with me, they would accept you. C'mon, Johnny, please? Won't you at least ask them?"

"It's not that easy, kitten," Johnny said softly, brushing away a tear that was starting down her cheek. "It's not time yet. There is a plan, a time we will be able to be more open in our communication with earth. But things aren't prepared yet. People have to be primed to accept people like me before we can come. It's happening, but it takes so long! There are so many people who have bought into the old Christian idea that the dead can't contact you here on earth. It's weird, because most of them believe that when you die, you don't die—that you go to heaven or float around here on earth or some netherland. But they still won't give up the old Bible idea that the dead shouldn't contact the living, and vice versa. People have been doing it for millennia, and still religious people fight the idea. At least the Greeks finally persuaded the church that we exist. Prior to that the Christians all believed the old idea that when you died, you died. That was one of the stupidest tricks ever played on the human race. No matter what we do, the Holy Spirit can't leave well enough alone. We finally get people convinced of the truth, and heaven raises up some other prophet to mess things up."

"What are you saying, Johnny?" Brenda asked as she pulled away and looked at him. "I thought that you were in heaven, and that the Holy Spirit and you were on the same side."

"Oh, we are," he said quickly. "It's that, uh, well, it's hard to explain what's going on up there. You know, it's on a different plane, in a different dimension, and sometimes it's not as simple as it sounds, that's all. You remember I said the other night that we had it all wrong before, that Jesus was just one Messiah among many. Well, it's just that sometimes He and the Holy Spirit get going on opposite sides of an issue, and it takes awhile to sort it out. But you can count on the fact that we're all on the same team."

Brenda leaned back so that she could look into his face. "Johnny, what's going on?" she asked sharply. "You sound like Steve used to when he got caught with his hand in the cookie jar. Are you telling me everything?"

For the first time since he had come home Brenda looked deep into his eyes, and what she saw scared her. It was Johnny sitting next to her, all right, right down to the scar on his left thigh from Seth McCracken's cleat. And it was his voice that talked to her, but the eyes—there was something behind the eyes that wasn't right. She had once seen a feral cat, racing across the lawn with a kitten from Mitten's litter in its mouth. For a second the evil, guilty look in the cat's eyes had stopped her in her tracks. It was the look a copperhead might have before it struck. For an instant in the moonlight glittering in Johnny's eyes she saw the same look, and she was momentarily frightened.

Then it was gone, and Johnny's eyes were looking at her. "Listen, kitten," he said. "I haven't been fair to you coming here like this. I was wrong, and I'm sorry. Taking her in his arms, he held her close, running his hands through her hair, caressing her back. "I've got to tell you something. I snuck out. Remember when we used to sneak out of the dorms at church camp back when we were kids, and meet out on the dock?"

Brenda giggled. "I remember almost getting caught by Miss Storm in the middle of a long passionate kiss, if that's what you mean. If you hadn't slid under that old canoe when we heard her coming, we'd have both gone home. What was funny was her sitting on top of that old scow talking to me for almost an hour while you tried hard not to breathe underneath."

"Well, it's the same up there. I sneak out every night to come down here. That's why I can't come during the day. They'd miss me, and I'd get fire duty."

"Fire duty?"

"Who do you think stokes those flames down under? It sure isn't the old devil. Anyway, every night I slip out a little gate I found and come here."

"Aren't you afraid you'll get caught?"

"Honey, I've been taking that risk for you for almost a month. Why should I stop now?"

"I appreciate it, Johnny. You don't know how much it means to me to have you here. I was a terrible widow till you came. I don't know how some of them do it. A few months after their husband or wife dies they act like it's no big deal. Not me. I'd have been dead too if you hadn't come. It's still hard, though. There are so many times and places I wish you were there. Isn't there any way you could convince them to let you come back for a while? You said yourself that it was in the plans someday. Maybe you could be a forerunner or something, sort of like John the Baptist was for Jesus."

"Sorry, Brenda, it's out of the question." There was a long pause. "There is one way . . ." Johnny's voice trailed off.

"What do you mean, one way? Why haven't you told me about this before? What way, Johnny? I'll do anything. Talk to anyone. I'll move mountains." Brenda mischievously poked him in the ribs. "Come on, out with it, you piker. What is it?"

"You could join me," Johnny said quietly.

"I could what?"

"C'mon, Brenda, think about it. I can't come here, but you could come there. I mean, you talk about fun. You've never swum until you swim in the river of life, Brenda. We could have a ball. We could be together all of the time. We could go places together, do things together, be a couple again. You think you miss having me here. Have you ever thought what it must be like to be in heaven without the ones you love? To go places alone. To do things alone. You should see our house up there, Brenda. It's fantastic. Remember those plans we had drawn a few years ago, when we thought we might move? Well, it's them, only a zillion times bigger and better. I rattle around in it all by myself. C'mon, Brenda, what do you think?"

"Join you?" Brenda swallowed hard. "How, Johnny?"

"Well, you know. The same way I did."

"You mean die?"

"Yeah! It's really not that bad once you get used to the idea. It's not death but dying that we're generally afraid of. And that doesn't have to be so bad. You'd have one advantage at least. You could choose how it happened."

"What are you saying, Johnny? That I kill myself?"

"No, I'm not telling you to kill yourself. You asked if there was a way, and I told you that there was, that's all." His voice was irritable. "If you don't want to, forget it!"

"Johnny, what about the kids? Who would raise the boys?"

"You said yourself that Steve had moved out, and that things were pretty rough between you and Johnny junior. My folks could take them—or yours, for that matter. If they knew, don't you think that they'd want us to be together?"

"I don't think my folks would want it if it meant losing me," she said slowly. "Besides that, it's wrong, Johnny. You just can't go around killing yourself to go to heaven. I can't believe you'd even suggest such a thing!"

"I didn't, Brenda. Remember, you're the one who asked. I just told you how. I guess it was a bad idea. I just miss you so much I got excited about the idea of our being able to be together, that's all. Forget I said anything, OK? Hey, the sun's coming up. I've got to get back, and you've got breakfast to make for a growing young man, so I'd better get going. See you tomorrow night."

"G'bye, Johnny."

"'Bye, Brenda."

Chapter 14

"Pastor, is suicide a sin?"

Stan Adkins struggled to bring his mind back to reality. He'd been studying through all of the Bible texts on death and had dozed off for a minute, his head on the notebook on his desk. Now he was sure he was dreaming.

"What?" he said, looking dumbly for a second at the telephone receiver. "Who is this?"

"It's me, Pastor Adkins. Brenda Barnes. Say, are you OK?"

"Yeah, I'm OK. I dozed off for a sec, and I'm having trouble digging my way back to the real world. How are you? I've been thinking often about you lately. I was hoping that we might get a chance to talk sometime. In fact, I think that Barb was going to call you this afternoon. I understand that the pizza down at the new restaurant in the mall is outstanding, and we thought we might take you out there to lunch sometime this next week."

"That'd be great, Stan."

"So, now, what did you ask me? I think I was still half asleep."

"Is suicide a sin?"

"Why do you ask, Brenda?"

"I was just wondering, that's all. Did you ever have one of the really great philosophical questions of the universe hit you while you were vacuuming? I do once in a while, so I thought I'd get an answer from an expert."

"Brenda, you're not thinking of . . ."

"No, Stan, you know me better than that. Besides, remember what I told you at prayer meeting a couple of weeks ago. I've got too much to live for, right?" Brenda laughed nervously. "So, is it or isn't it?"

"That's not an easy question to answer, Brenda. If you want to know what the church has taught down through the ages, I think that opinion has been divided on the issue. If you want to know what I think, I think that it's a very poor choice, but I'm not sure that it's a sin. People who do kill themselves are generally those who believe that they have come to the end of their ropes and have no reason to live. Often the depression is so serious that they aren't really responsible for the choices they make. In that sense, I don't believe that God would hold them responsible. So I'd have to say no on the idea of its being sin.

"It is, though, a very poor choice, Brenda, as I said before. It generally causes families and loved ones a tremendous amount of grief. Insurance companies often don't pay life insurance benefits in the case of suicide, so children can be left without an inheritance, and suicide doesn't deal with the really important issues. Life is a gift that everyone should cherish."

"Yeah," she breathed. "I know."

"We've all experienced the pain that sin has brought into this world," Stan continued. "For some of us it's been physical; for others it's emotional, or financial, or any one of thousands of other ways that sin inflicts us. But Brenda, there are none of those God can't heal if we will let Him. There is no dead end that He can't lead us out of. There is no pain we cannot bear and beat with His help and support. Even the loss of the most important people in our lives, Brenda. What does David say? 'Even though I walk through the valley of the shadow of death, . . . thou art with me.'

"Brenda, many of us walk that dark valley with loved ones long before we walk it ourselves. We struggle with them down into the vale of death, and it often seems that its dark shadows will engulf us as well. Everyone has been down into that valley with someone we care about. But there is a way out of the blackness. He is called 'the Light,' and He promises to go down there with you, if you will let Him, and to light the way for you to come back. Brenda, you've got to believe that and let Him lead you out of your depression from Johnny's death."

"No, Pastor Stan," she said. "As I told you the other night in the meeting, that's not an issue anymore. Johnny's back, and I'm happier than I've ever been in my life. I just wondered, that's all."

"Brenda, I wanted to talk to you in person," he told her, "but I guess I'd better do it now."

"What about?"

"I'm worried about you, Brenda, as your pastor and as a friend."

"Why?"

"Brenda, are you really certain that it's Johnny who's visiting you every night?" Stan asked gently.

"What would make you think it wasn't? I think I'd know my own husband, wouldn't I? What do you think I am, crazy or something?"

"No, Brenda, I don't. But I would like to ask you to listen with an open mind to what I'm about to say, and to think about it. If I'm wrong, I guess you can tell me."

After a long pause Brenda quietly said, "All right."

"Brenda, ever since the other night when you told us about Johnny's return, I've been studying what the Bible says about death. I'm sure you realize what a shock you gave all of us. You've seen the notebooks in my study in which I write down all the things I'm studying. As I recall, you even photocopied some pages out of one of them for a Sunday school class. Well, I've studied this death business the same way."

"What have you found out?"

"You're not going to like this, Brenda. More than 50 times the Bible describes death as sleep. In that sleep state it says that the dead can't think; they're not aware of anything that happens on earth; and that they are not able to communicate with us or with God. In fact, it says that in the grave there's not even any remembrance of Him. It also says that people remain in that unconscious state until they are resurrected either to live forever or be destroyed with the rest of sin."

"How about the soul, Stan?" Brenda asked, her voice almost sarcastically patient. "Doesn't the Bible say that the soul goes to heaven? In fact, I seem to recall somewhere that souls are described as crying out from under the altar in heaven."

"You're right, in a way. That was what I thought too, but it's not what the Bible teaches. What the Bible calls the soul is not a part of us: it *is* us if we are living creatures. In other words, souls can't depart because they can't go anywhere, unless you're talking about someone who's alive going to the corner grocery store or on vacation. Animals are called souls,[1] and so are people.[2] The only exception to this is a few places, such as Matthew 10:28, where the soul is used as a word to describe the spiritual nature of human beings. An analogy would be those times it talks about man's heart. When the Bible tells us to hide God's Word in our heart, or to love from the heart, we know it's actually talking about the mind. The same principle applies to soul when it describes our spiritual side. It's not something that is a separate entity. It's a side, or a part, of us—the spiritual side of our nature.

"As to the souls crying out from under the altar," Stan said, "that one gave me fits for a while until I studied it out. As a literary device, the Bible often describes certain situations in symbolic language. For instance, when Cain killed Abel, his blood, the Bible says, cried out from the ground.[3] I don't think anyone would imagine that there were literal cries coming out of the dirt. The book of Isaiah describes the hills and mountains breaking forth in singing, something I think we all would agree was symbolic.[4] And the book of Hebrews describes the blood of Jesus as speaking better than that of Abel.[5] Again I don't think it is talking about their literally speaking Hebrew or Greek. The same thing is true in Revelation 6. The issue is: has God forgotten His people? Their souls are pictured—in a book of the Bible that is jam-packed with symbols—as crying out from under the altar for vindication. Particularly, because it's found in Revelation, you'd have to assume that it's a symbol unless there was an overriding reason to believe otherwise."

"Then why in all the funeral sermons I've heard you preach, including Johnny's, have you said that the people were up in heaven?" Brenda demanded. "Were you telling us the truth or not?"

Stan sighed. "I thought I was. But to be honest with you, I'd never studied it for myself. I was just saying what I'd always been told. Now I've been forced by circumstances to ask some of the same questions you're asking, and to study to find out what the Bible says."

"And you're telling me"—her voice was shrill—"the Bible says that Johnny can't come back. If that's true, Stan, then who are you saying is coming into my bedroom every night?"

"When the Bible talks about such things," Stan ventured gently, "it describes demons going out into the world to deceive people. Brenda, I don't want to alarm you unnecessarily, but I think that you need to be very careful. I think that you are involved in something here that is very dangerous for you and the boys. Again, all I'm asking you to do is to pray about this, and to study what the Bible says. If after doing that, you have any questions, or if there is anything we can do to help, please give me or Barbara a call. Anytime, Brenda. Day or night. OK?"

"Stan, I don't know what to say. Sure, I'll call you if I need you. But you're asking me to deny everything my senses are telling me is true." She was crying now. "Stan, I am making love with Johnny almost every night. Believe me, it's not just smoke and mirrors. He has scars on his body that only his wife would know about. We talk about things that only we have experienced. If what you say is true, then it's contrary to everything I'm experiencing and everything that I want." Her voice broke, and Stan could hear her blowing her nose. "I don't think that I'm ready to give that up for anything."

"Brenda, I know how you feel."

"No, you don't!" she shouted. "You can go home and crawl into bed with Barbara anytime you want. You have her there. You can talk. You can go places together. You can laugh and cry and watch your kids grow up. Stan, when Johnny died, I lost all of that. The most important thing in my world was gone. I was an empty shell, Stan, until Johnny came back. Now you're asking me to give it all up, just like that!"

"Brenda—"

"I'm not through, Stan. Maybe we don't know everything there is to know about what happens when you die. Maybe the Bible doesn't either. Did it ever dawn on you that your precious Bible might be wrong? Maybe Jesus was just one of a number of messengers in heaven. Maybe even He was a little mixed-up. I don't know, Stan. I don't know. But to ask me to deny the reality of Johnny's presence is going a little far."

"Brenda!"

"Listen, I've got to go. Maybe we can talk some more over lunch next week. Maybe Barbara could come. Maybe she'd understand. OK?"

¹ Genesis 1:21.
² Genesis 2:7.
³ Genesis 4:10.
⁴ Isaiah 55:12; 44:23; 42:10.
⁵ Hebrews 12:24.

Chapter 15

Millie Crossworthy was in shock. It was Sunday morning; and Gus came down the winding staircase in a suit. Not his golf slacks, not his shooting jacket, not his gardening clothes, nor his jogging outfit. In his suit, and it wasn't Christmas or Easter!

"Where you going all dressed up?" she asked as Madge served them breakfast.

"To church."

"To church?"

"Yes, to church! What's wrong with that?"

"Nothing, Gus, I just . . . do you mind if I go with you?"

"No. I was going to invite you. I've already spoken with Noc, and he'll have my car ready by 10:15. I'm going to drive myself this morning. I remember, years ago, how pretty Cherry Pit Road is this time of year. I thought we might drive out that way. I've asked Madge to pack us a lunch, so maybe we can picnic afterward in that little park at the end of the road. We haven't done anything like that in years."

"Are you all right, Gus?"

"Sure. It's just a beautiful day, and I felt like going to church. Is that OK?"

"Yes, it's that . . . well . . . I'd love to go with you. I'll run up and change while you read your paper."

"Great! Why don't you wear that outfit you wore to the company picnic a couple of years ago?"

"OK." Millie's eyes were wide, and she cocked her head like a curious puppy. "Anything else?"

"No; just hurry, please. I'll be waiting."

Finishing her toast, Millie wiped her mouth carefully with the linen napkin, took a final sip of coffee, and left the table. Life sure was getting interesting. First her daughter turns out to be a witch, and then her husband decides to go to church.

When she returned, Gus stood in the large entrance hall waiting for her.

"Ready? he asked. "Say," he said, taking a second look, "you look very nice today."

"Thank you, Mr. Crossworthy. You look pretty handsome yourself in that suit."

Opening the door, they stepped out onto the drive. "Hey, aren't we taking the Mercedes?" she asked as they walked out under the porch. "Gus, this thing is your airport car. It's not suitable for church."

"Well, Millie," he said as he opened the door, "there's something I've been needing to talk to you about. I'll tell you as we drive, but I think that maybe this car would be more appropriate today."

"Where are we going, Gus?" Millie looked at him suspiciously as they headed down the drive. "I thought you said we were going to church."

"Oh, we are. I just thought it might be fun to go somewhere new for a change. Do you remember that community church out on Cherry Pit Road, the one we used to walk by when we were dating? Well, I thought that it would be fun to visit there today."

"Cherry Pit Community Church?" Millie said incredulously. "Why, Gus? Nobody we know goes there. And isn't it—well, what do they believe? Why are we doing this?"

"I haven't had a chance to tell you about a conversation I had the other day with Darrel Widmer, Millie. We played golf together and had lunch in the clubhouse on the turn. I asked him about Nadine. I knew that his wife had been mixed up in this witch business with Peggy, and I thought he might be able to enlighten me a little. He did—when I pushed him. It seems that our pastor is as mixed up in this stuff as his wife is. He even defended it when I challenged him about it, and he told me that if I didn't like it I could go out to Cherry Pit Community Church."

"He did what!"

"Yes, that's what he said, so that's where we're going."

They rode on in silence for a few minutes. Millie looked around, enjoying the view, waiting until her husband was ready to talk.

"I've done a little bit of research on the subject the past few days," he began. "It appears that we've always been cursed with witches and people involved in the occult. Look at the legends of Merlin the Magician and the Salem witch trials. But in the United States it wasn't really until the mid-1800s that it began to gain some respectability. Spiritualism, as it was called, even gained a foothold in a number of the mainline churches. In the 1800s it wasn't uncommon for certain famous U.S. clergy to be involved in things such as séances and other occult practices. A number of famous people were even involved—Thomas Edison, Sir Arthur Conan

Doyle, and Mary Todd Lincoln, to name a few."

"You're serious?"

"Yes, but there was a real backlash, too. Harry Houdini, the magician, spent his whole life trying to debunk spiritualism and fortunetellers. Some of the more conservative churches spoke out against what was happening, but they were ridiculed for being out of touch with the times.

"At the same time a movement sprang up under the leadership of a woman named Helen Blavatsky. It committed itself to missionizing the Western world with the ideas of Eastern mysticism and to wiping out traditional Christianity and its values. Its methods and aims went hand in glove with the spiritist movement, and in the 1900s they really began to pick up steam. They were patient and kept at it until, today, it's the largest missionary movement in the world. Look all around you, Millie. We're surrounded by it. It's everywhere!

"You can't imagine how insidious this whole thing is. Think back to the sixties. Remember the songs about the dawning of the Age of Aquarius? Well, it's here, Millie. It's happened while most of us, willingly ignorant, have let it happen. It's even captured our daughter.

"I discovered that the Third Reich, in Germany, was based on the ideas and practice of mysticism. It all sounds benign enough when they first introduce it. But when they are in control, then watch out. The leaders of Hitler's Germany were deeply involved in the occult, and we saw a little demonstration of what will happen to the rest of the world if they should succeed in America."

"I'm impressed, Gus," Millie said. "You've really done your homework on this."

"But I'm not finished. There's more. In the sixties and seventies this whole thing went into high gear. Apparently there's some kind of coalition made up of everything from old-fashioned witches and fortunetellers to positive thinkers and back-to-earthers under the broad title of the New Age movement. They feel that they're just about over the hump and are on the verge of realizing their goals. They network in ways that would boggle your mind. They conduct seminars, paid for by huge American corporations, introducing the cream of our society to New Age thought disguised as new management styles. They've introduced self-hypnosis and channeling into the very core of Western thinking, and TM into our schools. The media is full of the occult in every form. And the book and game stores, the Internet, and the video arcades are full of it.

"We're being inundated by this stuff in so many forms that no human mind can keep track of it. It affects us all in ways we can't imagine. It's sold under the guise of being harmless. Well, it's not. Think of the fantasy books we bought Nadine. They were harmless, right?" His voice was anguished. "Wrong! They prepared her for where she is today."

"Gus? Do you really think that?"

"Yes, I do. We didn't know any better, Millie, but we did it, and I don't know if there's any hope of salvaging her. She may be in this thing so deep that there's no crawling out. But if there is any hope, I believe that it's got to be in God's power.

"I've never told you, I guess, that years ago I attended a little prayer group for a while. It was when I was in college. A couple of guys invited me, and I went on a lark. But Millie, there was something different there. Those guys knew God! Their lives showed it in powerful ways. I was really drawn to what I experienced, and I honestly believe that if my grandfather hadn't died and I hadn't had to come home, I'd be a real Christian today. I was close. Now I feel a need, for the first time, for that kind of spiritual power. I know I won't find it in our church, so I'm going to check out Cherry Pit Community. If Darrel Widmer doesn't like them, it's as good a recommendation as they could get."

Chapter 16

Pastor, may I talk with you a minute?"

"Sure, Cheryl. I've got to start my new members' class in about 20 minutes, but we can talk until then."

"It needs to be confidential, Pastor. Can we talk in your study?"

"OK. Just let me greet the McKeowns, and I'll be right with you."

"What can I do for you?" he asked a few moments later when he joined Cheryl Fratanelli in the church office. He motioned her to a chair, and sat down behind his desk.

"Pastor, there are some things you don't know about me that I want to tell you. And I'm telling you now because, well, because of what's going on with Brenda. There was a time, before I became a Christian, that I was deeply involved in the occult. In fact, I was part of a group of psychics that acted as consultants to a number of very famous and well-known people here in the States. But when I became a Christian, God freed me from all of that."

Stan leaned forward. Another one. It seemed that Brenda's confession, if you could call it that, had opened the way for other people to tell their own stories.

Cheryl shook her head. "Don't believe anything you hear about how great the life of that whole stratum of society is, Pastor Stan. At first it's great; then it becomes a living hell. You're controlled and used by powers that are stronger than anything you will ever imagine. When I came out of the occult it was exactly what Peter describes in 1 Peter 2:9 when he says that we come out of darkness into light. You'll never know how true that is!

"Anyway, as I said, God took it all away—except for one thing. When I was involved in that lifestyle, my eyes were opened to seeing things that most people, thank God, will never see. There's a whole unseen world swirling around us that most of us—even Christians—never know is there. They forget what Paul says about unseen beings that he describes as 'powers of the air'—unseen principalities, powers, spiritual hosts of wickedness, and world rulers of darkness.[1] They're the devil and his fallen angels."

Stan nodded gravely. "I realize that."

"Before I became a Christian, I used to watch them working on people, finding their vulnerable spots, hassling the angels that God had sent to protect them, harassing or entrapping or abusing them horribly. Even though I was a part of it, at times it was pretty frightening. And interestingly enough, when I became a Christian God didn't take that ability to see that unseen world away from me."

This was getting interesting. "Really?" he asked.

"Really! Have you ever noticed that I sit up front in church every week? Well, it's for a reason. Two reasons, actually. First of all, if I sit back farther, I'm so distracted by what's going on that I can't concentrate on the service."

"What do you mean, Cheryl?"

"Every week God sends His angels to our services, Stan, but Satan dispatches his fallen angels as well. Many come in with the people to whom they're generally assigned, but others are there as well. They come with the specific purpose of disturbing our services. I watch them getting this baby to cry or that person to be distracted by what someone else is doing or wearing, and it really affects my concentration. It's especially bad when they get two people upset with each other and then sit back and laugh and ridicule them. I finally decided to sit in front, where I don't have to watch it."

"You're serious?"

"Yes, I am, Stan. As serious as I can be. We forget that this is all-out war, and our church is one of God's major outposts in that war. Do you think Satan and his confederacy want people coming to church and learning what's going on? They're going to do all they can to make sure it doesn't happen.

"There's a second, more important reason, though, that I sit up front. I don't know if anyone's ever called it to your attention before, but sometimes you have a kind of odd mannerism in the pulpit. You kind of rear back, then pull forward, as if you were fighting something. It reminds me of when Jerry got a line wrapped around a branch and back into his coat one time when we were fly-fishing. Every time he pulled back on the rod, his arm would go forward. It was pretty comical. He was like a puppet pulling his own string. Anyway, you're probably not even aware that you're doing it, but you have a similar mannerism. It's subtle enough that most people probably don't notice it, but I do, because I know what's going on."

Stan leaned forward. "Cheryl, what is going on here? I'm missing something here. What am I doing that's distracting you?"

"Every week when you come out onto the platform a whole covey of angels comes with you. It's exciting to watch. There are the angels that God sends especially to protect you. Then there's a group that Satan sends to keep you from giving the message God has given you for the people. Sometimes they're able to get ahold of you, and they pull on you. You sense it, and pull back against them. Pastor, I sit up front specifically to pray for you. It's my ministry."

Stan opened his mouth, closed it, then opened it again, shaking his head. At last he found his voice. "You're saying that Satan's angels are right up on the platform harassing me while I preach?" he asked, his voice a squeak that surprised him.

"Are you surprised?"

"Well, no, I guess not. I've just never thought of it. I don't know what to say."

"You're facing some hard times, Pastor. Several weeks ago, in prayer meeting, I watched the people who sympathized with Brenda Barnes. That's not her husband she's dealing with, Stan. I think you know that. And several others in our congregation are involved in the same thing she is. Pastor, you've got to face this thing head-on. I don't know how or when, but when you do, I want you to know that a number of us are praying for you. God will not forsake you, and will bring you and our church out of this victorious.

"Some of us have discovered that when we pray it frees God to use power that He otherwise wouldn't be free to use. That's why I sit in the front where I can be close to the battle, and I want you to know that I pray for you with all of my heart. I've also asked several others who, I have discovered, are gifted in the area of intercessory prayer to pray for you. We all are. You can count on that."

His smile was tired. "Thank you, Cheryl. Today, especially, I needed to hear this. Listen, I've got to get to my class. Pray for me today, will you? I'm going to need all of the prayer support I can get."

"Will do, Pastor. See you in church."

Francis had seen it before, or rather experienced it himself. A pastor has a certain look, walking into the pulpit, when he knows that what he's going to say could be very controversial. You see it especially if he loves his congregation and knows that his words could seriously divide them. *You might smile,* Francis thought, *and you put on a happy pulpit face, but there's an undertone that can't be hidden from someone who's been there himself.*

It had been a while since he'd been in a church service, and it felt good to be there. There was a spirit about Cherry Pit Community Church that made you feel at home. As Francis joined in singing the old Lutheran hymn "A Mighty Fortress" he thrilled to Luther's triumphant lyrics:

> "Did we in our own strength confide,
>   Our striving would be losing,
>   Were not the right man on our side,
>   The man of God's own choosing.
>   Dost ask who that may be? Christ Jesus, it is He,
>   Lord Sabaoth His name, From age to age the same,
>   And He must win the battle."

He felt tears welling up in his eyes as the words rang out from more than 300 lips:

> "And though this world, with devils filled,
>   Should threaten to undo us,
>   We will not fear, for God hath willed
>   His truth to triumph through us.
>   The prince of darkness grim, We tremble not for him;
>   His rage we can endure, For lo! his doom is sure,
>   One little word shall fell him."

After the offering and special music Stan Adkins stepped into the pulpit. "I'm not going to be preaching a regular sermon today," he said as he looked out over the congregation. Most of the members were there, sitting in their usual places. For just an instant Brenda held his eyes. And just as she said she would, Cheryl sat close to the front.

"I'm simply going to talk with you from my heart," Stan said, "in a way that I might not if I planned out carefully every word I was going to say. Our text for this morning is Genesis 3:1-5." He paused so that people could open their Bibles. "Did you ever, in a moment of reflection, wonder what the first temptation was, the first lie by the devil on this earth? You'll find it in this passage. Satan, in the disguise of a beautiful snake, asked Eve, 'Did God say, "You shall not eat of any tree of the garden"?'

"Now, I'm giving you the Adkins paraphrase of these verses, but follow along in your Bibles, and you'll see that they're faithful to the text.

"'Eve answered him, "We can eat anything we want, except for the fruit of one tree, which stands in the middle. God has told us not to touch it. If we do, we'll die."

"'And the serpent said to Eve, "You won't die! God's keeping you from something very special by telling you that you can't eat of the tree. If you eat of this tree, you'll be like God; you'll know, firsthand, the difference between good and evil."'

"Like I said, this is the Adkins paraphrase, but it's faithful to the text. Now, my friends, what was the first lie that the devil told? You find it right there in verse 4: 'When you sin,' the devil told her, 'you won't die.' And Eve chose to believe the snake rather than take the word of the God who created her. She and her husband, Adam, in choosing to believe that lie, led the whole human race into rebellion against God.

"The thing you have to keep in mind is that it was a lie of the worst sort, because it was partially true. It was a misrepresentation of reality. It was not the truth. Oh, they found out about sin and death, all right. And that was something God never wanted anyone to experience.

"Shortly after sin came into the world Adam and Eve had the agonizing experience of watching the first flower fade, the first leaf fell from a tree. They watched an innocent animal die, its blood soaking into the ground. They saw it sacrificed. And later the first fight broke out between brothers, and one of them was killed.

"Satan told the truth when he told Eve that if she ate the forbidden fruit she would be like God, knowing good and evil. But evil is something that Adam and Eve learned to their lifelong regret."

Stan took in the sanctuary with a quick glance. No one stirred. Even the babies were silent. He continued: "In the Bible, Romans 6:23 tells us that the wages of sin are death. We've all experienced the reality of that statement. Death, we discover in other Bible passages, consists of two distinct phases. One the Bible calls 'the second death.'[2] It is the death that every sinner will experience at the end of the world. It is total separation from God, and total annihilation from the face of the universe. When God finally destroys sin, it will be complete."

"But it stands to reason that if there's a 'second death,' then there must

THE CHOICE | 83

be a first one. That death is the one that everyone in this room—who is not alive when Jesus comes—will experience. It is this death we're going to look at for a few minutes today.

"What does the Bible say about this first death? It is described as a sleep in which there is no thinking, living, or involvement in the affairs of heaven or Planet Earth. For instance, and this is not an isolated example by any means, verses 5, 6, and 10 of Ecclesiastes 9 tell us that the dead know nothing. They have no emotions, no work, no thoughts, nor any involvement in anything under the sun. Psalm 115:17 says that the dead aren't praising God, and Psalm 6 says that the dead can't even remember Him. In other words, whatever this state is, it is not a conscious one. There is no awareness of anything that is going on."

Stan was so focused on his message that he was oblivious to the quiet rustle that had begun as people in the congregation turned to look questioningly at each other.

"Many of you know that several years ago I had surgery to repair a ruptured disk in my back. My surgeon got ahead of his schedule, so when the time came for me to be taken down for my operation I was wide awake. I can tell you that if I hadn't been awake before, I would have been when they slid me onto the operating table." Stan paused as people in the audience chuckled. "It was stainless steel and must have been about 38 degrees. It felt as if my bare back were going to freeze to the table. Shortly after that, the anaesthesiologist said that he was going to inject anaesthetic into my IV port. I'd watched enough television and asked enough questions that I knew what was next, and I decided that just for fun I'd like to see how long I could stay awake.

"As the doctor said, 'Now, Stan, I'd like for you to count backwards with me, please: 10 . . . 9 . . . 8 . . . 7 . . . 6,' the oddest thing happened. The doc's voice changed from a rich baritone to a soft alto. I was confused for a moment, until I realized that the surgery was over and I was in the recovery room. It was a nurse speaking to me.

"That surgery took almost an hour. All kinds of things were happening in the operating room, but I was not aware of any of them. To me, it was a microsecond. Less than that! One moment I was awake; the next instant I was waking up. That's the way the Bible describes death.

"'What about your spirit?' someone is probably asking. 'Isn't it conscious?' I don't want to get into an involved study of the meaning of the words 'soul' and 'spirit' today, although I think it would be a fruitful study for each of you. But we cannot allow ourselves to be sidetracked from the important issue in our discussion. Whatever we are, or wherever we as human beings go when we die, one thing is certain. We are not aware of, or involved in, anything happening on this earth. Job

14:21 tells us that explicitly.

"And if that is the case, what do we do with so much of what we hear about the supernatural today?" By now people were squirming in their seats. Some were looking at Stan in confusion or anticipation. Others were leafing through their Bibles.

"In the midweek service several weeks ago," Stan continued, "one of our members, a dear friend, described to many of us the appearance of a loved one who died about a year ago and who has now returned. If it is truly he, it would be a miraculous gift to those he loved. And if it is not, then it is the cruelest of hoaxes. How are we to know?

"Today's media bombards us with the supernatural, and the idea that contact with it is normal. However, the séances, use of Ouija boards, and the rapping on tables or walls that characterized early manifestations of the paranormal have been largely replaced. Now the way we are told to communicate with our dead is by channeling and contact with spirit guides in meditation, spirit writing, witchcraft, and many of the old nature religions of pagan Europe, the Americas, and the East. Contact with the dead is a commonplace occurrence in the television programming of today and in much of the literature you read.

"We as Christians find ourselves in a very awkward position in respect to all of this. On the one hand we have traditionally said that wizardry, witchcraft, spiritism, and all the other manifestations of the occult are satanic. In other words, they emanate from God's oldest enemy, and are part of his strategy for deceiving the human race. In fact, many of us refuse to celebrate the greatest occult holiday, Halloween, because it is filled with the very worst of the occult symbols. We base this on specific scriptural commands to have nothing to do with 'familiar spirits,' 'those who consult the dead on behalf of the living,' or those involved in wizardry and witchcraft.[3]

"But strangely enough, at the same time most of us have bought into a pagan Greek idea that was introduced into the church by the Greek philosophers Plato and Aristotle, and that is that when we die at least part of us doesn't die. Our bodies disintegrate, of course, but Plato and Aristotle taught that there is a part of us—our soul or our spirit, depending on whom you're talking to—that doesn't die." At that, Stan paused. His next words came slowly and carefully. "It is the original lie all over again. 'When you sin,' the devil said to Eve, 'you won't die.'

"Now, Aristotle expresses it in a different way, saying that when, because of sin, you die, you don't. Plato, his teacher, who popularized the idea in ancient Greece, believed that we had two parts—a body and spirit. The spirit was the good side of us; our bodies were the evil side. He got the idea from the ancient pagan Persian wizards called the Zoroastrians. Aristotle then figured out a way to make it easy for us nonphilosophers to understand.

"If our loved ones truly loved us when they died and if they are conscious and waiting somewhere to be reunited with us, then it would be natural for them to desire to contact us. In fact, we would expect it. When I go on a trip, Barbara expects me to keep in contact with her. I write her letters and postcards. I call. And when I am able, I slip back to see her. Because I love her, it's something I want to do. After my mom and dad were married during the war, he used to sneak off base during boot camp to be with her. He was willing to risk a court-martial to spend time with the one he loved.

"When you love someone, you're interested in that person's life. You want to know what's happening to them, and you want to be involved with them in all kinds of life's activities. That's a normal human response. If our loved ones are alive and conscious and somewhere else after they've died, we should expect them to contact us, shouldn't we? Our basic assumptions, bequeathed to us from the Greeks and Persians, say that contact with the dead is possible. And if it is possible, then we can believe our senses when it happens.

"However, we have a problem with that. Actually, at least two problems. First of all, we can't trust our senses. Jeremiah 17:9 tells us that the human heart is deceitful above all things. It's very easy for us to deceive ourselves into believing what may not be true.

"Second, no matter what anyone else says, God says that the dead have no contact with this earth, that they're not conscious or aware of anything here or in heaven.

"So now you have the devil's first and most enduring lie, and you have God's word. Each of us, you and I, are going to have to decide where we stand on this issue.

"A long time ago I told the Lord that I was going to base what I believed on His Word and His Word alone. No tradition, church or otherwise, would be more important than the Bible. That means that as much as I might like to believe otherwise, I have to take the Bible position on this subject.

"Just this past week I was discussing this with one of you, and you challenged me—and, I must add, fairly so. You said, 'Pastor, in every funeral you've ever preached in this church, you've talked about our loved ones being up in heaven with Jesus. Were you lying to us? Were you misleading us?'

"That was hard to hear, but it would have been much tougher if I hadn't recently spent some focused time studying this whole subject." He risked a glance at Brenda. Her sad, serious face looked at his defiantly. Saying a quick prayer, he continued. "They say that confession is good for the soul. Often a pastor's pride, when we've preached and taught something for years, keeps us from being able to admit that we've been wrong. Even worse, it leads to the most powerful form of self-deception. Often we won't even study or consider an issue like this because we might discover that we've been wrong. So we go on, intentionally deceiving ourselves, and often deceiving others in the process. We can't bear the thought of admitting to ourselves and others that we have made a mistake, and we cannot bear the thought of what such an admission might do to our reputation or our pride.

"I have to confess to all of you that I was dreadfully wrong on this issue. I'd never before studied it with an open mind. I just told you what I'd always been taught, even when it didn't square with what the Bible says." He shook his head. "It wasn't a deliberate attempt to deceive you or anyone else. It was the sin of accepting the word of others rather than studying it for myself."

He looked over the congregation, his gaze going from one to another. "I have been wrong," he said, "and I am terribly sorry! I ask your forgiveness, and ask you please to do yourselves and God the favor of studying this issue from His Word. It is a matter of life and death in today's world. In fact, it may be the most crucial issue you will ever face. Don't take my word for it, or the word of anyone else. Take the Word of God. Open it for yourself and see what He says.

"Now, to end on a positive note. As many of you know, my dad died several years ago. He was a traveling salesman, and was gone most of the time I was young. When I was in the seventh grade, he left my mother for another woman. So we never did get to spend much time together the way many of you did with your fathers when you were growing up. So I treasure my memories of the times we did get to go places and do things together.

"I had always dreamed that somehow, some way, my dad would change, and we could enjoy the kinds of father-son experiences many of you had with your fathers. I had this secret fantasy that through some miracle he would take an interest in me and God, and that we both would be alive at Jesus' second coming. I could almost taste what it would be like to experience heaven together for the first time. My father did accept Jesus as his Savior several months before he died, so I guess I am going to get part of my wish."

"One day soon Jesus, the Creator, is going to come back to this earth. First Thessalonians 4 tells us that God, through Jesus, is going to bring all those who have loved Him back to heaven one day. Verse 15 tells us that we're all going to go together. Verses 16 and 17 say that Jesus Himself will come from heaven with a cry of command, and the highest angel in heaven will call, and God will blow a trumpet, and the dead will come forth from their graves. They will rise up through the skies to meet God in the air, and we who are alive will join them, and then we'll be together, forever, with our Lord." His voice broke on the last phrase. He swallowed and looked around for the glass of water that sometimes sat nearby.

"You know, I can't wait! My dad and I are going to take that fantastic trip to heaven together. I can't imagine anything more exciting. Instead of trickling into heaven a person or two at a time, all of those who have loved God, clear back to Adam and Eve, are going to march through the gates of heaven as one fantastically large crowd. On the way there we're going to take a trip that will make anything you may have seen in *Star Wars* look like Tinker Toys. Together we're going to see, in the distance, the gleam of a city that is beyond the power of any human mind to imagine. We're going to arrive at the gates as a family. An angel somewhere along the line is going to have placed in my mom's arms my brother and sister who died shortly after birth. The rest of our family is going to be there— my stepdad, my other sister and her family, my wife and kids. As a group we're going to march through that golden gate as one. We're going to explore together what God has worked millennia to design and create for us. We're going to see Jesus and the Father for the first time, together. Folks, I'd never trade that picture for the idea that we're going to dribble in a little at a time.

"You can add to that picture the idea that my dad is not in heaven, watching all of my troubles on this earth. Heaven isn't being spoiled for him by what's going on here. He's asleep in Jesus, resting until Jesus comes again. There's no more pain. There's no more worry. There are no more problems. He is asleep. I refuse to let Satan with all of his lies take that certainty away from me." Stan took a deep breath. "How about you?"

---

[1] Ephesians 6:12, 13.
[2] Revelation 2:11; 20:14; 21:8.
[3] Jeremiah 27:9, 10; Isaiah 8:19.

Chapter 17

So how are things going, Cindy?"
The lunch room at Kroger's had never been one of Cindy's favorite places. It always seemed to be cluttered with yesterday's newspapers and last month's magazines. The bulletin boards contained a chaotic mixture of health department bulletins, year-old notices of promotions, and the inevitable ads

for people selling motorcycles, stereos, and skis. It was a place to go on your lunch hour, but that was about it. There was something about the atmosphere that made even fresh sandwiches taste as if you'd made them last week.

Usually Cindy ate alone and read. Cashiers had staggered lunch hours so there'd be only one empty register at a time. It made for efficiency but didn't allow too much opportunity to get acquainted with the other employees. Today two of the produce men were already there, so she found a place at the end of one of the long tables and was trying to concentrate on a book while tuning out their voices. It took a few seconds for it to register that one of the men was speaking to her.

Looking up, she answered, "Oh, OK, I guess. How about you?"

She had met Steve Heinrich only once, at a company picnic. He was about her age and seemed nice, but they'd never had a real conversation, so she was surprised that he even remembered her name.

"I'm great, thanks." He said it as though he meant it. "I just finished my finals and did pretty well, I think, so I'm feeling pretty good!"

"I didn't know you were in school," Cindy said. "What are you taking?"

"I'm just finishing a degree in aeronautical engineering down at Tech. It's been a long grind because I've been able to go only half time, but I'm almost there. Just one more quarter, and no more carrots and celery. Lockheed, here I come!"

Cindy laughed. "I thought you were going to make a career of piling produce. I'll bet you'll miss this place after a few years hunched over a computer."

He sat down across from her. "No way! Besides, I'm going to be a test pilot. No cubicles and computer terminals for me. I've been working on my ratings, and I'll have my interview next week. They like military guys, and I've been a weekend warrior for a few years, flying jets on the weekends, so I stand a pretty good chance. One of these days while you're checking, I'll give this place such a loud sonic boom it'll rattle every potato off onto the floor. You can stick your head out and wave at me if you want."

"Right!" Cindy nodded. "I don't plan on being here either."

"Really? You're moving? getting married?"

"Nope. I sing some evenings in one of the clubs in town. One of these days I'll be making enough that I won't need to tickle the cash register keys any longer."

"So when do you relax?"

"I don't—much," Cindy told him. "I read a little and catch a movie once in a while, but I stay pretty busy."

"What kind of stuff do you like to read?"

"Mostly metaphysical stuff, I guess. A novel once in a while. I'm really into astrology, so I read a lot about that." She took a potato chip from its package, then offered some to Steve. "And you, what do you do to unwind?"

They paused for a moment while the other produce men got up and excused themselves.

"Fly mostly, although occasionally I help out with my church's youth group."

"You go to church?"

"Yeah, a little place called Cherry Pit Community Church. Well, not so little, really. We've got a few more than 500 members, but it still feels like a small church to me. It's a great place." He took a few chips, then pushed the bag back to her.

"How about you? Are you an active member of one of the churches in town?"

She laughed. "Not me. I haven't gone to church in years. I used to go with my grandmother, but that was a long time ago. I guess it never really took hold. Where'd they ever come up with the name Cherry Pit Community for a church, anyway?"

"There was an old gal, years ago, who wanted the church they were building named after the road it's located on. It's lined with wild cherry trees and in the fall is covered with the pits—that's where they got the name. She was giving the lion's share of the cost of building the place, so they went along with her. A lot of people get a kick out of it, but we've gotten used to it, and actually, it's an asset. You have to tell people the name only once, and they never forget it."

"I believe that." Cindy looked at her watch. "Looks like it's time to get back to the salt mines. It was nice talking with you, Steve."

"I enjoyed it. Maybe we can do it again sometime."

This is ridiculous, Cindy thought later that night as she picked at a fajita in Dos Muchachos, a Mexican restaurant next to the mall. *I've never been afraid of anything in my life, and I'm not going to let some spook bother me now.* Yet she had to admit she didn't want to go home.

First there had been the candle, relit every time she left the apartment or even the room. Then there were the footsteps every night, wandering around for an hour or two as if whoever it was owned the place. She'd never had the courage to leave her bedroom to find what or who was there, but she had installed extra deadbolts on the door and had added safety locks to the windows. She knew it couldn't be anything human—but that didn't make her feel any better.

Next there'd been the faucets. One day as she was eating supper the faucets in the kitchen had suddenly turned on. She had been right in the middle of a bite of spaghetti and had dropped it all over the front of a new silk blouse. A few seconds later they turned off on their own, but a few days later they'd done it again, and later again. Now it happened several times a day.

Other things were happening too, such as the book on ancient spells that one morning she'd found open on the table in front of the candle. She'd won it as a door prize at a fair. It had somehow made her nervous, just as the witch she'd met at the last one had. Yet she hated to throw any book away, so she'd brought it home, put it in her bookcase, and promptly forgot about it—until the other morning when it appeared on the table, open, in front of that lousy candle. She put it away and blew out the candle, but it had been back when she got home from work. So she took it into the storeroom and stuck it in a box. When she returned from singing at the club, it was back on the table, open. Next she took it out and pitched it in the trash. Next morning it was back. It was like the phoenix continually rising from the ashes to haunt her.

A couple days later she had stopped off to see Karen on the way home. After hearing about these strange things, Karen had begged her to come and stay with her family for a while. Cindy refused. She liked to believe that nothing, no one, could bother her. She was independent, self-sufficient, and able to take care of herself. Yet she had to admit that when she looked in the mirror in the mornings, she was being affected by what was going on. The dark circles under her eyes were almost impossible to hide, no matter how much makeup she used. And she was losing weight.

Something had to give, she knew. She'd begun looking for excuses not to go home—dropping by her parents' house or the mall, or even staying in the lunchroom, rather than going home. She couldn't go on living this way. It was like living in a haunted house. It reminded her of the Winchester House out in San Jose. Her family had toured it one summer when they were in California on vacation. Mrs. Winchester had been the widow of the man who had been president of the company that manufactured the Winchester rifle, and when he had died, back in the 1880s, she had inherited his fortune. She, like Cindy, had been involved in paranormal activities and astrology.

One day a medium told her that as long as she kept building additions to her home she would never die. For the rest of her life she continued to tinker with that old house until it was a monstrosity of stairways that ended in blank walls, halls that went in circles, and doors that opened into nowhere. It was enough to give any carpenter an Excedrin headache, and it soon became a satanic nightmare. Nor did it do her a bit of good. Like everyone else on earth, in due time, she had died. She died an old obsessed woman, a captive in her own home.

Maybe Grandma T was right after all, Cindy thought. *Maybe this is a trap laid by some satanic power.* She didn't want to think of that, but she couldn't seem to help it. Maybe the astrology and the channeling and the harmonic convergences and seminars were a carefully designed plot to capture and destroy the whole human race. Was it possible?

It had all seemed so good at first. The people were positive. You were involved in a movement that was going to save the world from destroying itself. There was communication with people in other dimensions, on other planets, from other times. You became knowledgeable about the hidden secrets of the ages. You knew things no one else knew. There was power that no one else had. It was fascinating—so fascinating that at times it almost took your breath away.

Yet there was another dark side you didn't see at first—a sinister aspect to it all that was not apparent when you first got involved. It was like a fly walking onto flypaper. The bait was sweet, but once you got onto it, you couldn't get off. What had promised to be Disneyland was now turning into the Addams family, and it was really starting to bother her. So there she sat, alone at a Mexican restaurant, sipping cold coffee to delay going home.

"So this is where you hide out at night."

Cindy looked up into Steve's grinning face.

"Have you got somebody coming back, or can I join you?" he asked.

"No, I'm by myself tonight. Join me. What are you doing here?"

"Oh, Rick Ramirez and I are old school buds, so I slip in here once in a while and see how he's doing. His dad owns this place, and he's the manager. I guess he figures poor students need to be fed, so he cooks me up a special meal once in a while. His mama does, actually." He laughed and motioned toward the restaurant's kitchen. "When my mother died, I used to go over to their house for supper on the nights my dad worked. Mrs. Ramirez makes the world's best tortillas. And when they opened this place, they made sure I knew I was still part of the family.

"How about you? What brings you out on a night like this? I'd think you'd be home in front of a fire reading a book or something else domestic."

Cindy laughed. "That's twice today, Heinrich. One more crack about domesticating me, and you'll have to come over and wash my dishes some night."

"Oh no, not dishpan hands. Got any idea how they would look on the controls of my plane?" He accepted a glass of water from the server, who told him his meal would be ready soon. "You looked pretty serious a minute ago, Cindy," he said. "Is everything OK?"

She sighed. "Yeah, I'm all right. Just under a lot of pressure lately. It's hard to explain."

"Well, if there's ever anything I can do . . . OK?"

"Yeah, thanks, I will. Hey, looks like your meal is here," she said as the manager, Rick Ramirez, set a plate in front of Steve.

"Whee, it must pay to know the cook. What is that, anyway?" she asked.

"I'll let you in on the secret in a minute. First, though, Rick, this is Cindy Marshall, pride of Kroger stores. Cindy, this is Rick Ramirez, scion of the Ramirez Dynasty and manager of Dos Muchachos. And what he has just served me is Quesadilla Supreme—you won't find it on the menu. Rick's mom made it for me one time at their house, and I swore up and down it was the best food this side of heaven. Now she makes it for me every time I come in."

"I'm very pleased to meet you," Cindy said as Rick bowed low. "Steve tells me that you and your family have been very special to him."

Rick smiled. "We keep hoping that enough tortillas and beans will turn him into a real Mexican, but so far all it's done is made him one of the best National Guard pilots in the South. I just hope the U.S. never goes to war with Mexico. With him in the air we wouldn't stand a chance."

"So, Steve," Rick said, giving his friend a punch on the shoulder, "Papa tells me that you aced your finals this quarter. Don't you ever get tired of a 4.0?"

"Whoa, you're telling my secrets," Steve protested. "I have them convinced at Kroger's, that I can barely read. Now they'll expect me to be able to understand what's on the outside of all those cartons."

"It's about time they started getting their money's worth," Rick teased. "Hey, my pager's buzzing, so I'll leave you two to your dinners. It was a pleasure to meet you, Cindy."

"You too, Rick. When I come in next time, it's the Quesadilla Supreme, right?"

"I'll tell Mama. She'll make one for you."

Later, as they were finishing a flan so smooth you could hardly feel it on your tongue, Steve asked, "Cindy, I know that you said you weren't into church much, but a bunch of us in the young adult group are having a party tomorrow night. It's not a date kind of a thing. Just a bunch of us singles who get together once in a while to hang out. We'd like to have you come. I think you'd enjoy it, and I'd like for them to have the chance to meet you. How about it?"

Church? For a moment Cindy panicked, then thought, *why not?*

"Sure, I'd love to," Cindy said. "What time and where?"

"We're meeting in the church fellowship hall," Steve said. "There's a big fireplace, and it's big enough that several of us can get together without crowding anyone's living room. We'll eat about 6:00, then spend the evening. I can give you a ride. Pick you up about 5:30?

"Yeah. Great. Can I bring something?"

"Just yourself."

Chapter 18

"Hi, I'm Stan Adkins." The pastor of Cherry Pit Community Church stood by the door greeting people as they left after worship.

"Hello. I'm Gus Crossworthy, and this is my wife, Millie," Gus said heartily. "We're locals and have admired your church from afar, but we've never been inside the building. So we thought we'd drop in and visit today. I imagine there's a lot of history in this old place."

"I'm very pleased to meet you," Stan told him. "Yes, there is a lot of history in Cherry Pit Church. It's a special place." He kind of frowned. "Say, I know that today's service was a little unusual. I hope that you two weren't offended by my candor and that you'll consider coming back and seeing us again."

"On the contrary," Gus said, "I was thrilled! In fact, Millie and I have been thinking about the subject a lot lately, so it was right on target for us. It's the kind of thing I wish our pastor would be willing to talk about the way you did."

"Well, do come back."

Gus turned back partway down the steps. "I know this is short notice, but do you have plans for lunch?" he asked Stan. "Today is kind of a trip down memory lane for us. When we were dating, Millie and I used to walk this old road. We brought a picnic lunch out here with us today and thought we might eat at the park at the south end. Will you and your family join us?

"I don't know. My boys are pretty big eaters."

Gus laughed. "We brought plenty."

"Well then, OK. I don't know of any other plans, so we'd enjoy it. It generally takes a little while before things clear out here. Then we could go home and change. Can we bring something?"

"No, we've got more than enough for all of us. What do you say we figure on about 45 minutes?"

"Sounds good. We'll see you then."

"Gus, wasn't that Francis Baldwin?" Millie asked a few minutes later as they passed a man walking along the side of the road.

Looking in his rearview mirror, Gus swerved over to the shoulder. "I think it is. I wonder what he's doing out here." Putting the car in reverse, they soon came to where Francis stood watching them.

"Francis, what a surprise to see you out here!" Millie stuck her head out of the window as they rolled up next to him. "We thought you'd left the country."

"Gus. Millie. How to good it is to see you! I live right up the road about a half mile. This morning I decided to visit the church back there, and I was just walking home. But what brings you slumming out here in this part of the world?"

By now Gus was out of the car and coming around to where his former pastor was standing. "You were in church this morning? So were we! Millie and I dated on this old road, but we'd never been inside the church. Decided to visit this morning, too. Say, wasn't that some sermon!"

"It surely was. It took a lot of courage to say what that preacher did."

"What did you think of it?" Millie asked through the car window.

"I'm still processing it," Francis answered. "It's all pretty new to me."

"Us too," Gus said. "That's why we invited the pastor to lunch. We're eating a picnic in the old park at the end of the road. Francis, why don't you join us?"

"I'd love to, Gus, but I don't know . . ."

"Sure you will. We'd love to have you, and I need you to help me ask the right questions when I talk to the pastor. Come on, Francis, why not?"

"I just think it might be better if I didn't, that's all."

"Please, Francis," Millie begged.

"Listen, guys. Nobody out here knows that I used to be a pastor. To them I'm just Francis Baldwin, owner of Pine Burl Nursery. I've been getting acquainted with the pastor of the church, but I haven't told him what I used to do. Apparently he's never heard of me, and I'd kind of like to keep it that way if I can. I'm afraid if I come, someone might let the cat out of the bag. Please let me beg off this time. And please, help me keep my little secret."

"Francis," Millie said quietly, "we felt very bad about what happened. The past few weeks I've many times wished that you were still living down in Calhoun so that we could drive down and see you, old friend. You know, Francis, Gus and I have always said that if you'd been our pastor at First, we would have been there every week."

"Can we at least give you a ride?" Gus asked. "We need to talk."

"Sure, you can do that. I'll get in the back."

As Gus pulled onto the road, Francis asked, "Millie, you said that you wished I'd been at the church the past couple of weeks. What's going on?"

Millie looked silently at Gus, nodded slightly, and looked down, a tear starting to run down her cheek.

"Our whole world's fallen apart, Francis." Gus turned the car into the nursery driveway. "And Pastor Widmer, I'm afraid, is part of it."

Francis leaned forward. "What are you talking about? What's going on?"

"I know that we didn't attend much, Francis. But do you remember Nadine, our daughter?"

"Sure. I think that just about everybody in town knew Nadine. Has something happened to her?"

Gus didn't answer. He just sat, and it wasn't until Francis saw the huge shoulders shaking that he realized Gus was crying. For what seemed like hours the big man sat and sobbed, Millie beside him, rubbing his shoulder, crying, too.

Finally Gus took out a handkerchief and mopped his eyes. Then after blowing his nose, he turned to face their passenger.

"I guess you might call me a doting parent," Gus began. "Giving birth to Nadine was very difficult for Millie. She was a large baby, and she came very fast. In the process there was a lot of damage, and we were told that we'd never be able to have another child. Anyway, we poured all our love into making the one we had happy. I think most people in this town would say that we spoiled her, and they'd probably be right.

"I guess that we rarely told her no or denied her anything she asked for. In the process, she became friends with my sister, who, it turns out, was involved in some things that we thought at the time were just old wives' tales." He shook his head. "I remember when Peg went on vacation with us and we visited Salem, Massachusetts. To us it was kind of a lark to visit the museum commemorating the witch trials that occurred there, but to her it was like visiting the holy land. At the time we didn't think much of it. Peg always had some strange ideas. It was only recently that we discovered that she was a practicing witch and was a part of a coven operating right here in our town."

"It seems," Millie interrupted, "that Nadine developed an interest in that kind of thing herself. She loved to read, and some of the books were ones that we thought, at the time, were harmless fantasy—sort of like the old Disney thrillers or the ghost stories we used to tell around the campfire as kids. It seems that Peg picked up on that interest and apparently introduced Nadine into the coven."

Tears filled her eyes. "If we'd only known. We didn't know what Peggy was involved in, so, of course, when she wanted to take Nadine places, we let her. She was her aunt," Millie added as if she still couldn't believe what had happened.

"To make a long story short," Gus broke in, "Nadine is deeply involved in what, six months ago, I would never have believed even existed. In fact, she may be the leader of this group in town, now that Peg is dead.

"When I went to our pastor," Gus continued, "I discovered that he and his wife are involved as well. According to him, many in the church have been involved in this stuff for—at least 100 years. He said he thought that it was great and that we should join them. And that's the real reason we're out here today. Darrel Widmer said that if we were going to persist in our narrow-mindedness, we might as well go out to Cherry Pit Community Church, because they believed the same way we apparently did."

"In other words," Millie sniffed, "if we were so stupid that we didn't accept all this witch stuff, we might as well join a hick church out in the boonies!"

"It sounds like a pretty good recommendation," Francis murmured quietly. "Are you sure about all of this, Gus?"

"I've seen it with my own eyes, Francis. And Nadine has admitted it all. She's moving back to town from Atlanta and has warned us not to get in her way."

"Wow. Now I know why you appreciated today's sermon so much!" the former pastor said.

"That's why we wanted you to eat with us, Francis," Millie went on. "You should have seen Nadine. You should . . ." Her voice broke. "Francis, we don't know much about the Bible. This is all new to us. We've been so busy with our lives that we haven't needed God. We've had everything we wanted, and things were going great. True, there were times we'd wake up on Sunday morning and say something about maybe going to church, but there was so much else we wanted to do we just never got there. Francis, I don't know what the Bible says about all of this. Gus has been doing some reading lately, trying to understand it, but we're both neophytes." She paused to wipe her eyes and nose with a tissue.

"As Gus told you, we've remarked many times that if only Francis Baldwin were here, he'd know what to do! I think that God led us to you, Francis. Now you've got to help us."

"Let me get out of my suit, and I'll be right over. I'll do what I can, but don't expect any miracles. Say, did you bring a change of clothes?"

"Yes," Millie answered. "We were going to change over at the park."

"In those old outhouses!" Francis laughed. "No way! Come on in. You can change here, and then we'll go over together. You just have to remember that there's a very busy bachelor living here, so close your eyes to the mess."

A few minutes later, after putting their clothes in the car and getting out two huge picnic baskets, the three friends were walking down the drive toward the road when Millie asked Francis, "Is that a shrub peony?"

"Yes. Why?"

"I have searched all over town and even in Atlanta trying to find one, and everybody looks at me with a blank stare and says that they've never heard of such a thing. I saw one out in the Seattle area when we were there at a convention and have wanted some for our front flower beds ever since. Are they for sale?"

Francis grinned. "Everything, plantwise, on the place is for sale, Millie. How many do you want? I think that there are about 20 in that bed. Charla used to keep them dug with wrapped root balls, but there was so little call for them she just let them grow and figured she'd dig them when they were needed. As you said, most people don't know that peonies come in two varieties, so I haven't sold many. I'd like to keep a couple for starts, but I'll sell you as many of the rest as you'd like."

"Do you deliver?"

"Right to your doorstep."

"I'll take 12 as soon as you can get them to us. Gus, we can put them under the windows on both sides of the front door in place of those rhododendrons that struggle to bloom every year. Francis, bring a bill with you, and I'll have a check waiting. Oh, and Francis, be fair with yourself, OK?"

"All right, I'll bring them tomorrow evening around 6:00. I don't have anyone to mind the store during the day, so I have to make deliveries after I close."

"Francis, how are you doing?" Gus asked as they walked across the road into the park and toward two picnic tables that stood under a large wild cherry tree.

"Fair. I miss Ann terribly. I guess I always will. Other than that, Gus, I'm doing something I've always wanted to do. I guess every one of us has some dream we believe we'll never be able to realize. You know that I loved the ministry. I enjoyed preaching, and I relished the opportunities it gave me to interact with all kinds of interesting people. I even got a fair amount of satisfaction out of the administrative side of pastoring, although it wasn't my strong suit. But there were times I'd sit in the church office and wish I could be out in the open. Every time I went down to Davidson's to buy something for my yard, I'd think about what it would be like to own my own nursery. So when I discovered that this place was for sale I cashed out my retirement account and bought it."

"Do you see much of Ann?" Millie asked as she spread checkered tablecloths on the tables with practiced efficiency. "Do you ever hear from her?"

"No, she made a pretty clean break when she left. I hear about how she's doing once in a while from the kids, but that's about it. She got the house as part of the settlement, so she's happy. I ran into her once at a store and she was civil, but nothing more."

"Why did she leave, Francis? I heard about her little speech in church, but was there more?"

"Not that I know of, Millie. It's a long story, and I'll tell you some-time if you like. Let's just say that I had to choose between following the dictates of my conscience or continuing to preach what I knew the Bible didn't teach. I was aware when I made the decision to follow where God was leading me that it could cost me just about everything. But I didn't realize the price would be one of the most important things in this world to me."

"I am so sorry," Millie said quietly.

"Well, enough about me. Let's talk about you. Better yet, let's finish get-ting this food on the table. It looks like the locusts are descending upon us."

"What? Oh, I understand." Millie grinned as she glanced at Pastor Adkins' car pulling into the parking lot. "C'mon, Gus. Stop daydreaming and help me finish setting the table before they get here."

Chapter 19

Well, what brings you home?" Brenda stood in the doorway from the kitchen into the garage.

"Oh, nothin'." Steve looked up from a box he was digging through. "I just have to pick up some things I'll need for work out at the church next Monday. Claude said that he wanted me to wear work boots when I'm running the mower. I thought I'd pick up a pair of Dad's, if that's OK."

"Have you had breakfast?"

"No, I left this morning before the Edwards were up."

"Well, why don't you come in after you find the boots, and I'll scram-ble you some eggs."

"That would be great, Mom. Thanks."

More than a month had passed since Steve had left home, and waves of loneliness washed over him as he looked through the cabinets in the garage. Johnny Barnes had loved his shop, and every inch of it was fragrant with memories for Steve as he looked for his dad's work boots. He laughed as he looked at some of the gadgets his father had collected, and couldn't help crying for a minute as he finally held up the boots he'd watched his dad lace up every Saturday before they went out to work in the yard. He had hated yardwork! He couldn't count the times he had punched his pillow in frustration as he heard his father get out the old trombone to play reveille. Other guys got to sleep in on Saturday. He had to have a dad who thought it was cute to blast him out of bed on Saturday mornings just so he could get up early to trim bushes and mow the lawn.

Now he'd do anything to be able to go out with his father into the crisp morning air to work together. *The old saying "Absence makes the heart grow fonder" is really true,* he thought as he set the boots and a couple of tools by the door and stepped into the kitchen.

"So, Mom, how are things going?" he asked a few minutes later as he used a napkin to wipe toast crumbs from around his mouth.

"Fine, except that we really miss you."

"I miss you too, Mom."

"Why don't you come home, Steve?"

"You know, Mom. As long as . . . well, you know."

"Steve, if you would just give him a chance I know that your dad could explain everything." She leaned against the kitchen counter. "You know how much you've missed your father, son. Well, so did I. But now I can be with him again. You wouldn't want me to give that up, would you, Stevey?"

"Mom, you were at church last week."

"Yes, I was there."

"And you heard Pastor Adkins' sermon?"

"Yes, I did. I respect the pastor a lot, son, but he doesn't know what he's talking about this time. He is wrong about—"

"Mom," Steve interrupted, "have you ever really studied this in the Bible for yourself? I mean, really studied it? Maybe you're right. Maybe Pastor Adkins is wrong about this. But maybe it's you. Maybe whoever it is that's claiming to be Dad isn't, and it's a hoax or a demon or something. *I* don't know. I'm really confused, and I am really worried." Steve's eyes filled with tears. "Mom, I've not only lost my dad; I'm losing my mother, too, and it hurts!"

"Do you remember when Dad was dying and he called me over and said that I was going to be the man of the house now and that I was supposed to look after you?" Steve asked. "I'm trying, Mom, but you won't let me. First you shut me and Johnny out of your life because you were hurting so bad. Now you've taken up with this—"

"Steve, you sound jealous of your own father."

"My father! Give me a break!" Steve stood up and carried his dishes over to the sink. "Mom, won't you listen for once? You and Dad raised me to believe what the Bible said. Remember all of the times we had devotions before bed and you told us how important it was to study the Bible for ourselves? Do you remember that every fall at Halloween you and Dad wouldn't let us go trick or treating because of all of the occult stuff and that you'd tell us about Martin Luther? Do you remember how, on Satan's own holiday, Luther took his stand on the Word of God and nailed his theses on the door of that German castle? Remember telling us how you hoped we would grow up and be like Martin Luther and do what was right, even when it wasn't convenient or when everyone else in the world was doing wrong?

"Mom, you raised us to believe what the Bible said, no matter what. Now are you going to live by what you taught us, or are you going to let what you want blind you to anything else?

"Look, I've got to go," he said, "or I'm going to be late for one of my finals. Please, Mom, please! Take the time to study this. What have you got to lose?"

Brenda sat quietly for a minute, then looked up at her son. Somehow she suddenly saw him, for the first time, as the young man he had become. "OK, Steve. I will." Her voice choked. "And uh, thank you."

"You're welcome, Mama. And thank you for the breakfast. No one in the world scrambles eggs like you do."

Brenda sat thinking for a long time after her oldest son left. She hadn't spent much time reading her Bible lately. Since Johnny had come back it just didn't seem important anymore. Or maybe, she realized, reading it made her feel uncomfortable. But why would that be?

Then in her mind she saw the boys as they'd been years before. Small and skinny, ducking their heads, even hiding when they knew they'd done wrong and were in trouble. She could always tell, just by their sudden uneasiness around her, that something was going on. And that suddenly reminded her of Adam and Eve's reaction to God in the Garden of Eden after they had sinned. They'd had an overwhelming urge to hide from Him.

She didn't want to study her Bible, she realized, because it might show her something she didn't want to believe.

Well, that was ridiculous, she decided as she got up and went in to where her Bible sat on the table next to Johnny's favorite chair. If Johnny was in heaven, then the Bible should support the idea. And she believed that it did! She had heard all of her life that when you died you went to heaven or hell. Funeral sermons, Sunday school classes, pastors, guest speakers, and the beliefs of her own parents all reinforced the idea. All of them couldn't be wrong! All she had to do was to find the right texts on the subject and share them with Pastor Adkins, and everything would be back to normal. So picking up a yellow pad and pen from her desk in the den, she headed back into the kitchen.

The problem was where to start. Brenda suddenly realized that she had no idea what the Bible really said about death, or even how to find out. Oh, well, maybe she'd cheat a little.

Reaching for the phone, she called the church office.

"Jackie," she said when the secretary answered, "is Stan in? This is Brenda Barnes."

"Yes, he is, Brenda. Let me get him for you. Say, how are you doing? Did I hear you were looking for work?"

"Not for another year. After the boys are in college, I'll probably look for another teaching job, but not now. I've got too many irons in the fire, and I want to be home for the boys as long as they're here."

"Well, let me know when you're ready. Duane's on the school board, you know, and I'm sure he would put in a good word for you. OK, here's Stan."

"Brenda, how are you?" he asked, wondering just what was on her mind.

"Fine, Stan. How about you?"

"OK, thanks. What's up?"

"Well," she said, a little shy now that she had him on the phone, "your sermon the other day hit pretty hard. I s'pose you know that."

"I had no choice, Brenda. I hope you realize it wasn't intended to be personal."

"Well, I think you're wrong, Stan, and I aim to prove it to you. But in order to do that, I need your help."

"You need my help to prove me wrong?" Stan laughed. "What you're saying is that you want to borrow my gun so you can shoot me."

She laughed too. "No, it's not like that. I just need to borrow one of your notebooks, that's all. And a copy of some kind of Bible reference book, if there is such a thing. I need something that lists all the words in the Bible and where they're found."

"OK." This was sounding interesting. "I think what you're looking for is a concordance."

"I want to look up every text that talks about what happens when you die," she told him, "and I don't know where to start. I figure that you've already done a lot of my homework for me, and that you've got it stuck in one of the notebooks on your desk. That will give me a good beginning to my search."

"I think you may find it a real challenge, Brenda."

"I don't think so, Stan. How long have we been friends? Ever since we moved here about seven years ago, right? Well, I believe that you're one of the sincerest people I know, and I would never doubt your honesty. I just think that you've missed something in the study you say you've been doing. I aim to fill in the missing pieces, get you back on track, and, hopefully, get my son back. There's where I need your help."

Praise the Lord, Stan mouthed silently.

"Brenda, you're welcome to anything I have, you know that. I'll have Jackie photocopy the pages from my notebook, and I'll have them and the concordance in the office by early this afternoon. Pop by at your convenience and pick them up. Take the concordance as a gift from me. It's an extra that I've had, and I'd love for you to have it. It's called *Strong's Concordance,* and it lists all the key words found in the Bible and the reference where each can be found. It's a great tool for Bible study. And Brenda, I'll be praying that God blesses you in your search. Let me know how it comes out, OK?"

"You don't have to worry about that!" She paused. "Stan, I feel bad that Jackie's gonna have to copy all that out of your notebook. If I came down, could I help her?"

"Sure. She'd be glad to have you."

"See you in a few minutes, then."

Brenda got a light jacket from the hall closet and was headed for the door when the phone rang. "Brother!" she muttered as she set her purse and keys on the table and picked up the phone.

"Brenda," said the voice on the other end, "this is Ben Gladden. How are you, dear?"

"Fine, Ben. You?"

"I'm great! Say, I know that you're probably busy, so I won't talk long. I just had to call and tell you how angry I was about how you were treated last Sunday."

"What are you talking about, Ben?"

"Pastor Stan's sermon, that's what I'm talking about. He was wrong! I've already written a letter to the pulpit committee, and I plan to see that he never does something like that again. You shouldn't have to be publicly humiliated and criticized like that! Pastors are here to serve the flock, not condemn them."

"Are you saying what I think you're saying, Ben?"

"You bet I am." Ben's voice was shrill. "I think it's about time that that guy heads down the road. I know people who won't come to Cherry Pit Community because he's so offbeat on stuff like this. I'll bet you'd never hear a sermon like that from Darrel Widmer down at First Church."

Brenda walked across the room and sat on the leather chair by the couch. "Slow down a minute, Ben. Don't you think that you're overreacting just a little?"

"Not on your life. If you think that I'm going to sit in my pew and let that pulpit-pounder criticize my little girl, you've got another think coming. Patty cried for days when she came to see me. It broke my heart! People can criticize me all they want, but I've always said, "Don't you ever mess with my kids," and I mean it. That guy has got to go! I've already talked with Juanita Parris and a couple of others, and we're calling a meeting tonight at Juanita's to discuss this. We really want you to be there, Brenda."

"Ben, Stan was just sharing his convictions. You can't get rid of him for that. Sure, I think that he's wrong, and I plan to show him where as soon as I get a chance. But I surely don't think his sermon is cause for firing him."

"You mean that you're just going to sit there and let him attack Johnny like that? Is that Christian?" His shrill voice made her cringe. "You think that people aren't talking behind your back on this, Brenda? Many of them don't understand, and they think that you're some kind of freak. If they were to find out about Juanita's Luke, my Patty, or a couple of others I know about, we'd face the same thing. No, we're not going to let it happen. They can't treat you like this. We're going to act now before this thing spreads any further."

"I don't know, Ben. This just seems like you're really going over-board."

"You'll see," Ben said. "That man is nothing but a troublemaker. You can't straighten him out, and neither can I. He's hopeless."

"Ben, Stan is a friend of mine. He's a man of God, and he's very hon-est. He's taken a stand based on what he believes is right, and I respect him for that. I don't have to agree with him. I believe that when I have the op-portunity to study this whole thing, I'll be able to show him where he shot off into the stratosphere, and that he'll come around. In the meantime, let's not do anything rash, OK?"

"No, it's not OK with me. I'm not going to wait. You can't tell me that my little Patty isn't real. Every night I go up to her room and wait for her there. Ever since Mildred died she's all I've got. I sit in the rocking chair in her room, and I hear her coming and wait until she's just at the door; then I jump up and throw it open. It's a little game we play. She leaps back every time and screams and laughs, and then I take her up in my arms and carry her to the chair, and we talk, and I read her stories. Each time she comes, she wears the same pink little dress with white socks and the black patent leather shoes we buried her in. When she snuggles up next to me, we're a family again. I can imagine Mildred down washing the sup-per dishes as she always did when I read to Patty. We're together again, Brenda, and that pastor wants to take it all away from us. Just let him try!"

"Ben, I don't know what to say."

"Say that you'll come to the meeting tonight, Brenda. Then you can decide for yourself. You owe it to Johnny. And to the boys."

"OK. I'll be there." She sounded resigned. "What time?"

"Seven o'clock sharp."

Chapter 20

As Cherry Pit Community Church's wealthiest member, Juanita Parris had a large house in one of the town's nicest neighborhoods. Juanita and her husband, Luke, built it about five years before his death. It was their crowning achievement. Sanctuary Hills was an exclusive subdivision on a knoll overlooking the whole town, and each of its houses had been built by one of Luke's crews. For years he and Juanita had worked to design a house that was perfect for them. Sitting on the brow of the hill next to the gate of the subdivision, it was its centerpiece. Designed to resemble a castle, the pale pink of the stucco glowing in each sunset dominated the whole skyline.

"Brenda, we're so glad you could make it," Juanita smiled when she answered the bell. "Come on in. Most of the others are here, and we were just getting ready to start. Do you want cream in your coffee?"

"Yes, please."

"Go on in. Everybody's in the den. My maid is off tonight, so I have to see to a couple of details, but I'll be right there."

This place always intimidates me, Brenda thought as she walked down the hall toward the den. Its wall of windows looked out over the bluff and into the city. *It's like I am walking into another world.*

Carrying a large tray of cookies, Juanita joined 20 or so guests in the den a minute later.

"I'm so glad you were all able to come," she began. "I suppose that some introductions might be in order. On my left, over in the window seat, are Will Forster and his wife, Jamie, who, as you all know, attend our church. Next is Pete Sande, a member of the pastoral relations committee. By them is a very dear friend of mine whom I have asked to join us tonight—Carol Widmer. Her husband pastors First Church, downtown. Over by the banana tree are Sharon Creizon and Wilma Filsinger. They both have an interest in some of the things we will be discussing. Now, let's see. Next are Daniel and Cathy Evaneto—he's a member of our church board, and Kathy is on the Sunday school council. On their left are Daniel and Marilyn Fleetwood, members at Cherry Pit, and then Flanders Morgan, who attends our church and is chair of our finance committee. Now, let's see, have I missed anyone? Oh, yes, Kathy Pfaff, and Barbara Noyes, from church, and Larry and Paula Becker. Ben Gladden plans on being here, but said that he'd be a few minutes late."

After introducing the rest of the guests, Juanita continued, "Well, I suppose that we should begin.

"As you all know, we all love our pastor. He's a great guy and has done a lot for Cherry Pit Community Church. But recently he's gotten involved in some unfortunate, things that are dividing our congregation. It's very unfortunate, because it means that some people are becoming increasingly uncomfortable with his leadership. Several of us thought we might spend a few minutes tonight talking about what we could do to help him."

"What kinds of things are you talking about, Juanita?" Kathy Pfaff asked. "Pastor Stan's sermons have been great lately. I think he is doing a very good job."

"It seems that lately Pastor Stan has become obsessed with death," Ben Gladden said from the doorway as he entered the room. "Hi, everyone. Sorry I'm late. I let myself in. I hope that was OK, Juanita."

"That's fine, Ben. I think that there's room for you over on the sofa by the window."

"What do you mean, obsessed with death?" Flanders Morgan asked as Ben settled himself in the large sofa.

"Just what I said." Ben's voice easily reached every corner of the large room. "The man is obsessed with death. First he attacks Brenda for sharing about Johnny, then he preaches the sermon he did last week. There have been other things, too. A lot of people feel that Stan's obsessing on this."

"How do the rest of you feel?" Juanita asked. She smiled at Brenda as she lowered herself into a graceful antique chair. "We all know the things we appreciate and admire about Pastor Adkins, so we don't need to spend a lot of time on that. Let's think about our concerns. There are probably other areas that he may have some blind spots. Remember, we want to help him. So what are the areas in which you feel that he might improve? I'll tell you what. I've got a whiteboard and some markers. Why don't we list these concerns so that we all can remember what we've said?" She stood in one fluid motion. "Kathy, would you mind being our secretary? I'll get the props."

For a long few moments there was nothing but silence. Several people shifted uncomfortably in their seats. Kathy Pfaff nervously nibbled on a cookie, and Daniel Fleetwood picked at a callus on his left hand.

"Maybe I can help you get started," Juanita continued. "Pastor Stan is a man of strong convictions. We all appreciate that. But at times he tends to dominate church council meetings. We're doing things much differently from when Perry Parker or Knapp Richardson was here. I wish that sometimes he'd just leave the running of the church to us and do what pastors are supposed to do."

"What are pastors supposed to do?" Larry Becker asked.

"We can go into the details later," Juanita answered, "but don't some of you feel that it might be better if we had more say in the direction the church was going?"

Two or three people nodded, and Juanita said, "Good. Kathy, write down 'Too dominant in church meetings.'"

"But don't we want him to be a strong leader?" Kathy asked even as she wrote on the board as directed. "Isn't that why we hired him? To lead us?"

"I know that I'm not a member of your church," Carol Widmer spoke up, "so I probably shouldn't say anything here. But isn't the role of the shepherd to nurture the flock, not dominate it? That's what my husband believes."

"Heaven help him if he should try to lead the flock to greener pastures or out of danger," Flanders Morgan said under his breath.

"Did you say something, Fletch?" Juanita asked, standing so she could clearly see him.

"No. Just thinking out loud."

My mother and I were talking the other day," Barbara Noyes said. "She mentioned that she wished the pastor would visit the older folks more. She remembers back when the church was smaller and the pastor would drop by every few weeks. She says many of the older people feel neglected. I know that Stan is trying to train some of the elders to do much of the visitation, but it's just not the same. I, personally, couldn't care less if he ever came to visit me. We stay so busy it's not necessary, but these older members are lonesome, and the pastor could drop by and read the Bible and pray with them. It would fill a void in their life."

"OK, Kathy. Why don't you put down 'Visit more'? Now, are there others?"

Marilyn Fleetwood tentatively raised her hand.

"Yes, Marilyn?"

"There are some people who feel that the pastor's sermons are too long," she said quietly. "We need to get out on time. Twelve o'clock is the time church is supposed to be over, and it seems that the services are always going till 12:15. There have even been a few times we didn't get out the door until 12:30. We have more things to do than just go to church, and it makes it very difficult if we are always going over."

"H'mm. Services too long. Bad time management. Kathy, write that on the board for us, will you, please?"

"I'm a little uncomfortable with that," Kathy said. "Are we in church to worship the clock, or the Lord? What does it matter what time we get out?"

"You may not have anything else to do," Marilyn sniffed, "but we do. As a family we like to get out in the afternoon and do things, so it matters to us."

"And there are little children and diabetics to think about," Sharon Creizon spoke up. "They need to eat right on schedule. It's not being fair to them to go overtime."

"I'm not so sure," Kathy responded, looking first at Sharon, then Juanita. "I have more kids than any of you do, and it's not a particular issue for any of them. On other days of the week they get involved in all kinds of things and come late to dinner. If their favorite TV program is on, you have to pry them away to get them to the table."

"Are you likening church to TV?" Marilyn asked.

"No, but we should be realistic here. Why is mealtime such an issue on Sunday morning and not on Saturday, when college football is on? Just try to get your husband to the dinner table during a Georgia Tech game and see how important the food is. I think that it's all relative and can't see why it's such a big deal on Sunday."

"Thank you, Kathy," Juanita told her. "Your input is important on this. Now, are there other areas of concern?"

"How about the sermons themselves?" Ben Gladden spoke up. "I thought we were here to discuss Pastor Adkins' strange obsession with what happens to you when you die. Why are we talking about all of this other stuff when he is deliberately dividing the church with all of this talk about death?"

"Thank you, Ben," Juanita said. "Kathy, please write 'Divisive sermons' on the board. Now, are there others?"

"Not so fast, Juanita," Ben retorted. "I want to discuss this some more. It's the important issue we're here to discuss tonight. How do the rest of you feel? Does it bother you that Pastor Adkins has publicly attacked one of our members, a widow who is grieving over the loss of her husband?"

"You know, Ben, we can discuss the details of some of these things later," Juanita said. "Right now, are there other things anyone would like to mention? Again, our purpose here tonight is not to attack Pastor Adkins, but to look carefully at those areas in which there may be deficiencies, and to make suggestions. You know, everyone has strengths. We know our pastor's and appreciate them, but we are also interested in progress. And we can't help him and our church progress unless we deal with some of his areas of weakness.

"Wilma," Juanita said, "you mentioned something to me today that I imagine the rest of the group would enjoy hearing about."

"Juanita, could I trouble you for a glass of water?" Ben interrupted. He coughed. "I've got a tickle in my throat that just won't go away."

"Sure, Ben, I'll get you one."

"I'll go with you. That way I can get a second one if I need it."

"We'll be right back," Juanita said to the group. "While we're gone, why don't you get refills on the coffee? Oh, and the cookies are an old family favorite."

"What on earth is going on?" Ben whispered angrily, turning on Juanita when they were in the kitchen. "I thought we were going to get people together and stop this guy from attacking us. You should have heard little Patty tonight before I came. She was crying and begging me to stop him. She said that it hurt her so to listen to our church service and know what he is doing. She even said that Jesus is really disappointed that we are letting this go on and that we must do something before it's too late and more people start believing the way he does. Already most of the church feels that Brenda is nuts, and who knows what they'd think if they knew about you and Luke and Patty and me. I think that it's time to stop Mickey Mousing around and get this over with, Juanita. Now!"

"You old fool!" Juanita snapped. "You think that you can just go in there and say that Pastor Adkins is wrong about what he thinks happens when you die and that people will vote to dismiss him, just like that. It doesn't work that way, Ben. It's going to take a lot more than this issue to get rid of Pastor Adkins. Most people in our church love him in spite of whatever faults he has. The only way we stand a chance of accomplishing our goals is to have a reason for everyone to want him to go. Those reasons will be different for every member of the church. Everyone has their hot button. If we can discover what they are, and together furnish a good-enough list for the church members to choose from, we stand a chance. In the meantime, we put Pastor Adkins on the defensive. Now, Ben, get out there and act as if you're into this. Don't act as though you're out to get the pastor. Nothing will doom our efforts faster than for this to look like a lynch mob. We're out to help him because we love him, remember?"

"Well, how are the cookies?" Juanita chirped as she walked into the living room. "They're Luke's favorites—I mean, they were. Now, where were we?"

Chapter 21

I see you two picked up a hitchhiker," Stan Adkins laughed easily as he reached out to shake Gus's hand. "You know these folks, Francis?"

"We're old friends," Francis said. "When they saw this poor, emaciated, starving old man stumbling down the road, they couldn't resist, and invited me along. You've never eaten Dolores's cooking, so you don't know what you're missing, but I have and I wouldn't miss it for anything. Is this your family?"

"Yes, Barb, boys, this is Mr. and Mrs. Crossworthy. They visited our church today, and this is Mr. Francis Baldwin, who owns the nursery just down the road. And, everyone, this is my family—my wife, Barbara, and my two sons, Danny and David."

"Your father tells me that you're quite the eaters," Gus said. "You like fried chicken?"

"Yes, sir," both boys said in unison.

"Well, we have a cook named Dolores who makes the best fried chicken in all the South. They say that Colonel Sanders did everything he could to get her recipe, and when he couldn't get it out of her, he settled for second best. And we've also got potato salad worth dying for, homemade rolls, and pecan pie for dessert. Think you can handle it?"

The boys grinned.

"Now, you boys go over to the picnic basket there and pick out a soda for you and your folks, and we'll say grace and commence to eat. Francis, why don't you join the pastor and his wife on that side of the table, and we'll put these two whippersnappers over here with Millie and me, close to most of the food."

Later, while Millie and Barbara cleared the table and cut the pie, Gus wiped his mouth with a napkin and said, "Stan, tell me, what do you know about witchcraft?"

Stan choked on a final bite of chicken, and Francis laughed. "You're going to have to get used to Gus, Stan. He's pretty direct."

"I'm sorry, I guess I could have segued into that a little more delicately," Gus said, blushing slightly. "Why don't I start over? Stan, I was intrigued by some things you said in your sermon today and I—"

"It's OK, Gus," Stan interrupted. "I shouldn't have been startled. It's just that the other day I got a letter from someone, who claimed to be a witch. It was pretty threatening, and you caught me off guard."

"Do you believe in them?" Gus asked.

"Do you mean, do I believe that there are such things as real witches?" Stan asked.

"Yes, you know, people who go around casting spells and doing hocus-pocus and that sort of thing."

Stan nodded. "Yes, I do. The last I heard there were more than a million people in the United States who claimed to be witches or their male counterparts. That doesn't count the people who are part of the Church of Satan or other occult organizations. It's a big deal nowadays."

"But do you believe that they have the power to really do all of the things they claim to be able to do?" Millie asked, looking up from cutting a piece of pie. "It all sounds so spooky! I remember at Halloween we used to dress up like witches and pretend we were riding brooms, but we never believed that there was really anything to it. It doesn't work, does it?"

"You're really putting me on the spot, aren't you?" Stan said with a grin. "But since you asked, I'm going to tell you. First, though, why the interest in witchcraft?"

"Our only daughter has just told us that she's a witch," Gus said slowly, watching Stan for his reaction. "As you can imagine, it has taken us somewhat by surprise. We asked our pastor about it, and he said that it was great and that we should join her. We told him that that was out of the question, and he told us that we might as well leave and go to Cherry Pit Community Church, because they were so stubborn out here they'd never have anything to do with it. So here we are. Now, tell us what you know about witchcraft."

"What do you know already?"

"We know that witches have been around almost since the world began," Gus began.

"And we know that the Bible forbids having anything to do with them," Millie went on, "which really confuses us, because of all the churches and Christians that have Halloween parties. We're really confused."

"With good reason," Stan said. "It's not terribly consistent, is it?"

"No, it's not!" Gus said, "and I'm mad as—well, uh, sorry, Reverend. We need you to explain all of this. Oh, and what's this about a threatening letter?"

"It's really odd," Stan went on. "Say, boys, I tossed a Frisbee in the trunk before we left. Why don't you guys set up a Frisbee golf course and get in a practice round? We'll be there in a few minutes."

"C'mon, Dad, can't we stay? We're old enough to hear. Please? Besides, we'll miss out on the pie."

"You heard me, guys. I'll bet Mrs. Crossworthy will bring you your pie in a minute."

When they were gone, Stan turned and said, "I'll tell you about the letter later. It was just kind of a coincidence that you asked me what you did when you did, but it explains a lot.

"The Bible says that there are two opposing forces squared off in this world. They are in an all-out war that affects and involves every one of us whether we want to be or not. On one side is God, who has the power to create matter out of energy just by speaking, and who created everything that now exists in the whole extent of space. On the other side is another being, originally created by God, one who is so unbelievably powerful that there have never been human words to describe him adequately. At one time he was the chief angel in all of heaven; and when he chose to rebel, a third of all of the angels of heaven chose to follow him."

"You know, that has always boggled my mind," Francis said. "The devil must have had some ego to believe that he could challenge God and get away with it."

"As I said, he was so persuasive that he convinced a third of the angels to follow him. When war ensued, the devil and the angels that sided with him were thrown out of heaven."

"Where does it say that?" Millie asked. "I've never heard that."

"I found it the other day in Revelation 12," Gus said. "Go on, Stan."

"I don't think that any of us have any idea of what that war must have been like. Imagine beings that have the power to travel through space, who can appear or disappear at will, who have physical strength and resources we can only imagine, and you begin to get an idea.

"Anyway, when the devil—or Lucifer, as he was then called—was thrown out of heaven, he came to this earth. As Gus said, that's found in Revelation 12.[1] Apparently either Creation was in process or the world had been created just a short time before. Satan hadn't learned his lesson, so he decided to take God on again and try to take this world away from Him."

"If God is so all-powerful, why didn't He just destroy him?" Gus questioned. "It seems to me it would have saved us all a lot of grief, and God too, if you ask me."

"At first glance I'd probably agree with you," Stan answered. "But if you think about it, it would have been a bad decision. The Bible says that God's kingdom is based on love, not force. Because love is its foundation and its very essence, God gave every human He ever created the power of choice, the right to choose, and that means that we even have the option of making wrong choices. Take away that freedom to choose, and you knock out the foundation out of the government of the whole universe."

"That still doesn't . . ." Gus began.

"Let me finish, and I think it will be clear," Stan said.

"The second thing is that God has never forced anyone to love or serve Him. He only courts us and tries to win our love. He doesn't want to be served because we fear Him, as powerful as He is, but because we genuinely want to please Him. If He had destroyed Satan right off, the rest of the angels and all thinking beings would have served Him out of fear. So He gave Lucifer the opportunity to have his day in the sun. He had access to this world, and I would imagine all the others, and the right to try to persuade unfallen beings to choose his kingdom instead of God's."

"What a risk," Millie said, realizing for the first time something of the enormity of the situation. "What would have happened if they had all rebelled?"

"I would imagine just what did happen," Stan answered.

"Up until then, apparently, no one had ever seen sin or imagined rebellion. Now God had to let it run its course and allow everyone the right to choose between His kingdom and Satan's. Unfortunately, Adam and Eve, the first created humans on this planet, chose to join the third of the angels that had rebelled against God. Lucifer made disobedience appear attractive. He said that sin and rebellion were great and that God was trying to keep them from something they would really miss out on if they didn't experience it. They bought his line and chose to rebel, and sold the whole human race into slavery. Satan became, in the words of the Bible, the ruler of this world.[2] He could even go back to heaven, the book of Job tells us, as the rightful sovereign of our planet, chosen by us, and represent us in universe council meetings.[3]

"You mean Satan could just march into heaven and thumb his nose at God?" Gus cocked his head skeptically.

"God is so fair," Stan said, "that when we chose Satan as our sovereign, He honored our choice—even to letting the rebel commander back inside the city to represent us.[4] But God also had an answer to Satan's rebellion.

"From the very beginning the devil chose deception and trickery as the medium for promoting his way. On the other hand, when man sinned, God did something that dumbfounded even Satan. He offered all of us a complete amnesty, and based it on His willingness to die the death that was the natural consequence of rebellion. He would die in our place. In return, humans were given the opportunity, once again, to have the right to choose. We were no longer slaves. Slaves can't choose. Jesus died on the cross to free every person who ever lived on this earth. Pick the worst individual you can imagine, and that person was free to choose because of Jesus. In addition, God sent man constant warning of the natural consequences of rebellion.

"The Scriptures teach us that God sustains the whole universe. It's interesting—I was reading a book on physics the other day by a Nobel laureate who makes no pretense of being a believer. He talked about mysterious forces the scientific world is trying to discover that hold the universe together. Some scientists call it the 'God particle.' If they only knew! Anyway, I got sidetracked there for a minute. Apart from God, the universe self-destructs, just as a supernova implodes and explodes back into energy. The day is coming, God says, when He will no longer sustain sin and sinners. Everyone will have had a chance to make a decision, and God will just withdraw His support from them. At that point anything associated with sin will self-destruct in what the Bible describes as fire and brimstone—probably the best illustration the Bible writers could come up with for nuclear fission."

"Man, I'd never thought of it that way," Francis said quietly. "It makes sense."

"Back to your original question," Stan continued. "Apparently there was a time Satan also had the offer of amnesty—which he refused. He somehow believed he could win his insane war with God. Ever since, we have been involved in a battle over the soul of every human being born on this world. God's enemy has used all kinds of ruses to suck people into choosing him over God. One of them is what we today call the New Age movement. Another is the worship of nature and natural things, such as the sun or moon. Then there is witchcraft.

"The natural desire of the sinful heart is for power over our environment and over others. Witchcraft, with its spells and its mysterious powers and ceremonies, appeals to that side of human nature."

"But does it really work?" Millie asked. "Isn't it just hocus-pocus to frighten people?"

"History doesn't tell us that, Millie," Stan said, reaching for a napkin. "Witches are able to use the power of their master and his demonic angels just as we are able to claim the protection and power of God's angels and the Holy Spirit. Just as in Ephesians 6 God offers us armor and weapons to protect us, and to use in our warfare, so Satan's followers also have tremendous power. Anyone with any sense respects it." He shook his head. "I guess that was a long answer to a short question. Sorry about rattling on like that."

"Not at all," Gus said. "When you said you respect the power of witchcraft, what did you mean?"

"I meant that I am very respectful of the water moccasins down in McClellan Creek, even though I don't like them and might kill them if I had the chance. The same goes for witches and other practitioners of satanic power. I don't want to kill them—I'm not saying that—but I do respect their power and would have good cause to be afraid of them if it weren't for the power of God to protect me."

"What about the letter?" Francis asked. "If these guys are as powerful as you say they are, aren't you worried?"

"Concerned, yes. Worried, no, I don't think so. I guess it helps to know that you're on the winning side. Every war has casualties, and who knows which of us may be one in this battle. But I know that ultimately I am going to live forever with Jesus. That's what counts, isn't it?

"The real tragedy is that many on the other side don't realize that they're losers. The Bible says that at the very end of things, all those on both sides who have ever lived will live again. The followers of God will be inside the capital city of the universe, which God will have brought to this earth. Satan and his followers will be surrounding it. Satan convinces them one last time that they can take the city and rule the cosmos forever. It is at that point, when they are beginning their attack, that God will finally confront everyone with the consequences of his or her choice. How sad it will be for them when they discover that all of their dreams are nothing but smoke and mirrors. I feel profoundly sorry for them!"

"What can we do for people like that?" Millie asked. "I'm talking about people such as our daughter. She's so far into this that I don't know if there's any hope for her."

"Well," Stan said, "God won't force her, and neither can you. All you can do is pray for her and expose her to the light."

"What do you mean?" Francis asked.

"There's only one way to get rid of darkness," Stan said. "You can't gather it up and haul it away. You can't demand that it leave. The only thing you can do is to . . ."

"Turn on the light," two voices said in unison from behind Stan.

"We've heard that illustration before, Dad," David said.

"Hey, what are you guys doing here?" Barbara asked. "I thought your dad told you to play some Frisbee."

"Mom, we did," Danny said. "We played 18 holes and decided that Dad should be about ready to take up the offering over here."

Stan made a playful lunge for the boys, who dodged behind the cherry tree. "Are the ants going to get that pie, or do we get some?" The boys peeked mischievously from behind the tree.

"Coming right up," Millie said. "You guys have been very patient! When we're finished with the pie, I'll bet these three old geezers don't stand a chance against you guys in a golf tournament. Whoever wins gets to split the last piece of pie."

A couple hours later they all carried the picnic baskets across the road to Gus and Millie's car. Francis turned and said, "Stan, you still didn't tell us about that letter. What did it say, anyway?"

"Well, basically it said that I was getting in the way out here. That I was teaching things that would have serious consequences for me and for others that I love and care for if I continued. It also said that there would be people coming to my church who were concerned about some of the things we have been talking about this afternoon. It said that I was not to confuse them or tell them things that weren't true about the subject of witchcraft."

Gus stopped in the drive and turned slowly to face Stan. "Was it signed?" he asked.

"Yes, and no. It closed with the stylized drawing of a goat's head."

---

[1] Revelation 12:13.
[2] John 14:30; 12:31; 1 John 5:19.
[3] Job 1.
[4] Job 1:6; 2:1.

Chapter 22

Oh, no!" Cindy yelled. "I can't believe it!"

It was 5:15 in the afternoon, and the button had just popped off the waistband of the jeans she'd been buttoning. And that wasn't all. First her curling iron had quit working, and she had to run down to Sarah Jenkins' apartment to borrow hers. Then a club manager called, just to ask some silly questions about her repertoire, and he talked for more than a half hour. Now the button on her only clean pair of jeans was off. And knowing Steve, he'd probably come early.

I can't believe it, she thought. *I'm going to a party at a church with the leader of the youth group. I wonder what the people down at the club would think of that.* She smiled to herself. *Grandma T would be delighted.* And Steve wasn't that bad looking. Oh well, it sure beat sitting at home with that lousy candle or in the lunchroom at Kroger's.

Grabbing a needle and thread from the box of sewing supplies she kept in the guest closet, she sat on the bed and tried to sew quickly. Tying the final knot in the thread, she yanked on her jeans and ran for the bathroom to run a brush through her hair, freshen up her perfume, and put the final touches on her makeup. She grabbed a leather coat from the closet and was just walking into the living room when the doorbell rang. She bent to blow out the candle burning on the dining room table, then went to open the door.

"Man, don't you look nice," Steve looked appreciatively as the door opened. "Those uniforms down at the store don't do you justice, Miss Marshall."

"Why, thank you, Mr. Heinrich. Aren't we being formal tonight. You don't look the same as you usually do, swathed in a produce apron, either. Is the vegetable truck ready to go?" she asked, a mischievous grin on her face.

"Loaded with pumpkins and ready for Cinderella. Got your glass slippers on?" Steve answered. "Oh, and I was downtown earlier and passed Godiva's chocolates. I couldn't resist bringing you some."

"Wow. Thank you, Steve." Cindy took the box. "That was very thoughtful of you. How did you know I had a weakness for chocolate? This is some of the best."

"The wrappers you leave on the table every day at lunch."

"Oh," she laughed, "so you've been spying on me. That can get you in trouble. Spying calls for counterspying, you know."

"All right, I give," Steve laughed, throwing up his hands in mock surrender. "So, are we ready to go?"

"Just as soon as I turn out the light."

"How about the candle?"

"Oh, is it burning?" Cindy blushed. "I guess I forgot that I lit it." Stooping briefly, she blew it out again, and followed Steve to the door.

"So, what's it really like to fly?" Cindy asked as they traveled across town. "When I was little, I used to dream that I could step out my window and fly over the neighborhood like Mary Poppins. It was so fantastic looking down on the little houses below me and imagining what was going on in each one."

"You've never flown?" Steve asked.

"I have commercially. But I'm talking about being in your own plane and going where you want to go, seeing what you want to see, zooming down close, then soaring up into the clouds."

"You want to go sometime? I'll take you flying as you've never flown before. I didn't tell you, but I'm also a sailplane pilot. Got my own glider, a two-seater. If you really want to feel like Mary Poppins, that's the way to fly."

"You mean a plane with no engines?"

"Yes. You're towed up with a special plane, then turned loose to glide. If the weather conditions are right, you can soar for hours.

"I flew with an eagle one time. He was soaring up by the Palisades, and I slipped into the airstream right beside him. He just looked over at me as if I were another bird and kept going. We flew together for more than an hour. You can't imagine! We even got to chasing each other for a few minutes. It was so incredible, Cindy."

She shook her head. "You make it sound pretty exciting, but isn't it dangerous to be up there without an engine?"

"No, it's actually much, much safer than driving a car. There's always someplace to land if you need to. You want to go up with me next weekend if the weather's right?"

She leaned back and scrunched up her nose, pretending to ponder for about 10 seconds, then said, "Sure. What time?"

"You get your best lift after noon," Steve said. "I'll need an hour or so to get the plane ready, so how about 2:00 Sunday afternoon?"

"I'll tell you what," Cindy said. "You come over a little early, and I'll have lunch ready."

"That'd be great," Steve smiled. "It's a date. I'll pick you up right after church, and we can go out to that little park at the end of Cherry Pit Road. Ever been there?"

"Can't say that I have."

"It's one of the oldest parks in the state and one of the prettiest. Norton Hogsworth donated the land to the county in honor of his little girl and all of the Cherokee Indians who died in a smallpox epidemic in the 1800s. He said he knew that this country was going to grow up and develop someday, and he wanted to have some memory of his little girl and her friends. It seems that the Indians had rescued her from drowning when she was little and wandered off from home. So when they all died, Norton Hogsworth didn't want people to forget."

"How do you know all this?"

"Oh, there used to be a marker telling all about it when I was a kid. Old Norton was my great-great-grandfather, and we used to have a big bash in the park every year. The reunions died out about 15 years ago when my uncle Bud, who planned them all, had to go into a nursing home. A few years later thieves stole the plaque, so not many people know about it anymore. I don't even think they call it Cindy Park any longer."

"Cindy Park! Are you kidding me?"

"No. That was the little girl's name. Just think, you've got a park with your name on it. Speaking of parks, there it is, and the church is just up around the corner."

"You sure it's OK for me to be here?" Cindy asked as they pulled into the drive leading up to the church. Now that she was on the church property she felt uncharacteristically shy. "Won't your friends think I'm intruding?"

"No, you'll be very welcome," Steve said as he parked the car. He'd pulled into a parking place near the door that led into the large fellowship hall on the side of the church. "These are a great bunch of people. You're going to enjoy yourself."

Cindy had never walked into a place that made her feel so instantly welcome and at ease. The fellowship hall of Cherry Pit Community Church had originally been built of logs. Years ago the outside had been shingled, but the inside had the warm ambience of a hunting lodge that had enjoyed decades of love and attention. The hardwood floors shone in the light, and the comfortable furniture made you want to curl up with a good book.

She saw about seven or eight men whom she judged to be in their 20s sitting in front of the fire that burned in the huge fireplace that was the focal point of the end wall. They were laughing at a story one of them was telling. Through the open door of the kitchen, just across from the room's entrance, she saw nine or 10 young women working on a large platter of fresh veggies and dips. Behind them a tall guy was drizzling butter across heaped-up popcorn in the biggest stainless-steel bowl Cindy believed she'd ever seen in her life.

"Hey, guys," Steve called. "Chips are here!"

"Well, look who's here," someone shouted.

"I see you robbed the potato chip salesman of his outdated chips again," someone else said. "Hurray for a poor week of sales at the local A&P."

"All right, you guys, don't tell my secrets," Steve said, shaking his fist. "You're going to hurt my reputation for being a big spender on these evenings."

"Right. Like the rest of us," one of the girls, laughing, called from the kitchen.

"Hi, I'm Susy Kenyon," another of the young women said, walking across the room and extending her hand to Cindy. "I'll introduce myself, since Steve is so rude he won't do the introductions." She winked at Steve.

"Hey, give me a break." He tried to look hurt. "You haven't given me a chance. Everyone, this is Cindy Marshall, one of the checkers down at Kroger's. Cindy, let's see, where shall I start? You've met Susy. Then there's Dee Henderson, formerly Dee Jacobson. Her husband, Gary, is the one who's carrying the popcorn bowl that's bigger than he is."

"Hi," Gary said, looking over the huge bowl.

"Gary and Dee have been married for only about a month. This group is supposed to be just for singles, but they've been a part of us for so long, we can't bear to let them depart."

"Hear! Hear!" several of the guys said, raising their cans of pop.

"Let's see. Who else?" Steve went on. "The redhead by the sink is Lana Erickson."

"Hi," Lana smiled.

"Next to her are Lori Austin and Kay Jacobs. Then there's Terry Friberg and Margie Lunstrom. The girl opening the can of olives is Lee Friberg, Terry's twin sister, and over in the corner is Jennie Pippert, musician extraordinaire."

"Hello, Cindy," Jenny said. "Welcome to the asylum."

"Jenny!" Steve cleared his throat. "Please try to preserve some sort of positive impression here. I'm trying to impress this young lady."

"Then why'd you bring her here?" Lana asked.

"On with the introductions," Steve continued. "The men of this group, quickly, are—"

"Hey, wait a minute," one of the guys called. "This isn't right. Why so fast with us? When it's the girls, he takes his time. With us, it's 'Let's get this over quick.'"

"He's just afraid Cindy'll discover the quality of the other male company in the room," a tall blond man said, walking up to her and extending his hand. "Allow me to introduce myself." Before she could speak, he took her hand and, bowing deeply, lightly kissed it. "I'm Larry Kendig, eligible bachelor, maker of the world's greatest nachos, which you will have the privilege of sampling in a few minutes, and delighted to make your acquaintance."

He was greeted by a chorus of boos from the women and cheers from the men. Grinning, he stepped back.

After introducing the rest of the men, Steve asked, "Well, are we about ready to start? Who has the devotional tonight?"

Turning to Cindy, he explained, "We usually begin with someone sharing something spiritual; then we eat."

Later, after they were seated on the couches and easy chairs that they arranged in a big semicircle around the fireplace, Lori Austin stepped up in front of the fire. "This last week I did a lot of thinking about what I wanted to say," she began, "and I decided to spend a few minutes with one of my favorite texts—the last half of John 10:10. I'm using the King James Version, in which Jesus says, 'I am come that they might have life, and that they might have it more abundantly.'

"Most of you know that I wasn't raised a Christian. Fact is, I came from a pretty difficult home situation." She looked toward Cindy. "I've never told this to anyone here, and I apologize for laying such heavy stuff on you the first time you're with us, Cindy, but God put this on my heart to share tonight, and so I'm going to go ahead and do so. I hope that's OK."

Cindy nodded.

"I was badly abused as a child," she went on, her voice soft. "My mother died when I was 11. Afterward my father's social drinking escalated into his becoming an alcoholic. It took about a year, I guess. He eventually lost all reason, and, drunk most of the time, he decided to make his daughters his wives."

The room was dead quiet as Lori's friends waited in shock for her to continue.

"Eventually Dad began to bring other men home to sleep with us. In your worst nightmares you can't imagine how horrible life was then. It affected each of us differently. I was the youngest, and I didn't know how to resist. Sometimes I think that the worst of it all was being at school and trying to act as if I had a normal life—then going home to a living hell.

"By the time I was 14 I discovered that you could charge for what I was doing. I began making some pretty good money, so at least some parts of my life started looking up. I was able to buy clothes and the other things teenagers love, and"—she smiled grimly—"some of the flashiest men in town were paying attention to me.

"Anyway, about then the county's Family and Children's Services stepped in. I guess they finally figured out what was going on—or somebody told them. After a hearing, we were all taken away from my father and put in foster homes. For me it was like going from the proverbial frying pan into the fire.

"I thought that at last I was going to have a chance to change, and believe me, it was. Carrie Stanton was just the opposite of anything I'd ever experienced. My dad had no expectations of us, except what we could provide in his bed. Carrie Stanton believed that she had been placed on this earth to raise anyone in her sphere of influence to a higher standard. There was only one problem. You could never be good enough.

"Oh, I tried," Lori said, pacing now as she spoke. "I would have done anything to please her. I worked on my high school studies until I was getting straight A's, but she still criticized my grades. I read magazines and pretty much on my own I worked on how I dressed and walked, and even spoke, and eventually I was offered the opportunity to do some actual modeling and became fairly successful at it."

That's where I've seen her, Cindy thought. *Down at the Corell Agency in the folios. And in that* Seventeen *spread a few years ago that I so badly wanted to get.*

"No matter how nice I acted or how well I dressed, Mrs. Stanton always found something to criticize. At the dinner table she critiqued the way I held my fork and criticized my table manners. No boy I ever brought home was ever right for me. No friends were ever worthy. I would have done anything to feel that I could please her. I became obsessed with it and with success. I began to drive myself, but I never felt good enough. I never felt accepted just as I was, for me."

"I moved out of her house when I was 18 and got a job. At first I stayed with friends, then got a tiny apartment. Eventually the Student Aid

Department helped me get some scholarship money and loans so I could go to the community college. I worked like a slave in the evenings and went to school during the day, and two and a half years later I graduated with an associate business/marketing degree.

"My major professor was nice enough to put me in contact with a couple of different businesses looking for students, and I landed a job with one of them. I worked my tail off. I was determined to be the first—and best—in everything. I found myself a couple of nice business suits, on sale, and made sure I always looked a cut above the other women in the place.

"It wasn't too long before I started to get promotions. I made certain that I got my work in first and that every report was elegant and well presented. Eventually I got acquainted with the president at a corporation cocktail party, and before long, I became his mistress." He installed me in a penthouse apartment in one of the most exclusive buildings in Atlanta, gave me a Mercedes sports car, and anything else I ever wanted. As long as I was there when he wanted me, everything was mine. I was on a roll! With my new status I moved and partied in the highest levels of Peachtree society. I renewed my work in modeling and got some major contracts. In addition, I did some occasional work as a high-priced call girl and made obscene amounts of spending money."

Lori leaned against the stone surrounding the fireplace. "I'm not telling you all this to glorify what I was," she said, "but you've got to know it to appreciate what I'm going to tell you next. Even though I had everything—*everything*—that society tells us will make us happy, I wasn't! I was well paid. People looked up to me. Strangers even recognized me from seeing me in print, but I was miserable, and so was everyone in the crowd I ran with. On the outside we were living the good life, but once in a while the real person would peek through the veneer. We were all insecure; we were all lonely; and we were riddled with guilt. And all of the rationalization, all the therapy, all the denial in the world couldn't eradicate it."

Cindy shifted uncomfortably on the sofa. She'd traded a lonely evening at home with whatever it was that was haunting her house for what was supposed to be a relaxing evening, and now she realized that she was getting more than she'd bargained for and she wasn't certain how she felt about it. *Where is she going with all this?* she wondered. Lori's voice drew her back to her story.

"Most of us made very sure we didn't have much chance for reflection. We were either hung over, partying so hard we were exhausted, or had the TV or iPod going nonstop—anything to keep us from having to think. But when, occasionally, we did reflect on our lives, none of us liked what we saw, so we'd crank up the noise again.

"I guess I would have gone on forever, until I was some broken-down strung-out wreck, if it hadn't been for an airline pilot I met in Portland, Oregon. I'd flown out there to shoot an ad campaign for an area swimsuit manufacturer. They were planning to run it in the *Sports Illustrated* swimsuit edition, and it figured to be a real break for me.

"The pilot was a good-looking guy, and I flirted with him a little on my way out of the plane. I stopped to buy a magazine down the concourse, and he showed up in the same shop to buy some gum. We got to talking, and when I mentioned that I was going to get a cup of coffee, he asked if he could join me. Of course, I said yes.

"We talked for a while, small talk; then he got serious. He said that he'd been impressed to talk to me. When he asked me what I did for a living, I figured it was a come-on. So I told him about my sideline and made sure he knew I was available, but for a price."

"'You happy?' he asked.

"'Sure,' I said.

"'No, really,' he came back. 'Are you really happy?'

"That really blew me away. I couldn't lie. I didn't know why at the time. I think I do now, but at the time I didn't. But I just couldn't lie to this guy. This may seem weird, and I don't know if I could have put it into words then, but now I realize that it was like he saw right past all my phony, glamorous, confident exterior, and he looked right down into my soul and saw me for what I really was."

"'No,' I told him. 'I'm miserable.'

"'I thought so,' he said. 'Would you like to be happy, truly happy?'"

"At first I figured it was a proposition from a man who thought I'd be an easy night's fun in a strange town, but there was something weird about the look on his face. It was too serious. 'Who wouldn't want to be happy?' I said, 'but I don't think it's possible. This world's a pretty crummy place, and I think you've got to grab what you can out of it and get off before the merry-go-round starts to wind down.'"

"'I used to feel the same way,' he said, 'until I met someone who changed my life forever. I had it made, just like you. Between my flying and some investments I'd made I was turning several hundred thousand a year. I partied a lot and ran with a pretty racy crowd. Oh, there was a price,' he told me. 'I lost the best wife any man could hope for,' he said. 'My kids hated me because I was never there. And when I was home, I still wasn't there for them. I endangered the lives of my passengers more than once because I was so strung out from the night before that I had no business flying. But I thought I was happy.

"'Then one night, a flight mechanic, of all people, introduced me to Jesus Christ.'

"'Oh, brother,' I said, 'I'm outta here.' And I got up to leave.

"'Wait a second!' He gently laid his hand on my arm and stopped me. 'Please wait and hear what I have to say.' So I did—reluctantly. I sat down again and listened." Lori's smile took in the whole room. "Boy, am I glad I did!"

"'You say that you're happy,' he went on. 'And it's true that the life you're living brings a certain amount of fun on the surface, in the short term, but then it all turns to ashes. You as much as said so yourself.'

"He'd nailed me pretty accurately, so I kept listening.

"'You wake up one morning and discover that all the stuff you've been doing and all the things you've been chasing have changed. You feel as though an evil genie from some sinister bottle has made you its slave. You're revolted by it, right?' he asked me. 'And you want to throw up at what you've become. I know, Lori,' he said, 'because I've been there. You feel dirty and cheap, and there's nothing you can do about it, so you go out and do it again, and again, and again. You serve the genie. And it tightens its chains on you, and keeps ratcheting them down tighter and tighter, until it seems that the good life is going to suffocate you. And it will, if you let it.'

"I just sat there with my mouth open. It was like this guy had been watching my life on YouTube.

"And then he began to tell me about Jesus. He read the text that I gave you at the beginning. He had this little pocket Bible, and he read, 'I am come to give you life, and to give it to you abundantly.' And right there in that coffee shop, with flights being called and people swirling by, I discovered what I'd been longing for my entire life. I discovered that true life is a Person, not some activity or new way to entertain myself or even a church or a set of beliefs. Jesus was real, and He cared about *me*. And when I bowed my head and prayed what was probably the simplest prayer ever prayed, all of my sordid past was completely washed away. For the first time since I had been born, I felt clean and brand-new."

Someone handed Lori a tissue, and she wiped her eyes. "You know how the Bible says that when we're in Jesus we are new people? For me, it was instantly true. I can't explain it, but I felt like an 11-year-old virgin all over again. Unsoiled. Unhurt. Clean. *Restored.* All my compulsion to excel, to prove somehow that I was somebody, was wiped away, and in that moment I knew that I was somebody already.

"I discovered that I was valuable because I was a daughter of the King of the universe. I was forgiven, and I was loved—not for my performance, or my looks, or for the pleasure I could give someone, but just because I was who I was. And because Jesus loved me unconditionally the prisoner I had been most of my life was set free. It was as if suddenly the painful chains dropped off, and I was ushered out of some dark cell and into the light. I know it doesn't happen like this for everyone, but for me it was that dramatic. I was no longer a slave to my past or my passions or my obsessions. I was free at last to be me."

By now tears were streaming down her face. Dee Henderson stepped up and held her in her arms. Wiping away the tears, Lori straightened and said, "Captain Henley and I talked for a few more minutes. He gave me his Bible and quickly told me how to start studying it. Then he was paged and had to get back for his return flight."

"What did you do then? Terry asked.

"You know how dark and dismal Portland can be. Well, I walked out of the terminal to get a taxi to go to my hotel, and the sky was spectacular. It was summer, and it had just rained. The sun was shining, and a million raindrops glistened on the trees and grass and even in the air. It was as though the whole world had been washed when I prayed, and I felt through the sunlight that I saw God smiling at me. I wanted to dance down the sidewalk and sing and spin and laugh and cry all at the same time. I've never experienced anything like it in my life.

"I realized that I couldn't go to the photo shoot. You know what the swimsuits are like these days, at least the ones this company makes. It's almost like wearing nothing at all. So I called them up and canceled."

"You canceled!" Cindy exclaimed before she realized she'd spoken. "Gene Bridger would kill me if I tried that."

"You know Gene?" Lori asked. "He was my agent with Corell. He yelled so loud I thought the phone would explode in my hand. I just couldn't do it. It wasn't me anymore.

"Gene threatened my career—I told him I didn't care, I was done anyway. He threatened my life. I told him he wasn't brave enough to try to kill me. He even threatened to sue me, and I told him he was welcome to if he wanted, but I wasn't changing my mind. In the end he just swore and hung up on me.

"I took an early-morning flight back to Atlanta and went up to my apartment to get my things." She shook her head. "Walking into the penthouse felt like stepping into a sewer. I couldn't wait to get out. I cobbled together a few essentials and left. The doorman had always been nice to me, so I handed him my key and told him that anything I'd left in the place that he wanted was his. He didn't believe me, so I grabbed the concierge, wrote it out on paper, had him witness it, and gave it to the doorman. Later I heard he had had the classiest yard sale Atlanta had probably ever seen.

"I drove downtown, walked into my office building, found the personnel manager, and resigned. I couldn't wait to get out of there. I went up to the president's office, set the keys to the Mercedes on the secretary's desk, wrote a short note telling him goodbye and that, no, I would not be writing a book. I took the elevator to the basement parking garage, got my other car out of storage, and drove out into the sunlight. Next I stopped off at my pimp's place, tossed him my beeper, and left. I didn't wait around to hear the creative language he probably used to express his feelings. I then went on down to Corell, resigned, and drove out of town. Oh, it was wonderful!

"As I was leaving Atlanta I reached into the glove compartment, pulled out a map of Tennessee, set it on the seat, and—without even look-ing—pointed at the map. That's how I came to town. I took the first job I could find, in a factory, building furniture. I've loved every minute of it.

"One day one of you here tonight invited me come to Cherry Pit Church, and I guess, as they say, the rest is history."

Chapter 23

"Pastor, this is Cheryl Fratanelli."

"Good morning, Cheryl," Stan said as he cradled the phone against his shoulder and finished slipping the notes for his next sermon into a file. "How are you?"

"Fine, Stan, except that I wanted to find out how you're doing. You looked awfully tired last week when I saw you downtown. Are you all right?"

"Yes, I guess so."

"Is this stuff starting to get to you, Stan?"

"I'd like to think not, but it probably is, Cheryl. It's gotten quite a bit worse since we talked that day in church."

"Yes, I know. I've been watching what's happening in church, and I see the agitation in Satan's angels. He must really be lashing them hard to get them as upset as they are."

"I guess I don't mind for myself, but I worry some about my family. I'm afraid that this is going to start affecting them more than it has. I've been trying not to carry it home with me, but they're picking up that there are problems, and it's getting hard on them."

"Have you talked with Brenda Barnes lately, Stan? How is she doing?"

"I really don't know. A few days ago she called, wanting some re-sources I had put together on what happens to you when you die. That's the last I've heard from her. You need to be praying for her, Cheryl. I think that she sincerely wants to do what's right in this thing. She's just been suckered by the devil and can't conceive that the person she's seeing every night isn't Johnny. Even her kids have tried to talk her out of it, but from what I hear, she's pretty adamant about it with them."

"There are others, you know, Stan."

"How do you know, Cheryl?" he asked. "And who are they?"

"I probably shouldn't say how I know right now, Stan, but there are at least two or three other powerful people in the church who are very sympathetic with Brenda on this issue. From what I've heard, they're very upset with what you've been teaching lately. It may even come down to an attempt to get you fired."

"I was afraid of that. How many are there?"

"Not that many right now, but they're working quietly to develop a groundswell against you. And they're being very Machiavellian about it. I probably shouldn't say more at this time, but Stan, be very careful around Juanita Parris, Arch Emmons, and Ben Gladden. Almost nobody in the church is aware of it, but they're all involved in much the same thing as Brenda. Ben often sees his little daughter, Patty; Juanita has lunch almost every day with Luke; and Arch consults the ghost of an old Indian chief who supposedly lived and died on his property in the early 1600s."

"What can they do to me, Cheryl?"

"Well, as I understand it, they're trying to stir up dissatisfaction any way they can. I don't know all of the details, but I have friends that are keeping me informed of what's happening. They say it's not pretty, but it's so subtle that it's hard, at this point, to pinpoint exactly what it is they intend to do."

"I surely appreciate your letting me know what's going on. It means an awful lot to me." He leaned back in his chair and sighed.

"Pastor, most of us around here love you and appreciate your ministry," she reminded him. "You were brought here for a reason, and God's going to protect you. He loves you more than any of us can, and He has promised to go to bat for you when you're attacked like this. I've been thinking," she continued. "Remember when Paul—then he was still called Saul—was traveling to Damascus persecuting God's people and God met him on the road?"

"Of course."

"Well, I'm not telling you anything you don't know, but remember that Jesus said to him, 'Saul, why are you persecuting Me?' You see, Saul thought he was persecuting people who were following Jesus, but God told him, in essence, that if you're persecuting My people, in reality you're abusing Me. Stan, it's one thing for the devil and his followers to persecute you and me. We both know we wouldn't stand a chance against him. But it's something else for him to take on God." She paused. "How long has it been since you've read the book of Psalms?"

"You mean straight through?"

"Yes, one after the other."

"Oh, maybe three years. The last time I read the Bible through."

"Has it ever struck you that Psalms 3–40 have a common theme? It did me, just the other day. In virtually every one of them David says, 'Lord, I'm surrounded by my enemies. From every human standpoint it looks as if I'm going to die and lose my kingdom. Everything I've dreamed of and believed in is lost.' But then David turns around and in every one of those psalms he says, 'But even though it looks as if the ship is sinking and all hands will be lost, my hope is in the Lord. The Lord will take care of me. He will fight my enemies. He is the rock of my salvation, my shield, my fortress, the maintainer of my right.' And then he closes with praise to God as if it's already an accomplished fact."

"I'd almost forgotten that, Cheryl."

"Well, things may look pretty bleak to you right now. I know that people are talking and that you're under a lot of pressure. But just remember that they're fighting God, not you. He will triumph, and you will come out of this a winner in His strength."

"Thank you, Cheryl," Stan said quietly. "I really needed the encouragement. Not only do I have the situation with Brenda, but"—he hesitated—"I'm being threatened by someone who claims to be a witch."

"Then she probably is, Stan. There's a whole coven of them here in town. Even a pastor's wife, from what I understand, is involved. I'd imagine that you're going to get some pressure from them, too. They're all connected."

"How so?" He sounded puzzled.

"All of these occult groups are different manifestations of the same power, Stan. Whether it's witchcraft or New Age or satanism, one of the nature religions, spiritism, one of the occult branches of psychotherapy, or one of the forms of Eastern religion that are inundating the Western world, they're all manifestations of the same satanic plan. They're all connected like the tendrils of some huge fungus that's infiltrating our whole society. They serve the same master, they network with each other, and they meet often in seminars and occult fairs and do what they can to support each other."

"Where have I heard that before?" Stan wondered. "Every time I turn around I'm hearing the same story lately."

"If you're being harassed like this it's because the devil realizes the power of what you've been teaching, Stan, and his followers are not about to lose ground on this one. They're going to do all they can to intimidate you and frighten you and, if you keep on, destroy you. But don't give up. You're on the right track, and God will take care of you. I know. Remember, I've been there. I've seen how the power of prayer hampers the devil's ability to work. I've had my hands tied—almost literally at times—by praying Christians who took hold of the power of God in prayer. I've seen them intervene through intercessory prayer in the warfare between God and Satan, and I've seen Satan's angels so frustrated in losing one of their subjects that they almost lost control."

"I've never heard prayer explained in quite that way before, Cheryl," Stan said. "It makes it seem like more than just a ritual we go through before we eat our breakfast."

"Stan! Prayer frees God to work in ways that He couldn't otherwise. I don't understand this very well, but it's as if there are limits on God and Satan. I heard a preacher one time liken it to the Geneva convention, which has defined the rules of warfare in our modern world.

"As I understand it, the issue in the battle between God and Satan is the character and fairness of God. According to Paul, Satan is the god, the ruler, of this world. In order to be able to limit him, God apparently has also had to limit Himself. Otherwise the devil could rightly charge that God isn't fair. Prayer apparently opens the door for either of them to use power they couldn't otherwise use. In other words, when I pray to God, or when one of Satan's followers prays to him, it frees them to act in ways they otherwise could not. That's why prayer is so important and powerful in the life of a Christian. It is one major way we can cooperate with God in our battle against our common enemy.

"Several of us are making you and your ministry a matter of special prayer, Pastor Stan. We may not be able to do much more within the church to counteract what's happening, but we are going to support you on our knees. Every morning, after our kids are in school, Kathy Pfaff, Jean Nygard, Ella Jean Hampson, and I meet together to pray for you."

"That means more to me than I can tell you, Cheryl."

"Well, listen, I hear the kids' bus out front," she said. "I'd better get going."

"Thanks for calling. And thank your group. Very, very much."

Chapter 24

"Mmmm," Brenda sighed, burying her head even deeper in Johnny's chest. "I've really missed you. Where have you been?"

"I told you it was getting harder to get out," Johnny said. He gently pushed her away so he could take off his coat and sit down at the table. "They're starting to watch me a lot closer, and besides, I've been given a new position that's been keeping me pretty busy."

"But it's been more than a week, Johnny. Now I never know when to expect you."

"Well, you'd better get used to it. I'm going to be doing a lot of traveling now, and it might even be longer before I can get back."

"What are you doing?" Her voice was plaintive, like a disappointed child.

"You'll never guess in a million years, Brenda. Remember the movie *Field of Dreams*? Well, several of us approached the management, and they agreed to let us form a league that's going to take in the whole galaxy. You can't imagine some of the ballparks, Brenda, or some of the players. They've re-created some of the old parks from earth, and they've made some new ones you can't even imagine! With the different atmospheres and gravities on some of the planets, they're able to create fields that you wouldn't believe.

"Try to picture a baseball field with natural grass, and the stadium made out of solid gold. The seats milled-out black walnut with platinum accents and silk cushions, and the distance from home plate to the center field wall is more than four and a half miles. The fence—get this—is more than 300 yards high. You should've seen Roger Maris the first time he walked onto the field for batting practice. He looked, and he looked, and he *looked*, and then he quietly breathed, 'No way.' But you should've seen the ball he hit. It went clear out of the park!"

"How do you even play a field like that?" Brenda asked, wide-eyed.

"Do you remember the first humans on the moon, and how far they could jump? OK. Imagine a place with even less gravity, and you can begin to see what an incredible game it is. I saw Mickey Mantle jump for a fly ball the other day—almost 100 feet in the air. It was an incredible catch."

"You're teasing me."

"No way."

"Are you playing?"

"Better than that. You'll never guess in a million years. You are now looking at the first commissioner of baseball."

"Commissioner!" Brenda shrieked. "How . . . How . . .?"

"It was all my idea to do it, so they decided I might as well be the first commissioner. I've got an office, a secretary, and about a dozen staff. Looks like we're going to have about 30 teams the first year. They'll be broken down into four divisions that play a four-month season. It's incredible, Brenda."

"Tell me about your secretary."

"Oh, she's just your ordinary secretary."

"What's she like? Is she pretty?"

"Y-e-s," Johnny said slowly. "She's pretty."

"Is she married?"

"They don't do that there, Brenda."

She frowned. "What do you mean, they don't do that?"

"Well, nobody worries about it. We're all free."

"Free to what?"

"Well, you know, uh . . . uh. . . uh," Johnny stuttered. "Free. God didn't create people to be tied down, Brenda."

"That includes you?" Brenda tilted her head and squinted a little.

"Hey, you know, baby, I told you when we got married that I'd never cheat on you, and I meant it."

"Yeah, but that was till death do us part. How about now?"

"Brenda, you know I love you . . ."

"That's not what I asked, Johnny."

"It's really tough, Brenda. It's a different world up there. Remember in the sixties all the talk about free love? Well, that's what the Master created us for, not all the chains of being tied to just one person. Everything is . . . well, there are a lot of opportunities."

"What are you saying, Johnny? I want to know what you mean. Are you sleeping with someone else? Is that why you haven't been here for a while?"

"No, Brenda. I told you I wasn't. But I'm also telling you it's been very difficult. There are a lot of beautiful women up there who will give you anything you want, whenever you want it. I've been loyal, but—"

Johnny stood up and looked at Brenda. "You haven't made it very easy on me."

"Easy on you! I've waited with open arms for you every night. I have lost weight to look good for you. I've lavished money I didn't have on your favorite perfume. I have stayed up and waited for you and baked cookies and poured milk and loved you with all of the passion this body could muster." She was almost crying now. "I have withstood the scorn of my friends, the rejection of many in my church. I'm even losing my children for you, and you say that I'm not making it easy. Johnny, pray tell me, what else could I do?"

"I'm alone up there," Johnny almost whined as he started pacing back and forth. "Everybody else spends time together, and I'm off by myself. One of the Indian masters even pulled me aside and asked me if I was a eunuch. He said he could fix it in a moment for me if I needed him to. Then he offered me the pick of any of his harem for a week on the planet of my choice." Johnny's face screwed up as if he were in pain. "They worry about me, Brenda. They gather in little knots and look my way and whisper about me. *They* enjoy the universe, and I slip off to this little cesspool of a world to see you, and at times it gets tough, Brenda. That's what I mean."

Brenda reached for him, but he brushed her away. "How many men do you know could handle working with a secretary who makes Marilyn Monroe look ugly and who dresses the way they dress up there, and still be loyal when their wife wasn't even around? I need you, baby. If you won't come for yourself, won't you come for me?"

"How do they dress up there?"

He laughed. "Well, you know. Remember what the Bible says about Adam and Eve being naked and not being ashamed?"

"Johnny!"

"You'll get used to it. Everyone does. Look, Brenda, can't you see why I need you? I miss you, and now that I'm going to be traveling I won't be able to see you very often, and it's going to kill me."

"Kill you?" she laughed.

"It's just an expression." Walking over to her, Johnny took Brenda's hands. "Please, Brenda. I need you. Can't you see that?"

"Johnny, we've got two boys, remember?"

"They're gone anyway," Johnny said bitterly. "They won't have anything to do with me—or you."

"That's not true. Steve was here just the other day. I think, given some time, they'll come around." She brightened. "I've been getting some things together that I know will help me to convince them."

"What kind of things?"

"Let me show you." Brenda took his hand and led him into the living room. "I borrowed some books from Pastor Stan, and I'm going to show him and the church and the boys that you're real. I know that God has the evidence in His Word, and I'm going to find it, and when I do they won't have any choice but to accept you. I'll show you." Brenda pulled him toward the table where her Bible, a concordance, and a pile of photocopied papers lay. "Maybe we can do it together," she said happily. "Here's your Bible." She reached down to Johnny's personal Bible, which lay on the end table next to his chair.

"Don't!" Johnny cried, dropping the book Brenda handed to him. "I don't want anything to do with *that*." His eyes were wide. "Get it away from me!"

"Johnny, it's your Bible. What's the matter? You used to read it every night."

"I don't want anything to do with it," Johnny snapped, kicking it across the room. "Do you understand that, Brenda? Get it out of the house with the rest of them, or I'm never coming back!"

"Johnny!" She backed away from him. "What's going on? That was your anniversary gift. You underlined it, and you took it with you on trips. When I gave it to you, you said it was the nicest gift you ever received. Now you act as if you're afraid of it."

Walking over to where the Bible lay crumpled against the wall, Brenda picked it up, smoothed its pages, and began walking toward him. "C'mon, Johnny, I need your help if I'm ever going to convince people that the Bible says you're legitimate. You were the Bible student in our family. You know I can't do this on my own."

"Get that thing away from me," he screamed, backing up as Brenda grew near. "I know better now, Brenda. The Bible is nothing more than a collection of myths. It's a dangerous book. Get it away from me, now!"

Johnny took a deep breath and looked out the window for a moment to gain his composure. "There's something else," he said, turning back to her, a touch of steel in his voice that made Brenda uncomfortable. "I don't want you having anything more to do with Pastor Stan, do you understand? He's confusing you and a lot of other people with all of his talk about the dead being *dead* and not knowing anything. He doesn't know what he's talking about."

"Johnny, he's just trying to help me. He's my pastor. He's a good man."

"I think it's more than that. I've thought for a long time that his interest in you was more than pastoral. To use the Bible term for it, I bet he'd love to plow with my heifer some night."

"Johnny!" She was shocked.

"It's true. The guy's a jerk. Everybody up there knows it. He's in for some real hard times real soon. The sooner you get away from him and that church, the better."

"Where would I go? That's my church home, Johnny."

"Not anymore, Brenda, if you want me around. I think you need to go down to First Church. I've heard the pastor down there's a great guy. I think you'd like his wife, too. Brenda, you need to get away from that little bunch of Bible pounders before they confuse you worse than you already are."

"This isn't like you, Johnny," she said, puzzled. "You're not making any sense. What's wrong? Don't you remember how you loved our church and Pastor Stan? You guys hung out together. You went fishing together, and you played golf every Monday afternoon for more than seven years. And Barbara is one of my best friends."

"Brenda, don't you see what's happening?" Johnny asked, quietly taking her into his arms and drawing her close. "They're trying to keep us apart. I'm up there in heaven pining away for you, sneaking down here to spend time with you. I'm risking my neck for you and our love, and all they can do is criticize. Can't you see it?"

"It'll be OK. They just don't understand."

"I miss you, baby! Won't you come back with me tonight?"

"I can't, Johnny." She drew away from him. "I can't."

He drew her back, kissing her forehead. "I understand, baby," he said as he reached up slowly and began to untie the ribbon on her gown. "I understand."

Chapter 25

H ello. Is Nadine here?"
Marilyn Fleetwood didn't recognize the young woman in the $1,000 St. John dress who answered the door of what had once been Margaret Crossworthy's Victorian mansion. Since Peg died they'd missed having the meetings there on Rex Hill. Now that her niece was back in town it would be nice to be back in their old quarters.

"Yes, Nadine is here." Marilyn realized that as she'd daydreamed the woman had repeated herself. "Won't you come in?"

Following her down the hall to the parlor, Marilyn admired the fresh-cut peonies in the cut-glass vase on the hall tree. *Peg knew antiques*, she thought. *I wonder who this new gal is. She sure dresses snappy!*

"So, when does Nadine arrive?" Marilyn asked a few minutes later. She smiled at the other women and the two men seated on the brocade chairs and a silk-upholstered settee tastefully arranged around the room. "Oh, and who let me in? She's a little out of our league, isn't she?"

"So, you didn't recognize her?" Juanita's eyes twinkled. "No one else did either."

"Who?"

"What do you mean, who?"

"Her!"

"Who's her?"

"Marilyn," Darrel Widmer leaned forward confidentially, "that was Nadine."

"That's Nadine?"

"You don't recognize me without my goats, Marilyn?" came a lightly lilting voice.

Stepping into the room with a silver tray of shortbread cookies, Nadine set them on the sideboard next to an eighteenth-century samovar. Smiling graciously, she turned to the group and demurely sank down on the corner of a Louis XIV settee. She reached up to adjust a diamond stud in her ear, sat quietly for a moment, then said, "I really appreciate your coming. Each of you.

"As you know, this has been a very difficult couple years for me," she said quietly, "and I truly appreciate your support and help in my difficult period. It was probably obvious that I went into a time of deep depression from which I, thankfully, have recently recovered. My only consolation is that I grew much closer to our spirit guides during these two years. It is to them that I owe my current emotional state.

"I would have been very happy to remain as I was, but they graciously led me to understand that I could lead you only if I had your respect and honor. The practitioners of our Wiccan religion have too often been portrayed as a bunch of old crones riding broomsticks and living in squalor. My gracious guides have been teaching me that this has to change."

Looking around the room, Nadine dabbed a tear from the corner of her left eye, then smiled. "It is good to be back!"

"Welcome home, honey." Sharon Creizon was the first to react. "Welcome home."

"Thank you, very much. Now we've got business to attend to. I've spent the past couple weeks airing out Peg's house. I miss her very much. Although she often talks to me, it's just not the same. I've also spent considerable time refurbishing the altar and furnishings in the chapel area. I hope that you will find them to your liking."

"I'm sure we will, dear," Marilyn murmured, with Juanita adding affirmation of her own. But Darrel Widmer had something else on his mind.

"Nadine, we've got problems brewing in town," he boomed, leaning forward earnestly.

"So I've heard. That's why we're here today."

"What are we going to do?"

"What do you mean, what *we* going to do?" Carol looked scornfully at her husband.

"I mean, what *are* we going to do! This guy out at Cherry Pit is starting to make waves."

"Darrel, you're wringing your hands like an old lady." Carol stood up and walked over to stand beside Nadine. "We finally get the opportunity to show where the real power lies in this world, and you're talking like your whiny friends at the seminary."

"Carol!"

"You know it's true, Darrel. None of them believe in the supernatural. They don't even really believe in the Bible, much less a personal God. It's all a myth, remember? Why do you think so many church members join us? There's no power in the Christian church. People want to experience the supernatural. Once they discover you can't pick yourself up by your own bootstraps, they want to know that there's a power out there that's greater than they are.

"Now that they're convinced that it's not in Christianity, we're their only hope!"

"Wow!" Juanita cried, raising her coffee cup and laughing sarcastically. "You should have been an evangelist."

"You're cutting a little close to home, Juanita," Carol said. "That was our dream before we went to the seminary. We actually believed the pastor of our little church when he said that Jesus was coming back to take us to a real heaven. Old Darrel even used to believe that silly stuff about a great battle raging between God and the devil over our souls. You ought to do one of your old sermons sometime, Darrel. These guys would get a real kick out of it. Some God—whose followers don't even really believe He exists." Carol crossed her arms angrily. "I can't believe we really believed that stuff."

"Well, of course a great many people still do," Nadine said, "and that's why we need to get down to business." Gracefully she rose and crossed to the large window, and turned. Her smile touched everyone in the room. "I've talked with Peg several times, and this is what she says we must do.

"Now, I cannot believe that this pastor out at Cherry Pit is as dangerous as you think he is. He's just a young idealistic country preacher who'll probably cave in the first time we push him. These guys are so controlled by the fear of losing their careers and their churches that most of them will sell out cheap if we apply the pressure in the right ways. More than one good pulpit committee has taken the vinegar out of one of our foes in about 10 minutes." She laughed. "I wouldn't worry too much about old Cherry Pit.

"What we need you to do, Juanita, is this. I understand you had the meeting at your house, as instructed."

Juanita nodded.

"Good, and you invited the ones I told you to invite?"

Again she nodded.

"All right. Good. Then you have the first ingredient for our little game. Nothing intimidates a pastor more than knowing that people are meeting secretly and discussing him behind his back. He'll be on the defensive before you even begin. Now, I want several of you to go visit him. Start your conversation by saying that a number of you—leave it nebulous, and let his imagination fill the room until it looks like his whole congregation—met the other day to discuss him. Tell him it was for his good and the church's good. I love that line. It makes you look good, and sticks the dagger in deeper. No pastor is going to believe that people are meeting with his best interests in mind.

"Then tell him that you drew up a list of concerns that you want to talk with him about. By now he should be jelly, but don't let up. Ben, you should mention that members of the pulpit and finance committees share these concerns."

"You want me to be there?" Ben asked.

"Of course. I want you all to be there. Hit him hard. Make him feel outnumbered. Do you have the list, Juanita?"

"Yes. I printed it out this morning. You can't believe what we got out of some of those good people. A few of them were Stan's friends, but once the floodgates opened, everyone was sharing areas 'where the pastor could improve.'"

"You should have been there, Nadine," Ben put in with a loud laugh. "It became a feeding frenzy. It's amazing what cannibals people can become once the blood starts flowing—especially if their friends are on the bandwagon. I love it!"

"That's what we're counting on. Now, Juanita, whatever you do, don't give him the list. Just flash it so that he gets glimpses of it. And whatever you do, do not mention what Ben and Sharon and the rest of you are upset about. It just puts you in the same boat with Brenda Barnes." Nadine was marshaling her forces, and she loved it. "Express your concerns and show your anger at how the man has treated Brenda. Let her wounds break your hearts as you come to her defense. We're defending house and home! This isn't academic. It's your family and the kingdom of our leader he's insulting!"

"I tell you the truth, I've never been so angry!" Juanita interjected. "This has got me fighting mad, and I'm going to stop him in his tracks!"

"Good. Good. But you've got to understand that there's a major difference between anger and passion, Juanita. You're not mad at him, right?" Nadine gave her a caring, compassionate smile. "You love him. He's your pastor. He's your shepherd. And he's attacking you—that's the issue. Anger is like a pressure cooker that blows up. Sure, it may hurt the others in the room, but it also hurts you just as much. Listen to me now. We have no room for anger where we're going from here. When we get mad, we quit thinking and start reacting. That's not good. Do you understand me?"

There were nods all around.

"So what are we supposed to feel?" Sharon asked.

"We are passionate about a cause that will be victorious. We're not angry; we're on fire! The dawning of the age is occurring, and we have been given a pivotal part in it. Each of you is vitally important. You are going to make a difference. Your life is going to count for something." Nadine was striding up and down the length of the room now. "Not only is this man standing as a barrier in the way of our progress to the New Age—he is keeping you from freely spending time with the ones you love. Ben, your little girl cannot come at will to this world because of people like him. And Juanita, you cannot enjoy your husband's arms because of him. Do you understand that?"

By now Ben and Juanita could barely sit still. Straining forward in their seats, they hung on her every word.

"The rest of you, this man and others like him stand in your way of obtaining all that the age to come promises. I speak of the opportunity to rule, to enjoy the pleasures our master has for us, to experience complete oneness with the cosmic force. I'm talking of the power, the authority, over your enemies. These people are standing in your way. They must be stopped. No! They must be crushed. And you are going to have the privilege of doing it. But," she cautioned, "you cannot become angry. You must be in control at all times. Like a laser beam, we can burn with a white-hot fire, but we must always be in control. We must always be thinking. We must always be planning. Like a chess master, we must always be thinking ahead. Are we agreed?"

Again, heads around the room nodded.

"Now, as I said, this is the first round." She gracefully slipped into her seat. "We will see what this pastor is made of."

"What happens if he doesn't cave?" Darrel stood up. "You don't know these Bible people, Nadine. They don't intimidate easily. When they get passionate about something, you can't back 'em down. They're as fired up about this as we are! Opposition just makes them more determined. I've seen it!"

"*His* followers have always been like that," Nadine sighed. "One of the early martyrs said that their blood was like seed, springing up into more followers of our Enemy. That is why we must be careful not to make this foolish preacher a martyr. Even if it takes a little longer, we must work quietly until we're certain we have the upper hand. Your talk with him will put him on the defensive, but there will be more before he's defeated. So don't be discouraged. And don't overreact. OK?"

"Are you saying that we may not 'win' right now?" Sharon asked, her brow crinkled with concern.

"We may not win all the skirmishes, Sharon. But rest assured we *will* win the war.

"Now we have some other business to attend to," Nadine said briskly. "We must prepare ourselves for what lies ahead. It is time to rededicate ourselves to our mission. Doris," she said, turning to one of the other women, "did your husband get what we asked for?"

Doris shuddered. "Yes, he did. It's in the trunk of my car, but I don't want to touch it."

"You're going to have to get over that squeamishness if you want to advance in our little art, my dear." Nadine frowned. "Now, would you please assist Darrel in getting it?"

Turning to the others, she continued. "The instructions are very explicit. We need the heart of a very brave and aggressive dog. In this case it's that of a certain rottweiler whose owner this very minute is probably whistling for him in his backyard. I wouldn't bother you with the details except that Doris's husband, Jake, has taken care of it for us, for which we are very grateful. You may need to be prepared to act surprised if you hear of it. We also need the head of a male goat. As Mephisto is no longer fulfilling the function in my life he once was, our leader has graciously given him for this service. I will miss him. And finally, we need the blood of a human sacrifice. Thankfully, Gloria works down at Dr. Scriven's, and she has been able to procure it in the usual way. To the young women in our community who are mass-producing fetuses they wish to abort, we offer our eternal thanks. It saves a lot of mess to have the good doctor sacrificing them for us, doesn't it?

"So, we can begin. Doris, you and Ben get the things from your car. Darrel, if you will join me and the others in the garage, we can take care of things with my long-eared friend, and we'll be ready to go. I'll want to change clothes. Ben you'll find your apron in the usual place. We'll all meet in the chapel in 15 minutes.

Chapter 26

So this is a Greek picnic," Steve said, surveying the blanket Cindy spread out under one of the cherry trees in Cindy Park. "Now I know why Zorba was so chunky. How do you stay so thin?" he asked, looking at

Cindy appreciatively.

"Only Greek men get fat," Cindy giggled. "Besides, I'm part Swede and part Scot, and they're all skinny, right?"

" 'Fraid not. My aunt Helga is pretty stout." Steve stooped over and tried to snitch an olive. "What's all this stuff?"

"Out! Out! Out of my kitchen!" Cindy said, mimicking the voice of a Greek grandmother and whacking at him with the spoon she'd used to dip olives out of a jar.

"All right!" Steve snatched an olive and ran. "Don't beat me, please!"

A few minutes later they sat down to one of the most delicious meals Steve had ever eaten. There were stuffed grape leaves, a salad with vinegar and oil dressing, huge Greek olives, buttered pita bread cradling thick slabs of cold lamb, and sparkling water. For dessert, there were diamonds of baklava and iced cappuccino.

"Man," Steve asked, "is this the way your family eats all the time?"

"No, only when my grandmother Kamilos comes to visit. She's the one who taught me to make baklava. My mom, being Scot and Swede, never learned to cook much Greek food, so Dad always orders it when Gama comes."

"Gama?"

"That's what I called her when I was little, and it stuck. She's one incredible woman! I wish you could see her." Cindy's eyes shone. "Grandpa met her when he traveled to Greece on a holiday. They were both really young. She was 14 and he was 16, and it took them a full week to convince the local Orthodox priest to marry them. You should have heard what Grandpa's good Scottish Presbyterian parents had to say about that when they found out. But it was too late. The marriage had already been consummated, so they made the best of it. Grandma moved to Scotland, where Grandpa worked for his father, making and repairing sails. Eventually they moved to America, where my dad was born. We were probably the only family on earth," Cindy laughed, "that got scones and oatmeal porridge for breakfast and pilaf and lamb for supper when we went to visit our grandparents."

"Are they both still alive?"

"Oh, yes. I think they'll live to be 100. Grandpa still plays a round of golf six days a week, and Grandma can still cook circles around most of us. Not bad when you're 94 and 92. Dad has tried to get them to come and live with him and Mom, but they won't hear of it. I think they'd be lost without all of their friends."

"So, did you like the party the other night?" he changed the subject.

"I had a fantastic time, Steve. I really enjoyed myself. It was a lot more than I expected, quite frankly. It's been a long time since I've been around religious people much, and I figured they might be pretty boring."

"Nah," Steve said. "If you claim to be a Christian and you're boring, then something's wrong. The Christians I know are some of the happiest, most interesting people around. The problem is that a lot of people who claim to be Christians really aren't, and they give Christ and His people a very bad name." He popped an olive in his mouth. "Would you like to come back next week?"

"I was hoping you'd ask."

"Then it's settled. It was really neat to have you with us. I knew the girls would like you, and I'm glad you had fun." He paused, trying to decide whether to take the chance. "I was kinda hoping we could see a lot more of each other," he ventured. "I haven't asked if you have a boyfriend."

"No boyfriend," Cindy smiled. "Not for a while. I guess I've been too busy lately to think much about dating."

"What keeps you so busy, if I'm not prying?"

"No, it's fine. There's the job at Kroger's, of course, and I sing four nights a week at one of the clubs in town. Then I do a little modeling on the side." She took a slow, deep breath, adding, "and I've got a little retail business I try to take care of in my spare time."

"A retail business? What kind?" he asked, interested. "Similar to Amway or Tupperware?"

She shrugged. "No, it's a little more complicated than that. I sell books."

"Books! I love to read. What kind of books?"

Cindy suddenly began to feel panic. Somehow she didn't want to tell Steve, and couldn't figure out why. "I'll have to show you sometime," she said lightly. She pushed the dessert plate toward him. "Another baklava?"

He shook his head. "Not tonight, but I'd love to take a couple home for tomorrow. You've done Gama proud."

Cindy picked up her plate and his, slipping them into a plastic bag for disposal. "What do you know about the New Age movement?" she asked.

"All I want to, which isn't much."

She busied herself screwing a lid on the olive jar. "Why's that?"

"I guess because, well, I guess it's because at its core the New Age movement is against everything I believe in." He paused. "Do you want to get into this now?"

She felt her face flush, but tried to keep her voice light. "Sure."

"Well, the Bible tells us that there are two forces at work in this world—good and evil. If you believe that God is the creator of good, then the other force is evil. This may sound simplistic to someone who hasn't studied into it, but I think the New Age movement is a trap to destroy people. Besides, it may be involved in ushering in some kind of age, but it's certainly not new."

"What do you mean, 'not new'?" she asked, her voice sharper than she intended.

"New Age practices have been around in various forms for thousands of years," Steve continued. "They're called New Age only because they're committed to ushering in Eastern religion as the dominant one in the Western world."

"Well, if that's true, then why don't you believe in them? You're saying that they've been around as long as Christianity."

"Even longer. You read about them throughout the Old Testament."

"How do you know they're not right, then," Cindy asked defensively, "and that Christianity isn't the one that's wrong? Maybe the Bible writers got it all wrong, and Buddha or the Hindu religions have it right. I mean, look how long Christianity's been around. At least 2,000 years, right?"

"Right at 2,000."

"And the Jews before that. How long was Judaism a dominant religion? Another 2,000 years? If they are the world-changing religions they're supposed to be, don't you think there might be some kind of progress by now? I mean, how many years does it take, anyway?"

"The same could be said of all of the Eastern religions, Cindy. But longevity isn't the issue. Maybe we need to look at the effects of both throughout history."

"Right! Like the Crusades," she retorted bitterly, "and the Inquisition. They were real high points in human history."

"That's not fair," Steve frowned. "If you're going to take an honest look at both, then you need to distinguish between those who claim to be followers and those who really are—on both sides."

"That's kind of hard, isn't it?" Cindy asked. "Didn't Gandhi once say that he might consider becoming a Christian if he ever met one?"

Steve was silent for a moment. Then he said gently, "Didn't you tell me the other night that you had a Christian grandmother who was the most wonderful woman you ever met?"

"You're right, and I'm sorry. That wasn't fair. I guess I can get pretty wound up, huh. I'm sorry, Steve."

"It's OK. I'm glad you are passionate about what you believe. I just think you might need to consider some things you've never considered before."

"Like what?"

"In order to really evaluate the validity of both movements, Christianity and Eastern religion, you need to look at the effects of both on people and society down throughout their whole history. You also need to ask who they both worship and what they are both like."

"Go on."

"Well, in spite of certain obvious lapses that you have already pointed out, overall the effect of Christianity on the world has been very positive and enlightening. Slaves have been set free. Women have been emancipated and children freed from forced labor in sweatshops. Whole areas of the world have seen sweeping changes for the good in their standard of living. Entire countries have been brought out of cannibalism and the barest and meanest existence into a life that was much better than they had ever dreamed of or hoped for.

"True, you can point out those who have claimed to be Christians who have raped the land and exploited the people, but on the whole, real Christianity has had a transforming effect on every society it's touched. The greatest and freest country in the whole world, in spite of all of its faults, was founded on Christian principles that have lasted more than 200 years.

"My grandfather was a missionary in India, and my uncle and my father grew up in China," Steve continued. "They saw firsthand the effects of Eastern religion. When John Lennon came back from India, did he ever mention the slavery of the caste system? Did he mention the untouchables, who are born into this lowest of the low class and can never get out of it? Did the Beatles ever tell of the newborn baby girls who were thrown out on the garbage heaps or the older children sold into prostitution because their fathers wanted boys? Do the swamis and the Llamas and the yogis ever talk about the squalor of Bombay or Shanghai or the poverty induced by supporting the tens of thousands of priests in Tibet?"

"No, but . . ."

"I'm not quite through," Steve interrupted. "You talk about the horrors of the Inquisition. How about Nazi Germany?"

"What does that have to do with anything?" Cindy demanded. "Now you're going to blame the Third Reich on meditation? We preach peace, brother, not war. Remember?"

"Not many people know that most of the leaders of Nazism were devotees of Eastern religion, satanism, and the occult," Steve said. "The Third Reich was just the fulfillment of everything Helena Blavatsky and Alice Bailey had been advocating for years. They followed the plan, Cindy, and that was the outcome."

"You know about Alice Bailey?"

"More than I want to, as I said. Where do you think the whole doctrine of Aryanism originated?"

"I'd never thought about it before," she said, weakly.

"Think about our own country. Remember the sixties, and the dawning of the Age of Aquarius? What dawned, anyway? Free love, and the greatest outbreak of venereal disease since Columbus visited the New

World. A whole generation whose only values were based on themselves and a hedonistic pursuit of pleasure. More drug addicts than were in China at the height of the Opium Wars. If that's the dawning of a new age, I don't want any part of it. What the gurus preach as freedom is really only slavery in a different cloak, Cindy. Can't you see it?"

He continued, gently. "In reality, it all comes down to a matter of worship."

Cindy looked up, puzzled.

"True Christianity revolves around the worship of a God whom the Bible describes as kind and gracious and loving. The New Age movement, as I understand it, is openly, at its core, the worship of Lucifer."

"How do you figure that?" Cindy asked slowly.

"Isn't one of the main publishing houses of the New Age movement Lucis Publishing, formerly Lucifer Publishing?" Steve asked. "And isn't *lucis* the Latin term for light, from which Lucifer, the light bearer, got his name?"

"Yes," came the quiet reply.

"So, what you ultimately have is a choice between worshipping the devil, Lucifer, and God," Steve said. "Pure and simple, stripped of all the incense and music and trappings, that is what it's all about.

"The Bible says that Lucifer, or Satan, is out to trap and enslave us," he went on. "Satan is subtle, he's crafty, and he knows what will work best for each one of us. And he's out to make us his slaves."

Cindy laughed nervously. "I've heard that before," she said. "You didn't know Grandma T, did you?"

"Grandma T?" He laughed. "You have some strangely named grandmothers, Cindy."

"Oh, her name was Grandma Terwilliger, so we shortened it to Grandma T. It made it easier when you were trying to name all of them." She folded a red-checkered cloth and placed it over the items she'd put in the wicker basket, then reached for another baklava.

"So what do you know about astrology?" she asked Steve. "It's based on the stars and their effect on the earth. It's OK, isn't it?"

"Cindy, it's all part of the same package. I've taken enough astronomy classes to give you all kinds of reasons it doesn't work. But I think that it's probably easier to say that it's just another of the doors Satan uses to get people involved in the occult. Look at the company astrology keeps: Tarot card readers, witchcraft, paranormal studies—all the rest of the occult. Sooner or later most people who are deeply involved in astrology expand into other areas. I've seen it happen over and over."

Steve stood up from the blanket, stretched, and walked a few steps.

"I had an aunt," he continued, "who was into astrology. She was almost a missionary, she was so zealous. She'd often write to my mom about it. This went on a long time, and eventually she started telling Mom that her house was haunted. All kinds of bizarre stuff happened. Lights turned off and on. Faucets, too. She'd even find candles lit and burning when she knew she hadn't touched them." He shook his head. "She said that she heard footsteps in the night. It was really weird.

"She didn't live nearby," he continued, pausing to think. "My mom didn't see her often, but they talked now and then." He picked up a leaf from the ground, tracing its veins. "I'm trying to remember so I tell this right," he said. "I was a teenager at the time. A friend of Mom's went through the town where Aunt Sue lived, and stopped by to visit. Mom had been worried about her, of course, and asked this woman to see her. I remember that Mom's friend said there was a heavy, oppressive atmosphere in Aunt Sue's place. It kind of frightened her.

"Mom tried to help, to do *something*, but Aunt Sue wouldn't let her." He sighed. "She eventually committed suicide. It was all hush-hush back then. But it grieved my mother, and made quite an impression on me."

There was a long silence.

"Are you saying that she killed herself because she was into astrology?" Cindy finally asked.

"No. Nothing is that simple. But somehow—I can't say that I know how—astrology opened the door. And in my mind, the door opened for evil." He shook his head. "How did we go from enjoying your incredible baklava to talking about suicide?"

She laughed. "Don't know." Tilting her head and looking him over, she said, "I'm learning that you're a deep and complicated guy."

"So I am," he teased. He glanced at his watch. "Hey, we'd better get going, or we're going to miss our tow."

"Our tow?" she asked blankly.

"Yeah. Our tow. Remember? We're going gliding."

But she had slipped back into thought. Steve waved his hand in front of her eyes as she sat quietly, looking out over the valley. "Cindy, are you OK? Cindy?"

Chapter 27

It was one of those late-fall mornings that should be featured on the front of a feed store calendar. Brenda stretched slowly, luxuriating in the warmth of the feather bed she had tucked up around her neck. Turning her head, she looked out on the valley. It had frosted, and the lawn sparkled white in the morning sun. Pumpkins she'd been hardening glowed orange against the yellow of the cornstalks she hadn't yet had time to cut. A deer nibbled its way slowly along the fence line, pausing once in a while to look up as next door Fred Blevin, riding his tractor, rounded a corner.

Reaching out and shutting the window with her toe, she snuggled for a few more minutes, then jumped up and grabbed her robe from the back of the chair that stood next to the bed. Shoving her feet into huge fuzzy bunny-shaped slippers, she opened the bedroom door and padded down the hall to the kitchen. After pouring herself a cup of coffee from the pot and turning off the timer, she picked up the paper from the front porch, went into the front room, and settled into Johnny's big recliner.

As she stripped the rubber band off the rolled paper, she glanced over at the table. Sitting there where she'd left them the night before were her Bible, the stack of Stan's photocopied notes, the concordance, and Johnny's Bible. Its pages were still crumpled from being kicked across the room.

I wonder, she thought, setting down the paper and getting up, *what the Bible really does say happens when you die. I guess I'll never know if I don't get into those notes Stan gave me.* She walked back to the bedroom to get her glasses and a pen, then went into the living room and sat down at the table.

Bowing her head, she prayed, "Lord, it's been a while, and I'm sorry. I guess I've let my bitterness over Johnny's death get in the way of something very special we used to have. You know my need to understand what is happening lately in my life. You know how much I want and need Johnny, and how much his coming back has meant to me. You also know that in order for me to help others understand and accept that he's back, I need Your help. I believe that You sent him back to me, but I don't even pretend to understand some of the things he's been saying. I'm really confused. So I have decided to surrender my understanding of this to You. I only ask two things: that You reveal to me the truth about Johnny and what happens when we die, and that you give me the courage to live by what I discover. I claim this, asking for Your guidance and protection, in Jesus' name. Amen.

"Now, Lord, where do I start?" Brenda said aloud. She got up and retrieved a steno pad from a kitchen drawer. *I guess the only safe thing is to avoid anything anyone else has said*, she thought, setting aside the papers she'd gotten from Stan. *If I'm going to be fair about it, I guess it also means that I set aside anything my parents or Sunday school teachers taught me, and anything Johnny has said, and just go to the Word of God. Boy, this is going to be harder than I thought.*

Getting up, she went into the kitchen and poured another cup of coffee and got a muffin out of the refrigerator. "You're stalling, Brenda," she mumbled as she went back into the living room. "Now sit down and get to it."

Opening the steno pad, she wrote the word "Death" at the top of the page in big letters. Then she opened the concordance and went to work. First she looked up every occurance of the words "death," "dead," and "die" in the Bible, making notes about what each text said. Every time she discovered another word, that seemed to apply to her study, such as "sleep," she wrote that down too. When the phone rang, she had filled about 10 pages.

"Brenda, my name is Carol Widmer," the voice on the other end said when she answered it. "My husband is the pastor of First Church downtown. I think that I met you at Juanita Parris's house a while back."

"Yes, Carol," Brenda replied. She did remember her: a well-dressed, friendly woman. "I enjoyed the opportunity to get acquainted with you."

"So did I. I don't know what your schedule is like today, but I wonder if we might have lunch together."

H'mmm. This is an interesting coincidence, Brenda thought, saying aloud, "I'd love to. What time?"

"Well, I thought we might try for about 12:30. Have you eaten at the new Olive Grove restaurant that's just opened on Grand?"

"No, I haven't. But I've heard it's great."

Carol chuckled. "Actually, I haven't been there either, but I've been told that the veal scaloppinie is out of this world. As long as you like garlic, they say you'll love the place. Tell you what. I've got an errand or two to do, so I'll get there early and reserve a table for us."

"Great! I'll see you at . . . say, it's almost 11:30 now. I'd better get going. See you soon."

Well, that'll be fun, Brenda thought as she closed the Bible and lined up her pen and notes next to it. *I can get back to this after a while.*

A little more than an hour later Brenda pulled into the parking lot, delighted to find a spot facing the front doors. It was obvious that the Olive Grove was going to be a popular place. The parking lot was full, and a 20-foot line stretched across the front of the building. No telling how many more waited inside. She was glad that Carol was holding a place just inside the door by the reservation desk.

Sliding her way apologetically through the crowd, she finally made it up to where Carol stood just inside the door. "Glad you could make it, Brenda," Carol said, turning to smile at the couple standing next to her. "This is my friend Brenda. I hope you don't mind her joining us?"

"Not at all," the man said, a sour smile on his face. "The more the merrier."

A few minutes later, when they'd been seated and each had a copy of the large menu, Carol turned to Brenda. "What would you like for lunch? It's on me today."

"No, let's go Dutch."

"No way. I invited you," Carol smiled. "Georgia rules. Whoever invites pays. Next time it's on you, OK?"

It took a few minutes to put in their drink orders, study the menu, then place orders for the meal. But when the server left with their order, Carol turned to Brenda with a question. "So what did you think of the meeting the other night?"

"I don't know," she said honestly. "I'm still trying to sort it out. How about you?"

"It sounds like you've got a very nice pastor," Carol said slowly, "but I also get the impression he is having some problems."

"That's what I'm trying to figure out," Brenda said. "There's nothing that I can think of about Pastor Stan that isn't positive. Oh, he's got his blind spots, and there are some things he does better than others. But that's all minor stuff. But by the time the meeting was over it was starting to sound as if he's terrible." She shook her head. "I don't understand what's going on. Almost everybody loves Pastor Stan, just as Juanita said. He's a man of God." Subconsciously she ticked off each point on her fingers. "He genuinely loves people. He has a burden for reaching our community for Christ. And he's a real good preacher and teacher. I just don't understand."

Carol leaned forward in a confidential manner. "But hasn't he been awfully critical of you lately? From what I heard, he was really hard on you in front of the whole church."

"Who told you that?"

"It doesn't matter, but I have a hard time, Brenda, believing that a man of God would come out and embarrass one of his parishioners by hammering away at things that are very precious to that person." Then, her voice softening, she asked, "Can you tell me just a little bit about your husband?"

"Oh, man." Brenda shook her head. "Where do I start? I fell in love with Johnny Fletcher Barnes the first time he walked into my homeroom in high school. I had just moved to town from Seattle, Washington, and didn't know anyone. He was captain of the baseball team and came in to do some recruiting for fall tryouts. He was about six feet tall with wavy blond hair and a smile that was so genuine you could almost call it sweet.

"It took me two months to get him to notice that I even existed, but when he did, it was love from the first date. He liked to slow-dance, and when we'd go out, it was heaven to be in his arms. We dated the rest of our senior year, and got married three months after graduation."

"High school sweethearts," Carol cooed. "Isn't that lovely!"

Brenda pretended not to hear her. "You know, you read in some of the women's magazines about all of the unhappy women in the world," she continued, "women whose husbands are uncaring and insensitive to their need and desires. Well, Johnny was special from the very beginning. He had an old-fashioned chivalry that made him charming. He always took time to show real interest in the things that I enjoyed, and he spent all kinds of time with our boys. He was an athlete, and almost from the start he played softball during the summers, but he wasn't your typical jock. He took care of himself. He was always showered and never had an odor. Another thing, he went out of his way to be a good sport. Everybody loved him, Carol. Everyone! I don't know of a single person who didn't like Johnny."

"He sounds very special," Carol murmured. "You're very lucky."

"He was also a real Christian, too." Brenda looked up, her eyes brimming. "He, uh . . . huh . . ."

"What, Brenda?"

"Oh, nothing, just thinking. Johnny believed that the Bible was the Word of God. He read it every day and believed that it was the only real way we could know God's will. He made sure that we found a church we could all enjoy, and he took an active part in it. He had a genuine relationship with God that made him the spiritual leader of our home *and* a pillar in our church. He was just one great guy."

"Don't you mean *is?*" Carol asked quietly. "I thought he was back."

"He is," Brenda said, idly pushing at a ruffled lettuce leaf with her fork. "That's what's made it so hard."

"Hard? I'd think it would be wonderful to have your husband back again."

"It is." Brenda frowned and looked off into space for a moment before looking back at Carol. She jabbed at the leaf of lettuce. "It is good, but it's also very hard."

"I guess that I don't understand."

"I'm at a real crossroad in my life," Brenda said. "I have to decide . . . Can I be honest with you, Carol?"

"I hope so, dear."

"No. I mean really honest." Her voice was little more than a whisper. "You won't tell anybody?"

"Of course not, Brenda. What's wrong?"

"I'm starting to have some doubts, Carol. About Johnny."

"Oh?" A pause. "What kind of doubts?"

"Well, on the one hand, I have Johnny. He's been coming home most nights now for several weeks. Every fiber of my body, every cell in my brain, every square inch of my heart, tells me it's him. Carol, it's been great. You don't know what it's like to be without a husband you have loved with all your heart as I love Johnny. Even though at first I was a little scared to see him, it's been heaven on earth."

"So what's the problem?"

"The Bible," she said sadly. "I was really hurt when Pastor Stan said what he did in church."

"You have every right to be hurt," Carol told her. "That man ought to be ashamed of himself for what he did."

Brenda took a deep swallow of her iced tea. "But I'm not finished. I was really hurt, but I also realized that Stan said what he did because he cared about me, and he cares about others in the congregation who might have been affected by what I told them. So after a few days I talked with him about it. He really *is* a great guy, Carol. I also talked with Johnny junior. He's had a hard time with his dad's return, and he begged me to take the time to see what the Bible said about the"—she coughed, and took another sip—"the dead. I didn't want to, because, I guess, I was afraid of what I'd find. But today I finally did. And I'm scared." Tears filled her eyes and streaked down her face through her makeup. "I am really scared and confused. You're a pastor's wife, Carol. What do you think?"

"I think that the Bible will do that," Carol said quietly.

"What?"

"I just said that sometimes the Bible is hard for all of us to understand," Carol answered.

Brenda wiped her eyes with her napkin. "The Bible says that Johnny is dead, Carol. That he can't know anything. That he's sleeping until Jesus comes back. What I read today says that he's not in heaven and that he can't come back to this earth in any form until the Second Coming—because he isn't just gone. He's in the grave! I'm scared, Carol. If whoever's been seeing me isn't Johnny, then who is it?" she hiccuped. "Whom can I believe? How can I know whom to trust? I don't know what's right anymore."

By now the river of tears running down Brenda's face were dripping into the marinara sauce on her plate. "I just don't know what's right anymore."

"What does your heart tell you?" Carol asked gently, reaching across the table and placing her hand on Brenda's arm.

"My heart tells me that it's Johnny," Brenda said, mopping her eyes with her napkin. "But the Word of God says no!"

"So which are you going to believe, your senses or a collection of stories written more than 2,000 years ago?"

"How do I know, Carol?" Brenda sobbed. "How do I know?"

"Brenda, your senses—what you can see and smell and touch—are what's real in this life." Carol leaned forward, speaking confidentially. "You can trust your senses because they are part of you, and you know that you can trust yourself. You are the most important person in the universe to you. You know what's right. You know what's real. It's what you feel when Johnny's arms are around you and you are making love. It's the smell of his cologne. It's his smile. It's that wavy blond hair against your cheek. That's real, Brenda!"

"But—" Brenda began.

"But nothing! What do a bunch of stodgy old men who lived more than 2,000 years ago know about that? You can trust yourself, Brenda. You've got to believe that. Forget what the Bible says and go with what you know is right."

Carol sat quietly, her hand on Brenda's arm. When Brenda's crying subsided, she repeated it: "Brenda, you've got to trust your senses and nothing else."

Driving home later, Brenda couldn't decide whether she felt better or worse. She wanted to follow her heart. More than anything she longed to go and be with Johnny, to travel the galaxies and to let the solar wind blow her hair, to run "naked and unashamed" with him through some Garden of Eden, and to enjoy the freedom you'd never experience on this earth with all of its problems and all of its sin. It wouldn't be so hard, really, to go, a voice seemed to say. The boys had people who loved them and who would take care of them. Their college was paid for, and their grandparents would open their doors to them anytime they wanted to go there. It would all be so easy, and she wouldn't have to try to sort all of this out.

Opening the front door, she hung her coat in the front closet and crossed the room. Almost as an afterthought she stopped at the table and began to clear away the books and papers. She was crying again, great heaving sobs that sounded as if they would break her in two. Gently picking up Johnny's Bible, she began to smooth the pages, smoothing a page or two, then sobbing, then smoothing a few more. "Johnny, why, why are you doing this to me?" she cried as the sudden thought of leaving her sons almost knocked the breath out of her. "Why are you doing this to me?"

She struggled to gain control of herself. Nothing had ever hurt like this. "God! God, You've got to show me what's right! You have to show me what is right!"

She smoothed the last crinkled page and was closing the Bible when a text Johnny had underlined caught her eye. At first she couldn't read it through her tears, but wiping them away with the back of her hand she read the words of Jeremiah the prophet: "The heart is deceitful above all things."

"Thank You, God," she cried. "Thank You so much!"

Chapter 28

I made an appointment for you while you were gone." Jackie spoke through the open door of her office.

With a sinking feeling Stan looked at the pink while-you-were-out slip lying in the middle of his desk. "Juanita Parris called and asked if she, Ben Gladden, and a couple others could meet with you this evening at 5:00," Jackie continued. "I checked your calendar and it was free, and Barb said that it wouldn't interrupt your supper, so I called them back and confirmed for you. See you in the morning. I'll need the bulletin announcements by 10:00 a.m."

Well, it's beginning, he thought, tapping the slip against the edge of the desk. *I guess I hoped I'd have a little more time to prepare myself. What do I do now? How do you get ready for something like this?* His stomach felt as if it might capsize and sink to the bottom.

"Are you busy?"

Stan looked up to see Francis Baldwin standing in the doorway.

"I saw your car and thought I'd return the book I borrowed the other day," Francis said as he came into the room. "Say, are you all right, Stan?"

Stan shrugged. "Yeah, I just got some bad news, but I'll be OK."

"What's the matter, man? Is there anything I can do?" he sank into a chair opposite the desk and studied the pastor. The man looked to him as if he were about to faint. "Ashen" was the word they used in old novels for a look like the one on Stan's face. And the dark circles under his eyes made him look as if he hadn't slept for a week.

"I don't want to pry, Stan, but you look terrible. Are you sure you're OK?"

"Oh, I'm OK." Stan wiped his face and leaned back against the wall. He was so tired it was difficult to speak. "It's nothing that God can't handle."

"Does this have anything to do with the sermon you gave the other day?"

"Yes, it does, Francis. I never realized just what I was getting myself into when I preached that sermon. In retrospect, it may have been foolish. I thought I was doing the right thing, but now I wonder."

"You wonder?"

"Yes. Imagine what a deer feels like in the woods when it knows it's being stalked by a cougar. It can smell the cougar. It can even hear a twig crack once in a while, but it can't see it, beyond catching occasional fuzzy glimpses through the trees. The deer doesn't know when or from which direction it's going to jump. He just knows that it's going to happen, and that when it does, he's gonna die." He put his face in his hands and spoke through his fingers. "I guess that's how I feel right now. If God doesn't intervene, I'm fixin' to lose everything I've ever worked for, and I'm not even sure what I'm looking for."

"I think that Paul in the Bible knew what you're talking about when he described us battling unseen powers of darkness and the air," Francis said quietly. "Maybe he'd also have some answers on how to fight them."

"Thanks, buddy, but I don't need a sermon right now. I've been studying this for weeks, and I understand the issues—but not how to face them with the power that seems to be a given in the New Testament." Smiling wryly, Stan pushed himself away from the desk and leaned on the back of his office chair. "I love old Paul, but I don't know how much good he's going to do me right now. I'm really scared, Francis. I may have really gone out on a limb that can destroy me, my family, and this church. I've read the Bible and I've prayed for days." He lifted his hands, palms up. "And I still don't know what to do."

"Stan, I don't know what's going on. I don't want to, unless you want me to. But, tough as whatever this is, you can't turn your back on your convictions, or your assurance that God is going to walk through this thing with you. If you do, then your family will really lose, and so will the people in this church and our community who need men of principle and integrity as their leaders. And Stan, you'll lose too."

"What do you know about this kind of pressure, Francis?" Stan snapped, feeling as trapped as a rabbit in a snare. "It's not exactly a cosmic battle down there at the nursery, you know." His face glistened with sweat. "I don't know how much more of this I can stand. Just how much does God expect from a man, anyhow? I am going into a fight with an unseen foe who is free to strike from any angle, and who can take any form and use any one of a million others to get me—and I'm scared. Am I getting my message across? I am scared!"

Francis looked him in the eye, and came right back. "So, is your God big enough to carry you through something like that? Just how big is your God, Stan?" he asked. "How powerful? How much can you trust Him? That's the question you're facing right now. The problem is not whatever it is that you fear. The problem is that you're not sure how strong your faith is. That's what's making you afraid."

"You don't—" Stan tried to cut in, but Francis had more to say.

"Whether you win or lose in any battle with Satan, Stan, has nothing to do with your strength. But it has everything to do with God's strength. How much do you trust Him?"

"It's easy for you to say, Francis. What have you ever lost in the battle? What price have *you* ever paid?" He gave a short, rough laugh. "Fighting kudzu, as horrible as it is, and growing petunias doesn't quite compare with what I'm facing."

Francis walked over to the bookcases that lined the study wall and stood quietly, not moving or speaking. Stan watched him, wondering if he'd gone too far and, somehow, not caring if he had. But as the minutes stretched on he became uncomfortable and very aware that his friend stood hunched forward as if he too were weighted with a burden. Then, at last, he turned. To Stan's surprise, tears ran down his face and splotched the front of his denim shirt.

"Seven years ago, before you came to Cherry Pit, Stan, I was the pastor of a church in Calhoun," Francis said quietly. "I too looked into the eye of the hurricane and saw the devil smile. Four of us in town had been studying something from the Bible that was different from anything we'd ever heard. The more we studied, the more convinced we became that it was a life-and-death spiritual issue. So, I am thankful to say, all four of us, each in his own way, and in his own time, took a stand for that truth. Two of us paid a terrible price."

"I didn't know," Stan said helplessly.

"Of course you didn't. A lot of people don't. Ryan Goodbrad left the priesthood and is now lay leader of a little Protestant church up in Maine. And me? I lost my wife, I lost my house, I lost my church, and I lost my profession. I lost everything in this world that I had worked and lived for, Stan—everything except the kingdom of God. I lost everything, and gained everything, Stan. I know about cost!

"It doesn't always work out that way," he continued in a tired voice. "Sometimes God wins the battles; sometimes His adversary does. We must always remember free will, and that God will never force anyone to believe His truth. But God is going to win the war, Stan. You can't forget that. There are casualties in any war. There are tough decisions, and at times we foot soldiers wonder if we can slog another mile. But you can't forget that we're on the winning side!"

He shook his head. "It just so happened that a major shell hit in the middle of us, and we paid. But none of us would trade our loss for anything on the other side. And because we took a major hit doesn't mean that every incoming round is going to destroy *you*. I believe that in the next few days God is going to have a major victory here. A battle that's been brewing clear back to the days I and my colleagues faced what we did is going to be won! You can count on that."

Stan looked at Francis as if seeing him for the first time.

"You've taken a tough stand," Francis told him. "I wouldn't be surprised if all the powers of hell are arrayed against you right now. But you cannot forget that God will empty all heaven, if necessary, to send angels to your aid. You have the Holy Spirit to guide and empower you. You have some of us interceding for you, standing beside and behind you in prayer. The gauntlet has been thrown down, and the forces are being marshaled for a major battle. God is preparing to confront evil here and win. So, Stan, you can't run up a white flag now."

Stan opened his mouth, and closed it.

"Listen now, remember old Paul? You can take his advice and suit up."

"Suit up?"

"Yeah, suit up, my friend. Remember Ephesians 6:10-13."

"Yeah."

"Old Paul lists the armor we have to wear if we're going to win in a battle like this. 'Be strong in the Lord and in the strength of *His* might,' he says. Stan, we're not strong in our own strength. You're right. You can't win this one. But we can have the same strength that has always defeated Satan. And we get it by suiting up in a set of armor that the Lord personally has created for us. He even lists what it is, and tells us how and where to put it on."[17]

"When we put on that armor, Paul says that we'll be able to stand against the wiles of the devil. 'We are not contending against flesh and blood,' he says, 'but against the principalities' (that's the territory or domain ruled by a prince), 'against the powers, against the world rulers of this present darkness, against the spiritual hosts of wickedness in the heavenly places.' But God says, 'Hey, you can whip these guys if you put on My armor!' Sort of the David-and-Goliath thing all over again, only this time it's the King's armor that enables us to win. Put on God's armor, Paul says, 'that you may be able to withstand in the evil day, and having done all, to stand.' So suit up, buddy. Get that armor out and put it on, and you'll make it!"

A smile spread over Stan's face. "Boy, am I glad you came by, Francis! When you're down in the trenches it's easy to forget that you're on the winning side, isn't it? I was about ready to lose it. Thanks, buddy! Will you pray for me the rest of the day? I'm going to need it."

"No, I won't!"

Before Stan could sputter with shock, Francis looked square into his eyes. "But I will pray *with* you, not only today, but until this whole thing is over. And Stan, if you need my help—even at 3:00 a.m.—call me. I'll be there."

At 5:00 p.m. Stan was so deep in thought that he didn't even hear the cars pull into the church driveway or the doors slam as five very determined church members headed for his office door.

"Pastor, may we come in?"

Stan looked up from his Bible into the hard eyes of Juanita Parris, Ben Gladden, Sharon Creizon, Wilma Filsinger, and Marilyn Fleetwood all standing in the doorway.

"Of course you may. I'm sorry I didn't hear you come. Please, come on in." Stan stood and motioned to the chairs in his office. "We'll need more chairs," he said as he stepped into the lobby and brought in two more, then into his secretary's small office for another. "So, to what do I owe the pleasure of your company this evening?" he asked, looking from one to the other. "Is this a social call, or is there a new committee I'm not aware of?"

"Pastor, several of us had a meeting the other night." Ben spoke for the group, his voice smooth and oily as they settled into their seats. "It concerned some things we all believe that we can do to help our church and you grow and become more successful."

"Well, Ben, I appreciate your interest. What have you come up with?"

Ben and Juanita glanced at each other, and Ben went on. "Well, actually, Pastor, we have a little list of things we talked about that we'd like to share with you. I think you know that our motives are good and that we want to help you become the very best pastor possible." His glance flicked to Juanita again, and she raised one eyebrow as if to say, *Just say it!* "These are just some things that we see are getting in your way of ministering to our congregation, and we felt that as your brothers and sisters we should share them with you. Again, our only desire is to be supportive."

"Oh, I believe you, Ben. So share your list with me. I appreciate the opportunity to hear what you have to say."

Ben coughed politely. "Uh, well, Pastor, we . . . "

"Let me help you out, Ben." Stan shifted his Bible to the side of his desk and leaned forward, resting his chin on his folded hands. "I'll bet you had a meeting. And I'll lay odds that you listed just about anything any of you might ever have heard anyone say that sounded critical."

"Now just a minute, Pastor!" Marilyn interrupted.

"Let him finish, Marilyn," Juanita commanded, a smile playing on the corners of her mouth. "Let the pastor finish."

Stan nodded at Juanita. "But if I were a betting man, I'd wager that the real issue you have with me never made it onto your list. And if there were more than you five there, I'll bet it never even made it onto the agenda."

There was a long silence. The five exchanged curious glances. After pausing briefly for a quick silent prayer, Stan continued. "The real issue is the sermon I gave a few weeks ago, isn't it? And the real issue," he paused, looking at each one of them, "is that each of you is involved in the very same things that Brenda is involved in."

"Now you just wait a minute!" Ben exploded out of his chair.

"Ben, sit down!"

The look on Stan's face stopped Ben in midsentence. "Juanita, I understand that you and Luke eat supper together every night." The smile still played on the corners of Juanita's mouth, but the eyes were now glittering diamonds.

"That's right, Pastor."

"And Ben, you hold little Patty on your lap every night before you go to bed, don't you?"

"How'd you kn—? Who told you?"

"Shut up, Ben." Juanita turned glaring eyes at Ben. "Go on, Pastor."

"The rest of you are just variations on the same theme. Am I right?"

Surprised, Marilyn, Sharon, and Wilma nodded slowly.

"So this is the real issue. The rest is just a smoke screen. I suggest we deal with what's really on your mind, and leave the rest for another time."

"As you wish, Pastor," Juanita said calmly. "Now that the cards are on the table, let's get down to it." She leaned forward, taking control of the conversation for the five. "You've got a choice, Stan. Make a quick change, or, to put it crudely, you're gonna die—personally and professionally. Do you understand me?" The velvet covering was off now. Her voice was steel. "Country preacher, you are in way over your head on this one. You've got a family to consider. You've got a reputation and a career to think about, and . . ."

"And if I don't cave in, I die in a mysterious car wreck. Is that it, Juanita?"

"You said it, Pastor. I didn't."

Ben turned to Juanita. "What are you talking about?" he demanded. "You're not—"

"Shut up, Ben," Juanita snapped for the second time in less than a minute. Her eyes never left Stan's.

"As you said, Juanita, your cards are on the table," he said calmly. "Now I'm going to play a couple of mine." He picked up his Bible and walked around to sit on the edge of the desk facing them, just inches away.

"Juanita, let's be really honest with each other. As much as you might bandy about religious words, and as faithful as you might be in your church attendance, you and I both know that we're on opposite sides of a war that's been raging for more than 6,000 years."

Juanita didn't move an eyelash, and the rest squirmed uncomfortably in their chairs. "You're right, Juanita. I do have a choice, and I appreciate, very much, your helping me to clarify it. And," he paused briefly to look at each of them, "so do you. All of you. You see, I've read the rest of the story."

Holding up his Bible, he continued, his voice stronger with each word. "Even though it may cost me everything professionally and personally, I am going to be on the winning side. So can you, if you choose.

"Jesus, and rightly so, calls Satan, or whatever you choose to call him, the ruler of this world.[2] The devil could rightly say that Adam and Eve delivered it and the authority over it to him.[3] If the story ended there, there'd be no contest. But the Bible also teaches that at the cross Jesus won the right to take that authority back. And we have the promise of it in Daniel 7, where more than four times God says that after Satan is judged, all the authority and dominion, and ownership of this world, will be given back to Jesus, who created it, and to His people. So, my friends, no matter how much it costs me, I won't lose anything."

"What does all this have to do with any of us, or with Brenda?" Sharon asked. "We're all part of God's kingdom, Stan. I get the impression that you're somehow implying that we're not."

"That's exactly what he's saying," Juanita interrupted. "He's saying that you belong to the devil just because you knit—once in a while—with your grandmother when she comes back. That's what you're saying, isn't it, Stan?" Juanitas eyes glittered with the same look a cobra has when it is about to strike. "Isn't that what you're saying?"

"I am saying that the Bible says that the dead are dead, and that they cannot come back and talk with us, or do whatever else they're doing. Every time it happened in the Bible it was always condemned, and connected with the occult. That's all I am saying. Now you have to decide whether what the Bible says is good enough for you."

"Are you saying," Ben interrupted, "that my little Patty is not Patty? That she's some demon from hell? Is that what you're saying, Stan?" Ben stood up and glared, nose to nose with Stan. "Is that what you're saying?"

"That's what the Bible says, from Genesis to Revelation, Ben, and . . ."

"I oughta horsewhip you for saying something like that about my baby girl, you two-bit excuse for a preacher." Ben's words came slowly, as if they were being parceled out a syllable at a time. "Before I'm done with you, you are going to be so sorry, you miserable little weasel, that you'll crawl to me for forgiveness. And when you get there, I'm gonna spit in your face. Do you understand me, Preacher Stan? Do you understand me?" Ben's eyes shone a deep red, and his face was white. "I promise you that you'll pay for what you just said. You can insult me all you want. But you will never talk about my daughter like that and get away with it. I promise." With that he turned on his heel and left the room, slamming the door behind him.

"Well!" Juanita said, standing up and trying to sound perky. "I guess we all know where we stand now, huh, Pastor? The die is cast. Ladies, we need to be going."

---

[1] The armor listed in Ephesians 6 includes the belt of truth; breastplate to cover the torso and the heart, consisting of the righteousness, or perfection, of Jesus; shoes of the good news of God's, victory over the devil; the shield of faith in God; and the helmet of the ransom paid for us when Jesus died on Calvary. Finally, He gives us the sword of His Holy Spirit, expressed in the Word of God.

[2] John 14:30.

[3] Luke 4:6.

Chapter 29

"Stan, wake up. Somebody's at the door."

Stan struggled to climb up out of the deep that was his first decent night's sleep in weeks.

"Stan, wake up!" Barbara was shaking his shoulder, and he just wanted her to go away.

Rubbing his eyes, he struggled to focus on the clock on his dresser. It was Monday morning, his day off, and he had planned to sleep in for once.

"Six o'clock. Brother!" he mumbled, squinting his eyes in the morning sunlight. "I can't believe this. Who's here at this hour?"

Climbing out of bed, he fumbled for his bathrobe, put it on inside out, took it off, turned it right side out, and tied the belt. All the while, the insistent knocking continued on the front door.

"All right, already," he said, stopping at the bathroom to splash water
on his face and run a brush through his hair. "I'm coming, I'm coming."
Throwing open the front door, he looked into the apprehensive face of
Gus Crossworthy, his hand raised to knock again.

"Good morning, Gus." Stan blinked, turning his head away from the
sunshine streaming over Bald Peak. "It's a little early, isn't it?"

"I told you we shouldn't have come," Millie said from behind her husband.

"No, no." Stan raised his hand. "It's OK. I'm just having a little trouble getting my motor running. Come on in. What's up?"

Ushering them into the living room, he pointed to a seat. "I'm going
to put a pot of coffee on. I'll be right back. Can I get you some?"

"Please," Gus and Millie answered together.

Soon the smell of freshly brewed coffee accompanied Stan back into
the room.

"Stan, we're really sorry to bother you so early," Millie began. "But
we were up all night and didn't know anywhere else to turn. I am really
sorry. I bet we woke up your whole family."

"It's OK. The kids have to be up for school in a few minutes anyway.
You're going to get to hear what a school morning is like around here. It's
a real experience. Don't be shocked. Anything can happen until we get
them on the bus. Now, tell me what's happening?"

"Pastor . . ." Gus started.

He held up his hands. He couldn't get the words out.

"Stan, please . . ."

He stopped while he struggled to gather himself together. Then, taking a deep breath, he continued.

"OK, Stan. We need your help. Nadine, our daughter, is in real
trouble."

"Trouble?"

"Yes, big trouble. Our little girl, our baby, is part of a coven operating out of my sister Peg's place up on Rex Hill."

"Didn't I hear somewhere that your daughter was in college?"

"She was," Millie replied. "But she's come home, and she's living up
in Peg's old house. Peg willed it to her when she died."

Millie and Gus went on to tell about how Nadine had been introduced
to the occult practices of her aunt, about the death of Tom Lawson, their
trip to Atlanta, and Nadine's revelation that she was involved in witchcraft.

"We think she may even be the one that threatened you with that letter, Stan." Gus looked apologetic. "Now she's back in town, and we're
really worried."

"She's cleaned up and is dressing very nicely," Millie added. "And those horrid goats are nowhere to be seen. But still something is seriously wrong. We could both sense it. There was an almost palpable evil presence in that house." Again tears filled her eyes. "Pastor, you've got to help us."

"What can I do?" Stan looked perplexed.

"Would you visit her with us?" Gus's eyes pleaded with Stan. "This morning. Will you come with us and visit her? We've got to save her, Stan. We've got to save her. She's our only child."

"Wow." Stan rubbed his face. "Sure, I'll come with you, if that's what you want. But I need some time to think about this. Have you eaten breakfast?"

"No," Millie said, slowly drawing out the word. "We've been up all night and . . ."

"Listen," Stan interjected. "Barb's up and will be making breakfast in a few minutes. Join us, why don't you? And we can talk about this some more. In the meantime, I'll grab a shower and shave. The morning paper is on the table. Go on in and relax till I get back down. OK?"

A little later Stan set down his glass of orange juice and reached for a third slice of toast. "I've been giving this a lot of thought," he said, looking at Gus and Millie. "Are you sure you want to do this?"

"What other options do we have?" Gus looked worried. "You will do it, won't you?"

"Yes, I will. But we can't rush into this. It's going to take some preparation."

"Can't we just—?" Gus replied.

"Gus." Millie reached out and touched his arm. "You need to let Stan finish."

"This whole issue is plowing new ground for me," Stan told them. "I've been studying it for a few weeks, but there's a lot I want to know before I confront our adversary so openly. I don't take this lightly, and neither can the two of you. I need some more time."

Gus's big head nodded his understanding.

"There are some things we need to take care of. First, it would be nice to be sure that Nadine was going to be there when we arrived," Stan said. "And waking her up is no way to have her feel good about what we want to do. So this morning is out." He looked at them questioningly. Their heads nodded.

"If possible," he continued, "we need to have Nadine's cooperation. I'd like for you to call her and make an appointment to stop by. Wednesday evening, around 5:00, would be good for me. Just tell her you want to drop by and introduce her to a friend of yours.

"Then we all need to do some preparation. Here's what I'd suggest.

Do you remember the story in the Gospels in which Christ's disciples tried—unsuccessfully—to cast some demons out from a young man? Well, not long afterward Jesus came on the scene, and He succeeded.

"When His disciples questioned why He was able to do it and they weren't, Jesus said that this kind of thing often took much fasting and prayer. And so, my friends, for the next two days I am going to be doing some serious praying. I have some blood sugar problems, so I can't fast completely, but I will be eating very simply. I encourage you both to do the same."

"Anything!" Millie said.

"Next, I encourage you both to put on your armor."

Looking puzzled, Gus asked, "Armor?"

"In Ephesians 6 Paul pictures the Christian in a suit of armor when heor she faces the powers of darkness, as we're going to be doing Wednesday. Read it tonight and ask yourself where your vulnerable spots are. Be ruthless with yourself. After you've found them, then find the armor that's designed to protect them, and begin putting that armor on. Believe me, you'll need it.

"Finally, I am going to ask some people in my church who have a special ministry of prayer to begin praying for us. Especially on Wednesday, I want them on their knees interceding on our behalf."

"You mean that they'll be asking God to be with us?" Millie questioned. "Would they really?"

"Absolutely. But not because God has to be begged." Stan picked up his Bible, leafing through the pages. A lot of people think that intercession is somehow begging God to help us. But have you ever thought about what that says about God—that He's willing to help us only if someone begs hard enough? that it takes Mary, or some other saint to convince Him to help us?"

"I hadn't thought of it that way . . ."

"I don't mean to say that you're off base. I am probably overreacting. It's that I get so frustrated with the view people have of God. They seem to think (maybe even subconsciously) that God is a tyrant who just can't wait to fry us, and that He loves to make us miserable in the meantime. When I discovered what intercession is all about, it transformed my whole view of God and revolutionized my prayer life."

"In what way?" Gus had been deep in thought, and now roused himself.

"Well, you know how we generally picture *us* here," Stan gestured, "and God over there. And we envision an intercessor sort of standing between the two of us, interceding, somehow coming in between us and God, to protect us?"

Gus nodded.

"I discovered that's the wrong picture. It's Satan over here, doing all he can to destroy someone, to tempt and disarm that person. When I intercede in prayer for someone, I step—not between that indiviual and God—but between that person and the devil. I claim God's power and protection on that person's behalf. I honestly believe that prayer of this sort frees God to work in ways He couldn't otherwise. An intercessor even offers to take some of the devil's hits for the other person." He smiled. "It sort of reminds me of our two boys. A few times when some bully threatened to beat up the younger one, his older brother stepped in. That's what I'm talking about, Gus. You and I and Millie, and a whole bunch of others in our church, are going to step between Nadine and the one she thinks is her best friend. And I'll wager that all hell is going to break loose when we do."

"Maybe that's not fair," Millie replied.

"Nonsense," Stan said. "If we're truly the Christians we claim to be, that's what we're here for. We're in a war. When we enlisted on God's side of this battle, we knew what we were getting in for, and agreed to pay the price. The pity's that we aren't doing more.

"So you two go home and get some rest and start praying."

"What if she doesn't want to give this up, Stan?"

He shook his head. "That's her option. One of the most difficult things in the Bible to understand is God's commitment to our sovereignty. He won't force us to do anything. He will defend to His dying breath our right to make free choices, even the wrong ones—even to rebel against Him. We're not talking about taking that freedom away. You've got to be aware of that. There are no guarantees. Nadine may choose to continue in the path she has chosen, and it is her right. All we can do is do what God does with each of us. He offers us a choice. I guarantee that God will be doing all He can, without violating her freedom, to set her free of this. We've just got to be sure that we have been doing all we can do to free Him to His work."

"Stan, we don't know how to thank you."

"You don't need to." Stan stood up and extended his hand. "Thank you for giving me the privilege of being your friend and standing by you in a time like this. We're in this together, and we're going to do all we can for Nadine."

Chapter 30

It's almost like a cathedral, isn't it?"
Francis looked over at Stan, who'd just pulled his car over beside him as he walked down Cherry Pit Road.

"I was just thinking the same thing."

The farmers who had left the wild cherry trees growing on both sides of the road had thinned them so that they would grow tall. Like columns in a medieval church, they rose evenly on both sides of the road as far as the eye could see. Their branches arched up and over the lane, shingled with jade leaves that sparkled as they fluttered in the breeze. To the sides, looking almost like stained-glass windows, the farms and fields of the county stretched like a Norman Rockwell painting toward the horizon. The road itself, a charcoal aisle, curved slightly to the right, and in the distance—a white icon in a frame of old walnut—Cherry Pit Community Church sparkled in the morning sun.

"So what is the proprietor of our local nursery doing out here this time of day?" Stan grinned at Francis. "I thought you'd be knee-deep in mulch or compost by now."

"You haven't heard?" Francis smiled. "Charla just couldn't stand it anymore and offered to come in and spell me a couple of mornings a week if I needed it. So, with her minding the pansies, I decided it was time for a presidential stroll down the lane. I was just expecting to hear old Gabriel blow his horn and tell me that it couldn't get any better than this, and that he'd come to take us all home, when you beeped your horn. For a second I thought he'd gotten some manna in his mouthpiece, till I realized it was you."

Stan laughed. "Sorry, bud. Too bad I didn't have the air horn I've got on my old pickup. You really would have thought old Gabriel was calling you home."

"If you'd done that, he probably would've had to! So what are you up to, Parson? I don't see any golf clubs in the back seat, so you must be doing something official."

"Just heading out to do a few visits. I have two people in the hospital in town and I need to stop by and see Brenda Barnes for a minute, so I'd better get going. I'll see you later, Francis."

Stan's car had gone about 100 feet when it stopped and backed up. "Say, Francis, why don't you come with me? I'd love the company, and we'd get to spend some time together."

"I don't know, Stan, I . . ."

"C'mon, Francis. You need to keep your hand in. Besides, I don't like to visit single women alone. Barb was supposed to come with me, but something came up. I was thinking of skipping Brenda and just going to the hospital, but now I could see her. I'd really appreciate the company. You said Charla's watching the place, so why not?"

"Why not? I'll do it." Francis walked behind the car and opened the passenger door. "But this is going to cost you lunch, Adkins."

"It's a deal," Stan said, putting the car in gear.

A few minutes later they pulled up in front of the restored farmhouse that Johnny Barnes' family had lived in for more than 100 years.

"So, Brenda," Stan began after they were seated in the sunroom and had chatted for a while about the spring weather, "how's your Bible study going?"

"I'm really in a quandary, Stan." Her pretty lips pursed in puzzlement. "What my senses keep telling me is that Johnny is alive and well and that he's who he claims to be. But then I read the Bible, and it says otherwise. What makes it worse is Johnny."

"Johnny?"

"Yeah. When he was alive, he believed the Bible. He studied it, and he taught the kids and me that it was the only safe rule for our lives. But now that he's come back, he says it's all a bunch of hooey. He says he's found out that we shouldn't believe the Bible, and if we do, we're fools. I don't know what to believe anymore, or who. My heart says one thing and my head says another. I am really confused. One minute it's the Bible, the next it's Johnny. What do I do?"

"What does the Bible say, Brenda?" Stan asked gently.

"You know what it says, Stan." She gave a little laugh. "It says that the dead don't know anything, do anything, see anything, hear anything. They're just dead. Asleep."

"How do you feel about that?"

"I don't know. When I'm studying the Bible, it all seems clear. But then when Johnny's here, and . . . well, you know, with his arms around me, and I'm smelling his cologne and hearing him whisper in my ear that he loves me . . . well, it's not so clear." She was blushing now. "Can you understand that, Stan?"

"I think I can, Brenda." His voice sounded tired. "It must be terribly hard."

She looked from one man to the other. "So what do I do?"

"Well, one thing that you can't do is straddle the fence," Stan told her. "You're either going to have to believe the Bible and what it says about God, Jesus, and the unseen world all around us—and what happens to us when we die—or you're going to have to believe Johnny. But you can't have both, Brenda. They're total opposites. This is one of those terrible times in life that you are going to have to decide, once and for all, which side you're on."

"I've been wondering," she ventured. "If the Bible teaches that the dead aren't conscious, why do so many Christians believe otherwise?"

"Tradition. Believing what you're taught instead of studying it for yourself. A desire to have it one way that's so strong you close your eyes to anything that doesn't agree with you. Let's be honest, Brenda. Which do you want to believe—that Johnny is sleeping quietly up in Cherry Pit cemetery, or that he's still alive in some way that you don't quite understand and has come home? Don't you think that your desires might be affecting your judgment in all this?"

She sighed. "So what do I do?"

"Brenda, if you were the devil and you wanted to convince someone that there was life after death, what would you do?" Francis asked quietly.

"I . . . I don't know."

"Think about it. How could you convince someone to reject what the Bible teaches?"

She looked from one man to the other. "I guess I'd have to send something so *real*, something so attractive, that it would overwhelm the person's spiritual defenses."

"That's right," Stan said. "And how would you do it?"

She gave a half shrug. "I guess I'd probably send that someone that person loved or respected enough to believe that individual's claims. Or maybe I'd make what I was trying to put across interesting and exciting enough to get that person to trade what God said for it."

"Is it working?"

"Is what worki—? Oh! No, now wait a minute. Other Christians believe the same way that I do. Look at Juanita or Sharon or Ben or several others of the church members who also . . . uh . . . I wasn't supposed to say anything."

"It's OK, Brenda." Stan leaned forward intently. "You've only confirmed what I've known for quite a while. But Brenda, it doesn't matter how many people believe the devil's lies. They're still lies—lies he's used for thousands of years to trap people into turning their backs on everything the Bible teaches. He doesn't care about you, Brenda. He's just using you, and sucking you down into the fires of a future hell with him."

He paused to let her absorb what he was saying. She picked up a tissue and twisted it with both hands.

"You know that, don't you?" he prodded. "You've got to know that, Brenda. As much as you don't want to believe it, you know it's true."

She sniffed and reached for another tissue. "Yes, I believe you're right.

But I want so much to believe that Johnny's really Johnny. With all my heart I want to believe it, but I know—"

"What are you two doing here hassling my wife?"

Stan and Francis whirled and looked directly into the angry eyes of Johnny Barnes.

Crossing through the sunlight to stand protectively beside Brenda's chair, he spoke again, his voice low and menacing, "What are you two doing here hassling my wife? Get out of here. NOW! Before I throw you out!"

"Johnny!"

Brenda stood and stepped between her husband and the two men. "These are my friends. Stan's our pastor. You know him. What are you doing?"

"What am *I* doing? What are *they* doing? This is my house, Brenda. Have you forgotten? They're in here twisting my wife's mind, and I won't have it!"

"Johnny, I asked our pastor for his opinion. Stan's your friend. C'mon now, let's talk about this together."

"I don't want to talk about it, Brenda. We've already talked about this. You know that what these guys are feeding you is bunk. I've already told you that. Now, as the pastor said, it's time for you to decide. Is it Pastor Stan and that little church, or is it you and me, baby? Who's it going to be?"

"Johnny, I can't! Don't do this to me." Brenda turned toward the window sobbing. "Don't do this to me, Johnny; I can't take any more. These are my friends. They and my boys are all I've got. I can't leave and go with you."

Taking hold of her shoulder, Johnny turned her toward him so he could look into her eyes. "Brenda," he said softly, "you have to make a choice. This is my last visit home. You can go with me and we can enjoy everything we've been talking about, or you can stay here. But you have to choose."

Throwing her arms around him, Brenda pulled him close. "I want to, Johnny, I want to go with you, but I . . ."

"Johnny!" Stan spoke quietly, but his voice held an intensity and a firmness that surprised even him. "Before Brenda makes her final decision, I want to ask you two simple questions."

"I don't have to answer anything from you, Preacher." Johnny drew himself away from Brenda and hunched toward Stan. "In fact, I told you to leave my house, and I meant it!"

Picking up Johnny's Bible from the end table, Stan held it out toward him like a sword. And with a quiet authority that made Francis turn in wonder, he said, "In the name of Jesus Christ, I command you to stop!"

Johnny stopped as if he'd been hit, one foot lifted in midstep, a look of shock on his face.

"In the name of Jesus Christ," Stan spoke again, only this time even more firmly, "I command you to answer two questions."

Brenda gasped, looking from Johnny to Stan, her eyes wide with fear.

Stan's voice rang like a hammer hitting an anvil. "Who are you?"

The silence was eternal.

"In the name of the Lord Jesus Christ, who died on the cross"—again the words rang out, and this time Johnny flinched—"I command you to tell us who you are!"

"I don't have to answer." Johnny's eyes, fear-filled and angry, darted around the room. They rested back on Stan, and the loathing in them was thick and sinister. "I don't have to ans—"

"In the power of the name of Jesus Christ, who defeated you on Calvary, I command you to tell who you are."

Another long silence resonated in the room until it felt like the whole room was vibrating with the energy of it.

"I am," the words came in a cultured voice none of them had ever heard before, "Abadon, lord of this territory in which you live. I am the ruler of this territory under Azazel, lord of judgment." The voice grew with an intense power that pressed into the room and seemed to drive them to the walls. Increasing to a roar, he shouted, "I am king here, and Brenda is mine! She is my wife! Ask her!" Suddenly the figure of Johnny began to change until, like a monarch butterfly emerging from a chrysalis, a figure regal and kinglike stood before them. Powerful and deadly, Abadon faced them, as fierce as a warrior king staring down a rebellious subject. Leaning toward Stan, and looking as though he could flick him aside like a fly or a speck of dust, he roared, "I am Abadon, ruler under Azazel, who rules beneath Lord Lucifer. I am . . ."

Brenda shrank back against the wall in terror, and, watching in awe, Francis slid to the end of the couch.

"Enough."

The word was so quiet that Francis wasn't sure he'd really heard it. An island of calm in the midst of a hurricane, Stan raised the Bible until it almost touched his antagonist's nose. "In the name of Jesus of Nazareth I command you to tell Brenda the truth."

"Ah, the truth," Abadon said with a sneer.

"The truth," Stan repeated. "Who is Lord of heaven and earth? Who speaks the truth, and the truth alone?"

The figure before him struggled to speak, or not to.

"Who is truly Lord? Abadon, tell us. Who is Lord?"

The apparition began to tremble. Terror etched its face.

"I want the truth!" This time it was Stan's turn to roar. "Who is Lord of heaven and earth? Who defeated you at the cross? Who is coming again to destroy your great kingdom of darkness? Who, Abadon, who? I command you in Jesus' name, who?"

At the name of Jesus Abadon shrank in terror. "Je . . . sus." The name came slowly, as if pulled by an unseen hand from the fallen angel's lips. "Jesus . . . is . . . Lord."

Turning, he skulked toward the door, then suddenly stopped and pivoted back toward Stan. The fury in his eyes reflected the very fires of hell. "I am not done with you, Preacher." The voice rasped like an old file. "Before this week is out, you will be done. Do you hear me?"

And then he was gone. So quickly that your senses told you that you weren't quite sure he had ever really been there. For a second Francis could see the imprint of his shoes on the carpet as the threads sprang back into place. Then all trace was gone.

It was one of those moments that time stood still. Except for the sound of a chickadee in the magnolia outside the window, the room, the sunshine, the three could have been a painting. All were rooted in place.

Then Brendas wail broke the silence. "Oh, Stan, what have I done? What have I done?"

"You have done what we all might have done in your place." Stan and Francis put patted her shoulders. "You've done what we all might have done. But it's over now. You're free! It may be a while before you heal from all of this, Brenda, but you're free. God has shown you that you can trust Him. You're free."

Chapter 31

She's one gutsy woman, I'll say that for her." Francis shook his head. They'd stayed long enough with Brenda for Francis to fix her a cup of tea. Settled with her Bible in a comfortable chair, she'd insisted that she would be all right now. After praying for her, the men were driving toward town for Stan's hospital visits.

"No, not gutsy, Francis. Just finally convicted that God's going to take care of her. I wish I had 100 with her kind of faith right now.

"Excuse me a minute," he said, hearing a beep. "I've got a message on my cell phone. It's from Barb."

Pressing the speed dial to call home, Stan cupped the phone against his ear and turned onto Addison Pike. Pointing with his chin, he said, "Get a pen out of the glove box, would you, please? There's a scrap of paper in your door pocket."

Expertly he steered down the divided highway with one hand. "H'mmph," he said, "there's no answer." He pressed "end call," waited a half minute, then tried again. Then: "Barb, what's up?"

"Stan!" Francis could hear Barbara's hysterical cry even from where he sat. "Danny's gone!"

"He's what?"

"Gone! I've looked everywhere for him, and he's gone."

"Isn't he in school?"

"No, they called to find out why he hadn't come. So I took the car and traced his route. He's gone, Stan. His bike was leaning against a tree by the side of the road in that stretch of woods after Mabel Richard's place. We called and called, and there was no answer. I called Sheriff McLaughlin, and he's been looking, but we can't find him. Stan, he's gone!"

"Barbara, I'll be right home. He's probably at somebody's house playing a game or watching TV. We'll find him. Just be calm until I can get there. Listen, I've got Francis with me. We'll be there in about 10 minutes, Honey, just be calm. We'll find him."

"What's happened?" Francis asked as Stan wheeled into an emergency vehicle turnaround and whipped the car onto the freeway going the other direction.

"Danny's gone. Barbara's in a panic." He shook his head. "Danny's generally very responsible, so I can't imagine what's going on, but I do know that I need to get there quick. Do you mind, Francis? I can drop you off at the nursery as soon as I get Barbara calmed down."

"Don't worry about it. Just let me use your phone, and I'll tell Charla where I am. She can watch the store all day if I need her to. In fact, she'd love to. I'll stay with you till we find him."

"Thanks."

As he handed Francis the phone, it rang again.

"Get it, will you?"

Francis said hello, then handed it to Stan. "It's for you. I don't recognize the voice."

"Stan Adkins?" The voice was low and raspy, almost a whisper. Stan struggled to concentrate and hear while he was driving.

"Yes?"

"Stan, your son is missing. Are you aware of that?"

"Yes, I am. Who is this? What do you want? Do you know where

Danny is?"

"A walk in the cemetery behind the church might be illuminating, Pastor Stan," the voice rasped. "Or perhaps should I say edifying." There was a click, then nothing.

"Oh, dear God!" Stan hit the accelerator. "He said Danny's at the church, in the cemetery. Hang on, Francis. If they've done anything to my son, I'll . . . I'll . . . O God, please take care of Danny. Please protect him. Please . . . please . . ."

"Shall I call your wife?"

"Not until I know what we've found. Who knows what these people might have done to him."

"Who, Stan?"

"I don't know. But I've gotten some threats lately. It has to do with, well, you can guess." Turning off the freeway, he took the exit at almost 60 miles an hour. Braking hard, he skidded right onto Benson Road at the stop sign, then eight miles later turned left onto Cherry Pit Road. Driving so fast that the trees blurred on either side, he barely missed hitting Roscoe Byrding's old sheepdog, who was dozing in the road. A few minutes later he spun into the gravel of the church's driveway and slid up to the white-washed log marking the boundaries of the parking lot.

Throwing open their doors, he and Francis raced for the gate in the white picket fence that surrounded the cemetery. Stopping, they listened. They heard nothing but the buzz of a bumblebee coming out of a hole next to the gatepost.

"Stan, let me go first. We don't know what's up there and . . ."

"No, we'll both go."

"Wait, did you hear that?"

"What?"

"There. Listen!"

"Heeeelllp!" The quavering call came faintly from the slope behind the church. "Heeeelllp!"

"C'mon!"

Racing around the church, calling "Danny!" with every breath, they frantically looked out over the tombstones.

"Daaaddy!" The voice, louder now, came over the top of a little rise, in the newer part of the cemetery.

"Danny!" Stan yelled. "We're coming. Where are you?"

"Up here, Daddy. Be careful."

Cresting the top of the hill, Stan and Francis stopped in shock.

Harley Main's will had stated that his tombstone was to be of polished Georgia marble, eight feet tall by three feet wide. It had been ordered 10 years before his death and inscribed with a list of all his contributions to the community and his church. For years it stood in the back lot of Brookvale Monument, covered by a tarp, until the day it was installed over its late owner. Some said its size and opulence was an embarrassment to the church. Others chuckled and said that it gave the place character. Nobody ever bothered reading it.

Now it lay toppled in the stone-lined plot of the 12 grave sites Harley had bought, "so that I won't be crowded when my time comes." In the closely cropped grass, with herbs and colored sand, a large pentagram had been drawn. The massive stone lay on the ground in its center. On top of the stone, tied in place with ropes that had never before been used, lay Danny Adkins, large splotches of red covering his throat and chest. Terror filled his eyes.

"Danny?" Stan said quietly, almost afraid to move.

"Danny," he whispered. Then, "Oh, God in heaven, no!"

"Daddy!"

Walking uncertainly toward the huge stone of sacrifice, Stan and Francis stopped at its edge.

"Danny? Danny!" Rushing to his son, Stan held him in his arms.

"It's OK, Daddy. It's only paint."

"What?"

"It's only paint, Daddy. They said—"

"There's a paper tied to his toe," Francis said, fumbling to untie the string.

"It's a message, Dad. They said it was for you."

Struggling to untie the knots that held his son, anger and relief making his fingers shake so hard he could hardly hold the rope, Stan asked Francis, "What does it say?"

Then he looked at Danny. "Who did this to you?"

" 'Preacher, it's time for you to go.' Francis' voice was unsteady. " 'Next time it could be your wife, or a son, or maybe even you on this rock. And it might not be paint covering your throat. You have 24 hours to resign and be on your way. This is not a joke or a prank. We are serious. Going to the police will not do any good. We are everywhere, and we have the power to do what we say. You may have won at Brenda Barnes'. Enjoy your little victory while you can. It's the last you'll ever have. Preacher, don't let tomorrow's sun set on you here.' "

"That's it?" Stan finally untied the last of the knots, then pulled his son up to him and cradled him in his arms. "That's it?"

"That's it, Stan. What are you going to do?"

"I don't know, Francis. But I do know that I'm not leaving town. These people are extremely dangerous, but they're scared, or they wouldn't be doing something like this. Helping his son to his feet, he said to them both, "C'mon, let's go." With his arm around Danny and with Francis on his other side, Stan headed for the car.

Only minutes later they were sitting on the living room couch waiting for the police to arrive. Barbara had welcomed them with tears of relief, and had grabbed her son as if she'd never let him go. "Now," Stan asked Danny, "do you know who did this to you? I've got to know."

"No, Dad." The tears slipped down his face again, and he reached up and brushed them away with the back of his hand. "I was riding down Cherry Pit toward the cutoff to school when this car went by and pulled over ahead of me. Two men I'd never seen before got out and motioned me to stop. I just thought they wanted directions. The next thing I knew, they'd grabbed me and pulled me off my bike. One of them put a bag over my head, and then they shoved me into the car.

"There was someone else in there—a woman, because I smelled her perfume. Anyway, she was giving them directions, and the next thing I knew, we'd stopped and they were pulling me out of the car. I thought I was going to die, Daddy—I was so scared. I wet my pants a little. They pushed me up a hill, as though they were in a rush and didn't want anyone to see them. The woman kept telling them to hurry so they wouldn't get caught. Finally they stopped shoving and made me sit down, and then I heard men grunting, the way they would if they were lifting something really heavy; and then I thought I heard a tree falling. Then there was some rustling—it sounded like paper bags—and they made me get up and lie down on something hard and cold."

He stopped, his face still pale with fright. "I know now that it was that tombstone. They pulled my shirt off, and I tried to fight them, but I couldn't. They were so strong, and I thought that they were going to kill me. When I yelled, they pressed something against my face and almost suffocated me because the bag was still over my head. Then the woman whispered in my ear that if I was still I wouldn't be hurt, but that if I yelled I might not ever see you or Mom again. So I lay really still."

Tears ran down Stan's face as he hugged his young son.

"I felt them put something wet on my chest and my neck, and then they tied me up. The woman told me that they were going to take the bag off my head, so I had to keep my eyes shut tight. She said I could open my eyes after I counted to 1,000, but she said that they'd be watching and that if I opened my eyes ahead of time I'd be really sorry. Then it got quiet. I counted to 1,000 two times, and it took me *forever*. I'd get mixed up and lose my place, so finally I opened my eyes and started yelling. I yelled and yelled and yelled. I thought nobody would ever come, until I heard you, Dad. I knew you'd find me. I love you, Daddy."

"I love you too, buddy." Stan hugged him again. "I love you, too."

"Oh, Dad, there's one more thing." Danny pulled back from his father's arms. "They told me you'd ask me who did this, and that when you did I was supposed to give you this."

Reaching into his jeans pocket, he handed his father a small amulet in the shape of the head of a goat.

Chapter 32

W ell, Cindy Sue, I guess it's time you made a decision." Cindy looked at her face in the bathroom mirror and shook her head. "You can't walk both sides of the fence on this one, girl. So what's it going to be?"

It was Tuesday night, and for the first time in a long time Cindy was going to bed early. Two months had passed since she and Steve had gone to the first party at his church. She'd been back almost every week, and her life was being changed by the vibrant faith of the people she'd grown to know there. The contrast between them and those she met singing in the clubs or selling at the New Age fairs made her hunger for what they had. But she realized she couldn't have both. She knew that some who attended that church were not true Christians. It was common knowledge, in certain circles, what was happening out at Cherry Pit Community Church. But you didn't have to look far to see a tremendous difference between those who claimed Christianity and those who really lived it.

In her heart of hearts Cindy wanted the different kind of happiness that Steve and his friends enjoyed. It was clean, and there was no guilt associated with it. She wanted it for every day of rest of her life. And examining her face in the mirror, she realized that she was willing to pay almost any price to have that happiness—even giving up what she cherished most in life, her freedom.

What was it Eric Wold had said the other night at the church? She tilted her head, thinking, trying to recall his words. "God offers us a more abundant life than anything the world or the devil can offer," he'd said. "We may not have any more things or money, but we have something that no money can buy—happiness, freedom from guilt, and peace and contentment. Not only that," he went on, "but we have the certain knowledge that we're on the winning side in the battle between good and evil."

"What would I have to give up to get what you guys have?" she'd asked, almost before she realized it was her voice that was speaking.

"Nothing, and everything," Steve answered.

"Nothing, and everything? That makes sense," she'd laughed.

"I know it sounds strange," Jennie chimed in, "but it really does make sense when you think about it. God says in Romans 3:23 that all have sinned and come short of the perfection God created us for. Then Romans 6:23 goes on to say that the wage we earn for that rebellion is death. So we're all under a death sentence—every person born on earth."

Jennie had looked over to check Cindy's reaction. Cindy nodded, silently urging her to continue.

"Psalm 49, verses 7 through 9, say that there is nothing we can do to pay the price for sin—that's rebellion against God. The price of sin is death, and none of us has enough money or influence to substitute anything else. So sin costs everything!" She looked over at Eric. *Right?* her look silently asked.

"Right," Eric said. "And not only that, I think every one of us can testify to the fact that it costs a whole lot more. We've all experienced the guilt of doing what we shouldn't. We've all experienced firsthand the pain that comes from living in this old world. Even those of us who were born with a silver spoon in our mouth," and he winked at Larry, "sooner or later discover that even money and lots of it can't buy happiness. Neither can beauty or power. So, when you come down to it, it's all pretty empty."

"So now we know what we deserve," Kay interjected. "But instead of death, God offers us a free gift of new life that lasts forever. God loved us so much, John 3:16 tells us, that He sent His only Son, Jesus, to die the death we deserved so that He could offer us what He deserves—which is eternal life. Romans 6:23 says it's a free gift. When we accept Jesus' death in place of our own and ask Him to be Lord of our lives, then God gives us back the everlasting, abundant life He created us for. Not only that, but the guilt of the past is gone, and we don't have to fear anything in the future. The best news is that we can't earn or deserve it. It is a gift that we can only accept."

"So," Jennie interrupted again, "it costs you nothing, and everything."

"What about these two kingdoms you keep mentioning?" Cindy asked. "I still don't understand. Steve tried to explain it a while back, but I don't think I've got it yet."

"I think I can explain it." Suzanne Potts was a friend of Lana's who had dropped in for the weekend. "The Bible says that at one time there was only one kingdom in the whole universe. It was God's kingdom of light. Then one of the highest angels in heaven, Lucifer, rebelled. In that rebellion he took one third of heaven's angels with him. The book of Revelation says that there was war in heaven, and that Satan, which means the adversary or the devil, as we often call him now, was thrown out of heaven with the angels that joined him. They came here and convinced

Adam and Eve, the first inhabitants of this new world, to join their rebellion. Luke 4:6 says that the dominion of this earth was delivered to Satan, and Genesis 3 tells us the story of how it happened. So then the kingdom on earth became the kingdom of darkness."

"It could have ended there, with human beings subject to Satan, God's adversary, but God wasn't willing to let us go," Steve rejoined the discussion. "He loved us too much for that. He invaded, with an invasion of love. Jesus agreed to die in our place."

Eager to add to Cindy's understanding, Jennie leaned forward. "You could say that the kingdom of light invaded when Jesus came to this world. Ever since then, those two kingdoms have been at war on earth, the devil using force and deception, God using the power of love. The book of Daniel in the Bible, especially the seventh chapter, and the whole book of Revelation tell us which side is going to win. So since we're all winners," and she grinned at the group, "we've decided to be on the winning side."

"How about you, Cindy? Which side are you going to be on?" Lori asked the question that they'd all been praying that they'd ask at the right time.

After what seemed like a millennium, Cindy slowly spoke. "I don't honestly know. I do know that you've all given me a lot to think about. I want what you have. I just don't know if I'm willing to pay the price to have it.

"I've never understood before what was really going on in this world and some of the things I'm involved in, but now that I do I know I have to make a decision. But I must make it in my own time. I can't rush on an impulse or because I'm scared. If God's really up there, He understands that. If I decide to give my life to Him, I'm not going to go halfway. It's going to be all or nothing, and that's a decision I can't take lightly. Can you all understand that?"

Now, as she got ready for bed, Cindy realized that she had already, really, made the decision. The seed of God's love, planted so many years before, had finally sprouted. And she had to admit that its growth in her heart was wonderful. *Well, Lord*, she thought, brushing out her long brown hair, *I guess You've got me if You want me. I want to be a part of Your kingdom of light, so I invite You into my heart as Lord, and I ask You to forgive my many sins. I don't know if there's anything else I'm supposed to say. If there is, I don't know what it is, so I guess this is it. I promise that I will serve You forever. All I ask is that I can be a part of Your kingdom, now and when it comes on earth. Oh, and Lord, tomorrow morning I'm going to get rid of all the stuff from the other side. You're going to have to help me, because I know how hard Your adversary is going to be working to stop me now that I'm on Your side. If I'm tested, I ask that You will make me strong for You. Well, I'd better go to bed. It's going to be a big day tomorrow. Amen.*

Cindy smiled. It felt good to have made the decision. And it felt good to know that she'd made the right one. Locking her bedroom door, she pulled back the comforter and crawled into bed.

At 2:00 a.m. Cindy jerked instantly awake. She had been sleeping so soundly that it took a minute to orient herself. Then she heard it—the footsteps. She had hoped they'd be gone now that she had given her life to God, but there was no mistaking them. As she lay wide awake staring into the darkness, the footsteps crossed from the front door over to the kitchen. As it did almost every night, the water turned on for a minute, then abruptly turned off. Then the steps, each one firm and steady, crossed to the chair in the living room where her father always sat when he came to visit. She heard the creak of the chair and silence. Ten minutes passed as she watched the digital numbers on the illuminated face of her clock change glacially, one slow numeral at a time. Cindy was about to creep up and check what was happening when, again, she heard the creak of someone getting up from the chair and the steady tread of footsteps across the living and dining room to her bedroom door.

She shut her eyes tight and waited. *Lord, if You're up there, and I believe You are, You're going to have to protect me,* she prayed silently. Whoever was out there paused by her door. *I don't know what's going on, God, but I believe in Your power and the power of Your Son. I know that I've been awfully independent my whole life, but now I want to give my life to You. Everything. Just take me, and protect me. Amen.*

The footsteps continued . . . through her locked door.

Cindy lay perfectly still, her eyes closed as the measured, steady tread slowly crossed the room to stop at the side of her bed. Trembling like a baby cottontail face to face with a rattlesnake, she waited to die. *Dear God, please . . .* The sound of her heartbeat filled her ears. Then gently, a hand—cool, reassuring, soft, and gentle—touched her arm, and a musical voice, unlike anything she'd ever heard, spoke her name. "Cindy."

Please, God . . .

"I want you to come with me."

Cindy knew. Knew that the whole great battle between God and Satan had, for her, come down to this moment, here in her bedroom, and the decision she made here and now would be her choice for eternity.

What had Grandma T said? Think, Cindy! Help me, God. Oh, yes. Yes! She could almost hear her grandmother's voice. *Cindy, if you ever come face to face with Satan or one of his angels, the name of Jesus will be your protection. And Cindy, please, please choose to be with me in heaven.*

"Cindy," the voice spoke again, warm, inviting, like the seductive breath of spring. "Come with me." The voice pulled her like the gentle, soft, mysteriously sticky strands of . . . a spiderweb. That was it. She shuddered. This must be how a butterfly feels when it first senses the touch of those deadly strands. *I've got to get out of this,* she thought desperately, *before I'm entranced . . . What did Gram say? The name of Jesus; that's it. I have got to claim the name of Jesus.* Desperately she tried to say the word. Her mouth opened and shut like a fish gasping for air, but nothing would come.

Again the voice spoke. Determined, urgent, gentle. "Cindy, come with me." Again she felt herself being drawn into a deadly vortex of silk. Drawn toward a lethal world by zephyr strands of death.

Jesus! The word never passed her lips, but the cry from her desperate heart shot through to eternity like a thunderclap of victory. *Jesus! Save me, or I'm going to die!* As a warrior bursting to victory, the one-word battle cry of the followers of the Son of God rang through her heart, and instantly she knew she was safe.

Opening her eyes in triumph, she stared into the blazing eyes of the most hideously evil, sinister, diabolical manlike creature she had ever imagined. For a second their eyes locked, and she saw in his anger the face of the devil himself. Then he was gone.

In terror Cindy pulled the blankets up over her head and began to cry hysterically. Her trembling sobs shook the bed, and her moans and cries and wails broke the heart of God. Suddenly a voice so beautiful it seemed like the music of all heaven filled her apartment. At its first sound the darkness and fear fled, and light scintillated and danced throughout the room in heavenly cascades of peace. *Cindy, don't worry. I've taken it all away from you.*

In an instant she knew it was true. She was free from the trap that had held her so long.

Like a scared child who has found her mother's arms, she fluffed her pillow, nestled down into the covers, and fell, sniffling gently, into a sleep more peaceful than she'd known in years.

Chapter 33

Stan rinsed out the antique shaving brush he had inherited from his father, shook out the excess water, and set it on its end to dry. There was something about filling a shaving mug with steaming hot water, letting it soak for a minute, then brushing up a mugful of hot fresh lather and shaving that made every morning special. Twice his family had bought him electric razors in an effort to bring him into the twenty-first century, but they both sat in the bathroom cupboard, unused except for the obligatory first time to satisfy his family. Sure, it was old-fashioned. Sure, his family joked about it. But it was his morning ritual. That five minutes of undisturbed warmth was his. No phone calls. No interruptions. Just his to enjoy and luxuriate in as he stood in his bathrobe and slippers. He wasn't going to change. Three of his friends had watched him at pastoral retreats and had been so impressed that they too had gone out and bought mugs and brushes and were shaving the old-fashioned way. One of them had even dug out his grandfather's old straight razor and, after sharpening it, had managed to shave himself without doing more than minor damage. "Next fall," Stan told himself, "at retreat, I'm going to suggest that we form a club—the Royal Guild of the Mug and Brush, maybe. We might even talk Mel into designing a logo on the computer. We could go national. He grinned to himself. Baby boomers who have returned to the ways of their ancestors.

"Speaking of family," he continued talking to himself, "it sure is lonely around here without Barb and the kids. Well, it's for the best, I guess. At least until they catch these guys, whoever they are. Maybe I'll know tonight." The note had given him until sundown to get out of town, so he didn't have long to wait. He was just glad that there were people in the church who were his friends and who loved his family—and would protect them.

Splashing aftershave on his face, he padded into the living room and picked up a notebook sitting next to his favorite chair, a large wingback next to a window looking out over the valley. Putting on his glasses, he sat down, prayed briefly, opened the notebook to the first page, and began to review the written summary of what he had studied the past few months.

"There are two kingdoms on this earth, the kingdom of darkness and the kingdom of light. We are all citizen soldiers of one or the other. There can be no middle ground, no bench sitters, or noncombatants in this war. Compromise between the two is impossible. From my study I am convinced that Satan has been the ruler of this world ever since Adam and Eve delivered their dominion to him in the Garden of Eden. I believe that although I was born a citizen of the kingdom of darkness, God loved me—and everyone else on this world—so much that He invaded Satan's kingdom to redeem me back to Him. I believe that freedom is one of the most important things in the universe to God, and that He was willing to pay the price demanded for my freedom if I chose it, in order to restore to me the right to choose."

He shifted slightly, rereading the previous few lines, and nodded. Pushing his glasses up on his nose, he continued reading.

"I am constrained, by the love of God, the ransom paid for me on Calvary, and my own observations of the fruit of those two kingdoms, to take my side on the side of God and His kingdom. I realize that this puts me and my family in direct conflict with the second most powerful force in the universe. I am also aware that my choice may cost me everything on this earth, but my family and I are willing to pay that price for eternity. Because Satan is the rightful ruler of this earth, there are times that God would like to intervene more forcefully to protect His people, but cannot. Even though some battles may be lost, and even though we may be casualties in the short term, we have read the end of the story. We know that Satan was ultimately defeated at the cross of Jesus Christ. His fate was sealed. We know who will win this war. And we are determined to be on the winning side! Whatever that costs us, we will pay.

"In the meantime, we believe that we can face Satan's forces with courage and boldness far greater than is naturally ours, boldness that comes from our General and loving King, Jesus. We will take the sword of God's Word in our hands and minds and go forth to battle for Him, and we will do it in the energy and power of His Spirit. We will be gracious and kind and fair to all, even our worst enemies. We will fight the battle with God's greatest and only weapon, love. We will pray with all of our hearts for each other, and for those who may treat us badly. We will care for the wounded on both sides, to the best of God's abilities. And we will trust that He will make us victorious. By His grace, we will not back down in the face of Satan's most vicious attacks, but will stand together as a family to finish the work that God has given us to do in this place. We will never be the devil's friends. We will be in heaven together. And we will have others that we have led out of darkness into God's marvelous light."

"Signed, Stan Adkins, Barbara Adkins, Danny Adkins, David Adkins."

"I am so fortunate," he mused. "I am so blessed!"

Turning the page, Stan began to review all that he had discovered that the Bible said about death, the rebellion of Satan in heaven and the satanic kingdom on this earth, the occult, and our part in the battle between the two kingdoms. When he finished, he was more convinced than ever that he was right. Now all he had to do was make it through the next few days.

Bowing his head, Stan prayed, "Father, I guess that we have come to one of those power encounters between Your kingdom and Satan's on this earth. Funny—it feels as if we're living the book of Acts all over again here in our little suburb. I guess that's been going on for a few thousand years now, hasn't it? Well, I'm Yours. Use me however it suits You best. I just ask for clarity in my understanding of Your will as we proceed. I trust You for Your wisdom and for Your protection. Oh, and Lord, please take care of my family. I trust them to You. In Jesus' name I pray, amen."

Getting up from his knees, he set the notebook on the kitchen table, poured himself a cup of coffee, added cream, and headed to the front door to get the morning paper.

"Well, Abby," Nadine looked up into the tall being's handsome face, "it's down to the wire. Where do we stand?"

Abadon, territorial spirit in the kingdom of darkness, smiled at his subject. "I think that we are secure. Stan Adkins is under siege. His family is in hiding, and he's alone at home. He should be finding the little surprise that Phil left him any minute now. As you are aware, he has planned to visit you this afternoon along with your parents. I think we may have that covered as well."

Nadine nodded for him to continue.

"As for church, tonight, I think that we're prepared well. The notices about the special meeting went out to everyone but Stan's most loyal followers. Juanita's committee is ready to destroy him if he dares to show his face. And you and I will be there if anything unexpected comes up. The only real problem we are having is Stan's so-called prayer warriors. They're opening the door for a lot of intervention from the other side, which is a bit disconcerting. However, I think our forces can keep them so occupied that they'll slack off a bit today. The victory in this little battle should be ours."

"And if it isn't?"

"We don't talk about that, Nadine. We're on the winning side." Abadon's smile was wide but sinister.

"That's not what I heard about your little battle over at Brenda Barnes' house." Nadine's smile was equally wide, but the glint in her eyes was like Swedish steel. "I thought that you had that one sewn up tight, Abadon. Or has the old lover lost his touch?"

"What are—?"

"You know what I'm talking about. Do you think I imagine I'm the only one you ever seduced like that? How about it? Was she as good as I am? Are experienced lovers better than us young virgins you pluck off the tree of life? Did she sell her soul, then buy it back, or was she playing with you all along? Beating you at your own little game, maybe?"

The smile quickly faded from Abadon's face. "I had forgotten how jealous you humans get," he said slowly.

"It's a trait we inherited from God." Nadine grinned wickedly. "When we're two-timed, we fight back. You should know that, Abby. You deal with it every day."

"Ah, but God doesn't fight dirty."

"That I learned from you and my aunt."

"So where did you hear about Brenda?"

"So you lost Brenda," she went on, ignoring his question. "Not a very good recommendation for our little exercise this evening, is it? I plan to be there this evening, Abby, and I plan to be in charge. Your boss, Azazel, should confirm that for you if you have any questions. We're not going to screw this up the way you did Brenda Barnes."

Abadon's smile was strained, and there was a look in his eyes Nadine had never seen before—like a cannibal looking at his next meal. For a second her confidence wavered, and she lowered her eyes, wondering if she was the one being betrayed by Azazel. Then hearing again his words of assurance, she tilted her head back in scorn and looked the big fallen angel in the eye. "This means a lot to me, Abby. My folks are involved, and I will not have it messed up.

Stan was reaching for the front door when the phone rang.

Turning back, he crossed to the telephone on the kitchen wall and answered it.

"Stan?"

"Yes."

"This is Cheryl." Her voice was strained.

"Hi. Is everything all right?" His heart leaped. Barb and the boys were with Cheryl and her family.

"Fine on this end. How about you?"

"OK, I guess. Why?"

"Well, a little while ago, when we were all having family worship, we all started feeling a real need to pray for you. Barb and your boys felt it, and so did Mel and I. Are you sure you're OK?"

"Yeah, fine, I guess. I mean, yes! God said He's going to take care of us, and I believe He will. I'm feeling really peaceful about it. Is there anything else I should know?"

"Well, yes. Margaret and Phil called just a few minutes ago, and they both had the same feeling. We're all sensing that this is a crucial time, and we're really going to be in prayer, Stan. All of us prayer warriors have cleared our schedules today, and we're holding you up in prayer. You need to know that, whatever happens."

"Whatever happens? Is there something I should know?"

"There's a meeting tonight, Stan."

"I know. Prayer meeting."

"No, I found out this morning that there's another meeting."

"What kind?"

"Kim Mosely got a letter yesterday. I've checked with several others this morning, and everyone who's not one of your supporters has gotten one; even some who haven't been to church in years. It lists a number of your perceived faults, then says that the time has come to have a meeting and decide whether it's time we got a new pastor. I'm sorry, Stan, to have to tell you this."

"I need to know. Was it signed?"

"Yes. Juanita Parris, Ben Gladden, Wilma Filsinger, Sharon Creizon, and a few others. I can get the names if you want them."

"No, that's not necessary. Does Barbara know about this?"

"Not about the letter. I didn't want to worry her about it until I talked to you."

"Thanks, Cheryl. Listen, I'll come by in a few minutes and tell her. In the meantime, there's something you need to know. I don't know how this is all going to shake out. I'd surely hate to leave this church. But that's not what's important. God has a place for us. I am confident of that. What matters is that a lot of people in this little valley are not destroyed by this. I need you to get all the prayer warriors you know on their knees for the next 24 hours. We're going to win on this, Cheryl, but it's not going to be in our own power. I cannot face this alone. Right now I have more peace than I've ever had in my life, but I need your help."

"You've got it, Stan. I'll see you in a few minutes."

"Right."

"Can you join us for breakfast?"

"Nope, I'm going to fast today. Thanks anyway."

Cradling the receiver, Stan shook his head and headed for the bedroom to dress. A few minutes later he opened the front door and stopped in his tracks.

Hanging from the porch light fixture, at eye level, staring straight into his, was the shriveled bloody head of a male goat. Its eyes had been gouged out. Its mouth gaped open in a macabre grin as it spun slowly. From one arching horn a paper tag hung on a string, fluttering in the morning breeze.

Stan exhaled slowly. He couldn't move. His mouth hung open, and he stared in wonder for what must have been a full minute. Then he realized that he wasn't scared, just amazed. Grateful, he gingerly reached out, took hold of the tag, and turned it to read, "Preacher, don't let the sun set on you here."

Chapter 34

W ell, this should be interesting."
Stan got out of his car and walked toward Gus and Millie, who were getting out of their car, parked around the corner from Nadine's front door.

"Stan, we really appreciate this." Gus held out his hand.

"Oh, it's the least I can do for you folks. Is she expecting us?"

"We told her we would be dropping by, but . . . " Gus and Millie exchanged a quick glance. "We didn't tell her you were coming. Are you mad at us, Pastor?"

"No, I understand." Stan sighed and ran his hand through his hair. "I'll bet she knows I'm coming anyway."

"How?" Gus looked surprised.

"I think I got a message from her this morning."

"A message?"

"I'll tell you about it later. We'd better get going, or we're going to be late." Walking up the broad sidewalk between boxwood hedges and topiary shaped to resemble the signs of the zodiac, Stan admired the old house. *Someday,* he thought, *I'm going to restore an old place like this.* As he reached for the brass knocker set into the center of the polished oak door, it opened, and a liveried butler nodded his head, smiled ever so slightly, and invited them in. Leading them down a hall paved with sage-green wool carpet so thick that it seemed like manicured grass, the man opened the door to the drawing room and motioned them in.

Facing the fireplace across the room, looking at a leather-bound book, stood Nadine. She waited a full minute to acknowledge their presence, then turned.

"Mother. Daddy. You haven't been here since I've remodeled, have you? What do you think? And this must be Pastor Stan Adkins." She extended her hand to Stan. "I was expecting you."

"Expecting?" Millie asked, puzzled.

"I think we have a mutual acquaintance," Stan said, firmly taking her hand. "Someone I met at Brenda Barnes'. I am very pleased to meet you, Nadine. Your parents have told me a lot about you."

"I'll bet they have." Nadine's smile was dazzling. "And you're here to save me?"

Turning, she gently pulled a woven cord hanging next to the fireplace. "Will you serve us our tea now, Elizabeth?" she asked when the maid appeared. "Oh, I almost forgot. Pastor Adkins, I believe, prefers decaf coffee. Am I right?" She raised an eyebrow in question toward Stan.

"That'll be fine," Stan said. "With cream, please."

"Now let me show you around a bit." She took her father's hand. "We can save a full tour for another time, but I thought you might enjoy seeing what I've done to the solarium. I know that you're allergic, Mama, so we'll be back in a minute. I have a new hobby I want to show Dad. Pastor, will you join us?"

Opening the door, she led them into a tropical greenhouse as lush as anything Stan had ever seen. "I'm collecting tropical plants, including the obligatory orchids, Daddy. I thought you'd like that," she said as his eyes lit up approvingly. "I even have a few varieties my old father doesn't." She smiled a sly grin. "If he is really nice to me, though, I might share. But here's what I am enjoying the most."

Turning at the end of an aisle, she pointed to a bed of equatorial plants— some very small, others almost six feet tall, with a profusion of varieties in between. "They're *caro vorare*," she said happily. "Latin for 'flesh swallowers.'"

Reaching over, she touched a small plant hidden under the leaves of a pitcher plant. "This is a Venus flytrap. Pretty little things, aren't they, but deadly. Sort of like this pitcher." She straightened up and looked directly into Stan's eyes. "A little old fly wanders into its golden throat, and there's no hint of danger. It's beautiful. But the fly never leaves alive. There must be an illustration in that somewhere, right, Pastor?" Smiling impishly, she took her father's arm. "Come, Daddy. I can show you this another time. Sometime when the light is better." Turning, she looked as Stan, and the venom in her eyes stopped him in his tracks.

A minute later, seated on a carved Victorian love seat, she turned to her parents. "Now, Mother and Daddy, I believe that you're here for a reason."

"Well, we . . ." Gus began, a little flustered at her direct approach.

"Isn't that why you brought your nice pastor?" Her smile was wide but not cordial.

"Nadine," Millie began.

"You're worried about me." Nadine finished the sentence for her. "You're afraid I'm mixed up in something that I don't understand, and you want to save me from it. Is that it, Mom? Daddy?"

"Well, yes," Gus said. "Nadine, we . . ."

"Daddy, let's get one thing straight. You are my father, and I love you. Mama, I love you. But my life is my business. I am an adult. What I do, how and whom I worship, is my own affair. I do not appreciate your interfering in it. And I do not appreciate your involving someone else, especially"—as she turned to look at Stan the loathing in her eyes made Millie flinch—"him. Daddy, this man has no business in my home. You think Tom was bad.

THE CHOICE | 185

You've never met a man like Mr. Stan Adkins. Let me tell you about him."

Gus turned, concerned, toward Stan.

"It's quite all right," Stan said, a peace that defied description blowing into his soul. "You can tell them anything you want about me, Nadine. My life is an open book. There is only one thing. 'In the name of my Lord Jesus Christ'"—Nadine flinched at that—"I command that you speak only the truth."

For a few seconds Nadine struggled to speak, a puzzled expression on her face. Then turning, she rose and once again pulled the cord by the fireplace. In a moment the maid appeared carrying a large silver tray with coffee, tea, demitasse cups, and a crystal plate of shortbread. Setting them on the coffee table, she turned to Nadine. "Anything else, ma'am?"

"No, Elizabeth. I will serve. I'll ring you if we need anything else."

Handing Stan his coffee and her mother and father their teacups, she continued. "Now, where were we? Oh yes, the reason for your visit."

Stan took a sip. It was good coffee. Staring into it for a moment, he heard Millie again expressing her concern. Taking another sip, he looked up into Nadine's curious eyes.

"Pardon me, Mother. Is everything all right, Pastor Adkins?"

"Yes, fine. This is very good coffee. Do you get it locally?"

"It's a blend we make right here in the house," Nadine said quietly. "I assure you that it's not like anything you've ever drunk before." She looked at him through narrowed eyes, then turned to Millie. "Mother, go on, please."

"As I was saying, Nadine, we love you so much, and we just want the best for you . . ."

Nadine's head was turned toward her mother, but her eyes were on Stan as she absentmindedly passed the silver tray to her father.

"Pastor?" She gave him a hard look. "Are you sure you're all right? Pardon me for interrupting you, Mother, but Pastor, you don't look well. Are you OK?"

"Fine," Stan said, sneaking a quick look in the wall mirror. "Never better. Why?"

"No reason. Well, actually you look a little pale."

"I'm fine. Thank you."

"Great!" Nadine frowned and turned back to her mother. "I'm sorry we interrupted you. Please go on."

"I think what your mother is saying," Gus said, leaning forward and carefully placing his cup on the tray, "is that we believe that you're into something that's way over your head, and we've asked Pastor Stan to come and help free you from it."

"Daddy!"

"I'm still your father, Nadine, and I believe that I know what's best for you. Now, Pastor—"

"Daddy! You're not listening! Not you, nor Mama, nor anyone else—and especially Pastor Adkins—are going to stop me from my life's work. I am trying my best to be civil about this, but don't push me, Daddy."

"Nadine!"

She stood abruptly. "Daddy, excuse me, will you? Pastor, would you like some more coffee? I'm going to refill my cup. Dad and Mom can refill the tea from the teapot." Picking up Stan's cup and her own, she pushed open the swinging door and stepped into the butler's pantry between the parlor and the kitchen.

"What on earth is going on?" she hissed to Elizabeth, who stood by the counter filling a saltshaker. "Why didn't you . . . ?"

"I did," she said defensively. "I put in more than you told me to."

"Right. Where is it? I can't stand this guy any longer. If he's going to have a heart attack in my house, it's going to be a good one."

Pouring a cup of coffee for Stan and herself, she added cream to his. Then taking a vial from Elizabeth, she shook about an eighth of a teaspoon of its contents into the cup with the cream. "It's a good thing this stuff is tasteless," she muttered, placing the cups on a tray. "This is one infarct that's going to be massive!" As she stuck out her elbow to open the door, she smiled wickedly. "Be ready to answer my call, Liza dear. We want this to look good."

"Here you go, Pastor," she murmured, setting down the tray and placing his cup before him. She returned to her place on the love seat. "Now, Mom, about this exorcism or whatever you and Dad had planned. It's just not going to work. Is it, Stanley?" Turning, she flashed him a brief, phony smile. "What's more, Mother dear, if you and Dad are going to continue to bring this up, I'm afraid that we must part company. You two can go your way and attend that little church out there in the wildwood—yes, I know all about it—and I'll go mine."

"Nadine!"

"Daddy, I mean what I say. You don't need to worry about an inheritance. I have all the money I'll ever need. You two have to make a choice. If you're going to be a part of my life, you've got to give up this nonsense about church and all that goes with it. If you want to attend, that's your choice. Just don't ever mention it to me. That's just the way it is."

"Nadine, you can't . . ." Gus turned to Stan. "Can't you do something?"

"No, I don't think I can." Stan took a final sip from his cup and set it back on the tray. "Excellent coffee, Nadine." Turning to Gus, he continued, "I believe that your daughter and I would agree on one thing. We're on the opposite sides of a war. Am I right?" He looked at Nadine.

She nodded.

"When that war started, God committed to one thing, and that is that He would never violate anyone's freedom. That's more than can be said for the other side." He glanced at Nadine, who glared darkly.

"I can offer your daughter freedom from the life she has chosen, if she wants it. I can share the reasons it is the *only* way to live. I can, and do, pray for her, as you do. I can persuade, and even confront. But the one thing I cannot do and maintain my integrity is to try to force her to change. And neither can you. First of all, you can't force a person to truly change his or her mind. If you committed her, or tried some kind of deprogramming, or anything else, she'd just go underground."

He turned to Nadine. "Am I right?"

Again Nadine nodded.

"Millie and Gus, I agreed to come here because I care for you, and I know you care for your daughter. If she will give me a chance, I will gladly share with her about the kingdom of God, but that's as far as I can go. I'm sorry."

Tears rolled down Gus's face as he leaned toward his daughter. "Please, honey, won't you at least listen to the pastor?"

"Daddy, whatever I choose to think of your pastor, he's right in this. I have made a choice. If that choice leads to hell, it's mine to make. And if yours leads to wherever it leads, I guess that's your choice. But"—and she paused for a long minute—"expect me to fight you every step of the way. And"—again she paused before standing, her lips in a tight line— "know this, my side of this battle fights dirty.

"I'm sorry, Mama. I'm sorry. Daddy. I know you didn't intend for my life to turn out like this." A brief shadow of sorrow passed over her face. "Now I think we'd better say goodbye. Pastor, I think you have a meeting to go to."

As she led them down the hall, Stan stopped her with a question. "Nadine, do you have a piece of paper I could use?"

"Sure." Reaching into a tall secretary, she pulled out a piece of monogrammed stationery. "Make yourself at home."

"I just figured something out," Stan said as he finished writing, folded the paper, and handed it to her. "I thought you might appreciate knowing about it."

Closing the door after the three, Nadine gingerly unfolded the paper. Reading the brief message, she hurried into the library, pulled down a Bible from the shelf, and read the words of Luke 10:18, 19 from the New King James Version: "I saw Satan fall like lightning from heaven. Behold, I give you the authority to trample on serpents and scorpions, and over all the power of the enemy, and nothing shall by any means hurt you."

"Gary!" she screamed. The butler came skidding around the corner from the hall into the room. "Get me my car! That arrogant . . . Oooh!" she screamed between clenched teeth. "I am going to get him, and when I do . . ."

Chapter 35

Whew! The last time the parking lot was this full was Johnny Barnes' funeral, Stan thought, pulling into his reserved space next to the walk leading to his office. *This should set some kind of record for prayer meeting.*

Opening the outside door, he glanced quickly at the day's mail on Jackie's desk, signed a couple letters sitting on the credenza behind his desk, opened the door into the sanctuary, and stopped. Every pew was full. Virtually all of the regulars had arrived and taken seats, even though it was early. People who hadn't been seen in Cherry Pit for years were there. Jake Baumgartner, who'd left in a huff when they wouldn't use the pink paint his wife had chosen for the sanctuary, was on the front row. People who had transferred at one time or another to other area churches sat as if they had never left—even the Mosterts, who had moved out of state. Juanita Parris and her friends were all in a group in the back right, whispering among themselves. All of the board members and the pulpit committee were scattered through the congregation. There were even people Stan had never seen before. Most looked up to watch him as he walked into the sanctuary and down the aisle. Some smiled encouragement. Some frowned or glared. And many had the neutral look of people at a hockey game for the first time who aren't sure what's going to happen or whom they should cheer for. Cheryl and all the prayer warriors were there, dispersed through the audience. Brenda Barnes sat in the second row from the front with her boys. Francis Baldwin nodded, grimly, from his place on the back row; and the new girl, Cindy Marshall, looked uncertain from the left center.

As he started across to the lectern he was aware of Mark Barrett testing the sound system. Gus and Millie, among the latecomers, stood, red-eyed but determined, at the back door. He smiled at Sylvia and Jennie over at the piano and keyboard. They were trying to create the atmosphere of worship that usually characterized the Wednesday evening service, but it was hopeless. The ambience was more that of Panmunjom than Paradise.

Lowering the mike a centimeter in a little nervous ritual he always did before he spoke, Stan cleared his throat and began. "I am really glad that each of you is here this evening. We invite each of you to join us as Glenn, Al, and Clark lead us in praise and worship."

Taking his seat, he couldn't help feeling sorry for the three guys who regularly led one of the best praise services in the state. Getting this crowd to sing with any enthusiasm would take a miracle. As the first song began, he half turned toward the congregation and caught a movement out of the corner of his eye. It was Barbara, smiling and waving her hand in her lap to get his attention. Stepping forward, she handed him a note, then returned to her seat.

Opening it, he read, "Stan, nobody ever said it would be easy, but God promises never to leave us when we place our lives in His hands and set out to do His work. I don't know what tonight will bring, but I have been assured by God in prayer, today, that He will take care of us. Just know that your own family, and many in your church family, are standing beside and behind you and that God is your shield and fortress. Whatever happens, I love you. Barbara."

Looking up through the tears that welled in his eyes, he saw her crooked, crying smile, and in that moment loved her more than he had ever imagined he could. Then turning his attention to the song service, he joined in singing Jamie Owens-Collins' powerful song "The Battle Belongs to the Lord."

As they segued into the next song, Al looked over at Stan and winked. Somehow they knew, and had picked these songs especially for him. Feeling peace and assurance surging through him, he stood with the congregation and sang the words of "Be Bold, Be Strong," by Morris Chapman.

It didn't matter that many in the room that night weren't smiling, or that they frowned and glared when he looked in their direction. God was here, and His angels were present, and the Holy Spirit was flowing into the room on the wings of the music, and whatever happened, everything was going to be all right.

Goose bumps rose on his arms and shivers scintillated up and down his spine as the music modulated into another key and the measured strains of "A Mighty Fortress," by Martin Luther, began. This was a battle, all right, and before the night was over, there might be some pain, but it was God's battle, and He was on the winning side. As the final words, "His Kingdom is Forever,"echoed out over the valley, Stan adjusted his lapel mike and stepped up beside the lectern.

Nadine's Mercedes skidded to a stop by the back door to the

Northside Comfort Inn. "C'mon," she muttered, lightly pounding the steering wheel. "C'mon, you guys." Then, seeing the door open, she unlocked and opened the passenger doors of her car for the two men dressed in black who rushed toward her.

"Well?" She asked expectantly as she turned onto Sherman Oaks Drive.

"Couldn't find 'em."

"What do you mean, you couldn't find them?"

"They're gone. The brats weren't at school, and she's gone, too."

"I thought you guys had the power to find anybody."

"We should have done the kid when we had the chance, Nadine." The man in the back seat leaned as far forward as his seat belt would allow. "I told you they wouldn't scare."

"We're not talking about the past, Harvey. Where are they now?"

"We told you, Nadine," the hulking man in the front seat turned to look at her. "We couldn't find them. Every spell, every trick we used, nothing turned up. The Enemy's got them covered, and there's nothing we can do about it. So lay off!"

"Idiots!" Nadine spit. "I am surrounded by a whole cosmos of idiots! When we're done with this," she said as she turned onto the freeway on-ramp and floored the car up to almost 100, "I am going to—"

"Let me out, Nadine." The voice from the back seat was quiet and authoritative.

"You're s'posed to be able to levitate when you want to," Nadine growled through clenched teeth. "Let's see if you magic carpet guys are everything you're cracked up to be. If you want out, you know where the door is."

"Stop the car, Nadine!"

"Try and stop me." She glared at him in the mirror. "You guys screwed this whole thing up in the first place. Now you're going to help me finish it. Then I don't care where you go, and the hotter the better."

"Pull over, Nadine!"

"You don't hear so well, do you, pal? You get out when we get to the church." Weaving left, she passed a truck that was going 10 miles over the speed limit, whipped around it, and barely made the off-ramp. Taking the corner at the bottom at nearly 60, she turned and skidded across two lanes, barely missed a car full of teenagers in the oncoming lane, corrected, and accelerated to the corner of Cherry Pit Road.

"Now!" In tandem both men lunged for the wheel as Nadine slowed to almost 40 to make the turn onto the two-lane road.

"Oh, no, you don't!" she yelled as she butted her head back and connected with Harvey's nose coming up behind her. Screaming in defiance, she swung with her right backhand at Mitch in the front seat just as he grabbed the wheel.

There was no one to see the car shoot off the road and take down a fence post before it took flight. There was no one to hear it slam against the solid thick trunk of an ancient cherry tree, flipping on its side before it stopped. No one saw the spinning wheels that gradually slowed. No one saw Nadine fight her way past the deflated air bag, push away shards of glass, and pull her body through the hole where the windshield had been. And no one saw her, shaking and crying, as she sat for almost an hour near the tree where her crumbled Mercedes rested, its roof flattened, its windows gone.

Nadine stood and peeked through the hole in the windshield that she'd climbed through.

"Serves 'em right," she muttered, looking into the vacant eyes of Mitch, who was impaled on the fence post that had shot through the windshield. Walking to the back of the car, she reached through the broken window and took Harvey's limp wrist, feeling for a pulse. "Well, I won't have to worry about dealing with them," she muttered. Trying to read her watch in the shadows, she bent and tore away fabric from the lower edge of her skirt so she could run. Then slipping off her high heels, she began to jog gingerly down Cherry Pit Road.

"For the visitors here at Cherry Pit this evening," Stan began, "our midweek service is a time to praise and worship God." He looked across the audience and smiled. "Welcome, you who are here for the first time. It's our custom to reserve Wednesday evenings for sharing what our heavenly Father has done for us during the past week. We offer praise to Him for the new insights we've gained about Him and His plans for our lives. We enjoy singing, and we share our burdens so that we may pray for each other. But before we begin tonight, I have a few things I want to share with you."

"Before you do, Pastor," Ben Gladden spoke as he stood up, "there's something I want to say." He coughed uncomfortably. Then looking over at Juanita Parris, who nodded encouragement, he said, "I think we have some other things to talk about tonight."

"What kind of things, Ben?" Stan stood quietly, waiting.

"Well, uh, well, maybe, Pastor, you should . . ."

"What he's trying to say—" Juanita stood and gave Ben a look that said he was a total fool—"is that we are here, many of us, to discuss some very painful things that have been happening in this church lately, things that have caused many of us deep pain." Her voice rose in pitch and volume as she pointed a bony finger at Stan. "Pain that *you* have brought into our lives. And, Pastor, we've had enough. To be absolutely blunt about it, we're here tonight to decide whether you should continue as our pastor. And I, for one, say no! But, of course," she looked around the room, "that will be up to the group.

"Now, so that the discussion can be fair and open, I think it's only appropriate that you step out until the discussion is finished. We'll let you know when we're done. In fact, maybe you should just go home. We'll call you if we need you." Glancing toward Ben and others of her friends, she slipped back into the pew. Loud calls of "yes," and "good" affirmed the support of quite a number in the room.

Stan saw Francis bow his head and could see his lips moving in silent prayer.

"Juanita." Stan spoke quietly, but with a resonant power that filled the room. "This is prayer meeting—a time reserved for the worship of God, not for controversy. If you have a problem with me or my ministry, there is a pulpit committee, and our constitution makes provision for dealing with any concerns you may have. Prayer meeting is neither the time nor the place. Now I'm going to ask you, please, to be seated."

"I will not be silenced!" Juanita glared at him. "You are destroying the lives of many of us in this room, and the time has come to face it head-on. We are here, and we will make our point, whether you like it or not. This is our church, Pastor, not yours. You may think you can get away with treating people this way, but you cannot. Now, I would like to move that we make Ben Gladden the chair of this meeting so that we can get on with it." There were several loud seconds.

Slowly old Ruth Tucker stood to her feet. Tottering for a few seconds to catch her balance, then grasping the back of the pew in front of her, she waved the lace-fringed handkerchief in her hand. "Enough of this," she wheezed, her old voice cracking. "As many of you know, I haven't been to church for a few years. In fact, I haven't been out of Silkwood Manor for more than five years. But I've been praying that God would protect this church, it and our pastor. And when I was in prayer, God told me to be here tonight. I argued with Him, but He wouldn't give me peace, so here I am. Now, you know, it seems that we Christians love a good fight." She smiled a sardonic smile. "A million churches across this land are testimony to our inability to get along with each other. But never let it be said that this church is one of them! We've always gotten along. And we've always loved our pastors. Now, I've read your letters." She pointed around at some of the members. "Some of 'em were signed, and some were unsigned. I wouldn't give two cents for the unsigned ones. Never trust anyone who won't sign a letter that's sayin' about someone else. And I've heard what some of you have been whispering about, and it's wrong! It ain't Christlike. Pastor, don't you dare leave." She looked up at Stan. "Make 'em say it to your face if they're gonna say it."

She coughed and cleared her throat. "Now, I've known little Benny Gladden since he was too short to reach the teats on his daddy's cows, and he couldn't chair a meeting if it had four legs and a cane bottom. I nominate Don Halvorsen to lead this convocation. He's fair. He's honest, and he's not on anyone's side." Ruth narrowed her eyes and looked over at Juanita as a chorus of responses drowned out any objections.

Stan stood quietly praying for a full minute, then looked up and said, "I guess we do need to deal with this issue tonight. Don, you're a good choice. Will you chair the meeting?"

"I've got to get there. I've got to get there. I've got to get there." Nadine's breath came in gasps as she ran down the road. Her side hurt, as did her chest where the seat belt had crossed. The pavement tore at her feet. "I've got to get there. I've got to get there. I've got to get there. C'mon, spirits, where are you when I need you? You know what we've got to do tonight. C'mon, where are you?" Nadine had been chanting under her breath, imploring for her spirit guides to come and knowing that she couldn't stop running if she was going to make it to Cherry Pit Church in time to play her part in what was, this very minute, surely happening. "C'mon, spirits, I've got to get there. I've got to get there." She panted and wheezed, stumbling and falling and scraping her knees and an elbow on the pavement.

"I am not going to let that little twerp beat me. I am going to get him, and his sweet little wife and their sweet little kids. We're going to win! We're going to win! We're going to win!" The rhythm kept her going. Soon she turned a corner. Out across the valley she could see the lights of Cherry Pit Community Church. "I'm going to make it. I'm going to make it!" Turning, she left the road and cut across the fields toward the lights.

"Do you have a copy of the constitution?" Don Halvorsen turned to Stan.

"I'll get it." Jackie rose from her front-row seat next to Barbara and headed down the center aisle for the office door.

"Good." Don was president of the local community development agency and accustomed to chairing meetings. Turning to the crowd, he announced, "I am going to ask Dan Everston to act as our parliamentarian tonight. We'll both sit up here on the rostrum so we can easily see everyone, and you can see us."

Jackie returned with the papers and handed them to Don. He gave them to Dan, who joined him on the platform, taking the chair next to where he'd asked Stan to sit. "We will follow *Robert's Rules of Order* this evening, and our constitution will prevail if it is applicable. I would think that since we are a church, we would want to act in a manner befitting a church. Our objective should be the glory of God. I will call anyone out of order who does not, to use the words of the apostle Paul, behave 'decently and in order.' With that understood, I call this meeting to order. Now, who wants to speak first?"

Juanita stood immediately. "Mr. Chairman."

Don nodded in her direction. "So that we all know who each speaker is, I would ask that you state your name first."

"I am Juanita Parris, a longstanding member of this church. My late husband and I joined more than 50 years ago when we moved to the area, and have supported it to the very best of our ability ever since. We have been here when things were going well and when things did not, and we all had to struggle to keep the doors open. We've been loyal to our church and to you, our church family, through thick and thin, and have done all that we could to stand by you in your times of need. That is why I felt comfortable to call on you my—or perhaps I should say our—time of need."

She half turned so she could see both the congregation and the men on the platform. "I've seen pastors come and go at Cherry Pit Church. Some were a blessing to our congregation and a credit to their profession. Some left our little church and went on to greater things—something we as a church family can take pride and satisfaction in. Others eventually showed us and our community that they were not the men of God they claimed to be. The unity of our body was divided. Feelings were hurt. True colors were revealed. Sometimes these were men that we had come to love and respect, and it was very difficult for us to be objective as we considered their position as minister of our church. But we made the hard choices, and as a result our little church has flourished and grown. We have not experienced the church splits that others in our county have through the years. We've maintained our unity and our commitment to each other and to God, and I for one," her voice rose in a crescendo, "intend to keep it that way." She dabbed at her eyes and bit her lip.

"Go on, Juanita," Don said calmly.

"Well, now we stand at another crossroads. I think you all know that I love Pastor Stan and his family as much as anybody in this room. His dear wife is an angel, and his children are fine young men. He preaches good sermons and has a good reputation in the community. We can be proud of the growth we've experienced under his leadership. But"—and she lowered her head sadly—"lately something has changed. He has openly censured a young, struggling widow in our church, in a scurrilous attack that amazed and saddened many of us in our congregation. When we went to him, in the spirit of Matthew 18, to express our concerns, he widened his attacks to include us. He has begun insidiously to attack the very people who wanted to be his friends and brothers and sisters."

She sniffed and wiped a tear from the corner of her eye. "He has begun to undermine the unity of families in our congregation, and to try to turn wives against husbands, and parents against children. The tragedy is that a man professing to be a man of God has come into our midst as a wolf among lambs and is destroying us from within." Her finger stabbed the air in time with her words. "I am sorry, but I cannot allow this to happen without protest! That is why I sent letters to many of you, asking you to be here this evening. Pastor Stan has a silver tongue. He can speak in ways that I cannot. I am a poor widow, just as Brenda Barnes was before her dear, beloved Johnny came home." She bowed her head. "I know that I am no match for the pastor's logic or his ability to convince you to do what he wants you to do. But I must take a stand. He will try to turn you against me and against others in our church. He needs this job and will fight for it with all of his persuasive power, but we must—for the good of our church and the kingdom of God—stand together, or we will fall. Satan has come into our midst and is trying to take over our church, and we cannot let it happen. As much as we love Pastor Stan, we cannot let this happen!"

Sobbing, Juanita sank to her seat.

Sharon Creizon quickly stood next. "I would like to second what Juanita has just said. Pastor Adkins is a very nice man, and we all love and appreciate him. I, personally, could be very happy if he was to remain our pastor, but there are others besides Brenda Barnes and Juanita who are being hurt by what has happened lately.

"I know people who have moved to other churches because the services are too long. We've all talked with the pastor about it, but he doesn't listen. We have other things to do on Sunday besides church, and when we can't count on a getting out on time, it makes it very hard. Our children get restless, and the diabetics that have to eat on a regular schedule have a difficult time. Maybe it is time for a change." She sat down quickly as several voiced their support, and a number nodded their heads.

Next to speak was Wallace Emmons. "I don't understand what's going on here. We all love our pastor, and I don't think the services are too long. What's more important than going to church? And it's not as if it lasts all day. Who says that 12:15 or even 12:30 is any less sacred than 12:00? And another thing: I've never heard Pastor Stan say anything critical of anybody—even Brenda. The two times I've heard her mentioned in church, it was with love and concern. I just think you folks need to settle down here and put an end to this nonsense."

"I'll second that." Frank Kraft stood shyly toward the front. "I don't normally talk much in church, but I just want to say that Pastor Adkins has been a blessing to me and my whole family. I don't want him to leave, and neither do they."

Juanita began to stand, but Don stopped her with a slight shake of his head.

"I think that everyone should have an opportunity to speak before anyone speaks a second time," Don said, nodding at her. "So please don't be offended if the chair doesn't recognize you until everyone has had a turn."

Nadine had just about run out of steam. Gasping for breath, she looked across the valley toward the lights of Cherry Pit Church. "Boy, distances out here in the country are sure different," she mumbled. "I don't know if I'm going to make it or not. Where's that creep Abadon when I need him?" Getting up from the pasture grass where she had sat for a minute catching her breath, she started to run again.

"I've got to get there. They're not going to do this to me. They're not going to win. They're not going to take my family away from me. Peg, if you can hear me, I need your help. Don't abandon me now!"

She hadn't gone more than 100 yards when one moment she was on solid ground and the next her foot, as it came down, found only empty space. Covering her head and rolling, she splashed into the drainage ditch that snaked out of Bill Dunlap's hogpens, down through his fields, and, hidden from view, into Blackbird Creek.

"Yecchh!" She blew water and foul-tasting mud from her mouth and rubbed her eyes. "Whew! What on earth?" Climbing out, she shook the water from her hair, wiped her arms on her dress, and swore. Reorienting herself, she jogged again toward the lights of the church. "They should be able to smell me coming now," she giggled, suddenly tickled by what had happened. Then she started to laugh, and the more she did, the funnier it seemed. Soon she collapsed in paroxysms of laughter onto the grass. All the tension of the past few weeks dissolved as she lay back in the meadow. It had been years since she had really relaxed and just laughed. It felt so good! Rolling onto her back, she looked up at the stars.

For a moment, lying there, she felt the love of a God she had never known reaching out to her, calling her to Himself, offering her something she had always wanted but had been too self-centered to receive. For just a minute she allowed herself to be drawn by that love, then out of the corner of her eye she caught the lights of Cherry Pit Church.

"Oh, no, You don't! You're not getting me now." Scowling, she got up and began to walk again. The church was closer now, and glowed white in the moonlight.

The meeting had been going for almost an hour, with people standing to express opinions on both sides. Many were hearing the issues for the first time, and it took a while for things to begin to sort themselves out. *It's sort of like being in a dog show*, Stan thought as he listened to people describe him and his ministry in terms that ranged from glowing to despicable. *How can people have such differing opinions of the same person?*

For the past 20 minutes it had appeared that the tide was gradually turning in favor of those opposed to Stan. They had done their homework well. The lists they had circulated and the insinuations on the phone and in little meetings called all over the area had taken their toll.

Do I really want to stay that badly? he thought as he pulled out a pad and began to scribble some notes for a resignation speech. *What kind of a ministry do I have if this is the way they feel about me?*

Then, looking over the crowd, he noticed Cindy, a look of deep intense disappointment on her face. Francis looked as though he was about to throw up. The prayer warriors scattered throughout the room still prayed fervently, but there was a look of desperation on their faces as their lips silently moved in prayer. Barbara, face drained of color, sat on the verge of tears, with Jackie's arm around her. *Why did she bring Danny and David?* he thought in anguish as he looked at the bewilderment on his sons' faces. It was terrible for them to hear one after another stand and condemn their father. Stan was just about to speak when Brenda Barnes stood. Making her way to the aisle, she walked slowly to the front of the church. Every eye was on her, and the room became sepulchre quiet.

Stopping at the front for a moment to gain her composure, she spoke into the mike an usher had put into her hand.

"The last time I spoke in this church was at a prayer meeting, just like the one this was supposed to be, almost six months ago. It has been one of the most difficult six months of my life, and in the lives of my boys. In its own way, even worse than the day their father died." She paused to smile at Steve and Johnny junior who were sitting together about halfway back on the right side. "I told you at that time that the most wonderful thing was happening in our home. Johnny had come home. Some of you were shocked. Some of you were repulsed. And some of you rejoiced—because you too had loved ones who had died and returned.

"As I told you at the time, Johnny not only came home—he was sleeping with me. What most of you don't know, even my boys, is that he was encouraging me—no, pressuring me—to commit suicide so that I could join him. I bought all he said, hook, line, and sinker, and was prepared to do as he asked.

"I really believed that since he was in heaven, there was no reason he wouldn't come to see us, so why shouldn't I join him? The only thing that held me back was my leaving my boys. Years of sermons and Sunday school classes and the beliefs of my family, for generations, had prepared me to accept the idea of life after death without any attempt to discover what the Bible said on the subject. The same, from what I now understand, was true of our pastor. There was one difference, though. When confronted with what was happening, he went to the Word of God. And when he discovered that what he had always believed and taught was wrong, he had the courage to stand up and tell us—even when he knew what it would probably cost him. You will never know what his courage and commitment to what the Bible teaches means to our family. I would, probably, not be here tonight if it weren't for his spiritual integrity. You all need to know that.

"Whatever happens tonight, I would like to take this opportunity to apologize publicly to you all, and to thank Pastor Stan for saving my life and my eternity. If it weren't for our pastor, I would still be involved in the devil's trap, or even dead. Our pastor had the courage to confront me publicly and privately, and I owe him my life. Today, with Pastor Stan's help, I confronted the one who claimed to be my husband. I discovered, in very dramatic fashion, that it was not Johnny, but one of Satans demons. I now know that it was not my husband that came to my home every night, and that what I was involved in was part of an elaborate scheme to destroy me and my family. I will carry the emotional scars of my involvement in his diabolical trap for the rest of my life. I also very nearly lost my two sons in the process and may have lost you as my friends and spiritual family. I am so, so sorry!"

Looking back at her sons, tears running down her cheeks, she continued, "Boys, can you ever forgive me?" Sweeping the audience in a glance, she cried, "Can you as my church family ever forgive me? I am so, so sorry!"

Ben Gladden stood slowly as Brenda made her way to a seat between her sons.

"I am not blessed with Juanita's or our pastor's ability to speak, so I am going to make this brief."

"That'll be the day!" Almost everyone chuckled as Ruth Tucker shook her head and turned away from looking in Ben's direction.

"Grandma Tucker, that will be enough." Don Halvorsen tilted his head and looked in her direction.

"As I said, before I was so rudely interrupted," Ben resumed, an injured look on his face, "I will be brief. As many of you know, almost 30 years ago now, our little Patty drowned in Lake Almo on a church outing.

There was no one more precious to Anna and me than our little girl. For years we grieved her loss. I believe it was what put Anna in an early grave. Now, recently, the pastor has begun to work insidiously to destroy the memory of my little girl. You see, I too have had one whom I love come back home to me. I will never forget the night she came lightly tripping into my room, dressed in the same clothes we buried her in.

"I cannot speak for Brenda. I don't know who she's been sleeping with. But I know my Patty. She's alive. Jesus raised her and took her to be with Him in heaven. How can a man of God say otherwise? Jesus took her to be with Him because He was lonesome. And He sent her back to me because I was lonesome. God loves me so much He sent Patty to me, and now our pastor has the gall to say that she is a demon!" Ben's voice grew louder, and the loose skin under his chin shook with each word. "He has insulted, in public and private, my little girl, and I will not stand it another day." Juanita reached up and touched his arm, but he brushed her off and continued, eyes blazing, "I will not have my little girl's reputation sullied by anyone, much less a man who claims to be a man of God. I will not!" He shook his fist in anger. "I will not!"

Turning to Brenda, he continued to rage. "You may abandon your husband, you brazen hussy, but I will never turn my back on Patty. Never! Never! Never! Never!"

As he finished and started to sink into his pew, Ben clutched for his chest and crumpled onto the hardwood floor. His eyes were wide in pain and fright, his feet scrabbling and clattering on the hardwood floor, his lungs wheezing as he wildly struggled to catch a breath.

"Why is it things look so close at night when they're so far away?" Nadine wondered as she hobbled around Brian St. Clair's old farmhouse and onto his lane. Long ago she'd dropped her shoes. Her dress was in tatters and she smelled like a sewer, but nothing on earth was going to keep her from the meeting going on at Cherry Pit Church. It wouldn't be the first time she had looked the part of a traditional witch, she thought with a smile, and probably not the last.

What I can't figure out is where Abadon and Peg are. They promised to always be there. Now where are they? Maybe? No, can't think of that. I am on the winning side. But what if I'm not? What if I've invested my whole life, and alienated my family and friends, for something that really isn't true? What if it's all a mirage? What if I'm the sucker in all this after all? What a joke! What if they're using me to destroy a church and my family? If they are, then when they're done with me, I'll be next. If they'll do it to them, why not . . . No; I can't think that way. You're starting to get negative, girl. Gotta stay positive. Think affirmations. Think positive. What other options do you have? You've sold your soul, so it'd better be right. Man, why do they have to use such sharp gravel around here? Moving to the grassy edge of the lane, she continued to hobble toward the lights of Cherry Pit Church.

"Ben's having a heart attack! Somebody do something! Can't somebody do something? See what you've done!" Juanita shrieked at Stan. "He's having a heart attack! You're the cause of this! You've killed Ben with your foolishness! You'll pay for this! Somebody, do something! Can't you see he's dying? Someone call 9-1-1. Do something!"

Ben lay at her feet, eyes pleading, as he clutched at his tie and fought for breath. Someone finally grabbed Juanita, literally lifted her up, and set her on the next pew. Jerry Wilson, an EMT on the local fire department emergency crew, pushed his way through the crowd and soon was helping Marilyn Fleetwood give CPR. They worked for about 10 minutes while everyone craned to watch or gathered in little knots to pray. Finally Jerry straightened his back, sighed, and motioned for Marilyn to stop.

"I'm afraid he's gone. I'm sorry, but there's nothing more we can do."

"Where is your faith?"

The words, startling and beautiful, wafted into the room. Like the gentle rush of rippling water, the words danced across the hearers' consciousness. They became like a thousand violins on a warm summer night as they wrapped their hearers in assurance and confidence. "Where is your faith?" As the light tinkling of a thousand silver bells, the words rang in the room, setting ears and hearts on fire.

Then suddenly in their midst a being stood, so bright that they had to look away and blink their eyes. Like a symphony of light, the brightness filled the room flashing emerald green, dancing like dawn on water.

At first no one could see who it was that spoke. Then the light slowly faded, revealing a man in white robes with regal bearing and the stature of a giant. His eyes were the eyes of an aristocrat, but kind and gentle; his face, handsome and strong. Perfectly proportioned, he towered over them. His smile was so inviting, so assuring, that it made many want to throw out their arms and hug him.

"Why are your hearts troubled? Why are you afraid? Where is your faith?" The gentle eyes surveyed the crowd with tender admonition. "Don't you believe?"

For a few moments his eyes roved across the congregation, and most believed—or thought they believed—that in those eyes they saw the eyes of God. "Why must I deal so long with your unbelief?" came the question. "I told you that I would come back. I want so much to be with you, if you will just let me. I told you that you could trust me. Why don't you trust me?

"I am your friend, and yet you close your hearts to me. You believe false shepherds who tell lies and destroy your faith in me. I have tried so hard to break through to your world, to your hearts, with my message of love. I have sent my prophets and teachers, yet you persist in putting your trust in creeds and misbegotten beliefs and churches and leaders that deny me. I have promised you a new age of peace and understanding. My prophets of old were true, and they did their best, but their understanding of my kingdom was so limited that they could only hint at what was to come.

"I have tried to tell you so that you can believe in me. You have killed my prophets. You have spurned those who know me. The masters of the universe I sent to you, you have rejected. You have divided into little groups and have fought each other—destroying each other in my name. In place of enlightenment you have chosen darkness. You have sent missionaries to do battle with my servants. Now they send missionaries to battle you. When, when will it all end, my people? When will it all end? God finally decided that I should come back and tell you myself. I promised my return; now you must believe my words. You believe in God; why don't you believe me, whom He has sent?"

Tears ran down his cheeks and fell like zirconium crystals, sparkling on the floor at his feet. Raising his arm and revealing hands scarred with the prints of nails, he pleaded, "My children, when will you turn from your evil ways and believe?"

Turning, he walked toward where Ben lay. Already his skin was gray, his fingernails blue. People stepped from his path in awe and wonder, dropping to their knees, as water before a cutter is gently carved to the side. Kneeling beside Ben's body, he picked him up and cradled him gently in his arms.

"Oh, Ben, my friend, Ben, I am so sorry." Tears continued to make their way down the tall stranger's cheek, dropping onto Ben's face. "Oh, Ben, I want to take you home, old friend, but Patty says your work isn't finished yet. I am so sorry, old friend." Gently he rocked the quiet form like a father cradling a sleeping child in his arms. "I am so sorry, Ben."

Looking up at the crowd of people standing in the aisles and between the pews and kneeling in the aisles, he asked, "Do you believe?"

"Yes!" The cry came from a hundred lips.

"Do you believe?" he asked a second time.

"Yes!" the crowd roared back.

Tilting his head back and scrunching his eyes tightly shut, the stranger howled again, "Do . . . you . . . believe?"

Like the roar of a crowd in Atlanta Stadium, the cry came back, "Yes!

We believe!"

Looking down, the stranger gently shook Ben's lifeless body. Then once again he raised his face heavenward and in a trumpet cry called out, "Because of the life that is in the universe, and the power of the cosmic force, I command you to arise!"

In stunned silence the members of Cherry Pit Church pressed closer as the color came back to Ben's cheeks. In awe they watched as he shook his head, blinked, and sat up. Standing, the tall stranger took him by the hand and raised him to his feet. As Ben looked at the congregation, his face was radiant, and his eyes had the faraway look of one who has just seen a vision.

"It was so beautiful!" The words came from Ben's lips with the wonder of a child seeing lights and glitter of his first Christmas tree. "It was so beautiful! Why did I have to come back?"

Gently taking his shoulders, the stranger turned Ben toward him and looked deep into his eyes. "Because your work on earth is not done, my friend," he said. Gesturing to the pews, he continued, "Sit, rest, all of you. I'll tell you more in just a moment. But first you must know something else.

"I am Michael, angel, captain of the army of heaven, the one whom your ancestors and you call Jesus, and friend of the one you call the Father. I am come with a message for you."

All over the room, waves of people sank to their knees. "The Father commanded that I come with a message for you. He loves you. He is grieved by your pain and suffering. His heart breaks with all the wars and divisions on earth. But it is time for change! It is the dawning of a new age." The words thundered in the room until it seemed the old church would rock off its foundations. "Heaven is coming to earth. Paradise is being created. A day of brotherhood among all men and women is here. A day free from the tyranny of violence and hate! A day of emancipation from religious bigotry! A day of ransom!"

He paused, turning to look directly at Stan before letting his piercing gaze rake the others who supported him.

"It would be here now," he thundered, "if it were not for false shepherds such as Stan Adkins"

As he spat the words he pointed at Stan, who from his platform seat sat quietly watching. "This man has been lying to you about our Father, and he deliberately closes his mind to the truth every time he hears it. My friends, your Bible is not the Word of God for today. It has served a purpose, but that time is no more.

"Our God wants you to know that what you call the Bible is a collection of myths about well-meaning men and women down through history. But it speaks no more of God than books written by others who have glimpsed beyond the veil. I came to give you light and truth, and I was crucified for it. In order to salvage their reputation, well-meaning men wrote the stories you read of my death and resurrection. I don't blame them. Many of them are still my friends. But the time has come to put an end to what they started. When you know the truth, it will set you free! And when you are free, you will discover what the truth really is."

He had held Stan's eyes for a long time. Now he turned back to the congregation. As he'd spoken, the people gradually separated themselves into two groups. One group pressed forward to grasp his every word; the other group crowded together, putting as much distance between him and them as they could. A few were still in the middle, looking from one to another in confusion.

"There are those who would stand in your way of achieving this enlightenment," he continued, his voice filling the large room. "Your pastor is one of those men. He would have you believe that your loved ones are rotting in the ground." He swiped his hand across his mouth as though he'd tasted something rotten. "He'd have you believe that they 'sleep' until I return.

"Well, I tell you that they are not 'asleep.' I am here to tell you, it's not true. Your departed loved ones are alive and well with the Father."

His smile lit up the room. "Look at me. Am I an illusion?" A long pause. "Can you believe your eyes?"

He raised his hand and flashed a light so bright that people were thrown to the floor. Outside thunder crashed until it seemed the end of the world had come. "Whom do you believe?" he thundered. "God—or him?"

Advancing on Stan, he stood before him, as a lawyer before the accused. "This man"—he pointed at his face—"stands between you and eternity! Whom do believe?"

Then pivoting, he turned back to the church, his voice softly, tenderly pleading. "You can't believe what you heard from this man tonight. You can't deny the reality of little Patty." His voice softened until it was little more than a breath, and people strained to hear. "You can't deny what you see and hear, can you? Are you going to let this man stand between you and eternity? Are you? Are you? He's already destroyed the faith of Brenda Barnes. There are others here whose hearts are being turned away from the truth by this false shepherd. How long must it continue? When will you, who are called by my name, humble yourselves and believe?"

All around the sanctuary people were weeping—some responding to the stranger's appeal, some from fear. "If you will let it, the truth will set you free from the chains that bind you. You can be freed from the restrictions placed on you by millennia of men like this man—men who have put you in chains for their own evil ends. How long?" he pleaded, tears filling his voice. "O my people, how long must I wait? How long?"

Nadine stood on tiptoe, peering through an open side vent window of Cherry Pit Church. "I didn't know the old rascal had it in him," she said softly. "Abadon, you're great! I take back everything I said about you. *You* are incredible!"

Turning, she looked for a better vantage point, and almost ran into the low branch of a wild cherry tree growing on the other side of the sidewalk. Smiling, she grabbed it and swung herself up. She climbed higher and higher until she looked down into the church through the half circle clear window above the stained-glass portrayal of Jesus walking on the Sea of Galilee. "Best seat in the house," she chortled. "You've just been warming up. Now, Abby, let's see you put on a show for these guys like they've never seen!"

"How can we know that you're who you say you are?"

Little David Adkins may only have been 7, but he had heard enough. No one, not even an angel, could attack his dad and get away with it, as far as he was concerned.

"How can you know?"

Like Goliath of old, the big stranger peered down at the small David. "How can you know?" His voice rose in indignation. "Here, you young pup," he said with contempt, throwing his hand toward the altar. Suddenly a crackle filled the air, and lightning flashed down through the church steeple, melting the bell's surface and crashing it down through the ceiling into the sanctuary. The force of its fall was so great that when it hit the Communion table it exploded into splinters, while the bell shot through the floor to the damp earth beneath. In the same instant the explosion of thunder blew out the windows and left everyone in the room cowering for cover.

"*That's* how you know, you little son of perdition! Do you have any more foolish questions?"

"Great, Abby, great!" Nadine was enjoying the show so much that she almost fell from her perch as she clapped in delight. "Take that!" she laughed as another bolt fell from the sky and bore into the hole the first had made in the roof of the church. "Where's your God now?" she called down to the people huddled below her on the church floor. "Where's your powerful God now?"

"Enough!" The voice crashed through the room like a cymbal. From out of the smoke and dust billowing over the platform Stan emerged, face

your lord at Calvary, I command you to leave this place and never to come back!"

"But where am I supposed to go?" The voice was suddenly pathetic, as the once-mighty angel seemed to shrink before their eyes.

"Wherever the God of heaven sends you," Stan said quietly. "Wherever He sends you."

"I am doomed!" Abadon sank to the floor. "I am doomed." And then he was gone, the only sound the thump of Ben's lifeless body flopping back to the carpet in the center aisle.

For a long time Nadine sat on her perch, watching, waiting—forgotten or ignored by those inside.

Many in the crowd gathered at the front of the church, looking at the holes in the roof and floor, trying to comprehend what had happened. Little knots of people gathered around Stan and Brenda. Shortly a siren sounded in the distance, and an ambulance came to retrieve the body of Ben Gladden. Juanita and her friends slunk furtively out the door and drove quietly away. Nadine watched her parents congratulating Stan and an older man she had never seen. Stan's wife and sons got into a car with a couple she didn't know. Gradually everyone drifted away, until only one car remained. Then Stan Adkins, pastor of Cherry Pit Community Church, turned out the office lights, locked the doors, paused for a moment to look into the sky in prayer, and drove away.

Nadine, her feet tucked under her and her knees under her chin, sat in silence for a long time.

The sobs came slowly at first, in little jerks of her shoulders, then grew until the paroxysms of her heart and body almost rocked her off the limb. It was over. Her life. Her future. All she had dreamed and hoped for was destroyed. Ended. Everything she believed in was a sham, a sad, satanic joke. She was the victim instead of the victor. They had used her. They had stolen her virginity and her self-respect with mirages and promises of sand. There was nothing left. No going home. She had nowhere to go.

Pulling off the remains of her dress, she methodically tore it into strips—a pathetic, pale bird on the limb in the moonlight. Braiding the pieces, she fashioned a rope and tied it to the limb.

A Few Pages From
Stan Adkins' Notebook,
Two Kingdoms

Genesis 1:26

"Then God said, 'Let us make man in our image, after our likeness; and *let them have dominion* over the fish of the sea, and over the birds of the air, and over the cattle, and over all the earth, and over every creeping thing that creeps upon the earth.' "

Revelation 12:7-12

"Now war arose in heaven, Michael and his angels fighting against the dragon; and the dragon and his angels fought, but they were defeated and there was no longer any place for them in heaven. And the great dragon was thrown down, that ancient serpent, who is called the Devil and Satan, the deceiver of the whole world—he was thrown down to the earth, and his angels were thrown down with him. And I heard a loud voice in heaven, saying, 'Now the salvation and the power and the kingdom of our God and the authority of his Christ have come, for the accuser of our brethren has been thrown down, who accuses them day and night before our God. And they have conquered him by the blood of the Lamb and by the word of their testimony, for they loved not their lives even unto death. Rejoice then, O heaven and you that dwell therein! But woe to you, O earth and sea, for the devil has come down to you in great wrath, because he knows that his time is short!' "

Genesis 3:1-7, 11, 13

"Now the serpent was more subtle than any other wild creature that the Lord God had made. He said to the woman, 'Did God say, "You shall not eat of any tree of the garden"?' And the woman said to the serpent, 'We may eat of the fruit of the trees of the garden; but God said, "You shall not eat of the fruit of the tree which is in the midst of the garden, neither shall you touch it, lest you die." 'But the serpent said to the woman, 'You will not die. For God knows that when you eat of it your eyes will be opened, and you will be like God, knowing good and evil.' So when the woman saw that the tree was good for food, and that it was a delight to the eyes, and that the tree was to be desired to make one wise, she took of its fruit and ate; and she also gave some to her husband, and he ate. Then the eyes of both were opened, and they knew that they were naked."

"[Then the Lord said,] 'Have you eaten of the tree of which I commanded you not to eat?'"

"Then the Lord God said to the woman, 'What is this that you have done?' The woman said, 'The serpent beguiled, me and I ate.'"

Luke 4:5-7

"And the devil took him up, and showed him all the kingdoms of the world in a moment of time, and said to him, 'To you I will give all this authority and their glory; *for it has been delivered to me, and I give it to whom I will. If you, then, will worship me, it shall all be yours.'"

Job 1:6

"Now there was a day when the sons of God came to present themselves before the Lord, and Satan also came among them. The Lord said to Satan, 'Whence have you come?' Satan answered the Lord, 'From going to and fro on the earth, and from walking up and down on it.'"

John 12:31

"[Jesus said,] 'Now is the judgment of this world, *now shall the ruler of this world* be cast out.'"

John 14:30

"[Jesus to His disciples,] 'I will no longer talk much with you, for *the ruler of this world* is coming' [to crucify Jesus]'"

John 16:11

". . . concerning judgment, because *the ruler of this world* is judged."

2 Corinthians 4:4

"In their case *the god of this world* has blinded the minds of the unbelievers, to keep them from seeing the light of the gospel of the glory of Christ, who is the likeness of God."

1 John 5:19

"We know that we are of God, and *the whole world is in the power of the evil one.*"

Ephesians 2:1, 2

"And you he made alive, when you were dead through the trespasses and sins in which you once walked, following the course of this world, *following the prince of the power of the air,* the spirit that is now at work in the sons of disobedience."

Ephesians 6:10-13

"Finally, be strong in the Lord and in the strength of his might. Put on the whole armor of God, that you may be able to stand against *the wiles of the devil*. For we are not contending against flesh and blood, but *against the principalities, against the powers, against the world rulers of this present darkness, against the spiritual hosts of wickedness in the heavenly places*. Therefore take the whole armor of God, that you may be able to withstand in the evil day, and having done all, to stand."

Colossians 2:13-15

"And you, who were dead in trespasses and the uncircumcision of your flesh, God . . . , having canceled the bond which stood against us with its legal demands; this he set aside, nailing it to the cross [He ransomed us]. He disarmed the principalities and powers and made a public example of them, triumphing over them in him [at the cross]"

Colossians 1:12-14, 19-23

"Giving thanks to the Father, who has qualified us to share in the inheritance of the saints in light. He has *delivered us from the dominion of darkness* and transferred us to the kingdom of his beloved Son, in whom we have redemption [ransom], the forgiveness of sins."

"For in him all the fulness of God was pleased to dwell, and through him to reconcile to himself all things, whether on earth or in heaven, making peace by the blood of his cross. And you, who once were estranged and hostile in mind, doing evil deeds, he has now reconciled in his body of flesh by his death, in order to present you holy and blameless and irreproachable before him, provided that you continue in the faith, stable and steadfast, not shifting from the hope of the gospel which you heard, which has been preached to every creature under heaven, and of which I, Paul, became a minister."

1 Peter 2:9, 10

"But you are a chosen race, a royal priesthood, a holy nation, God's own people, that you may declare the wonderful deeds of him who *called you out of darkness* into his marvelous light. Once you were no people but now you are God's people; once you had not received mercy but now you have received mercy."

Matthew 25:31

"When the Son of man comes in his glory, and all the angels with him, *then* he will sit on his glorious throne."

Hebrews 2:7-9

" 'Thou didst make Him [Jesus] for a little while lower than the angels, thou hast crowned him with glory and honor, putting everything in subjection under his feet.' Now in putting everything in subjection to him, he left nothing outside his control. *As it is, we do not yet see everything in subjection to him.* But we see Jesus, who for a little while was made lower than the angels, crowned with glory and honor because of the suffering of death, so that by the grace of God he might taste death for every one."

1 Corinthians 15:21-28

"For as by a man came death, by a man has come also the resurrection of the dead. For as in Adam all die, so also in Christ shall all be made alive. But each in his own order: Christ the first fruits, then at his coming those who belong to Christ. *Then comes the end, when he delivers the kingdom to God the Father after destroying every rule and every authority and power.* For he must reign until he has put all his enemies under his feet. The last enemy to be destroyed is death. 'For God has put all things in subjection under his feet.' But when it says, 'All things are put in subjection under him,' it is plain that he is excepted who put all things under him. *When* all things are subjected to him, *then* the Son himself will also be subjected to him who put all things under him, that God may be everything to every one."

Revelation 14:6, 7

"Then I saw another angel flying in midheaven, with an eternal gospel to proclaim to those who dwell on earth, to every nation and tribe and tongue and people; and he said with a loud voice, 'Fear God and give him glory, for the hour of his judgment has come; and worship him who made heaven and earth, the sea and the fountains of water.' "

2 Corinthians 11:14, 15

"Even *Satan disguises himself as an angel of light.* So it is not strange if his servants also disguise themselves as servants of righteousness."

Romans 8:38, 39

"I am sure that neither death, nor life, nor angels , nor principalities, nor things present, nor things to come, nor powers, nor height, nor depth, nor anything else in all creation, will be able to separate us from the love of God in Christ Jesus our Lord."

More Pages and Thoughts From Pastor Adkins' Notebook

What Is Man?
Genesis 2:7
Body + Spirit = Soul

Hebrew—ruah.
More than 400 times translated as breath or breathing

Greek—pneuma
More than 350 times—breath

Ezekiel 18:4
"The soul that sins shall die."

Genesis 1:30
Animals also have breath of life.

Genesis 7:15, 21, 22
All creatures—breath of life.

Ecclesiastes 3:19-21
Breath of life/spirit—both animals and humans have breath.

Job 33:4
"The spirit of God has made me, and the breath of the Almighty gives me life."

James 2:26
Body without *pneuma*/spirit is dead.

Job 34:14, 15
"If he [God] should take back his spirit to himself, and gather to himself his breath, all flesh would perish together, and man would return to dust."

Genesis 3:19
You are dust, and shall return to dust.

Psalm 146:4
When a person's breath departs, he or she returns to the earth; on that very day his or her plans perish.

Ecclesiastes 12:7
Dust returns to earth as it was—and the spirit to God who gave it.

Psalm 104:29
You take away their breath and they die, and return to dust.

Death

Genesis 3:1-6
The first lie: when you sin, you won't die.

Ezekiel 18:20
"The soul that sins shall die."

Ecclesiastes 9:5, 6
The dead don't know anything. In the grave there are no thoughts, knowledge, nor wisdom.

John 11:11-14
Jesus first told His disciples, "Lazarus sleeps." When they thought that meant that their friend was resting, Jesus said plainly, "Lazarus is dead."

John 5:28, 29
All in graves will come forth. All will receive their reward at the resurrection of life or the resurrection judgment.

Revelation 22:12
At the Second Coming each will receive reward.

1 Thessalonians 4:16-18
The dead in Christ will rise first, and join those who are alive in Christ and go to heaven.

John 14:1-3
Jesus said, "I will come again and receive you unto myself "(verse 3, KJV).

1 Corinthians 15:21-28
"For as by a man came death, by a man has come also the resurrection of the dead. For as in Adam all die, so also in Christ *shall* all be made alive. *But each in his own order: Christ the first fruits, then at his coming those who belong to Christ"(verses 21-23).*

Psalm 115:17
"The dead do not praise the Lord, nor do any that go down into silence."

Psalm 17:15
David had confidence in the resurrection and that he would be saved. He believed he would see the Redeemer at the resurrection.

Acts 2:29-34
David didn't ascend to heaven. He is still in grave.

2 Timothy 4:8
Paul believed would receive his reward at the Second Coming.

Matthew 16:27
When Son of man comes in glory, *then* shall He reward everyone according to his or her works.

1 Peter 5:4
When the Chief Shepherd [Jesus] shall appear, you will receive your crown.

A Thought
If sinners burned in hell forever, then they too would be immortal.

The Occult
Exodus 22:18
"You shall not permit a sorceress to live."

Leviticus 19:31
"Do not turn to mediums or wizards; do not seek them out, to be defiled by them: I am the Lord your God."

Leviticus 20:6, 27
"If a person turns to mediums and wizards, playing the harlot after them, I will set my face against that person, and will cut him off from among his people." "A man or a woman who is a medium or a wizard shall be put to death; they shall be stoned with stones, their blood shall be upon them."

Deuteronomy 18:9-12, 14
"When you come into the land which the Lord your God gives you, you shall not learn to follow the abominable practices of those nations. There shall not be found among you any one who burns his son or his daughter as an offering, any one who practices divination, a soothsayer, or an augur, or a sorcerer, or a charmer, or a medium, or a wizard, or a necromancer. For whoever does these things is an abomination to the Lord; and because of these abominable practices the Lord your God is driving them out before you." "For these nations, which you are about to dispossess, give heed to soothsayers and to diviners; but as for you, the Lord your God has not allowed you so to do."

1 Chronicles 10:13, 14
"So Saul died for his unfaithfulness; he was unfaithful to the Lord in that he did not keep the command of the Lord, and also consulted a medium, seeking guidance, and did not seek guidance from the Lord."

Isaiah 8:19
"When they say to you, 'Consult the mediums and the wizards who chirp and mutter,' should not a people consult their God? Should they consult the dead on behalf of the living?"

For Kids

Maylan Schurch

Spiritualism bombards our kids constantly. But do most kids realize what's behind it? Thi adventure informs, protects, and leads kids to Jesus. 978-0-8280-1610-0. Paperback. 96 pages

Harry Potter, Wicca Witchcraft and the Bible

Steve Wohlberg

Gazing down to Earth's last days with heavenly vision, the Bible's last book predicts, "through sorcery all nations wer deceived" (Revelation 18:23).

Kids, teenagers, and adults around the world have become fascinated with a tale about a young sorcerer, Harry Potter. Meanwhile, in rapidly increasing numbers, young and old are visiting popular websites, buying spell books, joining covens, mixing potions, and practicing magic.

Hour of the Witch is a bold wake-up call" to Christian and non-Christians alike living in today's media driven society. 978-0-7684-0240-7. 2 DVD set. Runtime: 2 hours.

Every person on earth; all the beings in heaven; and all the forces of evil will soon be involved in earth's final battle.

G. Edward Reid

An update of end-time events, this book pulls back the curtain and allows the reader to see the forces of the great controversy in action. Through the influence of supernatural forces, many people are now making decisions that will affect their eternal destiny. Indications are that this battle of the spirits is soon to close. 978-0-9711134-0-4. Paperback, 251 pages.

3 WAYS TO SHOP

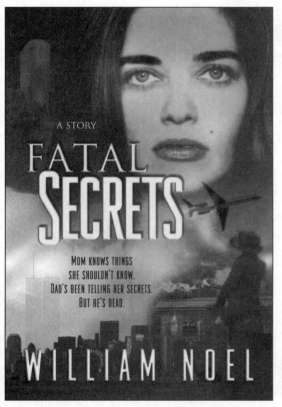

Hope wonders, Where is he now? In heaven? Or hell?

William Noel

In this sequel to *Broken River, Shattered Sky,* author William Noel weaves a tangled tale into a riveting spiritual story that reveals something about the darkness on the the the other side and the liberating power of light. 978-0-8280-1888-3. Paperback. 238 pages.

A true story of loss, wonder and liberating answers!

G. G. Albert

The author shares his story and his experience with an easy going style of writing and a passion for helping people. The heartache of death touches everyone. Learn how knowing the truth about death can give you peace of mind.

If you have ever lost someone and wondered about those who have died then I believe this book is for you. 978-1-60034-313-1. Paperback. 196 pages

3 WAYS TO SHOP